Inside Danger

Book Two of Outside The Ropes

ASHLEY CLAUDY

Cover by R.B.A. Designs.

We can easily forgive a child who is afraid of the dark; the real tragedy of life is when men are afraid of the light.

~Plato

1: The Other Side

THE GUN PRESSED INTO MY SKIN AS I climbed out of the cab. I tugged on my shirt, pulling it low with clammy hands, trying to keep the gun and my nerves covered.

I had no clue what I was about to get myself into as Silas approached dressed in a dark suit, but his sly smile reminded me that it wasn't anything good. Not that I needed a reminder; the gun tucked into my jeans, an almost burning presence, was enough.

His smile faltered as he dragged me away from the line of people waiting to get into the building. "What are you wearing Regan? I told you this was a club."

"I wanted to be prepared for anything." I pulled my arm out of his grip and shrugged.

He let out a puff of laughter and his breath clouded in the cool night air. "You're not turning criminal tonight. You don't need to be in all black." His eyes scanned over my dark top and jeans, a frown dropping into place. "Fuckin' eh. Did you bring a gun too? Give it to me."

My heart stopped at being called out so quick. The outfit was supposed to pass for dressy but also allow me to move. I wanted to be prepared for anything since this meeting was a mystery to me.

No one was in listening distance, but there were plenty of eyes from the line of people trying to get into this place.

Silas nodded his head to the side of the warehouse and we walked around the corner, out of view from everyone.

"I'm serious. Give me your gun and anything else you might have. These people don't know you and walking in armed could get you hurt. They're meeting with you because I said they could trust you. Don't make me regret it."

I didn't trust him, but I was going to have to follow his directions if I wanted to go through with this. And I did want to go through with this. Stepping further into the shadows of the building, close enough to touch him, I pulled the glock from the back of my waistband and handed it over.

He knelt down and slipped the gun into the top of his boot, covering it with his dress slacks. Rising, he cocked an eyebrow at me. "Good girl. Anything else you need to hand over?"

The pit in my stomach was bottomless, and I shook my head. I recalled Nan's tiny body in the hospital bed with machines hooked to her and let the fiery anger fill me, strengthening me.

"We can go in the back." He jerked his head to the side door at the far end of the building.

Each step into the darkness was bringing me closer to fate, and with each step I dropped any hesitation; there was no turning back. I needed to go in confident and sure. By the time I reached the door, I was.

Danger may be on the other side but it was better than the fear I lived with now. At least this way I was doing something instead of running. I was fighting for her, Nan, even if it was too late to do any good. But I was also fighting for him whether he wanted me to or not. I was done fighting for me, it wasn't worth it; nothing good ever came of it.

Silas pulled out his phone, thumbs gliding across the screen as he texted, and then the door opened. A man with a buzzed head and a smirk as dark as his eyes let us in.

"Come. Nick's waiting." His voice was flat and low with the hint of an accent. He nodded to me and then turned down a hallway with dim fluorescent lighting. The muffled beat of music and stale smell of alcohol filled the air, intensifying as we walked around a corner.

The man knocked twice on a door before opening it. He gestured for us to go in, sending a cold chill through me as I brushed past him. Even though he was only about my height with a slight build under his cream colored sweater, something in his face and the way he held himself was sinister.

But if he chilled me, the other man in the room nearly sent me into hypothermia. He had the size of Gage and a close resemblance, but was older, harder. His dark hair was pulled back in a low ponytail, and a fitted button up shirt covered muscles that were a bit softer than his nephew's but still held obvious strength.

He turned from the monitor he was looking at, surveillance footage from around the club in tiny squares on the screen, and his eyes struck me. Gages light blue eyes always seemed cold, but this man's dark ones were worse. I didn't need the introduction to know who this was, but it was given anyways.

Silas put a hand on my back, nudging me further into the room. "Nick, this is Regan. Regan this is Nick and that's Demetri." He gestured to the man closing the door behind us.

"Want a drink?" Nick asked us, eyes still locked on me.

My mouth was dry and stuck together, but I shook my head.

"I'll have one," Silas said.

Nick inclined his head to Demetri and crossed the room to sit on the couch, gesturing for us to sit in the two chairs opposite him.

I took the chair closest to the door and Silas sat in the other one.

Demetri made drinks from a small bar cart in the corner of the room. He set two glasses filled with amber liquid and ice down on the low glass coffee table in front of us. Sipping on one himself, he leaned against the desk off to the side of our sitting area. I didn't like how he was just behind my vision if I faced Nick, especially since his sharp eyes were on me.

Nick set his phone on the table and picked up his drink, sipping it slow. He watched me with narrowed eyes as he leaned back on the couch.

Holding the glass in mid-air he addressed me, "Silas told me a little about your situation. You're willing to help us, if we help you?"

I looked to Silas, but he nodded back at me. I needed to do the talking.

"Depends what you mean by help."

The corner of his mouth turned up, along with one eyebrow. "Well let's make it clear." He set his glass down. "Let's make sure both parties understand what they're asking for. It's important. Especially since I can't imagine a young thing like you wanting what Silas said ya wanted."

Pulling a cigarette out of his shirt pocket, he balanced it between his lips as he lit it. "You don't strike me as cold hard bitch," he mumbled around the cigarette and then pulled it from his mouth, exhaling in my direction. "So tell me, what exactly is it you want?"

"I want…" I flicked my eyes to Silas who nodded for me to continue. "There's a man I want dead." The nerves that tightened my throat made it hard to breathe.

Nick took another drag of his cigarette and leaned forward, resting his forearms on his spread legs. He pointed his smoke at me and shook his head. "You mean you want someone killed, murdered. Say it straight, 'cause wanting someone dead is different than wanting them murdered. Ya understand?"

I sucked in a sharp breath and nodded.

"Say it then." He relaxed back on the sofa and extended an arm along the top, but his eyes were full of challenge.

"I want him killed," my voice came out clear and emotionless.

His lips pulled up in a chilling smile as he nodded at me. "Who? Who has pissed ya off so bad ya think they deserve to die, little one?"

His condescending tone turned on my anger and steel ran through my veins, strengthening me. "Damien Jallow. He's involved with Rock, do you know him?"

"I know Rock. I don't know this Damien, but if he's one of his soldiers, then shits tough but I can deliver. Now I'm curious though, why?"

Nan's face flashed in my mind. "He murdered my friend."

Silas set down his glass and got our attention. "He's also been threatening Regan, want's her dead, but he wants to be the one to do it. Gave directions to have her brought to him."

Bile rose in my throat and I tried to meet Silas's gaze, but he avoided looking in my direction. He had only told me that Damien wanted me dead, not that he wanted me brought to him. I knew Damien was sick and dangerous but this took it to a whole new level. Unless Silas was lying, but I couldn't figure an angle as to why he would at this point. I had already agreed to this. I was here.

"Well fuck, then this needs to be done sooner than later. But first, let's work out terms. What do we get for doing this?"

"Silas said as long as I continued to fight for him." The minute the words were out I knew it wouldn't be enough.

Nick looked between the two of us and tapped the table with the tip of his finger. "Nuh-uh. Yes, ya need to keep fighting under our gym, but we need a guarantee of something more. Let's say a cash value. 'Cause what if ya lose and we end up with nothing?"

"She's good. I know she'll bring in money," Silas defended; it seemed like Nick had poked his pride.

"Maybe so, but we're gonna need ya to bring in fifty thousand dollars for this risk. We're in a tight spot with Rock as is, and this will stir it up if he finds out."

Silas and Nick ran over numbers and what I could potentially make for future fights. Silas already had one lined up for me in two weeks and another next month, but the time it would take to make their money was too long. It didn't surprise me when they started talking about setting up my fights, but I wasn't sure I could do it.

"I can't guarantee a win in a certain round; I'm not that experienced. I could throw a fight, but even losing in a called round—I can't promise that." And, again, I was amazed at how level my voice sounded. Inside I was a quivering mess, but I was keeping it together on the outside, where it mattered.

"How 'bout we practice first? This next fight, let's pretend. We have to wait till the odds come out to pick a round, but we'll see. You can't lose just yet, that's a ticket we won't cash till ya got a larger win column."

As he talked, his phone vibrated for about the dozenth time. He picked it up, pressing on the screen without breaking his conversation.

"So, do we have a deal?" he looked up from the phone, like everything had been worked out.

"I'm not quite sure I understand what's expected of me. What if I can't win in the rounds you choose? What then?"

Gage had won in the fourth but they bet on the third, and I hadn't seen him since. Silas assured me he had seen him, though, and he was okay. But it had been a week since he walked out of that hotel on me, and I wanted to know what was next. I was tempted to ask Nick directly. He was his uncle, he should be on Gage's side but I couldn't be sure.

"That's why we gave a cash value. You'll come up with it one way or another." Nick lifted his eyes from his phone to me. "Deal?"

"What about Damien? How will that be done?"

"Ya ask a lot of questions. Leave the details to us, we'll let ya know when and how after it's done."

I wanted to ask who 'we' was, he kept saying that, but he was dismissing me.

"If we're done here, I'll walk ya out." He went to his desk and slid on his jacket.

Demetri walked to the side of where we sat, ushering us to the door. I guess the deal was done.

Nick glanced at his phone one last time, then slipped it into his coat pocket and walked towards the door. "Before ya go." He turned back to us. "I have to introduce ya to someone."

Silas stepped to the side of me. "Who?"

"You don't have to come." Nick slid his eyes from Silas to me. "Someone wants to meet our newest fighter."

"Silas is my ride." I didn't want him to leave. He had my gun, and I wasn't about to go off with Nick alone.

"Then he can come too." He walked out the door, expecting us to follow.

Demetri left us little choice since he stayed behind us and kept us moving out of the room.

We walked down the hall and it became clear what type of club this was. A stage came into view and topless girls were up working the poles.

Nick opened a door to the right, just before we reached the opening to the main club. The room was full of people. It was its own mini club; a bar along one wall, three personal stages—each with half naked girls dancing on them, and a dark blue sofa that ran along two walls.

Men spotted the sofa and some stood in clusters. In the corner was the largest group and my eyes immediately found him, as if pulled by a magnet.

I froze. Stunned.

Gage was sitting back in a chair, laughing. It was unlike any expression I'd ever seen from him, and it's what shocked me the most. I had been going crazy this week, and there he was, beer in hand, laughing.

A man next to him clasped him on the shoulder and spoke into his ear. Gage's eyes rose up as he listened and they landed on me. Maybe for a split second something crossed his face, or maybe that was wishful thinking. Either way, he covered it with a swig from his bottle, and then his smile was back and he was no longer looking at me.

Silas leaned into me and spoke low, "Don't lose that poker face now. Stop staring."

I closed my mouth and pulled my surprise back in, along with all the other mixed bag of emotions Gage pulled out of me.

The man next to Gage gestured for us to come over with a single wave of his hand. He was tall, blonde, and kind of skinny, but his suit fit well and he seemed to be the center of this room.

We walked through the maze of people until we were standing in front of him. I never let my eyes go back to Gage, but he was still there in the corner of my vision, and it took all my strength not to stare and drink him in.

"This must be the new girl." The blonde rose to his feet, and the way his hazel eyes ran over me made my skin crawl.

"Everything's worked out. She's your newest fighter."

He directed his politician smile to me. "Sweetheart—"

"Regan." The word was out before I could think.

He cocked his head slightly. "Excuse me?"

"Regan. My name is Regan," I said it evenly, as if my heart wasn't pounding a hole into my rib cage. I didn't want to offend him, I could tell he held power here, but I didn't want to continue on with him calling me sweetheart either. I needed to make that clear.

"Regan?" His lip curled in amusement. "Well, Regan, I would love to stay and talk but I have somewhere to be. I wanted to introduce myself though, I'm Anatoli Rusnak." He stepped close and shook my hand with a firm grip, his other hand even firmer on my shoulder. "I've had a fortunate week. I'm the new owner of the City Center Boxing Club and we're glad you chose to stay on." He winked at me.

This was Rusnak. I hoped my shallow breaths didn't give away how uncomfortable he made me.

He pulled his hands away as Gage stood up.

"You can stay," Rusnak directed to Gage. "Demetri is coming with me." He gestured to Demetri and they both walked out.

All eyes followed his path as he left. He may have been skinny, but strength was clear in his movements and when he had touched me.

Nick stepped next to Gage, grabbing his shoulder. "Aren't ya gonna say hi? This is the girl ya jumped out of the ring to kiss, isn't it?"

His words dripped with sarcasm and I knew then, he wasn't for Gage. And the way his eyes lit up on me and his face twisted with a smirk, I also knew that I wasn't here to meet Rusnak or even for our deal.

They wanted me here for this moment, so Gage would see. I was a pawn they were using to get to him. I wasn't helping him. I had only made things worse.

2: Regret

MAYBE I WAS BEING OVERLY SUSPICIOUS. MAYBE Nick's comment wasn't the bomb I thought it was.

Maybe.

If I went off of others reactions, it was nothing more than conversation, but I wasn't willing to give any of them that benefit of the doubt.

I couldn't help but study Gage as he responded. He inclined his head to me with a slight nod of greeting before giving his uncle a questioning side look. "That was a fun night, but why is she here?"

He typically stood tall, confident, with his shoulders back, but not now. His shoulders were slightly rounded, a barely there change, but my heart dropped at what it could mean. Was he intentionally making himself less or had they beat out his confidence? This close, his bruises were visible. His bottom lip was swollen and cut, and a shadow of a bruise was on his cheek; those weren't from his fight last week.

I slid my hands into my back pockets to keep from reaching for him. They tingled with the need to touch him, to more than see that he was okay, I needed to feel it.

Nick laughed, ignoring his question. "What's the matter, ya don't want her here? I thought you'd like seeing your girl again. Never seen you put in so much work for one before."

Gage picked up his beer bottle, eyes on me as he took a sip. But there was nothing in them and that was holding me together. His guard was up and I didn't know when I had gotten so close that I could read the little signs. Or maybe it was my imagination again, but either way, I would follow his lead.

His gaze dropped over me, looking me up and down with a blank face, and then he shrugged and turned to Nick. "She was fun, but not worth the trouble." He sat back down on the sofa and nodded towards me. "I don't care if she's here though; I see her all the time at the gym. Just wondered why."

Heat burned under my skin. As much as I tried to keep cool and distant, I couldn't control the reaction, even when I tried to remind myself he wasn't being honest. This was all an act, it had to be.

Nick sat beside him and cocked his head, appraising me. "I could see that, she's got a little too much anger." He turned back to Gage with a grin. "I've always liked the sweet ones though. But that anger could be good for us, since she's going to keep boxing."

Gage took a sip and raised his eyebrow at Silas. "So what is this? A fuckin' company picnic? Any others coming?"

Silas took the seat next to Gage. "Just had a meeting with Nick to work out her contract, that's all. Have a seat Rea, now that work's done we can relax some."

I knew I should go. My muscles ached with the desire to flee, but something more intense, deep in my core, told me to stay. I didn't want to leave Gage just yet. So against my better judgment, I took the seat next to Silas, he was my ride home anyways.

"Cindy, get over here. I need a drink," Nick called over the chatter and music in the room.

A topless girl, with melon-sized boobs, slinked over. She sat on Nick's lap and pulled on a chain around her neck, revealing several charms on the end. One of them was a bottle opener and she used it to crack the lid on the beer in her other hand, then passed it to him.

"Can I get anyone else anything?" she questioned us with a sultry voice.

Gage lifted his beer bottle and wiggled it, signaling for another.

"Bourbon for me," Silas said.

"What about you, doll?" she asked, seemingly oblivious to Nick's face in her chest.

I shook my head and turned to Silas. "I need to go soon."

I felt pulled; I wanted to talk to Gage, but I knew it wouldn't happen tonight. Not here. And the more I sat, the deeper my unease grew, a nagging feeling in my stomach that I shouldn't be here.

Silas didn't pull his eyes off the server walking away as he responded, "Soon."

I slumped back in the seat and tried to put my mind anywhere else. Some girls were up dancing and some were rubbing on other men; some were naked, some wore underwear, but none were in clothes. I shouldn't be here.

The big-boobed brunette returned, leaning suggestively into each man as she handed off his drink. Nick hooked his arm around her, pulling her back onto his lap before she could walk away.

"Have ya sampled the new goods?" he asked Gage and Silas, maybe I was included, but I doubted it. He lifted the necklace from her cleavage and flicked through the charms dangling from the end. "The star, right?" He asked her and she nodded.

As Nick unscrewed the charm, she lifted her hand flat and he poured white powder onto the back of it, between her thumb and pointer finger. She brought it up to his nose and he inhaled sharply.

Gage was leaned back on the sofa, turned away from me, watching his uncle snort more off the girl's chest.

Nick sat up. "It's got to be the finest shit we've ever copped." He ran his hand up and down the girl's waist, then patted her hip and pointed to Silas. "Go give 'em some."

She sat on Silas's lap and I scooted myself away, snakes coiling in my stomach, knotting into a venomous ball of disgust. It wasn't even her I was disgusted with, the distance in her gaze made it clear she was just doing her job. This place and these people disgusted me.

Silas spread out the coke on her cleavage and buried his face as he inhaled. Nick nodded to Gage and she moved to him, straddling his lap, and I nearly threw up.

I didn't want to see this; I never wanted to think of Gage like this because, no matter what the excuse, this image would forever be burned into my brain. And I couldn't un-see it or forget it.

She braced her hands on either of his shoulders as she cooed, "How do you want it?"

His eyes connected with hers as he took the charm from Silas and grabbed one of her hands, tipping some out onto the space between her thumb and finger. She moved her hand to his nose and he breathed in, long and deep.

The knots in my stomach were unbearably tight, but they tore painfully as he moved her hand to his mouth and sucked off the residue.

She trailed her hand down his neck and rested it low on his stomach as he let his head fall back, closing his eyes as the high took over.

She turned to Nick, but inclined her head to me. "What about her?"

"No." I didn't give him the chance to answer. "I don't do that." I couldn't hide the contempt in my voice. I wanted to shout at Gage, see how easily I said no. Everything in me was boiling and burning.

Nick's gaze glazed over as he looked at me. "Fine." He turned to Gage, who still had the girl on his lap, and nudged his shoulder. "I thought ya said she was fun?" He asked with a low rumble of a laugh that reminded me of Gages.

I couldn't see his face as he responded since he was turned away from me, but his voice sounded light, teasing. "I also said she wasn't worth the trouble. She takes a lot of work." His hands slid around the girl's waist in front of him.

A part of me was still hoping that he was acting, that this was all a cover for him. But either way, I couldn't sit here and listen. And really, no matter what we meant to each other, I wouldn't let a person say that stuff about me.

I stood and faced Nick. "Whatever, I'm not here to make friends or have fun. We worked out what I came for. I'm leaving now."

Nick's slick smile was almost a sneer as he said, "Bye." He saluted me with two fingers to his forehead.

I glanced over the others, but Gage didn't even bother pulling his eyes off the boobs in front of him. Silas stood up and followed me.

He stopped at the door and pointed to the main club. "Go out the front, they can get you a cab. Here." He handed me a couple of twenties. "I'll see you Sunday morning, we'll talk and start training. Stay low till then." He turned away, going back to Nick and Gage.

As I climbed into the cab, I scanned the perimeter of the club, half expecting Gage to walk out, to talk to me. But he didn't. That shouldn't have surprised me or hurt me. But it did. I was realizing now I couldn't bet on him, he never comes through.

I returned to my hotel, a hotel in the suburbs, outside of the city. I moved out of the house with the girls when I made the decision to stick with Silas and fall in with Rusnak, I didn't want to drag anyone else down with me. But sitting in the room, alone, I hit an all new level of desolation. I had still held onto the hope that I had Gage, that I wasn't completely alone, but I knew now, I was.

While that realization hurt, a part of me was relieved to let him go. I felt weightless, untethered. I had nothing left to lose, and that made taking risks that much easier. And I knew there were risks I needed to take, there was no way I was getting out of this with my hands clean.

* * *

I make everything worse.

It's what Nan had said. It's what I knew.

Each choice I made snowballed into a worse one. And now, I was buried under them. Even the choices that didn't seem too bad at the time turned into the ones I regretted the most.

As I stared at the text I just received, I regretted ever moving into the house with the girls.

An unknown number sent a picture of Leona and Aliya walking into the house. The picture itself wasn't bad, they seemed oblivious to the car that must be parked at the curb. The clock on the dash was visible at the bottom of the screen, 6:38, letting me know whoever it was, was there right fucking now.

The shock to my heart jumpstarted me into action. I hit the contact button, searching for Leona's number, but before I found it my screen lit up with an incoming call.

Same unknown number.

"Where you?" an accented voice asked.

"What do you want? 'Cause I'm not there, you can leave." I stood up from the bed, unable to keep still with the jolts of fear shooting through my muscles.

"Where you? I leave then." His flat, level voice sounded familiar, but I wasn't sure. "Who is this?"

"Demetri. Now tell or I ask them."

"I'm at the Holiday Inn, in Timonium," I lied, but it was within walking distance, I could get there.

"Take picture. Send it now." He hung up.

My body was trying to escape, turning inside out to flee as my mind stayed put, trying to think this through.

I slid on my jacket and shoved my keys, pocketknife, and pepper spray into my pocket. Phone in hand, I made my way out of the hotel. What the hell was going on? I pulled up Leona's number as I hustled down the stairs and then abandoned that idea. Warning her might only make it worse, cause her to panic and tip him off.

My blood surged through my body, thick with anger and fear, anger at myself and fear for my ex roommates. The small knife and pepper spray in my pocket wasn't any reassurance, Silas still had my gun.

Silas. I found his number and dialed as I walked to the sidewalk lining the highway, toward the Holiday Inn. But his voicemail picked up as an incoming call broke through. Shit.

"Hello," I answered, breathless from my clipped pace.

"Send picture now. Important I find you. Nothing bad."

"Nothing bad?" I stalled, trying to keep him talking till I could get to the hotel, but also curious. "Then why are you sending threatening messages?"

His breathy laugh was like nails on a chalkboard. "That's no threat. I not waist time is all. My job, find you. Now send picture and stay till I come." He hung up again.

The hotel was visible now, so I took a picture of the street signs at the intersection and sent it. Then I sat down on the bench at the bus stop and waited. When a bus pulled up, I was tempted to hop on, but then what? He might return to the house, I couldn't risk that. This guy was part of the deal I made, I had to face him and find out what he wanted.

It was impossible to put my thoughts in order or make sense of them, they were twisted beyond recognition. By time the sleek Silver Lexus pulled up to the bus stop, I was close to melting down. I wouldn't let him know that though.

The passenger side window lowered, and he didn't even bother looking in my direction as he said, "Get in."

"Why? What do you want?" I snapped under my chaotic emotions.

He cut me a side look and his dark eyes flashed with irritation. "Not me, Anatoli wants to talk. Get in."

When I didn't move, he leaned over the empty passenger seat, lean arms flexing under his t-shirt as he opened the door. "It's about what you ask for; get in."

My skin burned to leave but I got in the car. I had asked for this, Leona and the others didn't.

He whipped the car into traffic and turned up his music, loud, a heavy metal song that fueled my anger.

"What?" I yelled over the noise.

He pressed a button on the steering wheel and the music cut off. "I take you to Olli's. That's my job, that's all."

He flicked the music back on, drowning out any response I might give. Not that I was going to give one, the lunatic next to me was just a deliveryman. I used the rest of the thirty-minute car ride to place a calm mask over my frenzied emotions, so I could face Rusnak.

My new calm exterior was ripped away the moment Demetri whipped out a pistol, placing it to my temple. I guess I should have expected it, but it happened in the blink of an eye; the moment he pulled into the detached garage behind a mansion, he had the gun out. And then he turned off the car.

He grabbed one wrist, demanding, "Give me other arm, behind you."

The tip of the gun pushed my head as he spoke and I did what I was told.

Demetri used a cable tie to handcuff my wrists together, the plastic biting into my skin. Leaning over me, his free hand swiped my body and he emptied my pockets, snorting as he tossed my knife and pepper spray to the side. His fingers slid around the rim of my shoes and then he grabbed my arm, yanking me out of the driver's side door with him.

When we were both standing, he slid the gun into the front of his waistband but left it exposed over his shirt.

The garage was dark, no windows to let the moonlight in.

He gripped my elbow, dragging me to a door in the back corner. My heart ricocheted inside me like a pinball but didn't pump any blood to my head. It was all in my feet and I couldn't think. He opened the door to narrow stairs and pushed me up them, nearly making me fall. I wasn't moving fast enough for him, he kept pushing.

Demetri flipped on the lights, revealing a sparse apartment—one sofa, one small dining table with two chairs. But I didn't get to look long; he pulled me through the room, shoving me into a bathroom.

The door closed, the click of a lock, and then silence. He had left me alone.

It was useless but I tried the door, pulling at the handle with my hands behind my back, it didn't budge. I scanned the claustrophobic box of a room that was now my cage. It was empty besides the sink and toilet, there wasn't even toilet paper.

Unable to sit and do nothing, I pushed at the door with my shoulder, a pathetic attempt. So I kicked at the door instead, using the bottom of my foot to pound at it, but it didn't splinter, it only boomed with the effort. It must not have been made of wood, not since it vibrated my leg with each force and didn't even shake.

I don't know how long I tried, but I kept at it until my legs were numb and unable to lift anymore. Tears were rolling down my face as I slumped to the ground, exhausted and confused. Sucking in air, I breathed down my panic. I needed a clear mind to think, not this jumbled mess.

I am an idiot, that was the only thought that made sense and was repeatedly screaming in my head.

The door opened, surprising me. I hadn't heard anything on the other side, and I had been listening.

Rusnak stepped in, his long limbs folding as he sunk to his knees in front of me. "I am sorry about this." His arms wrapped around me to cut the bands behind my back.

I stood up, away from him.

"Demetri, she is a guest, not a prisoner," he scolded, still on his knees as Demetri appeared in the doorway.

"She would have run, I saw in her face."

"She is a guest." He stood and smoothed his hand along his dark suit jacket. "Demetri was supposed to bring you here to talk to me. I have found out some rather disturbing news and wanted to make sure my newest boxer was safe." His eyebrow lifted and he nodded to the living room. "Let's sit and talk."

He walked away without waiting for a reply. But Demetri stayed, waiting for me.

Rusnak was a liar. He didn't care that I was locked up here or practically kidnapped. I ran my hands along my sore wrists as I shouldered past Demetri, a crazed sort of anger taking control.

I took a deep breath as I faced Rusnak. He was sitting on the only couch and nodded at the space next to him.

Pulling a table chair over, I sat a good distance away.

"Would you like a drink?" he asked with his smile, as if we were two friends talking.

"I want to know what the fuck is going on."

His eyebrows popped up, but smile stayed in place. "I brought you here for your protection. You will stay here, actually in the main house, until everything is resolved."

"My protection?" I popped up, incensed, "I was just held at gunpoint and tied up by him. So fuck you—"

Demetri took a threatening step forward, but Rusnak raised his hand ever so slightly, stilling the man. It was that little gesture, with his politician smile still in place, that froze me. This man held power in just the flick of his wrist.

I sunk back down onto the seat, the anger in me receding and leaving me hollow.

"I've already apologized for Demetri. Tell her, Demetri, that you're sorry."

Demetri met my eyes with a blank look. "I'm sorry."

"There. Now, as I was saying, Demetri has learned that there is a threat on your life. I think you knew this?" he didn't wait for my acknowledgment. "It seems that this man is more serious than we realized and this man has more pull than we'd thought. It's strange because I've never heard of Damien, but Rock seems to hold him in high esteem and protects him. That is something we're looking into as well." He looked to Demetri who nodded, and then he focused back on me. "Until we can ensure your safety, you will stay here. I take care of my employees."

His words burrowed into my brain. Was this really to keep me safe? Or just to keep me under their control? I was thinking the latter. "He can still be killed, right?"

Rusnak's smile dropped. "I am telling you only that we will keep you safe. If Damien happens to die, you'd be safe. Given the people he associates with, I wouldn't be surprised if he dies soon, maybe even this week."

Demetri inclined his head as Rusnak looked towards him.

I got the message, Rusnak was above the dirty work.

"Well, I have to go, I do have prior arrangements tonight but we will talk more in the morning. Demetri will take you to your room."

He stood up and nodded at me, eyes bright. "Enjoy your stay." Then he walked out of the room, leaving me alone with Demetri and taking any warmth with him.

"Let's go." His usual blank face was frowning. "I will kill Damien soon, then I be done babysitting you."

I smirked, getting a sick pleasure out of his unhappiness.

He walked me to the main house, in through the basement. I took in the opulent surroundings as we made our way upstairs, more to know the layout than for appreciation.

The hallway on the main floor was wide and long with white walls, gold trim, and dark cherry doors. One of the doors opened, and my heart leapt into my throat as Gage stepped into the hall, swinging the door shut behind him. He radiated anger, his face severe as he made his determined path down the hall.

Demetri continued to push me forward and my wrists still burned from the ties earlier. Gage didn't seem to notice me as he stormed past and I panicked, reaching out for him. I needed someone to know I was here, other than these strangers.

He ripped his arm away as if I'd burned him. When his eyes met mine, he shot me with a look of pure disgust. His hands flexed at his sides as he seethed, "You never could fucking listen, could you?"

He stepped towards me and I moved back, but it was Demetri's step forward that stopped Gage.

Lightning flashed in Gages eyes as he narrowed them at Demetri, then slid them back to me. He shoulder checked Demetri as he walked away.

3: The Devil You Know

GAGE'S WORDS AND ANGER RIPPED THE LID off my emotions, and now he was walking away with it.

Demetri shoved me towards the stairs and everything spilled out. I was a hopeless mess, sure I was being walked to my death.

I spun around, shouting over Demetri's shoulder, "What a surprise you're walking away, like always!" Gage turned the corner out of sight, but I continued to yell, "Can never fucking stick around, can you?" My arm burned as Demetri gripped it, pulling me down the hall.

Gage hadn't even looked back as I yelled at him. He hadn't even slowed his pace, and I felt like a ghost, already dead.

I whipped around to Demetri and shoved him, hard, but his grip remained. "I can fucking walk on my own. Stop pulling on me."

He dropped my arm with a smile and gestured to the stairs. I stomped up them, ignoring my shaking muscles.

"Turn right, last door on left," Demetri directed from behind me.

I took a deep breath, fortifying myself for the walk to the room that would be my new prison. No matter what Rusnak had said, I knew none of this was for my benefit. I couldn't believe his lies, not when I was stuck with Demetri.

I stepped into the room, a little taken back by the size and luxury of it. It was nicely decorated in greys and blues. Among the furniture, the king size bed and flat screen TV on the wall caught my attention.

Demetri stepped in behind me and all my focus went back to the mad man who stood with a smirk.

His dark eyes narrowed as he spoke, "You and Gage, have lovers fight?"

That was ice to my boiling blood. I walked to the opposite side of the room, to the window, checking out the view but also putting space between us.

"He's crazy. Better to stay away."

My eyebrows nearly sprung off my head in shock. Demetri calling him crazy scared me and only confirmed that I didn't know Gage at all.

Demetri walked to the nightstand by the bed. "Here is remote for TV. You stay here tonight, I come back for you in morning."

The window overlooked the side yard, and the forest beyond. There were no houses within view, not that I would run for help anyways. I had to finish what I started.

Turning back to Demetri I nodded. "How long do I have to stay here?"

"Only couple of days, maybe week." He shrugged one shoulder and then left, locking the door from the outside.

I did the only thing I could do. I took off my shoes and climbed into the soft bed. Leaving my jeans and T-Shirt on, I slept.

* * *

I'd been awake for hours. I took a shower, stared at the TV, and paced the room—a lot—before Demetri came strolling in.

"Breakfast waiting downstairs." He was dressed casual, in faded jeans and a coca cola t-shirt, but still managed to make his simple words sound ominous.

"I'm not hungry." I faked interest in the news on TV.

"Olli is waiting, too." At my questioning look he sighed, "Rusnak, Anatoli Rusnak. Come now"

Demetri took a step towards me and I stood from the bed, out of reach.

"I'm up; let's go." My hand went up to keep him away. I didn't need him yanking me around anymore.

Rusnak was seated at the head of the table in the kitchen. He stood as I entered and pulled out a chair to the side of his for me to sit in.

As I approached, I tried for confidence, but I was empty, drained.

When I sat, he pushed in my chair and rested his hand on my shoulder. "Did you sleep well?"

I nodded, keeping my eyes on the dark wood table in front of me, unable to look up at this man who was standing too close as I resisted the urge to knock his hand away.

His fingers curled on my shoulder, applying soft pressure. "Good." He released me and then sat in his own chair.

He was dressed down from the suits I had seen him in previously, but still formal in grey slacks and black button top. A thick gold watch wrapped the wrist he rested on the table and on his ring finger, a wedding band.

"I hated how things went yesterday. I came here first thing this morning to check on you. What are your plans for the day?" He was relaxed back in his chair.

Demetri sat down across from me and I glanced his way with a shrug. "What can I do?" The minute the question was out I regretted it. It sounded like acceptance.

Rusnak leaned forward and tapped one finger on the table to get my attention. "You can do whatever you want. Like I've said, you are a guest."

I held his stare. "I didn't feel like a guest when Demetri locked me in my room last night."

His eyes narrowed and he paused for a beat before a small smile tugged at his lips. "Demetri takes things too far sometimes. It won't happen again." He looked to the man and said, "You are her body guard, not prison guard." Turning back to me he added, "He has to stay with you, but you can do what you want. Tonight there is an event that I would like you to attend. It's to celebrate Gage's win, but also an announcement of sorts that I have taken over the Baltimore gym as well as opening the new one in D.C."

My heart stuttered at the mention of Gage, but I kept my blank expression easily enough.

"Do you have any other plans? Perhaps pick up things for your stay here?"

I nodded, eyes back on the table.

"I know this is a strange situation, but tonight I need you to put on a good face. You will be representing the gym." His voice was gentle but the demand was clear.

* * *

Demetri started up the Lexus. "Where to?"

"The Red Roof Inn, where you picked me up yesterday."

"I thought Holiday Inn." He backed the car out of the garage.

I gave up trying to keep where I was a secret, it's not like I would be hiding out there again. "I lied."

He snorted. "I figure."

We drove up the long driveway, pausing as the gate slid open. Demetri waved to the man in the guardhouse controlling the gate, and my stomach sunk as I took in the security of the place.

"Why not stay at your house? Why not tell anyone where you at?" Demetri pulled me from my thoughts.

I shook my head, surprised that he was talking to me. "I didn't want those girls involved in this."

"But anyone look for you, they go there." He shrugged.

I got his point, but him pointing out the flaws in my plan frustrated me. "I was only thinking about Damien, he doesn't know I lived there."

"Neither did I, but I found easy. You gave up where you were easy, too. It took one hour total to find you yesterday." His smug tone grated my nerves.

"Good for you," I snapped, then turned to stare out the window.

"Did you tell anyone else about the hotel?"

"No."

"What if something were to have happened? What if you died? Nobody would have known where to look for you."

He was much more talkative today, I wished he would shut up.

"If I was dead, that wouldn't be my problem."

He smiled and his dark eyes brightened. "Good point. And you said without flinching. You not scared?"

"No, not of dying." Dying almost seemed easy; it was everything else that scared me.

Merging with the traffic on the highway, he nodded. "Good." Then he accelerated and turned up the volume to the radio.

* * *

Demetri walked me to the VIP lounge where Rusnak was, already a full crowd surrounding him. I kept my face blank and body soulless, determined that nothing would touch me tonight—not emotionally.

Rusnak approached Demetri, and they spoke low to each other, too low for me to hear over the music beat and noisy atmosphere.

Demetri turned to me and leaned in to be heard. "I have to go now. I pick you up at end of night. Stay in this area."

I nodded, a mixture of relief and dread running under my skin. The devil you know vs. the Devil you don't. After spending the day with Demetri, I still thought he was a lunatic, but we had come to some sort of truce or understanding. I didn't know who was going to be responsible for watching me now.

Rusnak directed his smile to me and ran a hand down my bare arm, stopping at my fingers to bring them to his lips. "You look stunning tonight. I have a few people I need to introduce you to."

I had spent the day testing Demetri's orders to do what I wanted and bought a new dress as well as makeup. I figured following Rusnak's directions to put on a good face could only help my situation. My money was running low now that I wasn't working anymore though, so the dress was cheap but fit nicely; a blue strapless cocktail dress.

I stayed by his side for a while and met businessmen of the community, people who had something to do with boxing or were just spectators of the sport. My eyes kept scanning the room, waiting for Gage. I hated that there was still a part of me that wanted him near, but I couldn't cut it out of me just yet.

"Ah, there's the woman you really need to meet, my wife." He guided me through the crowd with his hand on the small of my back. We stopped in front of a beautiful lady standing at a cocktail table with another woman.

Her smile brightened as she saw Rusnak but there was something sharp in her eyes, and I got the vibe that this woman was a force all on her own.

After they embraced and kissed each other's cheeks, she turned to me.

"This is Regan Sommers, the gyms most promising female boxer. Regan this is my wife, Alessandra Rusnak."

She shook my hand, chin raised as she appraised me. She was taller than me and her toned body was shown off nicely in a form fitting black dress, her long sleek brown hair hung past her large boobs.

"Where is your most promising male boxer? I haven't seen Gage all night," she asked Rusnak the question that had been on my mind.

"He's in the main club mingling for now. Publicity and public image is important, but he will be joining us in here shortly."

They continued talking, ignoring me, so I took the opportunity to walk away and was surprised that I could. So far, no one had been hovering over me. Maybe I wasn't on watch tonight.

I went to the bar to order a drink when Silas slid into the spot next to me.

My body tensed as he leaned to speak into my ear. "I saw the missed call from you. I've been trying to call back but you haven't answered, everything all right?"

I shrugged, not sure what information I could trust him with. "Yup. Everything's fine but my phone's gone." Demetri took it yesterday and still hadn't returned it. I'd ask him for it tonight.

Lines formed between his brows. "So you'll be at the gym to start training tomorrow?"

I nodded and turned to get the bartender's attention. My mouth was dry and I needed something to drink.

Nick appeared to the other side of me, making me step away so our bodies wouldn't touch. He inclined his head, an amused look crossing his face. "Hello, little one. Ya having fun?"

I inclined my head in greeting and turned back to Silas, abandoning the idea of getting a drink. "I'll be there in the morning." I went to step away, but paused. Gage had finally arrived.

His large presence was easy to spot, but I didn't recognize him. His smiles seemed to come easy as he talked with a group of people. They all laughed at what was being said, including Gage. He finished off the beer in his hand and swiped another one from a passing server. Then his eyes landed on me, for one brief, heart shredding second.

Nick stepped in front of me, blocking my view. "Here." He handed me a glass with pink liquid. "It's cranberry and vodka."

"Thanks, but I don't drink." I set the glass down.

He cocked his head. "You might actually loosen up if you did."

"I'm not even twenty one yet," I said it like it made a difference.

His eyebrow lifted, surprised. "Damn, you are a baby. So young to be in so deep." He patted my shoulder as he walked away, joining Gage's group.

Silas turned to the bartender and ordered me a tea before leaving to go mingle.

I sat alone for a while, fighting against the urge to watch Gage move around the room.

As I exited the bathroom, an arm wrapped around me and pulled me back against a firm chest, a hand over my mouth.

"Shhh," the man breathed into my ear, slipping us into a small dark room.

I wasn't going to yell. I knew the moment the arms circled me it was Gage.

He turned me around, releasing my mouth as he held me against the closed door. His warm hands cupped my face, blue eyes glowing in the dark.

"Are you all right? Seeing you at his house yesterday—fuck. Have they hurt you or anything?"

I couldn't form words, my emotions choked me. This was the concern I wanted from him but I found it hard to swallow now. He had walked away yesterday.

His breathing was raspy and reeked of beer as it fanned over me.

I raised my hands to his chest, wanting to push him away but not able to find the strength. "I'm fine."

"Good." He let out a large breath and dropped his forehead to mine. "I've missed you."

I did push him away at that, but he barely budged. "Could have fooled me."

"It's not you I'm trying to fool." His hands gripped my shoulders, holding me in place. "Although, it would be best if you believed it, too. Everything is so fucked up now. I don't know what they're telling you to keep you there, but I guarantee it's not the truth."

The thing was, I knew that. I knew they were lying, but now I realized I didn't believe him either. I didn't trust that anyone was telling me the truth.

"I have to get back out there before we're noticed." His hands rubbed my shoulders as his head dipped towards mine, breathing me in, drowning me. "Damn, you make me crazy. I had to talk to you. Please, don't do anything till I talk to you again. Let me fix this." Then his lips were on mine with a frenzied need, and I kissed him back, clinging to this electric moment until his words sank in.

I pulled away from his kiss. "It's too late for that. I need to know what you know, so I can know what to do."

"Tonight. I'll be there tonight, just wait till then." He stepped back and caressed my cheek. "You go out first. I'll wait here." His heat and security vanished when he took a large step back, leaving me cold and weak.

Panic gripped my heart and muscles as I thought of leaving this space, going back out there, back to him treating me like nothing and everyone manipulating the situation. Sucking in a shuddering breath, I tried to fight back the swell of fear and burning tears just behind my eyelids. His promise to come tonight didn't comfort me. It felt like another lie, another ghost of a promise. I fought against every cell that demanded I pull Gage back into me, turning instead to open the door.

"Wait." His warmth was instant as he stepped close; his hand pressed on the door by my head, keeping me from opening it.

A wave of relief flooded me, and the tears that had been threatening to fall escaped. This was too much. He was too much. I'd lost control of everything and hated myself for allowing that to happen.

He moved his free hand to my hip, turning me to face him again. I fought against it, not wanting to fall apart in his arms, but I had little strength.

Both of his arms circled around me, holding me to him. "Babe, you've got to stay strong. Don't cry."

Stiffening at his words, I reigned in my emotions and shoved away from him.

"I am strong. You make me weak," I accused, squeezing my eyes against any more tears as I sucked in several calming breaths.

"Fuck," he groaned as he swiped a hand over his short hair, looking at the ceiling of the storage room that was our hideout. His voice was even, absent of emotion as he spoke. "I'll go out first. Wait a minute, and then you can come out. Go to the bathroom again and clean yourself up."

He lowered his gaze back to me, face unreadable in the dark. He pivoted on his feet, moving slightly towards me at first but then he sidestepped me. He slid out of the door and closed it behind him.

Without him in the room, I was finally able to take a deep breath and steady myself. I meant what I said, he only made me weak. I couldn't control myself around him; that had always scared me, but now it was dangerous and no good for either of us.

After breathing down my panic, calming the tingly sick feeling in my muscles, I stepped out of the room and ducked back into the bathroom to fix my face. There were others walking in the hall, but no one I recognized and none seemed to notice me.

* * *

"Where's Dexter?" Nick asked Silas.

We were back at the bar, Nick and Silas on either side of me. I pulled out of my haze at the question and looked to Silas for the answer.

He forced a shrug. "Gage said he's focusing on school now, not boxing anymore."

Nick's head bounced from side to side as he thought this over. "Kid was never great at it anyways, not like his brother. But damn, he was fun to have around." He raised his eyebrow at Silas. "He's still going to be around, right?"

Silas shrugged again as he brought his glass to his lips and gulped down the contents. "Not a clue. Talking about Dex doesn't go over well with Gage."

"He's old enough to make his own decisions." Nick set his empty glass on the bar behind me and stood up, glancing at his phone. "All right, little one, it's past your bed time. Demetri's out front."

I stood, eager to leave, even if it was only back to a prison of a room. At least I would be away from here and away from Gage. He was surrounded by people vying for his attention. Every one of his careless smiles pissed me off, and every time his arm slipped around another girl at his side a stick was added to the angry fire burning in me. But that anger was better than the weak feeling of need he caused in the storage room.

"Stop calling me little one," I demanded, facing Nick.

He laughed, unaffected by my snap. "All righty then. Let's go, I'll walk ya out front." His thumb slid across his phone screen as he texted.

* * *

I was twisted in my sheets from tossing and turning with frustration, on the edge of sleep, when the door creeped open.

Reaching under my pillow, I sat up at the same time, my hand wrapped around the ceramic wedge I hid there. I had carefully cracked the vase in the bathroom earlier to have something to defend myself with. Just in case.

"Fuck, there's no lock." Gage's hand fumbled on the knob of the closed door and my chest deflated with a relieved sigh.

"Only on the other side," I explained and dropped the ceramic piece to the ground

I had given up hope of him coming; by the look of the soft glow in the room it was near morning. But here he was, and he had just walked on in, like he could.

His eyes pierced the dim room, connecting with mine in a flash of intensity. "They've locked you in here?"

"Not tonight. Rusnak told Demetri not to do that anymore."

He crossed the space of the room in three long strides. He grabbed my hands and pulled me to the en suite bathroom, shutting and locking the door behind us. Dropping one of my hands, he turned the water on in the shower, his other hand kept us connected.

"What are you doing?" I wasn't taking a shower with him.

He grabbed my hands again as he stepped close, cornering me against the counter. "In case someone comes in your room. This covers us, you. You're in the shower, alone." His lips dropped to my ear as he whispered, "Just keep your voice low."

A current traveled through me, knocking my resistance over like a line of dominos.

His lips moved over my neck in rough kisses that sparked my passion. He dropped my hands and lifted me by the hips, setting me on the bathroom counter. My fingers glided inside the back of his t-shirt, running over his heated skin. He had changed from his dress clothes earlier, but I didn't dwell on it. The feel of him was like a drug, and I wanted more.

I rolled my head back so he could nibble at the sensitive skin at the base of my neck. He pushed himself between my legs, rubbing against me as he sucked on my collarbone and I let out a soft moan.

He broke away with a rumble and tugged his shirt off, whipping it over his head and tossing it to the ground. There was a hungry glint in his eyes and then his mouth was on mine, claiming me.

And my body was all too willing to submit. My back arched, pressing into him, and my hands traced over his muscles, recalling the pleasure they could give.

But when his tongue slipped into my mouth and I tasted him, my mind woke up, spinning with different thoughts. He tasted like alcohol and something else. My mind easily jumped to what that could be, recalling the stripper from the other night and the girls by his side tonight.

My stomach heaved, clenching in on itself painfully. I pushed him away, disgusted in myself and gasping for air while trying to still my traitorous body.

My push didn't do much, but he got the point. He stepped back, wide eyed with shock. His eyes flicked around, searching my face.

"Baby, don't do this. Let us have this moment." Cautiously, he stepped back to me.

I closed my eyes as his hands slipped around my waist, but I put my arms up, bracing them on his chest to keep him away. I could feel his heart pounding beneath my palm and it softened me. The beat traveled through me, keeping time with my own erratically beating heart.

His warm breath tickled my cheek, then his lips were there, and his forehead pressed to mine. "We don't have much time."

I had been weakening, about to cave in again. His body was an intoxicating poison, killing all of my common sense. But his words sobered me.

"Then we need to talk." I reached behind me and pulled his hands from my waist, resting them in front of us. I didn't let them go, I couldn't bring myself to.

"What have you been doing?" I whispered, our heads still pressed together.

He let out a sigh and straightened. His eyes cast down, staring at our linked hands. He moved his fingers to lace them with mine and rotated our hands, then froze and his face hardened.

"What's this? What happened?" He dropped my left hand and traced his finger over a raw line under my right wrist.

I shrugged one shoulder, watching his finger travel over the red skin. "Demetri used a plastic tie to handcuff me when he first brought me here. It must have rubbed off some skin."

His eyes closed as he inhaled and exhaled and his hand locked around my wrist. "I'm sorry." His icy blues popped back open. "What have they told you? Why do you think you're here?"

I broke the stare off we had going, letting my eyes drop over him. All my air escaped in a painful rush when I saw the sick yellow and brown splotches marring his skin. Large bruises marbled his ribs and sides.

Pulling my eyes back up to his, my voice came out strained, "I asked first, what have you been doing?"

His hand slid into my hair, cupping the back of my head. "Don't worry about me. I'm here for you, to get you out, but I need to know what they're telling you and what you've done."

Swallowing my stray emotions, I began, "They say they brought me here for my safety, that Damien was after me, wanted me killed, and put me on a hit list to be brought to him." I raised an eyebrow, "But you knew that, even before your fight. Silas told me you saw Damien that first night and he said things to you."

"That's bullshit." His low growl from cut off my words. His hands gripped the counter on either side of me, knuckles turning white. "He said things, but I'm taking care of that already, and Damien's not going to risk everything he has going on just to get to you."

I squeezed his hard forearm, leaning towards him as fear squeezed my heart. "You don't need to take care of this. That's why I'm here in the first place. They are going to kill him, and I am going to keep fighting for Silas. You don't need to do anything."

"What the hell, Regan?" His jaw clenched and he stepped back, out of my reach. "You promised to fight for these people to get Damien killed? I was already fucking taking care of this. That's why I'm here, doing more than just boxing for them, risking my fucking life to save yours, and then you go and do this!"

He seized me, gripping my shoulders tight, anger twisting his features. "You want to know what I've been doing? I've been Rusnak and Nick's bitch, just so I can get to the big jobs that'll get me close to Rock and his crew again. Close to Damien. You need to call it off. Tell them you've changed your mind."

I flinched back. "No. Why should you be the one to put yourself in danger for me? You can stop doing what you're doing, let them kill him."

"You don't fucking get it do you?" He dropped my shoulders as anger deflated from him.

"I guess not, but you never explained it to me. You just leave and expect me to know what to do."

The room was filling up with steam, my clothes beginning to stick to my damp skin. But I ignored it all as he leaned closer to me, all signs of anger vanished.

"You're right and I'm sorry. I've never been good about including people, never had to before. But you won't listen to me without an explanation, so I'll tell you."

4: Honesty

I SLID OFF THE COUNTER TO STAND in front of him. My movements were slow and cautious as if he were a timid animal I didn't want to scare away.

He brought his hand up, caressing my cheek, stilling me. "Promise that you'll listen to me. After I explain, you need to do this my way." He pleaded and then added in a whisper, "Please."

If it were anyone else I would have lied, I would have made the promise and took the information. But even after everything, I still wanted to believe that as much as he has kept from me, what he had spoken was the truth. I had to believe that, and if I wanted to continue to believe that, I needed to be honest too. And I sure as hell needed this conversation to be a truthful one.

"I can't make that promise, not yet."

His eyes narrowed and his hands dropped away from my face. His body tightened, making him appear taller, stronger, as he pulled away.

I reached for him, not wanting him to go, and wrapped my arms around his waist. I pressed my cheek to his bare, slick chest. The steam filling the room was choking me. "I'm trying to be honest. I will listen to you though. Every word, I'll listen."

One of his hands wrapped around me, stroking my hair, and I relaxed slightly. He kissed the top of my head. "All right."

Those two words caused a flood of emotions and I strained to breathe. Letting out a shuddering breath, I pulled away from him and flipped off the shower.

"I can't take the steam," I explained, moving to the door and unlocking it, I cracked it open and let the thick heat escape into the larger room. I stopped him from closing the door. "This way we can hear if someone comes in, but you're still hidden."

Picking up his crumpled shirt on the tiled bathroom floor, I handed it over without looking at him. "Put this back on."

He took the shirt, threaded his arms through the sleeves, and pulled it over his head. "Ready?"

I nodded and walked to the far end of the bathroom, opposite the door. I dropped myself down onto the tile, legs crossed and back against the wall.

He sunk down beside me and gripped one of my knees. "I did see Damien that night." His eyes narrowed as he watched his hand rubbing over my sweatpants. He pulled his hand away and looked up at me. "Why didn't you tell me he was there? When they robbed the gym?"

My body broke out in goose bumps as an electric fear ran through me. "It didn't seem all that important at the time." He shot me an incredulous look, so I elaborated, "considering everything else going on."

"That was important. He threw it in my face that night to try to get the upper hand, but it didn't work. I would've killed him right then, except one of his friends hit me in the back of the head with their empty gun and he got away."

That explained his bruised ear that night. I circled my arms around my knees and pulled them into my chest. "I'm sorry, I didn't—" I stopped myself and changed directions. "There's plenty you haven't told me though."

For one brief, intense moment he held my gaze, a fire growing, and then he broke away and looked forward. "He didn't— Did he—" He took a gulp of air and my stomach sunk, anticipating his question. "What did he do to you?"

"Nothing—"

"Bullshit." He grabbed my hand, angling his body to face mine. "He said… fuck what he said, I want to hear it from you."

I dropped my head to avoid his eyes, but he grabbed my chin and lifted my face.

"It's not your fault, none of this."

I flinched away, stiffening with anger. "Isn't it though? I chose my path, just like you chose yours. We're all guilty."

"Stop avoiding the question." His tone was sharp, but his hands were gentle as they trailed along my arm.

"He held a gun to my head, forced me to watch them beat up Dexter."

"But what did he do to you?" His whisper was strained with something. He was imagining it worse than it was, I had to tell him. But I hated him for making me say it

I shook his hands away. "He licked my neck." That alone burned to say, my stomach gripped thinking about the rest, but I forced out the acidic words with my eyes closed against Gage's probing glare. "And he put his hands down my pants, but nothing happened." I popped my eyes back open. "Another guy there stopped him, the one that seemed to be in charge, real tall guy, but I didn't know him."

When a few seconds passed without him saying anything, I looked up. His jaw was clenched but that was the only sign of anger, otherwise his expression was blank.

"Now it's your turn to share what you've been keeping from me," I prompted him.

He snapped out of the daze he was in and looked towards me with doubt. "That was really it? That was all that happened? I need the truth."

I glared back at him. "He said other things, like I chose the wrong side or he'd give me a job. He also told me to ask you, 'who can't fuck with who now?' but otherwise that was it. Nothing happened."

He let out a large sigh. "He told me something different, something that made me want to rip him apart, slowly. But still, that's not nothing, I should have never left you after court."

I gave him a hard look. "There's lots of times you should have never left, but that wasn't one of them. We couldn't have known. But what's been happening since then?"

His hands were back on my knees, it seemed to steady him so I let it go.

"Rusnak and Rock have worked out a weak truce. Rock's made a deal to get Rusnak back the drugs that were taken and punished the person responsible." When his eyes met mine, I knew the punishment was death. "Rusnak's letting him have the marijuana connection he made since that's not really one of Rusnak's markets. But for all other drugs, Rock has to go through him." His grip on my knee tightened. "That's what I've been doing, organizing a shipment that's coming here to get distributed out. That's why I can be here now with you. I'm staying downstairs."

I placed my hand over his. "What about boxing? What about you not winning in the third?"

He laced his fingers through mine and scooted closer to me, his legs on either side of me. "You saw the bruises. They were fucking pissed, but we're working it out. We're in negotiations now about what to do for future fights."

"Future fights?"

"Silas is setting up a fight between me and Ray Bridges and when I win that, I'll be in a good position to fight for the IBF cruiserweight title." This should have been great news, but he said it with such weight that it seemed doomed.

"They want me to win the title, then throw the next fight to one of their other boxers. I don't want to fuckin' do that. It's different when they want me to win in a certain round, I still get my win. But this… this is my record." His sad eyes focused on me. "I think that's the real reason they have you here, as leverage to get me to agree."

His hands slid around me, cradling me into his chest. "I can't let them know how much you mean to me, but I won't let them hurt you either. I'm playing it safe for now, but if it comes down to it, you have to know, I'll choose you. Can you trust that?"

In his arms, I could believe his words. I felt safe with his strength surrounding me and ignored the voice in the back of my mind that warned he didn't have that power, he couldn't protect me. It didn't matter anyways, I wasn't with him for protection. I just wanted him and I wanted to keep him safe too.

My hands slid around his neck. "I do trust you, but I don't know if you're right about why I'm here."

"I know I'm right." His head dipped towards me and his nose rubbed against mine. "But I'll find out more today and then I'll come back tonight." His lips brushed over mine. "I've got to go, but I don't want to leave you."

Our lips moved together, gentle to intense in a flash. He pulled me onto his lap so I straddled him, and his hands slid under my shirt, coasting up and down my skin.

He bit my lip and sucked it into his mouth with a growl, then flipped me onto my back. The cool tile floor chilled my heated skin as he slid up my shirt. He hovered over me and his lips dragged down my neck in fiery kisses. Grinding his hips into me, his hands pushed at the elastic of my sweatpants.

I kicked them off, consumed with the urgency of the moment. The bright sunshine streaked into the bedroom beyond us, he had already stayed too long. But I needed this moment.

Slipping my hand down his jeans, I rubbed the rigid length of him. He rose up to his knees, undoing his pants and slipping off his shirt in an instant. Then his body was pressed to mine and his fingers glided in and out of me. My body tightened around him, sensation already building, about to burst as the rhythm increased.

I guided him into me and he filled me in a quick motion. I bit down on his shoulder, stifling my moans of pleasure. He lifted my leg, slamming into me deeper than before. The knots of need in my core were loosening with each thrust, about to undo me completely. My legs vibrated with pleasure as his lips latched onto my nipple, hands exploring me. He controlled the fevered pace, and it had me spinning with the intensity, the speed, the pleasure. I absorbed every second, every piece of him. His hot release came as he rolled my sensitive bud between his fingers, and I collapsed, falling apart.

He rested his forehead against my neck, his breath tickling my skin as he sucked in air. "It's only you. All right? Despite how things may look." He raised his head, eyes pleading with me. "It's only you I'm thinking of. It's only you I want. It's only you that I love. Trust me." He moved his hand over my cheek and neck. "I probably shouldn't, but… I'll come back here tonight and check on you."

I nodded, distressed that he was saying good-bye, but knowing he had to.

He kissed my lips one last time, a soft kiss full of longing that squeezed my heart. Then he dressed and left.

* * *

I walked out of the locker room, freshly showered, and straight into Dexter.

"Rea, where the hell have you been? Leona said she hadn't been able to get a hold of you since you moved out."

I took a step back, surprised by his presence. "I thought you weren't boxing anymore. Why are you here?"

I looked beyond Dexter to the front door, Demetri was walking in to pick me up. He had dropped me off with Silas this morning and went off on his own. It felt good to throw myself into training, but now everything was coming back and the familiar tension pulled at my muscles.

"I came to work out. Plus, I was hoping to see you. This is your usual workout time, but I guess you came a little early today." He stepped close to me and spoke in a low voice. "Is everything okay? I was surprised to hear you came back to boxing with Silas."

Dexter finally noticed Demetri walking towards us. He looked towards the short, but fierce, man and back to me. "Regan? What are you into? Didn't you learn anything from me?"

"This isn't the same thing, Dexter. Stay out of it." Although I didn't believe my words, especially recalling my morning with Gage. I had unintentionally pulled Gage into my mess, just like Dexter had.

He stepped back as Demetri took up the spot next to me.

"Dexter." Demetri nodded to him and then turned to me and nodded to the door. "Let's go."

Before I could walk away, Dexter had me in a tight hug. It felt different than any of the hugs before; there was no humor or joy in it. His worry and concern pressed into me, transferring to me, I had to pull away or be suffocated in his fear.

Demetri turned towards me, sliding on his sunglasses against the bright sunshine of the unseasonably warm day. "I followed you yesterday while you shop. Today is my day. We do what I want."

I raised my eyebrow in question as I buckled my seat belt.

"Can you use gun?" he asked with a smirk.

5: Investment

PULLING AWAY FROM THE CURB, HE DISMISSED my hesitation with a shake of his head.

"Doesn't matter. You not shoot anyways." He checked his mirrors to get over into the next lane before slowing to a stop with the traffic. "I have one errand before we have day off."

I stared at him and leaned back against my door, putting distance between us. "What's the errand?"

"Have to collect something. Shouldn't take long." He turned onto another street.

The nice weather brought everyone out, and our drive was slow as people crossed the road with no sense of urgency. We took another turn and the taller buildings were replaced by row homes, many with boarded windows. Kids rode their bikes and groups of teens walked in the road defiantly. I recognized the neighborhood, stayed with a foster family here for part of fourth grade.

Another turn and the people were fewer, homes all abandoned. A tingle of nervousness skittered over my skin.

"Here." Demetri reached under his seat and pulled out a gun. He kept it low as he handed it to me. "Put in waist band, cover it up, but show if he talks to you."

I took the gun. It was light and made of a hard plastic, and my throat constricted like I was allergic. Trying to keep calm, I turned it over in my hand and checked that the safety was on, but there was no safety.

Demetri's raised brows could be seen over his sunglasses. "Glock 17, good gun for you. Put away now."

He took another turn as I slipped the gun into the top of my pants and covered it with my shirt, stomach on a spin cycle. "What are we doing?"

"Picking up someone. You just sit there and leave talking to me."

A group of three men stood on the run down corner, a girl with wild long hair exchanging something with the middle man. They looked up as our car slowed to a stop in front of them and the girl took off in the opposite direction.

Demetri wound down his window, keeping eyes forward. "Get in back."

The men traded glances, communicating silently, and then the one on the end stepped forward and slid in the back of the car.

"Demetri, how's things?" He questioned with a nonchalant smile.

He pulled the car away as he shrugged, one hand on the wheel. "Depends. How's business? Bad enough you dealing on the corner?"

The man in the back shifted, the smoky sweet smell of a black and mild filling the air as he leaned towards my seat, yellow eyes suspicious. "Who's the girl?"

"She's my associate." Demetri nodded towards me.

I wasn't sure if this was the moment Demetri told me to act on, but the sickly exciting rush pulsing through me made me move. Better to show it too soon than too late. I nodded to him and lifted the bottom of my shirt, just enough to flash the gun before covering it back up.

He saw it and sat back in his seat. "Nah, I don't sling on the corner. I got boys for that. So what do you want? I know you're not here just to lecture me on how I run my shop."

Demetri slowed at an intersection and took his time to look both ways before crossing the empty four way stop. "I came for what you owe."

"Well talk to Nick, he's given me an—"

"Nick sent me." Demetri raised his hand, silencing the man, but his voice stayed cool and level.

My heart thumped in my stomach and hands hovered over my gun as the man reached into his pants. He pulled out a money clip and I relaxed.

"This is all I got."

Demetri took it and then tossed it into the center console like the thick wad of green was nothing but cheap sunglasses.

"That's good start. I see you next Sunday for rest." He turned left onto a one-way street and pulled the car over.

The man exited the car but hesitated before closing the door.

Demetri's hand moved to his pants, but stopped as the door slammed. He chuckled, watching the man jog down the street in his rearview mirror.

"You did good." His hands were quick and he had the gun from my pants in a second.

I shook my head, confused. "Why did you bring me along?"

The corner of his mouth turned up. "It was on the way. Figured get it over now. Plus, wanted to see how you do." He inclined his head to me. "You passed." He tossed the gun onto my lap, and I flinched. "Didn't think you would be stupid enough to try something. But I wasn't stupid enough to give you bullets either."

I put the gun in the glove box in front of me to get it out of sight. All the tension from my body was travelling to my brain, giving me a killer headache. "I threatened a guy with an empty gun?"

Demetri put the car in drive and pulled away. "Not threatened. Just warning is all." His chest jumped with one laugh. "I didn't tell you to show gun as an introduction, but it worked."

"Don't ever take me on this type of errand again," I demanded with more authority than I possessed.

He shrugged as he pulled into heavy traffic. "Why? It can help pay what you owe and it's easy. You didn't show fear."

I swallowed down the bubble in my throat. The lure of money and getting out sooner only tempted for a second before my sense returned. "That's not me."

"Suit you."

"What?" I stared at him, unsure of what he said. His accent made it almost sound like, "shoot you."

He pulled a cigarette out and stuck it between his lips as he lit it. "I said,"— he cracked his window and blew out smoke—"suit you. I won't bring you along, even though I'm expected to watch you and get shit done."

It finally clicked and I spoke absently, without thinking, "The saying is, suit yourself."

He glared at me as he took another drag of his cigarette. "You don't go on errands, you still need to know to shoot. And I need to relax. Let off steam, is the right saying?"

I nodded, unable to read if he was angry or not.

* * *

I quickly learned Demetri owned a lot of guns, and knew a lot about guns, and had sniper accuracy when shooting guns.

My arm vibrated from my last round of shots. We were back at the prison, Rusnak's place, at the end of the sprawling property where stables were set up for target practice.

"You emptied in less than a minute. Let's check accuracy."

We walked over to the hay bale with the target paper on it. I could see the bullet holes cutting through the torso and head, but there were a few stray holes on the side of the paper.

Demetri dragged his finger through the air, counting up the shots. "Looks like two missed the paper altogether, but 6 are kill wounds. Not bad for so fast."

I resisted the smile bubbling up. It had been thrilling to shoot, but this didn't feel like a compliment I should be proud of.

Demetri cocked his head at me. "Enjoy this."

I wasn't sure if it was a question or demand.

"It's all right to like this." He nodded to me.

I kind of did like this, but didn't want to admit it to him. Instead, I nodded at the paper. "Not too bad then?"

"We'll keep practicing. But not bad."

* * *

"Where is Mrs. Rusnak?" I asked Demetri as we ate a sandwich around the counter in the kitchen.

A few people had been in and out, stopping to talk with Demetri, and I wondered how the wife felt about all these guests and my presence.

He swallowed his bite. "She's at home."

"This isn't their home?"

"Ollie likes to keep things separate. He has his office in the city, his home in the suburbs, and this… this is his compound for… his… side work."

Demetri had been decent today and while we were on good terms I figured I would get as much information as I could, without pushing too hard.

"Ollie? I haven't heard anyone else call him that."

"It's a family nickname." He took another bite of his sandwich. "My sister, his cousin, gave it to him in Russia."

"So you're family. Does that mean you're second in command?" I needed to know the order. Was it Demetri or Nick who I should worry about most?

He leveled me with his gaze, setting down his sandwich. "We're family. He wants to see you before he goes. If you're done, I'll take you now."

That killed my appetite, and I didn't want to put it off so I set down my sandwich. "I'm ready."

Demetri opened one side of a double door, admitting me into Rusnak's office within the house. The room was dim and masculine, dark cherry wood and gold, obviously expensive.

He walked around his desk to greet me, smile in place. "Regan, come in." He grabbed my hand and slid it to my elbow as he escorted me to a chair. His touch almost made my dinner come up.

He leaned on the edge of his desk directly in front of where I sat. His long legs stretched out so his feet nearly touched mine.

"How was your day? I trust last night was better?" he looked beyond me to Demetri in the doorway, "No locked doors?"

"No locked doors."

I didn't turn to see Demetri's reaction. I had to block the memory of last night, not wanting to risk thinking of Gage in front of them. "My day was fine."

"Good." He picked up a red rectangular case on his desk, it was slightly longer than his hand but he held it easily. "Demetri told me you two went shopping yesterday." He laughed, eyes lighting up as he looked behind me again. "I'm sure Dem loved that. You'll have to go again though, we have more parties coming up this weekend."

"She has dress already. She needs no more."

I nodded in agreement. I couldn't afford any more.

"Nonsense." He stood up. "Dem, we'll only be a minute. Go check on something else." He said it in a way that made it clear there was a specific something else to be checked on.

When the door clicked close, Rusnak reached into his pocket and pulled out his wallet. He fingered through it and then extended several hundred-dollar bills to me.

I gripped the chair rails to keep from reaching for it. I wasn't going to take money from him.

"For shopping this week, and to pay you back for what you spent yesterday. The gym will cover the expense of dressing up for our functions." He leaned forward, pressing the bills into my hand.

I swallowed hard and my hand shook as my fingers closed around the money. "Will I have to pay this back?"

His smile softened as he looked down at me. "No. This is our expense, not yours. Silas can fill you in tomorrow on the details, but needless to say, you're worth the investment."

He tapped on the box in his other hand as his eyes connected with mine. "My wife makes jewelry. Did you know that?"

I didn't know anything about them, nor did I want to, but I couldn't tell him that. I struggled just to shake my head no. It was hard to keep up a brave act in front of him. Even though he had never been mean, I knew everything wrong originated from him.

He sunk to his knees in front of me, and my heart lodged into my throat. He was tall enough that up on his knees he was eye level with me in the chair. He smiled at my stunned reaction and dropped his eyes to the box in his hand.

"This is one of her pieces, but it made me think of you. You should have it. Wear it." He opened the box and extended it to me to see before pulling it back and taking it out himself.

The bracelet was a thick leather band with a gold chain woven though and pearls braided into the design. I still couldn't find my voice, not that I had anything to say. My brain must have escaped and I sat stupefied.

He picked up my hand and buckled the bracelet on my wrist, murmuring, "It's strong, but beautiful, like you." He looked up at me with a new type of smile, one that cut into me like a sharp knife.

Rising to his feet, he tugged on my hand, encouraging me to stand. His fingers slid around my wrist as he admired the bracelet.

"Thank you." I found my voice with my legs. I wanted out of the room and feared I didn't hide my discomfort well.

"You can go now. Sleep well." His lips slid into a grin, but he didn't move as I walked out of the room.

I closed the door behind me, heart pounding and stomach crashing in waves. I needed to get to my room and process what had just happened. That man was the master at making me feel fear without saying anything. All he had done was give me a gift, from his wife, but it felt like more. A lot more. And I felt dirty, like I had done something wrong.

Speed walking down the hall, I turned the corner and bumped into someone.

Gage.

His hands grabbed my shoulders to steady me without even paying attention to who I was. When his face flashed with recognition, his hands dropped away at the same time.

My heart was still pounding, and seeing him only made the waves in my stomach crash with more force, especially when his eyes dropped over me. It was like he knew where to look, he zeroed in on my wrist and lifted my hand. His jaw clenched as his eyes flicked from my face to the bracelet and back again. He shook his head, dropped my hand, and stalked away.

I could have crumpled on the ground right then, the look in his eyes wounded me so. But I sucked it up and made my way to my room.

Curling under the covers of the bed, I closed my eyes against the chaos and tried to shut it all out with sleep.

6: In The Moment

I WASN'T ASLEEP FOR LONG BEFORE THE door opened, letting in muted light from the hallway. The brief outline of a shadow in the doorway was enough to let me know it was Gage.

Sitting up in bed, I paused as the door closed and shut out all light. Something pulled across the carpet. It took a moment for my eyes to readjust to the dark, he had a chair wedged under the doorknob.

Before I could slide off the bed, he was there, crawling over me, forcing me to lie back down. One hand wound into my hair, angling my head up as he dipped his down. His lips dragged across my cheek, to my ear.

"You're mine." His whispered voice was ruff with demand, matching his movement as he pulled me further up the bed and stretched out on me.

One hand squeezed my waist and his other hand tightened its hold in my hair. "Right?"

I hadn't realized it was a question, but the pressure of it was suffocating, almost as bad as the smell of smoke and alcohol surrounding him, choking me.

"Why are you doing this?" Fear was beginning to beat out the other emotions he caused.

He pulled his head back, his chest rising and falling with his breathing. His eyes narrowed as he looked down on me. "Why? You know why." His hand left my hair and slid down my left arm, to the bracelet. Pushing off of me, he pulled me up into sitting with him, fingers locked on my wrist. "This." He held up my arm between us.

"It doesn't mean anything." I tried to pull away, but my muscles were rubbery.

He tightened his grip and tugged me to him as he hooked his other arm around my waist. His lips were back at my ear. "You know that's not true."

Did I? I had been trying to convince myself that it meant nothing, but his words sunk that hope, drowning it. My merry go round of emotions hit sadness and I leaned into him for support, the only person who could help take away the pain, even just for a moment.

"Answer me," he pleaded, letting go of my wrist as he pulled me into his chest, both arms wrapped around me.

"How can I? In this room, yes, I'm yours. But—"

He pushed me away from him, hands on my shoulders. "Whose are you the rest of the time?"

I jerked free of his grip and sprung off the bed, standing, anger strengthening my body and words. "Nobody's. I'm my own person. And I take it back. Even in here, I don't belong to anyone, not even you. You selfish prick."

In a flash, he was standing and I took a step back. He snatched my wrist to keep me from retreating further.

"Good." His voice was filled with so much relief it stilled me. "Good. As long as you're not his or anyone else's." His fingers fumbled with the buckle to the bracelet until it gave and slide off my skin. He threw it into the darkness of the room. "That doesn't belong on you."

His warm hands cupped my face as he pressed his lips to mine, heat building between us as our kiss deepened. He walked me back to the bed, never parting from me. Our movements were broken and slow as we moved to lying. He was flush against me, hands caressing the skin on my back and sides.

He didn't pull away when he spoke, "You're wrong. I'm not selfish." Continuing his path down my neck, his lips moved against my skin as he went on, "I'd do anything for you. Anything." He looked up at me, eyes hard and serious. "And you are mine."

My stomach dipped as his words started a heat wave crashing into my core.

He slid further down me, lifting my shirt. "Your body is mine." His fingers dragged lightly over the skin on my stomach, leaving a trail of heat. "Your kisses are mine." His lips followed the path of his fingers, sparking electric shocks through me.

Lifting my shirt farther up, he slid his fingers under my bra and I sucked in sharply. My defenses returned and I tried to push his hands away. Away from the scars.

He grabbed my hands and rose up over me, shaking his head. "No, Regan. All of you is mine, including your scars. Just like I'm yours. All of me, even the darkest parts. It's all yours."

A reckless need took over, his words hitting something in me, something primal and passionate. And I crashed my lips into his, silencing him as I moved my tongue against his.

He undid my bra and I let it fall free as he pulled my shirt over my head.

It was exhausting keeping everything in, so for this moment I let it out and I let him in. And for the moment, we were each other's and I submitted to him as he submitted to me.

But it was only for the moment. We both knew in the morning it wouldn't be true. In the morning I would have to find that bracelet and put it back on. But for now, we lived in the moment, infinite and strong because we were together.

We were tangled in each other's arms, still sweaty and weak from our lovemaking, because that's the only way it could be described. We had made love, from the moment we connected, every movement, every touch, every kiss, had built this blanket of love that surrounded us and shielded us. I was still encased in it as his fingertips glided up and down my arm.

But the feeling was lifting as the sun rose, casting a pale, ominous light into the room.

"What did you do tonight?" I asked, not moving my head from his chest.

His fingers dropped away and he shifted under me, angling his head to look towards me. "Hm?"

"Tonight, when you came in, I could smell the alcohol on you. Who were you with? What did you do?" His natural fresh musk was all I could smell now, but it had been undeniable when he first entered. And I was a fool for not asking sooner.

"I was with Rusnak." His voice took on an edge and I tightened my arms around him, struggling between not wanting to know but needing to hear it.

"They talk so much shit. All the time. I know they do it to try to catch me, to get a rise out of me. They haven't acted on any of it so I've been able to play it cool, but seeing his bracelet on you—I know what he's doing."

His rant confused me. "What is he doing?"

"He's reminding me who's in charge, who has control." His hands tightened on me. "But as long as their focus is still on me, it'll be all right."

I pulled back from him, resting on my forearms so I could meet his eyes. "What are you talking about? You're not making sense."

He rubbed his hand over his head with a frustrated sigh. "You've been playing the game well. You even have Demetri saying you're all right and coming from him, that's big. So I don't think they'll actually try anything. I don't think they'll hurt you. Not when they still want me to fight for them."

My blood turned icy, spreading through my veins. "Have they threatened to? All they tell me is that I'm here until Damien is taken care of because he is the threat."

"Baby, I hope that's true." He dropped his hand onto my head and his eyes followed the path of his palm down my hair. "He will be taken care of soon enough, but I only have one more night of staying here before the drop off. I'm going to do what I can to get you out of here when I leave."

Tomorrow, or tonight rather, now that the golden glow of morning light filled the room, he would be done with his business here.

"Wasn't this supposed to get you close to Damien? What are you planning?"

He shook his head and leaned in to kiss my forehead, pausing with his lips on my skin as he inhaled. "He should be finished after tonight, too."

Everything became tight, my lungs, my throat, my stomach, but I forced the words out. "No. Leave it to them to take care of. I don't want you—"

Suddenly he sat upright and dropped his feet to the floor. "I'm taking care of it." He stood up, jerking on his clothes as he gathered them from the floor. "You just worry about yourself and keep low. Stay close to Demetri and try to stay the hell away from Rusnak or Nick."

Fully dressed, he turned to look at me and paused, softening. "Please. I need you to listen." He sat back on the bed and I moved to his side, pulling the sheets with me to keep covered. "Don't do anything, don't take any chances today. Tomorrow, things should be different tomorrow."

I nodded, hoping I could listen. But very little had been in my control since I got here.

He pressed his lips against mine, lightly, briefly, and then walked out of the room.

* * *

I slid into the passenger seat of Demetri's car and exhaustion pulled at my muscles, a combination of lack of sleep, my time with Gage, and the effort I had just used in the gym.

"Now that's done. What to do today? And don't say movie or TV." Demetri scowled beneath his glasses.

I gave him a wry smile. He was a mystery to me, but knowing that Gage thought he was the least of the evils to be around helped.

"How about coffee somewhere and then the shooting range again?" My hand vibrated with the memory and finger itched to pull a trigger again.

He smiled and nodded as he pulled out into traffic.

* * *

"Oy," Demetri hollered, keeping me from raising my gun. "Your phone is ringing again." He raised it up, showing me.

I spun towards him and reached for it. I hadn't seen my phone since he took it on Friday, three days ago.

"It's the prison, it's called before."

I shot him a stern look as I clicked the answer button. How was I supposed to know when he had my phone?

An operator notified me that a prisoner, James Baker, wanted to speak with me. I agreed to wait while they put him through. My feet stuck in the ground the instant his voice came through.

"Regan? Shit you're hard to get a hold of."

Demetri was watching me, not even pretending to give me space for this conversation.

"I didn't have my phone. What are you doing in jail?"

"I told you the cops were all over my apartment. They found a bunch of stuff, violated my probation so I got locked up. But listen, that's not why I called. You need to call Miguel, he has some news you need to hear. About Nan."

"Um," I swallowed, clearing my airway. "All right. What's his number?"

* * *

Miguel didn't want to talk on the phone, so we made arrangements to meet at the library later. Demetri approved the location and set himself at a table to watch over our conversation.

I met Miguel in between two rows of reference books.

He tugged at his dark hair, making it stand up in a wild wave. "I talked with James and I know what he wants with Damien. Hell, I don't blame him. It's awful what happened to Nan."

I crossed my arms, keeping a lock on the sadness that Nan's name provoked.

"But Damien says it wasn't him." Miguel's eyes widened as he whispered these words that stung me.

I shook my head, unbelieving. "You talked to him? And you believe him?" I seethed. Who cares what Damien says, of course he would deny it. Wouldn't he?

Miguel stepped back, hands up. "He came to me, I wouldn't have looked for that psycho. But he told me to tell James that he didn't do it. He said he was giving James this one chance to call off whoever he has after him, out of respect for his sister. But, if it's not called off, Damien will strike back."

Miguel grabbed my arm, with panic. "I'm just delivering the message so Damien knows I did my part. James said I had to tell you since he hasn't set up anyone to go after him, it had to be you."

I stepped out of his grasp. "Message delivered. Now you can go."

"Regan, he'll kill James if you don't stop whatever you're doing. And if he finds out it was you, he'll kill you too."

Not if he was dead, he couldn't go after anyone then. That thought kept replaying in my head, and it was so close to happening.

An angry confidence filled me and I nodded to Miguel. "I'm not doing anything." What I meant was I wasn't stopping anything, but I wasn't about to admit that to him.

I turned and walked out the front of the building with Demetri following close behind.

7: There You Are

THE MOMENT DEMETRI CLOSED HIS CAR DOOR I turned to him, barely containing my anger. "You need to fill me in now. How does Damien even know someone's after him?"

Demetri grunted, turning on the car. "I don't take orders from you. I don't need to tell anything."

I was about to fly across the seat at any moment and strangle him. "I hired you. And I'm paying for it. Tell me what's going on."

His lip curled as he laughed low. "Finally, there you are. I wondered how long." He shrugged his shoulder as he lit his cigarette. "Don't know how Damien knows. News to me, but it does change things."

"What does it change?" My mind was clicking, perhaps Gage had done something that tipped him off. Gage needed to know that Damien was aware that people were after him.

He slowed to a stop at a red light, the road empty around us. The lit end of his cigarette burned bright as he sucked in, he pulled it from his mouth and exhaled a cloud towards me. "Maybe nothing. Maybe everything. Probably speed things up. I'll take you to the house and then figure out." He flicked his barely smoked cigarette out the window as the light turned green.

We turned onto the back road that led to Rusnak's compound. The roar of motorcycle engines drowned out the heavy metal that Demetri listened to.

Turning around, three black bikes popped into view directly behind us, out of nowhere.

"Fuck." Demetri leaned forward, pulled a gun from under the seat and gave it to me. "Take the wheel."

He twisted back before I even responded. I grabbed the wheel as the car started to veer off the road.

One of the motorcycles broke from the pack and sped to our side. The helmeted rider reached one arm into his leather jacket, and I jerked the wheel, hitting the motorcycle before the man removed his hand.

The car ricocheted off the bike. I dropped the gun to grip the wheel with two hands and right us on the road, the impact vibrating through me. The bike, empty of the rider, skidded on its side off the road into the grassy ditch. The other two bikes were still behind us.

The back window shattered and I ducked low, but kept both hands on the wheel as Demetri accelerated the car, aiming a shotgun out the back.

I took everything in at once. The road in front of me, empty. Only one bike left behind us, but the rider had a gun aimed at our car.

Demetri fired, just as the gun in the motorcyclist's hand sparked. In an instant, the rider fell off his bike, rolling as it tipped over and flipped into the ditch. Demetri grabbed the wheel, whipping the car in a tight u-turn that forced me to grip the seat and ceiling to stay put, a hurricane of adrenaline tearing through me.

The car picked up speed as we approached the only human mass on the road, our headlights spotlighted on the man as he raised himself up on his elbows. Then he was under the car, a sick thump and squishy crack as the wheels rolled over him—front then back.

The car screeched as Demetri hit the brakes, slamming us to a stop. My arms were out, bracing the dashboard to keep from smashing into it, but not enough to keep me from whiplash.

He backed the car up and stopped, stepping out into the night with a gun in hand. He walked over to the body and shot once, it barely made a sound. Then he walked down the road and fired the gun into a ditch too deep for me to see in.

Sliding back into the driver's seat, he said, "One more, there."

He drove slow to the first driver, the one I had hit with the car. He didn't get out, but extended his arm out the window and shot down the embankment. The body jerked as the bullet hit the exposed neck, blood exploding from the spot. But the way the body was twisted, especially the angle of the head, made me think the bullet useless. He was already dead.

"Get out. Help me lift," Demetri said, exiting the car.

My adrenaline didn't leave much room for thought, it whipped through me, keeping me alert and steady.

He opened the trunk as I rounded the back of the car and handed me gloves and a box of trash bags. Opening the one in his hands, he lined the trunk then taped it down with masking tape. The fact that Demetri drove around with this stuff in his trunk gave me an odd sense of comfort.

Following his lead, we worked together to line the entire space with three layers of trash bags. Then we approached the body and Demetri checked the pockets and pulled out a wallet, sliding it into his own coat.

I held my breath as Demetri grabbed his arms and I grabbed his legs. We lifted the stiff body into the trunk and I forced my thoughts down, knowing I couldn't handle any of this if I paused to think. We did the same with the other two men, Demetri pausing to take their wallets as well. We tossed our gloves on top of them before closing the trunk.

Wiping his hands on his pants, he turned to me. "We'll come back for the rest later." He spoke as if we were talking about groceries instead of a wreckage that could link us to murder.

Murder. My mind clung to the word, taunting me. And my stomach heaved into my throat, choking me.

Demetri scoffed as I coughed and spluttered, unable to clear my lungs and take in air.

"Stop. Get in car. No time for that." He pushed me away from the trunk to the passenger side door.

My feet were moving, but I tingled with lack of air and couldn't focus on anything around me.

Once seated, I tried to get a grip on my breathing, but this was beyond any panic attack I'd ever had. It wasn't physical, it was mental. My body clashed with my brain, both warring for control, unable to blend together.

Frigid night air whipped around the car through the shattered back window as Demetri sped to Rusnak's place. The drive was short, we were less than a mile away.

Demetri was holding his shoulder at an odd angle; he didn't lean it back on the seat and kept it hunched forward. I scanned over him, his dark shirt was stuck to him and shredded.

"You've been shot."

He snorted. "Yes. Not bad though."

I kept quiet as Demetri stopped at the guard shack and the gates to Rusnak's slid open. After we entered, he drove off the driveway, over the grass, to a large barn by the shooting range we had been at earlier. He parked the car in the barn, getting out to open and close the doors manually by sliding them on their hinges.

Demetri walked me to my room in the main house. "Wash up, get changed, and meet me here." He disappeared into the room on the opposite side of the hall.

I hung tight to my adrenaline, burying my thoughts to get through tonight, and went into my room to follow Demetri's orders.

* * *

We were in a different car, cruising down the highway. Demetri had cleaned himself up but his shoulder was still stiff, although I only noticed because I looked for it.

"Who were they?" I asked, giving my brain an inch of room to function.

"That's what we find out now. I think I know."

I liked that he said we, it made me feel slightly stable in a very unstable situation.

"Does it have to do with Damien?" Maybe my meeting with Miguel had been a set up.

"Don't think so. They knew about Anatoli's place. I think is bad business."

Rusnak could be involved in all sorts of things, there was a good chance this had nothing to do with me or Gage. But, there was a chance it did. I pulled back in my thoughts, not wanting to get a head of myself.

"How do we find out?"

He met my eyes for a frozen moment and then said, "We talk to Ollie first."

The minute we turned into the warehouse district I knew we were going to that strip club. But I didn't care. I was determined to do what I needed to do to find out what was going on.

We walked through the back door, down the familiar hallway that pulsed with music and smelled of alcohol and bodies. Demetri led the way, confident in where he was going. He entered into the room that I had first met Nick in.

Silas and Rusnak sat on the couch, and Gage sat on the chair opposite them. They were huddled around the low coffee table in front of them but sat up as we entered, their gaze shifting from Demetri to me.

"Dem, you brought the girl along?" Rusnak lifted his brow with a curious smile.

I couldn't see Demetri's face from my spot behind him, but he grunted and shook his head. "We had incident tonight."

Silas closed the dark case they had on the table, zippering it up as he slid it beside him. But Gage kept his face blank as he leaned back in the chair, splitting his attention between us.

"Come sit, sweetheart." Rusnak's voice easily relit my fuse.

"Regan," I reminded him between clenched teeth.

His smile spread as his eyes narrowed. "Right, Regan. Sit down." He dropped his eyes to the spot beside him, but I stood still.

"Get her out of here. We've got business to discuss." Gage spoke up, deep voice even and low.

"I don't mind her staying." Rusnak flashed a look at Gage and then rearranged his face for me, back to smiling, but his voice had an edge as he repeated, "Sit."

"If she's going to stay, the least she could do is take off her clothes, give us a little entertainment. What else is she good for?"

I snapped my head to Gage. "Fuck you." My nerves were too raw from earlier events, my control nonexistent. I understood him having to ignore me, but he didn't need to be cruel. This was crossing the line.

He cocked his head, lips gliding up into a dark smile. "Fuck me? I'll be by your room for that tonight, sweetheart."

It took a moment to register, a second for the words to ignite and explode in me. Then I was all reaction, all my tension from tonight erupting. I lunged towards him, pushing him with a quickness and force that must have surprised him. He caught himself before he toppled over in the chair and rose to his feet. He towered over me as he grabbed my hands to keep me from striking him.

Demetri pulled me away, putting me behind him as he demanded, "Stop." He gripped my shoulders, making me meet his eyes before he continued, "You stop. We leave in moment."

I nodded and took in a deep breath, not daring to look at anyone else.

Demetri dropped my shoulders and turned back to the group. "These men," he laid three ID's on the table, "had issue with us, but they can't tell what was no more."

They leaned forward and studied the ID's on the table.

Silas tapped one ID. "That's the man from the other night."

Gage's eyes popped up, meeting mine for a heartbreaking, fire igniting second before moving to Demetri. "Where are they?"

"In car. But their bikes need clean up."

Rusnak stood up and walked Demetri to the door. "Call Billy, take her back, we'll be there soon."

He held the door open for us. As I passed by, he shot me a hard look and spoke with an even harder voice, "I'll talk with you tomorrow."

Demetri turned down the radio as we merged on to the highway. "Why you let him into your room?"

My simmering anger went flat at his words. "Who?"

"Lawson."

I shook my head, unable to form words.

"I never let someone talk to me like that. You shouldn't either."

"I don't. You saw that." My shock was receding, uncovering my anger again.

"I saw you act like child."

"I'm not exactly thinking things through right now, not after what happened." I tried to defend.

"You did good earlier, when it mattered." He inclined his head in recognition, but then gave me a disgusted look. "But you let him get to you. He had control."

I breathed through my reply, still stuck on Demetri knowing about Gage and I, trying to work out how to ask about that.

"I would kill someone who talks to me like that."

That snapped my attention back to him and what he was saying.

He laughed at my expression. "I've killed people for less." It almost sounded like a question as he smirked my way.

"Are you joking?" I honestly couldn't tell, but he was still laughing.

"What you think?"

I didn't have a clue. But I decided I didn't really want to know the answer so I shook my head, looking away. My clouded brain couldn't think of a tactical way to ask, so I just came out with it. "How did you know Gage came into my room? Who knows?"

He shrugged his shoulder. "Everyone that wants to know, knows." He tapped the corner of his eye, "It's my job to know."

After a moment of silence he added, "But nobody cares. I only mention because of how you acted tonight. I had thought you stronger is all." He turned up the volume, ending our conversation.

* * *

I sat in my room, trapped in my own mind, working out what I should do next. I needed a plan.

The door opened, and I jumped to my feet, anger blazing at the sight of Gage. Before he could close the door behind him, I pointed to the hall. "Get out."

He shook his head, but didn't step further into the room. "You know I didn't mean it."

"I don't care what you meant, you said it. And I'm done with this game you're playing." I crossed the room to him, shoving him out the door.

He gripped my shoulders, forcing me to stand still. "It's not a game. You know that," he whispered, determined.

I pulled away from him. "Whatever. It's over. If it's too dangerous for you to even treat me halfway decent in public, then it's just too dangerous." I was mocking him, speaking the words flippantly.

He tried to step back into the room but I closed the door, keeping us in the hallway. I knew I wouldn't be able to keep up my strength alone in the room with him.

"Don't" he breathed, stepping closer to me. "Don't push me away. You need me."

"Need you? You have my mind twisted more than anything else going on, and I can do something about that. I can't be two different people and you made your choice tonight. So walk away now."

"This is you lighting those fires you warned me about. Don't do it." He reached for me, his hand landing on my shoulder. "Lets—"

I shoved his hand away. "You lit this fire. I'm just cleaning up."

Demetri's door opened and he stepped out, pausing as he took in the scene. He cocked his head at me, a glint in his eye.

"Fuck off Demetri, this isn't any of your business," Gage broke the silence.

Demetri's smile broadened as he nodded at me. "She is my business. I leave if she wants me to."

Looking between the two of them, I stepped back to my door, hand on the knob. "We're done talking."

Gage met my eyes as he stepped back.

Then Demetri stepped in front of me, lifting his chin down the hall. "You go now, Lawson."

Gage walked away without looking back, but my eyes followed him until he turned the corner to the stairs, dropping out of view.

Demetri nodded to me and then followed behind Gage.

I walked back to my room, empty, but relieved that I had finally dealt with the one thing I did have control over.

8: Signs Of Life

THE CHILLY MORNING AIR SMELLED OF THE rain that came during the night. Puddles spotted the driveway and reflected the bright sunshine. All I kept wondering was if the rain had washed away the blood from the wreckage. Guilt was heavy in my stomach, a brick that wouldn't budge.

Demetri was as silent as ever as we walked to the car. He'd only spoke to order me to get ready, we had to go to the gym and he was driving me again.

As we drove down the road, I looked for signs of the accident. There were skid marks on the road and grass. Nothing else I could see as we passed by. But my mind was expanding, thinking about what might have happened after.

"Did everything go okay last night?" I asked.

Demetri tilted his head towards me with a frown. "Hm?"

"The cleanup." I swept my hand, gesturing out the window.

"Yes, finished." He kept his face forward, eyes on the road.

"Did you find out who they were?" I asked, patience slipping.

"None to do with you."

I guess he no longer considered me part of it. I decided to drop it for now and move onto my other concern of the night.

"What about Damien? Was that done last night?" Icicles formed painfully in my body, keeping me rigid as I awaited his answer.

He pulled his eyes from the road to narrow them at me. "Why you think that done last night?"

I gulped, air stuck in my lungs as I realized I'd almost caught myself. It was Gage who told me he was going after Damien last night when he did his transaction for Rusnak.

"Well, since we found out Damien suspected something, you said it might speed up." I quickly tried to cover my tracks and shrugged like it was just an assumption.

"Ah, that." He looked between the road and me a couple of times with narrowed eyes before settling back down. "No, that was not done. Not yet."

My almost slip still had me jittery. Demetri might have known Gage and I had some type of relationship, but I didn't want to reveal that it had been more than physical. So I kept my mouth shut on further questions.

* * *

My workout couldn't touch the turmoil in my brain. And Silas's anger wasn't helping.

"Dammit Rea, focus. You have a fight in two weeks, but if you keep this up you're not going to have any more."

I tried to shut down everything else and strike his hand, and it almost worked. But I still wasn't getting into my zone, and eventually Silas called off the training.

"Go finish up on the treadmill. Be ready for more tomorrow." He started to walk away and then stopped. Stepping back towards me, he dropped his voice, "I shouldn't need to remind you that this is important. Act like it."

I didn't even have the energy to argue with him. There was nothing I could say anyways. He was right, I had to do better.

* * *

"Where are we going?" At this point I felt less than human. I felt numb as I followed whatever agenda others had for me.

"Nick needs to talk to you." Demetri had his sunglasses on now, making his flat tone even more unreadable.

"What about?"

"He'll tell you." Once he merged onto the main road, he turned up the radio, his way of ending our conversation.

* * *

We were back in Nick's office in the club, it was much quieter in the morning hours.

"I'll cut to the chase, 'cause I don't feel like wasting time." Nick leaned forward on the sofa, forearms perched on his knees and tattoos showing under his rolled sleeves. His dark eyes focused on me and I tingled with anticipation.

"I don't trust ya. You've done very little to earn it. And now we've learned that the police are closing in on Damien, putting pressure on him." He raised his eyebrow at me, pausing for my reaction.

But I had no reaction. I couldn't put two and two together.

I shrugged. "Okay."

Demetri pushed himself off the wall he was leaning on and sat in the chair next to me.

"That's what Damien knows, that's what boy was warning you last night."

I shook my head. "Why would cops questioning him make him think someone's after him? He killed a person. The cops should be all over that."

"As far as I can tell from talking to Rock," Nick began, "he thinks someone's running their mouth to the cops."

My breathing was shallow. I could feel Nick's accusation in his glare, but I didn't know what it was.

"So," I stretched it out, gathering my thoughts. "Does that mean it's too risky? You're calling it off." I wasn't sure how to feel about that, but something like excitement sparked in me.

Nick and Demetri traded glances and then Nick stared me down.

"No. It means you're going to be watched even closer." He leaned back with a sneer. "We checked into ya phone records and know ya been in contact with the police. Tell us about that conversation."

I perched on the edge of the seat, ready to run at the first sign of movement. The already tense atmosphere collapsed into unbearable as what he was accusing me of sunk in.

"I only talked to a friend, a street cop, a nobody. I just wanted to see what he knew about my friend who was murdered." I looked to Demetri, hoping he believed me. "You've had my phone this entire time. I haven't contacted anyone. I wouldn't."

Demetri nodded to Nick. "True. I don't think she'd set us up. What she say? She hired us to kill someone?" He shook his head. "She's not devious."

Nick and Demetri stared at each other for a moment, then Nick shifted back to me. "Fine. Maybe Demetri's right. Maybe ya only talked to the cop before, but consider this a warning. We'll know if ya contact the police. And I hate killing police officers, especially when they're only involved because idiots don't know how to keep their mouth shut."

I gave a slight nod, acknowledging his words. Fear strangled me, fear for Anthony. He was another person I regretted ever knowing, because I don't only hurt myself with my choices, I destroy everything and everyone I come in contact with.

"Ya can leave now," Nick said, rising to his feet.

* * *

"Why didn't you tell me what that was going to be about? You knew about the phone records didn't you?" I questioned Demetri, my muscles shaking as my control slipped away.

Demetri scoffed, sliding his glasses from the top of his head to cover his eyes. "I don't have to tell anything. That's Nick's conversation, not mine."

I buckled my seat belt and sat back, trying to reign in my emotions, lock them away again.

He started the car and then turned to face me. "I told I believed you. I do. Don't make me regret that."

His words actually calmed me. Even if they were a halfway threat, they were also a halfway support.

"Gun range again?" he asked and I nodded. "After, I have to go, more errands to run, unless you change your mind about going?" He smiled at me, and it looked out of place on his face.

"No. Not tonight." I was beginning to think going on his errands might be a good opportunity to make money and cut ties sooner, but I needed sleep tonight. I had been getting very little since this man dragged me to this place.

* * *

Something woke me up a second before the door flew open, rebounding off the wall with the force.

I sat up, expecting to see Gage's shadow in the doorframe, at first I thought it was. But before my eyes could even adjust, rough hands yanked me from the bed, dragging me out the door.

Nick had my shoulder gripped by one of his large hands, pulling me down the hallway. My heart pounded, blood pulsing through me as I tried to stay on my feet and keep up with his pace. He hadn't spoken, but I could hear the anger in his breathing and it fueled his movements and grip.

"What are you doing? Let go of me." My voice caught up with the moment. I spoke loud, hoping Demetri would come out of his room.

He jerked me forward, knocking me off my feet but yanking me up by my arm in a burning grip as he pulled me down the hall. "Shut up," he commanded.

I scrambled back to my feet as we reached the stairs. He didn't care if I walked or was dragged, it didn't slow him down.

The frigid night air hit my skin, my t-shirt and sweatpants did little to block out the cold. My bare feet burned. The rocky surface cut into my skin as he forced me over the fields to the barn that Demetri and I parked in the night before. The arm he gripped had lost all sensation as he jerked me around to make me keep up with his long strides.

My nerves fired and pulsed as he slid open the barn doors, never lessening his grip on me. The coppery sent of blood was the first thing to hit me, and then the ground as Nick tossed me down. My palms burned as they scraped the wood floor, catching myself. But the pain was quickly forgotten.

The world lost focus, the edges bleeding into darkness as I took in the sight in front of me. Laid on his back, shirt blood soaked, eyes wide open but empty, Demetri.

My hands moved over him, checking for signs of life, a pulse, breath, anything. But he was stiff, and cold, except the blood covering his shirt held warmth.

Tears burned my vision as I looked around for anything that might help. There had to be something.

Nick grabbed the back of my neck, forcing me to look at Demetri. "See what ya did? I want ya to see what talking does and what ya cost us."

I couldn't breathe. Shock, sadness, fear warred inside me, shattering any coherent thoughts. Nick continued to yell at me, shaking me as he pushed me closer to Demetri. Then, suddenly, he dropped me.

I landed on Demetri's slick, sticky shirt, his chest unnaturally solid and hard beneath it. I pushed off of him, scooting away from his body.

"What the fuck is she doing here?" I wanted to run to that voice.

Gage stood with Rusnak at the barns entrance, and I could finally take a breath.

"She needed to see," Nick seethed, taking a step back towards me.

"Stop," Rusnak ordered, clear and emotionless, freezing Nick in place.

Rusnak walked over to me and stared down at Demetri, face blank. "He is not a message to be shown off." His fists curled at his sides and he turned to Nick. "I need to hear what happened, but first," he bent down, hands light on my arms as he lifted me to standing. His hazel eyes were soft but demanding. "Go back to your room."

I nodded, a heavy relief dropping over me as he let me go, and I walked out without looking back.

9: Falling Into Place

I LIFTED MYSELF UP, STIFF FROM LAYING on the floor. The pillow and comforter did little to soften the hard, cold tile. My shoulder ached from the poor sleep and Nick's rough treatment, but I paid little attention to it.

Not wanting another surprise attack, I locked myself in the bathroom for the night, but I knew I was going to have to face them. Now, faint noises were coming from the bedroom.

A knock vibrated the door as Rusnak's soft voice spoke, "You in there?"

I should have run the minute I left the barn. Hearing his voice made me wish I had, but I knew I wouldn't have gotten far and it would have only provoked them more. Instead, I returned to the room, washed away Demetri's blood, and made a pallet for myself on the floor and tried to erase his face, grey in death, from my mind.

With a sinking heart, I opened the door. Rusnak stood tall, put together in suit and tie. He looked beyond me, at the pillow and blanket, then back at me. "Clean that up. Then pack up your things. You're leaving."

He walked over to the bed, to the suitcase laid out on it and unzipped it, pushing back the lid.

"You can use this." He looked back at me. "When you're done, come down to my office." He didn't look away until I nodded in agreement.

Scooping up the pillow and blanket, I breathed deeply, trying to rid myself of the nervous energy pulsing through me. I paused before stepping back into the room, Rusnak was still there.

He stood by the nightstand table, looking down at the bracelet he had given me. He picked it up with one hand and slid it into his pocket.

I took a backwards step, deeper into the bathroom and out of his view as he turned and walked out.

Only when I heard the click of the door did I venture into the bedroom. I went through the motions of packing and cleaning, my dread building and heart faltering as I walked out of the room.

Rusnak grabbed the suitcase from my hand and walked outside, wordlessly. I followed behind him, lightheaded with lack of oxygen.

He opened the passenger door to his Audi for me. When I got in he closed it. The slam of the door made me jump, every movement from him made me jump. I kept waiting for him to say something or do something, to blame me for Demetri, because I knew it was my fault. I had sent him after Damien and now he was dead instead.

If Nans death lit an angry fire in me, Demetri's extinguished it, leaving me ruined with nothing. It all felt pointless.

Rusnak drove away, still not speaking, and every minute that passed a dark sense of foreboding spread through me. When the screaming silence became unbearable I spoke, but kept my eyes on the passing tree line outside my window. "Demetri, what happened to him—"

"He went back to Russia," he cut me off with a sharp tone.

I snapped my eyes to him, taken aback by his response. He shot me a hard look, challenging me to deny what he said.

"He had never planned on living here for long," he continued evenly, but his knuckles turning white as he gripped the steering wheel gave away his concealed emotions.

I should go along with his story, I knew. But if he was going to kill me, this may be my last time for any answers. "Was it my fault?"

"That's not clear. If I knew it to be your fault, we wouldn't be here right now. I will find out though."

My hold on sanity was slipping as my panic took over, and all I knew was I wanted out. I didn't care what happened to Damien anymore.

"I didn't mean to do anything. I don't need Damien killed any—"

"Tcht," He shushed me with a flick of his hand, dangerously close to my face. "Damien is not my concern, never was. Except to keep him from hurting you." He pulled his hand back to the steering wheel and his voice became level as he continued, "You can talk to Nick about those details."

My breathing thinned as I considered having to talk with Nick. If Rusnak didn't want me dead, I knew Nick did.

"You were too close to everything where you were, I heard it was affecting your training. You'll have a new trainer at our DC gym. I'm taking you to an apartment near there to live at until this is cleared up."

* * *

The elevator dinged our arrival on the fourteenth floor and the doors slid open, letting me escape from the small box. Rusnak strolled to the end of the hall and the door opened before he even touched it.

A slight woman, probably in her late twenties, held onto the door. Her camisole top rode up as she leaned on the door jamb. Stretching one arm out, she pulled him to her by the collar of his coat and pressed her lips to his.

Their brief kiss ended and she swiped her green eyes to me. Her face hardened as she stepped back, letting us enter.

I followed Rusnak down the entry hall. He stopped at the second door and pressed it open. "You can sleep here." He set my suitcase down inside the door but kept walking to the living room at the end of the hall.

I glanced in the room, it was sparse but a decent size bedroom, and then I continued to the living room.

The girl ran her fingers through her dark auburn hair with frustration. "How long does she have to stay?"

"She'll stay as long as I please. This is my place, not yours." He pushed the laundry basket on the floor with his foot. "And clean this place up and put on some damn clothes." He sneered at her tiny pajama shorts.

I hadn't seen him yell before and the girl rightfully flinched away. But her small chest began to rise and fall as she stepped close to him with a glint in her eye. "I remember and I will," she spoke low as she rubbed her hand over his chest. Her gaze travelled past him to me for a second. She pressed closer to him and cooed, "Why don't you come help me in my room?"

He dropped his hand onto her hip and nodded.

"Make yourself at home," she tossed the words as she passed by, leading him into a room attached to the living area.

I went back to the bedroom Rusnak put my bag in and sat on the bed. I wouldn't unpack. I let my surroundings sink in, but I couldn't allow myself to believe this was it.

Considering my recent arrangements, this didn't seem bad at all. My life had prepared me for new places and the awkwardness of living with strangers who weren't always thrilled at your presence. I knew I could take that tiny girl in the other room if need be, and she could be useful with the way she distracts Rusnak. Something else had to be coming.

After a while, Rusnak walked into the room followed by the girl. She had changed into a dark wrap dress and was making a show of adjusting it as she entered. But Rusnak looked as fresh as ever, not a hair out of place, as he tossed my cell phone onto the bed.

It bounced in front of me once before I snatched it up.

"You'll be getting a call from your new trainer and Nick."

I twisted my phone in my hand, watching it carefully.

"If you choose to go anywhere, keep that phone on you. I'll contact you later." He crossed his arms, waiting for me to acknowledge his words.

I nodded, speechless, and then he walked out of the room.

The girl introduced herself as Kiera, told me I should clean up the living room and even pulled out some cleaning supplies, then shut herself into her own room. I cleaned for something to do. Plus, putting my space in order always helped me feel better, even if it was only slightly better.

I put the vacuum back into the hall closet as a knock on the front door echoed around the apartment. My muscles shook with the sound.

Kiera popped out of her room and raised her brow at me. "It's going to be for you."

She walked past me, checked the peephole, and opened the door with a sigh.

Nick didn't even wait for her to speak before he strode in.

I forced myself to stay completely still even though I wanted to run and lock myself into another room. But Gage followed behind him, taking away my ability to move. He nodded to Kiera as he passed by her.

Nick paused in front of me, dark eyes staring me down. Kiera shut the door, it snapped him out of it.

"Don't you have somewhere to go, get out of here," Nick stretched some money out towards Kiera as she walked towards us.

Her gaze travelled between the three of us, Nick and I practically at a face off and Gage beside her.

"Take it." Gage inclined his head to the money Nick held out.

My body ticked, a bomb counting down the seconds until destruction. Gage's nonchalant look didn't hold any promises, but Nick's dangerous glare did.

She snatched the money out of his hand. "Fine. But you better not mess up anything."

When the door clicked closed, I moved before Nick could, wanting to keep space between us.

Nick followed me into the living room and Gage leaned on the wall near the hallway, blocking that exit.

"Sit down. Rusnak told me ya had something to say, that's the only reason I'm here."

With shallow breaths, and shaky knees, I sat on the couch.

Nick sat on the opposite end of the same couch, body turned towards me. "Speak now, little one, before I lose all patience."

I swallowed, trying to unstick my tongue. "I, uh." I took a breath and started again with a clearer, stronger voice. "I want to call it off."

He circled his hand, gesturing for me to continue.

"After last—" I cut myself off, not wanting to remind anyone of last night. "I don't need Damien killed. I want it called off."

Nick's loud laugh made my heart speed up.

"What do ya think this is? Ya can't set events in motion and call it off because ya lose the stomach for it. I warned ya from the start." He paused, licking his lips and narrowing his eyes as he leaned closer to me. "This isn't your call anymore. Damien will die. Not for you, but for what he did last night. But you, you still owe us." He leaned back with a laugh, eyes scanning over me. "Stupid little girl got in over her head."

I leaned forward, head in my hands, my thoughts and stomach swirled. So it was Damien who killed Demetri. Now I knew it was my fault, but I couldn't get out of anything. I was trapped, with no hope.

Nick pulled one of my arms away, making me stumble before I caught myself and looked up at him.

"I don't buy this innocent act, little one. This was your choice. You started it, and when I prove your part in what happened, I will end it. Demetri should have never trusted you."

Something clicked in me, a puzzle piece finally falling into place, a piece I didn't even know I was missing. But it strengthened me. I hadn't been putting on any act and I needed to, it was expected. If I was stuck in this now, I needed to be sure that I wasn't viewed as an easy target. Plus, I had nothing left to lose.

I ripped my arm away from his grasp. "Don't fucking touch me."

He snatched my upper arm, yanking me across the couch, dark eyes going black with anger. "Ya need to learn some respect, little bitch."

In the same second, Gage was there, between us. He pulled Nick up to standing and pushed on his chest, forcing him back.

"Cool off," he demanded, eyeing him down until Nick took his own step back.

I sat myself up, watching this exchange, taking gulps of air to calm my racing heart.

Gage whipped around to me, leaning over me with his hands on my shoulders, pressing me back into the couch. "Watch your fucking mouth before you get yourself hurt." He shook me once and leaned even closer to me. "Regan look at me."

I slid my eyes up to meet his piercing blue ones, lit with anger.

"Watch what you say and who you say it to." His voice was a low warning, laced with a threat.

He released me and straightened himself up. "Let's go," he commanded to Nick, still not taking his eyes off me.

When Nick began walking to the front door, Gage finally turned away, ripping his eyes from mine. Then he disappeared down the hall and the door slammed shut.

10: On A Leash

MY MIND WAS SPINNING, BUT GETTING NOWHERE. I sat on the couch, trying to figure out the maze I was stuck in and what path I should take. But every direction seemed to be a dead end or riddled with obstacles.

When the front door opened, I didn't move. I waited for whatever was coming next with a mounting agitation. I didn't want to keep waiting, especially when it was only going to get worse.

Kiera's heels clicked as she walked into the living room. She tossed her purse on the side table as she looked down at me. "You're still here? I was wondering what I'd come home too." She sat in the chair to the side of me and began removing her shoes. "Well, if we're doing this roommate thing, I think we need to get some rules straight. This is my home, my stuff, and you need to ask before you touch any of it. And for food—" She cut herself off as I stood up.

I wasn't about to sit and listen to her giving me orders. I had enough people I had to listen to and she didn't rank with them. Without saying anything, I walked away. I stopped by the room I was assigned, picked up my cellphone and book bag, then walked out the front door.

My heart thumped, skipping beats, as I made my way to the street. I didn't pause in my path till I reached the corner. I didn't know if I was allowed to leave, but at this point I didn't care. I half expected to be tackled to the ground any moment. But as I kept walking, a tingly excitement pulsed through me.

Street lamps and shop windows lit up the sidewalk as the evening sun barely glowed. I turned left onto a main street, people walked all around me and traffic lined the roads. If I stayed in populated areas nothing could happen. I would have to return to the apartment, I knew that, but the brief freedom was enough to encourage me to keep walking.

My phone vibrated in my pocket, jerking me back to reality. I was on a leash.

I didn't recognize the number on the screen. Stepping away from the main path of foot traffic, I stood just to the side of the entrance to the subway system. Street performers began playing music, a loud banging, and I had to grip one ear shut to hear the voice on the phone as I answered.

"Where are you going?" a male voice I didn't recognize asked.

"For a walk. Who is this?" I tried to put an edge to my voice, but my shallow breaths made it difficult.

"That doesn't matter. You can go on your walk. You can go wherever you want." Satisfaction was evident in his voice as he added, "Within reason."

A cold chill skittered over my skin, but it only made me tense and defensive. I started walking again, but felt eyes on me everywhere.

"You're going to have to be more specific." I sprinted through a crosswalk as it counted down the last seconds before it turned red.

"Careful now," his voice was light.

I stopped dead when I reached the curb. Was he referring to my comment or my actions? I looked around as his breathy laugh reached my ear.

"What does that mean?"

"Stay within reach. You can figure it out," the silky voice instructed. "Luckily, Anatoli has a far reach. Enjoy your walk."

I hung up and gripped the phone in my hand, restraining the part of me that wanted to throw it into traffic. Sliding it back into my pocket, I decided to test the limits some. If they weren't going to tell me how far was too far, I'd figure it out myself.

The dimming light of the evening made a familiar anxiety begin to rise in me, but it was easier to push down now. I wouldn't let the darkness control my actions anymore, not when I had real threats at all hours.

With no real direction, I walked wherever the crowds were, finding safety in them, but still kept a watchful eye. DC was larger than Baltimore and the streets unfamiliar, I walked slow, making sure to memorize my turns.

After several blocks a storefront sign sparked my attention, DC Small Arms Range. The neon sign shown a smoking gun, and I stepped into the shop.

A round man waddled from a back door. "What can I do ya for?"

Walking in had been a compulsion, not a thought. I licked my lips and walked along a glass display case, looking at the guns laid out. "Is the range open?"

"Sorry Miss, just closing it down for the night. But we'll be open tomorrow day, if you come back." He stepped over to the case where I stood and cleared his throat with a phlegmy cough. "You own a gun? This one here," he jabbed a fat finger at a gun with a pink handle, "just came in. An STI Elektra." His cheeks squished up in a smile as he opened the case and took out the gun.

"It's the right size for you. Small, but unlike other 1911 9mm's, this one can shoot."

I watched him with the gun, my palms tingling. He must have seen something in my face because he continued his pitch.

"It has an aluminum frame, beveled magwell, fixed tritium sights." He stopped and eyed me. "We have it in black, too."

"How much?" I was all for getting a gun of my own and I still had Rusnak's money in my bag.

"Fifteen hundred, but you can apply for credit. All I'd need is your permit and license."

I blew out a low whistle. "I don't have one. How long does it take to get a permit?"

His face dropped and he placed the gun back in the case. "You have to take a class first, we offer them here, then fill out the paperwork and get fingerprinted." He walked to the register and pulled out a pamphlet. "Here's the information about class dates and times. Give this number a call." He circled the number with a red pen. "We can always put the gun on hold if you like?"

"That's all right. Thanks for the information." I took the paper and walked out, another dead end.

I walked around a bit more and then went back to the apartment. So much for taking control of anything.

* * *

"How did you like the new gym? The new trainer?" Rusnak was in the apartment, sitting at the kitchen table.

I continued my path to the refrigerator, pretending his presence didn't unsettle me. The past couple of days had been easy without

Rusnak or his goons around. Kiera mostly stuck to herself, but always spared a moment to glare at me if we happened to see each other. I always had a returning smile; making her stomp away was easily becoming the highlight of my time in the apartment.

"Good." I limited my response as I grabbed a water out of the fridge.

Truthfully, the gym was a joke. It had Zumba fitness classes going on in a glass studio in the back, twenty-four-seven. My trainer taught boxing fitness classes there too. But he wasn't too bad, just a little hard to take serious when he put on his instructor voice and tried to pep talk me into being motivated, like smiling was a requirement in boxing.

"You'll be ready for next weekend then? I look forward to finally seeing you box."

I could feel his eyes on me, but didn't turn around to address him. "Yes." Closing the refrigerator door, I went to walk away.

"Wait." He raised his hand slightly from the table. "How's the shooting range? I hear you've been putting in time there too." His eyes held amusement, and a challenge, as he leaned back with a knowing smile.

I met his eyes, with a challenge of my own, daring him to say more. I wanted him to. I wanted him to tell me what the guidelines were. "Good."

Kiera popped into the entrance of the kitchen. "I'm ready." Her smile faltered when she saw me.

Rusnak stood up smoothly, but otherwise didn't acknowledge Kiera's presence. "Which is your favorite gun?"

"G37." I leaned back on the counter, trying to play off relaxed, but really wanting to give him space as he passed me by.

But he stopped in front of me, eyes gliding down me then back up. "I should have realized jewelry wasn't your style." He winked with a grin, then turned and walked out.

Kiera shot me one last glare before following him.

She wasn't gone but an hour before she came huffing back in the apartment, opening and closing doors just for the sake of making noise it seemed. After about twenty minutes of her tantrum she stopped in the kitchen. She had changed out of the knit dress she had on earlier and into a tight lacy thing and her makeup was darker.

Placing her hands on the back of the chair opposite me, she leaned forward and seethed, "If you're here to keep tabs on me for him, make sure you tell him that I left tonight to go out. And tell him how I looked, too. You can tell him, I got the message loud and clear and won't ever mention it again."

I set down my fork and leaned back, not from intimidation but from the shock of realization. "You think I'm here to spy on you? I don't give him any messages. Hell, I prefer not to talk to the guy." I shook my head and straightened up. "I won't be telling him anything about this." I gestured over the length of her.

Dropping into the seat with a huff, she turned her big green eyes on me. "Huh, so why are you here?" She rocked her head back with a sick look. "God, you're young enough to be his daughter. He isn't sleeping with you too, is he?"

I shook my head and shrugged. "No." I wasn't going to share any information with her. "but I thought you were reporting back about me." I stood up with my plate and walked to the sink.

"I've only been told to call if you kill yourself or something," she said absently.

I turned around to catch her expression. She was serious.

"Yeah, he was really clear about that. I've got instructions to keep my medicine cabinets locked up and all drugs away from you."

She stood up and smoothed down her dress. "Well, I have a friend to meet up with. We'll talk more later."

* * *

"You're taking her?" I heard Kiera's screechy voice from outside my door.

I stepped out of the room, in the same dress I wore last week since I hadn't bought a new one.

Rusnak pressed her into the wall, lips moving to her ear. "I'll be here to end the night with you, don't worry."

She gripped his head and kissed him with passion, hands moving down his neck to back.

I closed my door, gaining their attention.

Rusnak pulled away, but kept his hands on her hips as he looked towards me. "Ready?" At my nod he ducked his head down to Kiera and promised, "later." Then we walked out.

I didn't want to go, but wasn't given an option. It was a charity event for kids' athletics and half of Baltimore was going. Rusnak said the boxing center was one of the main contributors.

After several minutes of silence in the limo, Rusnak shifted on the seat, pulling a familiar case out of one of the compartments. He cocked one eyebrow up at me as he opened it. "I know you don't wear jewelry, but for tonight you should."

My heart bounced around, looking for an escape as he slid over next to me.

I yanked my wrist out of his grasp, unable to bear the touch. "I'll put it on."

Sitting back, he handed me the case and watched as I fumbled to secure it to my wrist.

Once it was in place, he leaned close to me and picked up my hand with a force I couldn't easily pull out of. "I can be nice to you. Or I can be mean. You decide how this goes."

I stared at him, waiting for his next move.

Satisfied by my lack of response, he dropped my hand with a smile. "I have another gift for you, too. That gun you liked, you can practice shooting it on Sunday, at my gun range." He used one finger to move my hair off of my shoulder, sending a chill through me.

I shifted my shoulder away from him. "Save your gifts for Kiera."

He laughed, but his eyes narrowed. "We're picking up my wife now, so don't speak of her again."

I nodded and turned away, relieved when the car finally slowed in front of a home and he went in to get his wife.

They spent the ride discussing the event and who was coming, which sounded like everyone and anyone, including politicians. But Gage's name was the only one that sparked any life in me and I spent the rest of the ride trying to build up my strength to see him and ignore him as he would me.

11: Another Chance

FOR A KIDS CHARITY WITH A CIRCUS theme, there was a noticeable lack of kids. In fact, I didn't see one and I don't think it would have been appropriate for them to be there. Drinks were flowing and half-dressed entertainers went around on stilts breathing fire, juggling, and other strange things.

Pretending to be strong was easy. Pretending to be happy was beyond me, but that's what Rusnak was expecting. He warned me to put on a smile and be nice as he dropped me off at my seat. A back corner table, reserved for the no bodies probably. My smile was genuine when Rusnak walked away with his wife to the opposite end of the ballroom.

He had introduced me to some of the people at my table before he left, a mix of guys and girls whose names I had already forgotten. I ate in silence and let the others talk around me, watching my surroundings.

I didn't see him arrive, but I saw him in a group talking and my heart skipped. He wore a fitted black suit over a dark grey shirt, the same way he wore everything, with natural confidence and ease. Gage was comfortable in his skin, had faith in his body, and it showed.

Somehow he seemed even more confident tonight and stood taller than he had before. He made his way to Rusnak's table and people followed, wanting to talk to him, be in his presence. I guess that's what happens when you're a future titleholder, or was it his new association with Rusnak that made him so popular?

"That was a rude question, I'm sorry." The guy to my left leaned towards me, arms on the table and face slightly pink as he ducked his head.

Pulling my vision from Gage, I shook my head and focused on what was being said. "What was? I didn't hear you."

He picked his head up with a crooked smile. "Don't worry about it. I was being nosy and asked what else you did besides boxing." He talked with his hands in gestures that didn't make sense. "I know you can't make that much to start and I assume females make even less. And you don't appear to be beat up so I assume you don't fight much. I was just thinking you had to have another job, is all."

"You're right. I'm also a server." Well, I was trying to be, but I had to find a job first.

"Oh. A server. Well, yes, I assume you can do well with tips." He nodded, adams-apple bobbing as he swallowed. "I attempted to serve first year in college, but failed miserably. No coordination for it." His cheeks flushed and he dipped his head. "Probably shouldn't admit that to you."

His awkwardness was kind of cute, in a geeky sort of way, and I welcomed the distraction.

"I'm sorry, what was your name again?" I asked.

"Brandon." He beamed and extended his hand for me to shake. "Brandon Cutty. I'm interning in Senator Cardin's office."

Brandon rambled on about his work, school, his pet iguana, and all of his family. I was content to sit and listen, the pressure of doing anything removed.

Rusnak would look over sometimes as he danced with his wife or others, but otherwise he let me be and I wondered why I had to come.

"You should try the wine." Brandon handed me a glass from a server's tray as she came around. "Not that I know that much about wine, but the Riesling is good and I heard they are paying top price." He winked at me and leaned in conspiratorially. "Always take free things when the rich are paying."

Out of curiosity, I took a sip. But the taste was the same as any other alcohol I'd tried, and it left my tongue dry. I slid the delicate glass back on the table.

Gage slid the glass even farther away and sat down in the empty chair to my right.

"You'd prefer the ice tea," he said, setting a tumbler on the table with a lemon wedge hooked to the edge.

I didn't touch the drink. I didn't move. His sudden appearance surprised me and the churning in my stomach wasn't pleasant.

Brandon extended his hand to Gage with enthusiasm. "Hello. I'm Brandon Cutty. I intern in the Senator's office."

Gage looked from me to him and back to me with a smug smile. "Brandon? If you'll excuse us, I'm going to steal her away for a moment." He stood up and extended his hand to me.

Function and thought escaped me. I looked around at the plates on the table left over from dinner and then finally up at Gage.

Impatient, he grabbed my hand and pulled me up to standing, but I stepped away before he could walk me anywhere. I could have collapsed when his eyes narrowed at me.

Brandon stood up, bouncing with nerves. "You two can stay. I'll go and uh… get some dessert or see something…" He let his words trail off as he walked away, leaving Gage and I at the empty table. Everyone else had left to walk around after dinner.

Gage's eyes scanned around the room, and I looked around too but didn't see Rusnak anywhere. Then he stepped close to me, blocking everything else from view.

"Come with me, please. We need to talk," His low, deep voice sparked something in me. The part of me he had hurt wanted to deny him, to anger him, but my sense won. He might have information I needed to know and I wasn't sure when we would get another chance.

At my nod, he slid his hand to my back and guided me through the crowd, out of the ballroom. The lobby was just as crowded. We traveled down a side hall and turned a few corners before he opened a door to a library or office. There was a desk in front of a large curtained window and all the walls were lined with bookshelves.

He closed the door behind us and then stepped towards me, arms around my waist in one quick motion. His warm breath caressed my cheek as he dropped his head to mine.

"Are you all right?" He sucked in air as his hands traveled up my waist, over the blue silk of my dress.

His firm hold was overwhelming. I struggled not to cave in to him, but my hands slipped inside his suit jacket with a mind of their own. Before his lips could find mine, I ripped myself away, breaking my own heart, but I needed clarity and space to breathe. And answers, I needed answers.

"What happened to Demetri? What happened that night?"

His entire presence hardened, his face turning to stone as he shook his head at me. "Don't ask. I can't tell you." His chest rose and fell, his expression softening as he let out air. "There are some things it's better if you don't know." Crossing the space between us, he attempted to slip his arm around me again.

"That's bullshit." I sidestepped him and held my arms up to keep him back. "They've accused me of having something to do with his murder. I know it was Damien that killed him, so maybe it was my fault. I need to know what happened." He was the only person that might tell me anything I could half believe, he had to tell me. "Please," I begged.

"It wasn't your fault," he was quick to say, but he paused with a pained expression narrowing his eyes. "And it wasn't just Damien. It was group of them, they took him by surprise. It was a set up."

When it was clear he wasn't going to say anything else I questioned, "But what happened? Who set it up?"

He grabbed my hand and pulled me a little closer with such gentleness that I allowed him to. I needed him to open up. His fingers tickled my palm as he moved them over my hand. His thumb ran along the bracelet Rusnak gave me.

I stiffened, expecting him to react but he simply looked up at me with a sigh.

"We're trying to figure out who, but I know it wasn't you. Rusnak knows that too." His soft voice soothed me as he stepped even closer, leaving barely any space between us.

My breathing shallowed, but I still maintained control. "What about Nick?"

He slipped his other hand behind my neck, thinning my resistance even more. "You don't have to worry about Nick. He's the one that made mistakes. It was his deal that night, and he let them change the time and location, he let them set it all up so they would out number his crew. His mistakes killed Demetri, not yours." His fingers grazed over my bare shoulder and arm, and his head dipped towards mine.

His slow movements had me in a trance but I snapped out of it, clinging to what little strength I had left and stepped out of his hold.

He nearly buckled over as I pulled away, but his hand shot out to my waist, stilling me. "Stop. You can't still be mad at me. You know I'd do anything for you."

I jerked away, hearing the lie in his words. "Except treat me with a shred of respect in public."

He took in a deep breath, his hand gripped the back of his neck. "First, I knew they already knew about me going into your room, so I had to play that off as no big deal. Second, and most importantly, you couldn't stay and hear the meeting we were about to have. I had to do something to get you out of that room and I knew you would react. I saw how tense you already were." Dropping his hand to his side, he curled his fists. "I wanted to protect you. If you had stayed for that conversation, you would never be allowed out, not with your life, you would be in too deep."

An icy chill shook me, making my skin prickle with goose bumps, but I met his eyes, deathly serious. "I'm already not going to get out alive."

The look that crossed his face, a mix of regret and anger, only confirmed my words. He wrapped his arms around me and pressed me to him, filling all my senses and taking away the cold.

"No, you will get out of all of this. I'm going to get you out safe."

I stopped resisting and let myself sink into his warmth, but I shook my head on his chest. "That's not true. You can't promise that, you don't have that power."

His hands moved to my face, to make me look at him. His eyes steady as he spoke, "I can promise."

Realization dropped over me, crushing the security I felt with him. I pushed back feeling sick. "You were there for that conversation, that meeting. So that means you're not getting out."

He nodded once, jaw clenched. "I told you I would do anything for you. I haven't lied to you."

"Haven't you though? All that talk about belonging to each other? You belong to Rusnak now." I tried to wrap my anger around my panic, to keep from breaking down.

His eyes flashed with anger. "I did what I had to. But I don't belong to him. I work for him. I'm good at this and he's starting to trust me again. But you still come first."

I closed my eyes against the pain of stepping further away from him. "Except when he's around." I opened my eyes, having pushed down all my emotions. "We can't go on like this. It's killing me, waiting for these moments. It's better to stop altogether."

There was panic in his eyes, and desperation in his movements as he clung to me, trying to pull me back in. "Don't say that. I'll take whatever I can get, whenever I can get it. It's better than nothing."

I tried to push him away, but he wasn't letting me, and I felt drained of strength.

"That's not good enough. I can't do that. I can't let myself depend on you when you're not there."

He buried his face in my hair, his strong arms pulling me into him tighter. "I am always here. I am always thinking of you. This is all to keep you safe."

"No, you're keeping yourself safe. And I don't blame you for that." His grasp weakened at my words and I stepped away. "I'm just protecting myself too. That's why I need to walk away because this only makes me weak."

I started towards the door, but his hands circling around me from behind stopped me. His whispered breath sent a current through me as he leaned into my ear and spoke, "I'd give you it all." His hand spread on my stomach, pulling me back into him. "Don't go."

This tug of war was driving me crazy and it was my sanity that was slipping and losing.

"Let's leave." I turned around in his arms and wrapped my own around him. "We could leave and go away from here. Run away from all of this." Looking up at him, my brief bubble of hope burst.

The look of regret was back. "We can't leave." He locked his arms around me, keeping me in place. "Look around tonight. Do you see all the people Rusnak connects with, people of power? Even the police commissioner is on his payroll. And soon things will change and you can be mine openly. Just wait. I love you, believe that."

"You say a bunch of pretty words, but they don't mean anything without action." I pushed away one last time, headed for the door. "You're doing well in all of this, I can tell, and I don't want to bring you down." The way he spoke of Rusnak's connections merged with my memory of his easy smiles at these parties, and I realized this was him. Stepping further back, I cut lose my feelings, getting rid of them. "I have to do this on my own. It's better for both of us this way."

I pulled open the door as he grabbed my arm. "You'll see I mean what I say."

I twisted towards him. "You don't get it. I'm telling you not to bother. I want out and you don't." I yanked free and escaped the room, walking away.

As I made my way back into the ballroom Rusnak stopped me with a hand on my back. "I was beginning to worry. Where have you been?" He spoke in my ear with a smile covering his suspicion.

"The bathroom, I'm not feeling well." My head was swimming and my stomach was in a vice.

His eyes dropped over me. "You don't look well. Have a seat and don't go anywhere. We'll be leaving soon."

In the limo, his wife kept her hands on him, petting at his chest as they talked about everyone they saw and what new connections they made. When the limo pulled up to their house, Rusnak got out with his wife. Then he leaned back in to the car and spoke low to me. "You can tell Kiera something's come up." He winked with a sly smile. "I'll call you Sunday about the gun range." He closed the door.

12: Fate

I HAD SOMEWHAT CONVINCED MYSELF I WAS being dramatic when I told Gage I wasn't making it out alive. But as I watched Rusnak load an M16 assault rifle, I was certain my words were true.

My thoughts had already been spiraling down since I talked to Gage Friday. But I had thrown myself into training and wouldn't allow myself to form any assumptions about what Rusnak wanted.

The sinking realization that I would be killed started when he sent a stranger to pick me up from the apartment. Kiera had thought Rusnak was showing up and primped for him. Her face dropped when she opened the door to this other man and she sulked away to her room, just like she had done Friday night when only I came back. Except this time she didn't glare at me, she gave me a nervous, wide-eyed look.

When the man finally spoke, telling me to come on, a knot ripped in my stomach. It was the guy from the phone, the one that knew I was on a walk that first night here in the apartment.

As we pulled onto the back roads leading to Rusnak's, I fully expected him to pull out a gun and shoot me. It wasn't that he was mean, he wasn't. He was silent. I didn't exactly know why they would kill me now, but I figured maybe because of Demetri, or maybe Nick finally convinced Rusnak I was talking to the police.

I kept my hands on my legs, out in the open, and sat statue still, barely even breathing. I doubted I could move faster than him and a gun, but I would try. When the car drove over Rusnak's property, to his gun range, my blood was pooled heavily in my feet, leaving the rest of me freezing.

As I got out of the car, the boom of a shotgun sounded and I almost fell over thinking that was the sound of my death, but the bullet never reached me. Rusnak had shot a distant target in the tree lines.

He greeted me with a smile and told Boris, the stranger who drove me, to come back in an hour and then escorted me into the stables.

He had the M16 taken apart on a table. Putting the pieces together he tried to explain to me the history of the gun and the power, but I wasn't listening. All I could do was stand and stare as I contemplated if I should run or attack now before the gun was put together and operational. But my feet never moved.

"Have you shot a rifle before?" he asked, with the weapon now built and loaded, resting on his shoulder.

I shook my head, eyes on the gun.

He cocked his head with a ghost of a smile and lifted my chin up with his free hand. "Always so serious. You're much too young to be so serious."

I leaned away from his touch, but the tightness in my chest kept me from speaking.

"We have girls your age working at the club, they're always smiling and joking, always looking for the next good time. I don't think I've seen you smile yet. Those girls are fun to be around."

I shrugged and spoke through the strain in my chest. "Then go be around those girls."

If he was going to kill me, I wish he would just get on with it and make a move. This unknown anticipation was straining all of my muscles.

He clicked his tongue with a grin. "Sweetheart, I invited you today."

"Why?" I stopped breathing as I waited for the answer.

His smile grew and he nodded out the stalls, into the bright sunshine. "To shoot, so let's get to it."

* * *

"Ah, there's that smile." Rusnak took a step towards me as I lowered my gun, having shot all the rounds.

I dropped my smile. I should have shot him when he gave me the gun, but he always held one of his own too.

"Did you like the feel of it? That could be your gun if you like it." His long fingers slid over my hands, removing the gun from me, as he nudged closer.

I shot him with a look, hoping it would keep him back, but knowing it wouldn't.

He met my eyes, for an intense moment, a standoff. Then the corners of his eyes wrinkled slightly with his soft smile. "You have her eyes." It came out just slightly louder than a whisper. "And her smile. But she used hers more than you." His eyes dropped low. "At least when I first met her."

My skin broke out in goose bumps as a cold chill shot through me, my body was warning me for bad news. I took a step, only wanting to get away from him.

He gripped my shoulder as I turned. "Don't walk away from me." His voice was cold with the order, soft tone gone.

I turned around and crossed my arms, trying to protect myself from whatever was happening. "Who?" If he was going to make me fight this head on, then so be it.

His lips thinned as they stretched into a smile. "You're stronger than her though, that's a good thing."

I jerked away from his hand as he tried to tuck a stray hair behind my ear. "And she would never have worn her hair up like you, or jeans like you. She was always dressed up, in an appealing way."

It was like he was squeezing my heart in his hands, squishing it with his riddle.

He sighed. "But your mother didn't stick around to teach you any of that."

My heart exploded and I might have blacked out, but we were still both standing in the same spot when the spinning slowed.

"What the fuck are you talking about?" My head was pounding.

He gripped my elbow, maybe for support or maybe to keep me from bolting. "Let's sit down."

My thoughts were all in pieces I couldn't comprehend. Before I knew it, I was in a chair and he was dragging another one over close to me, so he could sit directly in front of me.

"I met Angela Sommers when I first moved to America, when I was your age."

I dropped the hand I was rubbing my temple with and stared directly at him in complete shock. No one besides social workers and therapist had mentioned her to me, ever.

"She was most men's type; soft spoken, sexy but classy. She was the boss' girl, but she always treated me nice." He slid his hands over the top of his thighs, his voice hardening. "I thought she was the perfect girl, but I didn't realize she was so weak. When the boss was done with her she went off the deep end and your mom became a common, drugged out whore."

Anger was boiling in me now, searing away the shock. "Don't call her that."

"Whore?"

"No. My mom." I spit the word out. "She was no ones mom. I never had one."

When he spoke her name, he released demons that I had trapped a long time ago. They took over my body and thoughts. I rose out of the chair, nearly knocking it over in my attempt to escape this conversation.

He was up just as quick, grabbing my arm, and I broke.

I spun on him and pushed him away. "Leave me alone. Don't fucking touch me."

He pulled his hands back, raising them palms up, but stalked towards me as I backed up further into the stables. I knew it was the wrong way, I needed the exit but I couldn't pass him.

"I didn't mean to upset you. I don't want to hurt you."

"Of course you do." My body was shaking as I stopped walking backwards. I'd soon be at the back wall and I didn't want to be trapped there. "What other reason do you have for doing all of this? Everything you do is to scare the crap out of me."

"Calm down." He stopped walking towards me, eyes wide as my sanity slipped away.

"Calm down?" I shouted. "I keep waiting for you to attack me. And I don't know if it'll be to kill me, hurt me, or rape me. How the hell am I supposed to calm down?"

His chest vibrated with a breathy laugh and I gripped my stomach. He was enjoying tormenting me.

"I'm not going to do any of those things. I promise and I keep my promises." He dropped his smile. "Now sit back down. We need to talk." He stood behind a chair and gestured for me to sit.

Falling apart in front of him was the last thing I should be doing. And I was trying my damndest not to, but holding it all together was like holding onto water, it kept slipping out. My rubbery muscles somehow carried me back to the table, but I walked in a wide arc from him and chose the chair on the opposite side of where he stood.

I couldn't cover my breathing, it felt like I'd been drowning, maybe I still was, each gasp only gave way to another with no relief. And my heart felt weak as it fluttered in my chest. I couldn't take my eyes off Rusnak, he may have promised not to hurt me, but his promises didn't mean anything to me.

I sat up in the chair and counted internally, trying to calm myself. I had already shown too much weakness. He had to have known he scared me, but telling him was something I wish I hadn't done. But when he said her name, he demolished every roadblock I had placed in my thoughts.

"Better?" He moved his chair to my side of the table and sunk into it.

I took one last big breath and nodded.

Eyes absorbed on me, he spoke softly, "Those eyes. So haunting, yet beautiful. Just like hers." He shook his head, as if clearing a thought, and then began again with a smile, "She would have loved events like I took you to Friday night or the bracelet I gave you. The difference is I can do more for you than he ever did for her."

I glared at him, feeling my newly found restraint faltering. "I don't want anything from you. And I don't care about," I took a gulp of air and had to force the word out, "her." Even that burned.

The corner of his mouth turned up. "Well—"

But I cut him off, my words already flowing. "But who is he? Who are you?" I wanted to add "to me", but the words dried up in my throat.

He inclined his head, acknowledging the question. "He was the boss, my cousin, Nikolai Rusnak. I came here to work with him, learn the business. Your mother—" He stopped at the look I shot him, but leaned forward towards me, conversational tone gone. "She was your mother. She may have made some mistakes, but she was your mother."

"Mistakes? How can you say that, if you knew…" I stopped myself and wrapped my arms tighter around me, one hand on my scars.

"I do know." He nodded at me, his voice soft with sympathy that only grated on my nerves. "She wasn't always like that. You were probably too young to remember the better side of her."

I pushed away from the table, anger charging through me, making my muscles jump. "I don't remember any side of her. I was only three when she killed herself, but the bitch failed to kill me first. She doesn't deserve any of my memories."

He leaned back in his chair, index finger pressed to his lips as he watched me. "I know."

His calm demeanor and simple words stunned me and drained some of my anger. But I couldn't allow it all to slip away because I knew tears and grief were just behind it.

I shook my head trying to bring the conversation back into focus. "What about that guy? Is he… is he my—"

Rusnak shook his head no, saving me from uttering the rest. "Sit back down."

Weak with confusion, I dropped back in the seat.

"Are you?" I asked and prayed the answer would be no.

He laughed, a loud, harsh laugh. "If either of us had been your father, none of that would have happened and you would have been raised in this family. Not by the state."

I slid my hands to my temples and pressed, more confused than ever. "Then what are you going on about? And why now? Why are you telling me this?"

"It's fate. That's the best answer I have. When Silas told me your name, it sounded familiar, but when you walked in to my club that night, I knew. Or I thought I knew, but I checked into it all just in case." His look of pure amazement seemed honest.

Fate. That would be mine. An ill-fated connection. The first time I meet someone who knows her, and it's him. She always was the source of everything bad in my life, it shouldn't surprise me that she would be involved in this too.

But now, I didn't know what to do. I wanted to suck up whatever information I could, but couldn't stand talking about her. Given my situation, this felt like a card I could use so I needed to get it together. I tried to let my brain take over and fought my emotions.

"So you just wanted to let me know you knew her? That's it?"

His hazel eyes crinkled with amusement. "Yes and no. I wanted to let you know, but it's more than that." He scooted his chair closer to mine, our knees almost touching. "She was… amazing. Sexy, sweet, perfect. But when Nikolai replaced her, it destroyed her. And then she killed herself." His hand slid to the edge of my knee. "I couldn't help her. But I can help you."

The slow drip of ice in my stomach quickened and I shifted my knee away. "Where was I? Did you know me then?"

He shook his head. "I had heard she had a kid. She had already had you before meeting Nikolai. I never knew who the father was." He answered my unspoken question. "She was a server at a restaurant he went to and I guess he took an interest. I was his driver then, so I would see her frequently. But she never brought you around, never talked about you."

That didn't surprise me, yet it still managed to sting.

"They didn't last long though. Maybe a year and then he took up a new girl, one who eventually became his wife. That's what finally broke Angela."

"What about you? What was your relationship with her?" I bit out my question.

He shrugged, nonchalant, but his eyes lasered into mine. "I had been young and was mesmerized by her. She stood up for me against Nikolai one time, it was only something small, but still. And there was a moment, after they broke up, that I thought maybe we could be more. But I had very little to offer then." His fingers scratched the table as anger slowly crept into his voice. "And I didn't realize she gave her affection away like a whore. It was never real."

The tender way he spoke at first gave me hope that I could use this, but he ripped it away with the venom in his last words. Maybe this gave me no leverage at all.

He sighed and let his eyes drop away from mine. "When she did what she did, it made me sick to think of how far gone she was, that she would do such a thing to her child. But you weren't any of our concerns. I figured you would have gone with family, but I guess she had none."

I tried to block out the deafening static of my chaotic thoughts and pushed down the bile in my stomach as I put on a brave face.

"What is it you want then?" I spoke clearly, with his same simple tone.

His lip curled up on one side. "Want? What makes you ask that?"

I was done and laid it out. "My deal never involved you from the start. It could have stayed between Nick and Silas and I, but you took over everything. What is it that you want from me?"

"With Nikolai in prison, I have the control. And that's how I like it." His hands shot forward and he grabbed my knees, bracing his elbows on his legs. "I want to see what parts of her you have and what parts you don't."

An engine rumbled, Boris must have arrived.

Rusnak released me and pulled his phone out of his coat pocket. "So tell me, what is it that you want?" His fingers moved over the screen as he split his attention to me.

"To be left alone." My reply was immediate.

His thumbs hovered over his phone as he looked fully at me. "All right. Done. Once you finish your business with Nick, you'll be left alone."

He nodded his head to the exit. "You can go, Boris will drive you home."

I stood, heart stuttering in my chest. I paused when Rusnak's voice stopped me.

"We'll talk more later. After your fight on Friday."

13: Taking Over

I BATTLED MY OWN THOUGHTS, AND TRIED to keep them down, avoid them. But blocking memories of the distant past only gave room to my present. Images of Demetri were still fresh in my mind and I didn't want that to happen to anyone else. I should have never let my anger decide for me that day in Silas's office. I had blamed Damien for everything, now I knew it was me. I had to be cursed. Rusnak had called it fate, but whatever label it was given, it was clear that my life was doomed from the start.

I went to the gym for the second time that day. Training was the only thing that might move me forward and out of this pit, everything else only dug me deeper. The gym was bright and noisy with a fair amount of people working out. My new trainer, Kyle, wasn't there and everyone else left me alone. I threw myself into my workout, never stopping till my muscles gave out. They reached exhaustion before my brain, but at least my thoughts felt lighter. I had to keep this forward momentum and focus on what I could do; one moment at a time.

As I exited the gym into the night lit by the city lights, the familiar tug of anxiety began creeping in again. I sped up my walk as I made my way back to the apartment, looking forward to crashing in bed, my one sure escape.

Walking through the front door, I was greeted by Kiera in a fitted knee length ruby dress. She leaned against the wall across from the door of my room. She rolled her head in my direction, a look of frustration clear in the tight line of her lips.

Rusnak stepped out of my room.

"What are you doing?" My words were out before I could consider them and unfortunately I hadn't masked my frustration either.

He pushed my door open further. "You left something today. I put it on your bed." He tilted his head, gesturing into the room. His gaze held a spark, almost like he thought we were sharing a secret.

Kiera sighed, crossed her arms, and pushed off the wall. She tried to glare at the man in front of her, but he didn't acknowledge her. She marched away, slamming the door to her room.

I took off my jacket and shoes at the door, buying myself time to think, but it didn't help. Instead, my agitation rose as he continued to smirk at me, pleased with whatever he thought was going on. I walked past him into the bedroom, hating that he had been in there. A grey, hard cover gun case sat in the middle of the bed. I opened it with caution, the G37 I used earlier in the day was snug in the foam cushions. I closed the case, my excitement was tempered by my confusion.

"You don't like it?" Rusnak stepped next to me and glided a long finger over the case. "I can take it back."

"No, I like it. I'm just surprised that you're actually giving me a gun." I looked up at this baffling man.

His lips slid up into a slow smile. "Is there a reason I shouldn't?"

I shook my head, pressing my lips together to keep silent. He either thought I was inept with a gun or knew that those around me were much more skilled. But even still, it felt like a trap and I had to walk carefully.

"You wanted the gun." He shrugged. "I told you I could be nice to you, as long as you don't give me a reason not to be." He inched towards me, so close I could smell his spicy cologne and feel his warmth. His voice dropped, but still held a teasing tone. "Don't give me a reason not to be."

Forcing my feet to stay in place, I didn't move and maintained eye contact. I hoped he couldn't hear my heart pounding recklessly in my ribs. Running my hand over my hair, I hit my ponytail, reminding me that I was still sweaty and in sloppy gym clothes. But his eyes dropped over me and made me feel exposed even in my track pants and loose t-shirt.

"It's a strong gun for its size. I had thought maybe you meant to say the G27, but you handled it well today." He opened the case. His hands traveled over the gun, resting on the magazine. "There are ten bullets in it already and I added some into this side pocket, enough to get you started."

I tensed and focused on the gun. "Started with what?"

His hand slid to my shoulder, squeezing in way that might have been meant to soothe but had a very opposite effect. "Relax, I meant when you go to the shooting range again—unless you wanted to do more."

I couldn't tell if it was a question or not.

He released my shoulder, but trapped me with his eyes as he sat on the edge of the bed. "I know you asked to be left alone after your deal is done with Nick, but if there's anything you want in the meantime, all you have to do is ask."

I crossed my arms around my waist, trying to ease the spinning I felt there. I had been thinking about what I should have said to that very question earlier, but I hadn't expected to be given another chance. I had to take it.

"I do have something," I started tentatively, I wasn't at all sure this was a good idea.

His eyes sparked and his smile grew as he grabbed my hand in a warm, gentle grip. "What would that be?"

I pulled away, but sat on the bed next to him, closer than I would have liked.

"My deal with Nick? I don't want it."

He raised his hand in a quick, silencing gesture. "We already talked about this. That's between you and Nick. I'm not part of it." His voice was sharp.

I nodded, a hard weight dropping in my stomach, but I met his gaze with surprising confidence. "I know. He's not letting me out of the deal and since you asked what I wanted, I thought I'd try again." My voice was level and absent of any emotion.

His eyes traveled over me and a slight smirk tugged at his lips. "That's not my place to intervene. But," he grabbed my hand and pulled it onto his lap, his other hand dragging circles over the top of it. "Let's see how this Friday goes. It's only a practice fight, but if you don't do well, we will discuss this again."

The light pressure from his fingers on my hand was crushing, but I didn't dare pull away. I swallowed my nervousness. "Okay."

I was sure he would make me pay one way or another, but at least others may not die in the process. It seemed like the better deal to take.

"Are you ready for Friday? It's only five days away." He fingers trailed up my forearm.

"No. I don't know what I'm supposed to do. No one's told me what round things are supposed to happen in, I don't know what to prepare for."

I had already looked into the girl I was fighting and she was butch, strong hook but slower reflexes. Although, she could take hits and had never been knocked out in her eight matches.

His fingers stopped and his hand gripped mine tighter. "Nick hasn't told you anything?"

I shook my head.

"I'll talk to him," he promised and then his gaze softened. "What about the gym? Do you like it?"

I shrugged, tugging my hand away with the gesture. "It's okay."

"Tell me, what's wrong with it?"

I had to continue the tightrope act of being nice with him, but not letting him in too much. I might be willing to go along with his advances if they felt like I was gaining control, but every touch felt like he was taking over.

"Nothing really. I guess I just was used to the other one." I shrugged and added low, "But nothing's the same anymore."

He cupped my chin with his hands and it took all my energy to let him move my head so I was looking up at him. I clasped my hands together to keep them still.

"I don't want you unhappy here. I know things are hard, but know that I can help you."

I held my breath as he leaned in closer, his hot lips pressed to my forehead briefly. Then he stood up and relief washed over me.

He stood looking down on me, waiting for me to respond I guess.

I rubbed my hands over the slippery smooth material of my pants and stood up to meet him. "Thank you." I somewhat meant it.

He nodded, spark back in his eyes. Then he turned and walked out of the room; the front door opened and closed seconds later.

I took a shower to wash away my sweat and his touch, but also to think over a strategy. If I threw this fight and did horrible, Rusnak said he would come up with a new deal. Was that a risk I should take?

My phone rang while I was brushing my wet hair. Gage's name on the screen froze me, that hadn't happened since before everything went down a month ago.

"Hello," I answered, voice barely a whisper as I strained to talk.

"Regan, we're parked out front of your building. Come down now," his cold, hard tone burst any hope I held for his reasons of calling.

I nodded and hung up the phone.

The callback was immediate. He wouldn't have seen my nod over the phone.

I picked up and said, "I'm coming down now." Then I hung up again.

After throwing on worn jeans, t-shirt, and a hoody, I pulled my wet hair back into a low ponytail.

Pausing by the bed, I opened the case and pulled out the gun. The heavy weight of it still surprised me for the size. I slid the magazine into the handle and tucked it into my large hoody pocket before walking out the door.

Gage was leaning on the passenger side of a dark Cadillac as I stepped out of the building. He wore a leather jacket over a hoody with the hood pulled up over his head. The sky was spitting an icy rain and the wind held the same icy feel. The brief flash in his eyes as they met mine made me forget the cold. But then he pushed off the car and opened the back door, not looking at me. And the bone deep chill was back.

I took quick strides to the car and slid in the back. Nick turned to me from the driver's seat, dark eyes sucking any residual warmth from Gage's brief gaze.

After Gage was seated in the passenger seat, Nick pulled off. "We're going to park and talk."

We all stayed silent, tension thick in the air until he pulled into a nearby parking garage and parked at the top. He shut off the engine but his hands still gripped the steering wheel, knuckles white with tension.

Gage twisted in his seat to face me, hood pulled down now. His light brown hair was a mess. "Your fight this Friday, you need to win in the sixth round. Do you understand?"

"No one's really betting on it though, right?" I questioned with the same detached tone that Gage had used.

"Ya fuckin' know that already." Nick grumbled from the front and turned to glare at me. "Do ya not listen when I talk to ya? Or are ya that fuckin' stupid? I told ya I would give ya the information about this, but ya had to go whine—"

"Enough." Gage stopped his verbal onslaught with the one word and then turned back to me. "There will be bets on you winning, but not on the round, not this time. But you need to win in the sixth to show you can. It's still important you do this as if there was a bet." His eyes widened at me, trying to press the point.

I stared back, but kept all emotions buried. My hands were in my hoody, gripping my gun, grounding me in reality so I wouldn't get lost in his intense stare. At my nod, he surprised me by throwing open the door and getting out of the car.

When the door shut, Nick was back to glaring. "Ya can't be so stupid that ya think ya got any power here. Anatoli may talk to ya, but that don't mean shit. So don't fuck this up."

I barely paid attention to him as I watched Gage jog around the car to the back door opposite me. Besides, Nick was wrong, he was flustered because I had a little power now. They were here talking to me because of my conversation with Rusnak.

"The hell are ya doing?" Nick questioned as Gage slid into the seat next to me.

Gage didn't look away from me as he answered, "I need to give her some tips and turning in that damn seat was annoying as fuck." His knee nearly touched mine, and the slight, almost touch was both comforting and straining.

"She's strong so you need to keep pounding away at her from the start. Don't wait till the sixth round; you're going to need those rounds and the points. The sixth is the last round, so even if you don't knock her out, if you win overall by points that still counts as a win in the sixth. But try to knock her out, it'll help your rank and make future fights worth more."

I nodded, absorbing every last word and comparing it to Rusnak's promise. "How many more fights will I have to do this with? How long till I can be done?"

Gage ran his palms along his legs and then gripped his knees; the knuckles on his right hand grazed my left knee. That small touch took up too much of my attention, I shifted away from him.

His eyes followed the movement of my legs as I pulled them away. "If you play this right it could be as little as two more fights. And that could be done in two months."

"But from now on ya talk to me about this, ya don't go to Anatoli. I'm in charge of this."

Gage's eyes were drilling a whole into Nick's head, but he stayed tightlipped.

My fingers traced the trigger of the gun in my pocket, giving me strength and making me sick at the same time. "What about your end of things then?"

"I thought ya didn't want him killed anymore?" Nick's smile was patronizing.

"I didn't, but if you're not letting me out then you should stick to your side of things." And at the moment I didn't care if Nick was the next one to end up dead.

Gage's chest rumbled with a low growl and his fingers flicked slightly, I think in warning to me but I ignored him. He needed to speak up if he had something to say.

I was at the end of my ropes and was done silencing myself. I needed to be direct if I wanted to understand what was going on. "So what's that timeline? How long till that part's done?"

Gage narrowed his eyes at me. He wasn't impressed with this new tactic of mine. Too damn bad. He may have been involved in it all, but he didn't control any of it.

"I'm not fucking telling ya anything about that. I'll let ya know when it's done and that's it. Shit's not gonna go down the same way." Nick turned the key in the ignition. "Get back in the front seat. We're going."

Gage looked to me one last time and squeezed my thigh on his way out. The gesture surprised me, but I didn't allow myself space to think about it.

* * *

The next morning, I was met with another surprise as I walked into the gym to meet Kyle for our morning training.

Dexter was next to him, talking animatedly with a large smile as Kyle laughed at whatever he said. They both turned to me as I approached. Dexter was in gym shorts and a tee that had the words 'Blame Me' written across it in bold letters. And despite my agitation, I had to smile at it and the welcoming grin he directed at me.

I walked into his hug. I had missed his funny presence but knew this wasn't right.

Pulling away from him, I questioned, "What are you doing here?"

"I'm on spring break and was told you needed a corner man for your fight." He put his arm around my shoulder and pulled me to him. "I'm here for you."

14: You Mad?

"WHO TOLD YOU THAT?" I QUESTIONED DEXTER.

Leaning away from him, I looked up at his face. His nose had a slight bend to it now, but the imperfection somehow only made him more attractive, less cute but more man. It also reminded me that he was meant to stay away.

"Silas." He shrugged like it was no big deal.

"What about your brother?" I didn't even want to say his name, but my heart still squeezed just mentioning him. "I thought you weren't boxing anymore."

Kyle clasped his hand on Dexter's shoulder. "Looks like I win."

I narrowed my eyes at him. "What are you talking about?"

Dexter laughed and raised his hands in a calming gesture. "I told him you'd be happy to see me." He turned to the beefy blonde and gestured to me. "I didn't lose. This is Rea happy."

I rolled my eyes. "Shut up. Kyle, I'll be ready in a minute. I need to talk to Dexter first."

"Sure thing, Terminator." Kyle pushed his hair back from his forehead and I wanted to punch him in his thick throat for using that stupid nickname.

Dexter's lip twitched. "Terminator? Really? Sarah Connor maybe, but you can't go giving Rea nicknames. It won't fly."

My frustration from their banter was growing. Impatient, I grabbed Dexter's shirt and pulled him away, ignoring Kyle.

"Seriously Dex, what are you doing here?" I questioned once we were somewhat removed from others.

Dexter leaned on the large weight machine that we were talking behind. "I told you. I'm here to be your corner man this Friday. Silas told me that they wanted me to and I wanted to see you anyways, so here I am."

"Whose they? What about your brother?" I had a small hope that maybe Gage had sent his brother. It was a perverse happiness since I didn't want Dexter involved, but I wanted to see action from Gage.

He threw one hand up. "They. You know, they. Whoever they are. The powers that be." He gave me a side look as his lip curled. "And my brother? I told him and he said all right. He was all over my case, but he's let up some now." He kicked his foot at mine lightly and crossed his arms. "What about you. You mad… or nah?" He gave me his best innocent smile.

I shook my head and let out air. I hated to admit I was happy to see him, but he was always a good training partner and motivator.

"Let's focus on the fight." I started back to where Kyle stood. "Does this mean you're back to boxing, too?"

"Nah, not yet. Maybe in the future, but it was always just for fun for me anyways. And now with Gage on the rise, I'm fine with helping him and focusing on school." He kept pace beside me.

"Is he even training still?" I didn't know what he knew, but boxing seemed a safe topic.

"Yeah, of course. But he's got four months till his next fight. At his stage in the game, fights don't come quick."

"Oh." In four months, I'd be out but he wouldn't be. He already said he was in for life now.

* * *

The sun was beginning to set as I came back to the apartment on Thursday night, but I was ready to crash in bed. That had been my routine all week, early to bed, early to rise. It worked for me, especially since Kiera was typically on the opposite schedule.

I trained every morning with Dexter, spent the afternoons at the shooting range, and applied to different businesses and restaurants. If I was going to be here for at least two more months, I needed money, money that didn't come from Rusnak. I'd also found a health clinic to get my birth control shot; I didn't need any more complications.

Before going to my room I stopped in the kitchen to grab my typical evening snack of an apple and almond butter. It was a bit of a miracle that I was able to keep up this clean eating. But I'd been left alone this week and that made it easier, and I felt better for it.

Kiera sat at the table and pulled a wine bottle away from her already red stained lips. Her red hair was a tangled mess, and her eyes were blood shot as she glared at me.

I was used to a drunk Kiera and her angry looks never fazed me. I ignored her, like always.

She pointed at me with the wine bottle, voice abnormally whiney. "Were you just with him?"

"No, I wasn't." I continued to cut my apple into wedges.

"How many times have you been with him this week?" She stood up from her chair, wobbly on her feet. "Because I haven't seen him at all and I know that's because he's replacing me with you." She was near tears but I had no sympathy.

I transferred my apple onto a small plate and then turned to her with a sigh. "Kiera, I haven't seen him since Sunday. Get it together, he's not worth this." I gestured to her sloppy state.

Her face twisted as the tears began. "See, you don't even know how great he is. He's going to regret doing this to me. He can't put me to the side, I know too much. He won't answer my texts, so you be sure to tell him. I know he's more than just a businessman, he better start remembering me or—"

"Shut up." I stepped towards her, an unexpected concern taking control. "Don't say anymore. Don't tell me anymore. Don't tell that to anyone and for the love of God, do not threaten him with that." This girl was unhinged if she thought blackmailing him would get her anywhere good.

She sniffled, but her glassy eyes seemed to register the advice in my words for a moment. But then she took another swig of her wine bottle and tossed it into the sink. "You're just trying to protect him," she concluded and walked out of the apartment.

I blocked out the mini drama, it wasn't my concern. Especially tonight, the night before my fight, I couldn't spare thoughts to worrying about her out in the city, a sloppy, crying, mess.

* * *

Dexter and Kyle followed me out to the ring as the music blasted. The crowd and venue was larger than the other two fights combined but I was the opening match, so there were still plenty of empty seats.

I had tunnel vision, only focused on the ring as I walked out. But as I waited for my opponent to be introduced and Dexter rattled on words that were meant to pump me up, I turned and all my focus went to Gage in the front row.

His eyes locked with mine and there was nothing else, not at that moment. Only him. Someone bumped his shoulder and it snapped me out of it. Leona, Aliya, and Danny were in the seats next to him.

I gave a little smile to them and turned around, a new nervousness taking over, as I recalled the picture Demetri had texted me that first day. Even if they did nothing wrong, associating with me wasn't safe. I wanted to yell at Dexter for inviting them, but knew all my focus needed to be on the task at hand.

Gerri Luxman was in the ring. Her brown curls slicked back and tied in a pouf. She was standing in her corner, statue still, waiting for the fight to begin.

The first two rounds were uneventful. I landed only a few body blows, which felt more like hitting a brick wall; they didn't seem to faze her. She didn't get any punches though. I was able to block the few she attempted. We mainly gave each other space as we circled around the ring.

The third round started with a punch to my head. And I felt it. An explosion of pain and white that rocked my vision and snapped my head. But I stayed standing and blocked the rest of the combination she threw my way.

Retreating a few steps back, I blinked a few times, clearing the fuzzy spots. The pain throbbing in my left temple was welcomed as it took over my thoughts. The girl who delivered it became my only focus and I stepped towards her. The sting radiated through my body, alerting my muscles.

She jabbed in my direction to keep me back. But I slipped past and my gloved fist made contact with her stomach and then her chin. She hit my sides, lightning pain shooting through me with each blow. I was high off the pain, exhilarated. I was confident I could take it all and continue standing.

I took a few more punches to the side as I delivered two more to her ribs. Her strength wavered, her punches lessening and my fist now shook her body instead of hitting a wall.

The bell rung and we had to separate. Adrenaline pulsed in me, consuming and covering my pain.

Dexter pushed something cold to the side of my head and ear.

"How you feeling?" at my nod he continued, "I think you won that round too, you landed the better, cleaner hits, and more of them. You're making a dent in her." His words confirmed my thoughts.

"Only three more rounds. You got this," he reminded me.

I had to go three more rounds. I sucked in air. I felt good, plenty of stamina left. Rising to my feet, I pushed away the cold press and shook out some of my muscles.

The next round I came out swinging, eager to get back to where we were. It took a few more body shots till she dropped her arms enough to let me get a head shot. I took full advantage of the opening and landed a quick three punch combination, two to her left cheek and a slamming one to her right that sent her to the ground.

She bounced up almost immediately, but stayed on one knee taking advantage of the count to recover. The fire in her eyes as she drilled into me only made my own fire blaze higher. I loved the anticipation and smiled broadly in response to her sour look.

At nine she sprung to standing, lunging towards me with fist flying. She was losing control and I loved it. I ducked down, below her swinging arm and my fist sunk into her stomach. She buckled and retreated a few steps back.

She kept her distance, jabbing the air if I tried to get too close and I was fine with giving her space for now. I had two more rounds to go.

The fifth round, she had recovered enough to attack again, but she still tried to keep me away. She was taking advantage of her longer arm reach and as I tried to get inside them, she landed another punch to my left temple. The flash of light wasn't accompanied with pain this time, but a roaring thunder. I felt nothing as my vision tunneled.

I didn't retreat back, but stepped in close and took my own shots. A quick series of shots to her torso, each one pushing her back, inch by inch, till she was against the ropes. I raised my punches and connected several to her jaw. The ropes were all that kept her up. My body moved, continuing the onslaught, but my mind sparked a warning, it couldn't end yet. Stopping my swings was painful, and my excitement flashed to anger as I let my brain take control of my actions.

I stepped back some and slowed my punches, giving her enough space to pick herself up and block. I had to make it look natural.

The referee pushed me back further, standing in between a bloody Gerri and me. Then the bell rung and we each moved to our corners. Gerri's team stuck cotton up her nose to stop the bleeding.

Dexter wiped my face and gloves with a towel, and then he reapplied Vaseline to my face with a large, goofy grin.

"You're there. You got this…"

I couldn't focus on his words. My muscles sung with the need to finish this and I watched my opponent until the sixth, and final round began.

She stood back up, but I was thrilled to see the weakness in her slightly shaky muscles. I charged back in, her punches barely registering. My only concern was to get back into position, inside her arm reach. Once there, I didn't let up with my punches to her torso, and as her arms fell away, I connected with her face. Repeatedly. My arms moved over and over, my body vibrated with each impact, until she dropped to the ground.

As far as I was concerned, there was nothing beyond the ring. Only the ref's counting reached my ears. Only the sight of her trying to raise herself up filled my vision.

"Six."

She lifted up, her arms straight beneath her.

"Seven."

Head lifted, blood dripping from her mouth.

"Eight."

Her head rolled back down.

"Nine."

She dropped her arms. Giving up the fight.

"Ten."

I won. In the sixth. With a Knockout.

When Dexter jumped around me in congratulations, my mind opened back up to the outside world and the first thought was Gage. I turned to the spot he had been, but the seat was empty.

15: Delivered

I SCANNED THE ROOM, LOOKING FOR GAGE but never finding him. Even as a few reporters representing papers and blogs I never heard of questioned me, I still searched with the corner of my eye. I wanted to see him. I felt charged with energy but his disappearance again was an anchor, reminding me that tonight's victory wasn't worth celebrating.

The more time that passed, the heavier the realization became. I won. I did what Nick wanted. It changed nothing. But in time it would, I reminded myself. I had won. And I would do it two more times, and then I would be free of this. I could do it, I had to. But Gage would still be in.

I cut the reporters off, I was barely able to focus on the questions anyways. A buzzing filled my head, intensifying as the pain returned. My sides ached and ear throbbed. But it was a delicious ache that made me feel stronger. I could take whatever was thrown at me, head on.

Dexter pulled me back to a locker room, and after taking off my gloves, cutting away the tape, and giving me an ice pack, he left me to shower and change.

The cool water felt good on my heated skin, but I kept the shower short, my body too wired to stay in one spot. I dressed in jeans, t-shirt, and zip up hoody then checked out my face in the mirror, my lower left jaw was an angry red that traveled to my almost purple ear. I poked the offended ear and nearly laughed. She had hit me good, but it didn't matter.

It reminded me of when Gage had reprimanded me my first fight for celebrating a win where I was hit, twice. This time I had been hit a lot more, my ribs were evidence of that, but I couldn't stop the surge of pride I felt all the same. I just wish he had stuck around, even if it was to yell at me about it, I'd enjoy that fight.

I had to shake him from my thoughts.

The second I stepped out of the locker room I was surrounded.

"Fan-fucking-tastic fight," Aliya wrapped her arms around me.

Leona was the next to step up. "I would ask what you've been up to, but I can tell you must have been training."

"You killed it out there." Danny gave me a half hug. "You ready to party?"

I looked around the excited group, wanting to say yes, but doubting I should.

Dexter raised an eyebrow at me. "C'mon Rea. You need some fun." His bright smile was persuasive.

But the air was vacuumed from me as Gage stepped to my side. I hadn't been looking for him just then and didn't see him approaching. His eyes were bright, his dark grey shirt and dark denim jeans contrasted nicely with the light color. The fit of his clothes showed off his hard body, and I had to remind myself he wasn't mine to touch.

He looked down at me and one hand pushed my hair back from the side of my face as he inspected my ear.

"You did good. You feeling okay?" His voice was just as soft as his smile.

I shrugged his hand away and nodded.

"Are we watching the next fight or do you want to go out now?" Danny asked, rubbing his hands together.

"You should come with us," Aliya said to Gage.

But Leona frowned and looked to Dexter as she grabbed his hand and said something too low for anyone else to hear.

Gage hadn't taken his eyes off me, I knew because I could feel the intensity of his gaze as I looked anywhere else.

"Regan and I have other plans tonight," he spoke evenly.

I whipped my eyes to him, excitement building as we made eye contact. He grabbed my hand in his and heat traveled through me. There was no way I could say no, and I didn't want to.

Aliya grinned at us but nudged my shoulder. "Maybe another night then. But frickin' answer your phone sometimes."

I nodded to her, barely able to look away from Gage, and waved to everyone as he walked us out of the building.

The parking garage was filled with cars, but nobody was around but us. He kept me close to him, tugging on my hand if I slipped too far away as we walked to his SUV. We both hadn't spoken and I didn't know what to say or if I could even speak. I didn't know what I was doing. All I knew was that I wanted him. I wanted to share my adrenaline rush with him. I wanted to celebrate this small victory with him.

He pulled me to the passenger side door and opened it for me. I set my bag down on the floorboard of the seat, but the thought of letting his hand go, breaking our connection, gripped my heart. I looked up at him, taking a step towards him instead of into the car.

He moved towards me at the same time, and then his full lips were on mine and every wall I had tried to put up against him disappeared, like the imaginary blocks they were. He pulled me into him, our bodies pressed together, as his arms wrapped securely around me, heat radiating between us. My hands moved up his shoulders, neck, and then into his hair, fingers running through the silky thickness of it. I gripped his hair, angling his head to let my tongue explore his mouth further. I had missed this and finally felt like a piece of me was back in place.

His chest vibrated as he moaned into my mouth and then his arms dipped down, picking me up and guiding my legs around his waist. His hand snaked up my back and tangled in my hair as he held my head in place. Taking the few steps to his car, he set me down on the passenger seat, leaning over me. His lips dragged down my chin and neck with hot nibbles and licks. His hand unzipped my sweater but stayed on top of my shirt as he glided them over my curves, from chest to hip.

I pulled at the front of his shirt, wanting him to be on me, to feel his body pressed to mine again. His fingers ran along the edge of my jeans, tickling the skin underneath. I nearly cried out when I felt him slow his kisses and pull away.

My hands still fisted the material of his shirt, not letting him go, not letting him pull away, as I searched his face.

His features were broken with a mix of too many emotions to decipher, and his mouth kept opening to say something but he didn't. His face firmed with his decision made. He kissed my lips in a soft peck, but pulled my hands from him at the same time. Then he stepped away and closed the door.

A few deep breaths and he was in the driver's seat pulling out of the garage. I tried to get a grip on the ache in my chest. He was here next to me, he hadn't left me, only ended the kiss.

I licked my lips, taking in the remaining taste of him, easing the tightness in my muscles. As we turned onto the street, I questioned, "Where are we going?" I should have asked sooner.

His knuckles turned white as his one hand gripped the steering wheel; His other hand moved to my leg and squeezed my knee. "Trust me, okay?"

Those walls that disappeared at the touch of his lips began going up again, maybe they were more like sliding doors.

I ignored his question, like he had ignored mine. "Where are we going?" I asked with more force and tossed his hand off of my knee.

His heavy exhale was all the answer I needed. My heart clenched with the knowing, he was stabbing me in the back. I had been so stupid to walk off with him, to think that he was here for me, really for me, and not for Rusnak or Nick.

"To the club. Nick needs to talk to you." His voice was flat, but his eyes were watching me.

Tears burned behind my eyes. "I was so fucking stupid." I was unable to hold back my thoughts, he had sliced me open and it was all spilling out. "I should have known you only showed up tonight for them. You wouldn't come here for me."

"I'm here for you," he interrupted me. "I wanted to see you. I have to take you there, but I wouldn't do it if I thought it was dangerous for you. But I'll stay with you the entire time, I'll keep you safe. I wouldn't let them hurt you."

I knocked his hand away as he reached for me. "That's bullshit and you know it. Were you keeping me safe when I was with Demetri, when I was stuck at Rusnak's, or how about now while I'm at his girlfriend's place. Tell me how you're keeping me safe because I don't see you anywhere around."

His eyes flashed to me, lit with anger, and he pulled the SUV over to the curb and threw it into park. Cars zoomed past us.

"Are you fucking serious right now? I'm doing what I can. You're the one that pushed me away. You're the one that made the choice to get involved in the first fucking place, not me. I told you to stay away and what did you do? You made a deal with Nick and Silas. This is all your fucking fault and now you're throwing it in my face that I'm not doing enough?" He pressed his lips together, breathing through his nose, reigning in his emotion. When he spoke again his voice was calmer, but still strained with anger. "Don't take your mistakes out on me. I'm doing what I can."

I couldn't respond to what he said because I knew he was right. I had brought this all on myself and it wasn't his job to fix it. But I wanted to rip the truth from him, I wanted him to face it and admit that he had no control, just like me.

"But that's just it, you can't do anything. This is my mistake and you can't fix it, so don't act like you can."

He ran his hand through his hair and let out a frustrated sigh, then leveled me with a look. "I can do more than you think." The seriousness in his voice was chilling.

I shrugged, feeling the weight of the moment. I no longer wanted to fight with him, not when I had to let him go.

"Let's go. I want to get this meeting over with." I also wanted to get away from him. The physical pain I felt from my fight was nothing compared to the pain Gage had delivered tonight.

He was about to move the car to drive, but slid it back to park. "Wait, I have to know." He closed his eyes, hands gripping the wheel. "What's going on with you and Rusnak?"

The thick emotion in his voice nearly choked me. "Nothing." I didn't want to tell him how he knew me. I didn't want to talk at all. I didn't trust Gage anymore. No matter what his words, his actions have repeatedly shown he would choose them. I couldn't blame him, but I wasn't going to trust him either.

He gave me a side look, with narrowed eyes. "He usually lets his captains take over a deal and doesn't interfere. But he keeps stepping in on your deal with Nick. I thought it was to get to me, but I've worked my shit out with him now. So what's going on?"

I sat up. "You worked your stuff out with him? What does that mean? Are you throwing your fight?"

He shook his head. "I told you, I'm in now. I get to keep my boxing career, but I work for him." He shrugged. "He's not so bad. As long as you get your job done, he's fair. That's why I know he wouldn't hurt you. At least I don't think he would. He hasn't, has he?"

I shook my head, trying to process. He had said he wouldn't keep our relationship a secret once he didn't have to. It sounded like he didn't have to now, but I doubted he would do anything to jeopardize his place by Rusnak's side.

"Has he tried anything? I know he gave you gifts, but you can say no to him."

I stared at my hands. "Doesn't seem like the type of guy who takes a no very well."

Gages eyes flashed and his jaw clenched, but his phone beeped and pulled his attention before he could respond.

"Hello. We'll be there soon—Twenty minutes." His eyes slid to mine. "Yeah, maybe. We can talk about it when we get there." His thumb slid over the screen, ending the call. Then he slid the phone back in his pocket.

He put the car in drive, merging into traffic, and kept his eyes forward as he said, "you can say no. In fact, you should say no. He might give you gifts, but he won't interfere with Nick's deal with you. So don't think letting him touch you will get you anywhere."

I bit my tongue, tasting acid from my stomach. I wasn't talking to Gage about this. He was speaking with jealousy, that was clear in his harsh tone.

"Say something. Has he tried anything? Have you let him? Would you let him?" The disgust in his tone lit my anger. He had no right to judge my actions, not when he wasn't innocent either.

"I'll do whatever I have to do to get the hell away from all of this." I turned away from him to look out the window, but peeked back with the corner of my eye.

He jerked his head to look at me, but only for a moment before he had to focus on the road. The muscles in his jaw worked as he clenched his teeth, and the lines of his muscles in his arms flexed as he gripped the steering wheel.

We both stayed silent the rest of the ride.

Gage parked around the back of the building, tires crunching over the rocks as the drive turned to gravel.

"Regan," my name came out like a whispered plea. "I need—"

I shut the door on his words, sliding out the minute the SUV had parked. I wasn't going to be sucked in by his words anymore.

I gripped the strap of my bag on my shoulder and walked to the back entrance, not waiting for him.

His car door slammed, then his quick footsteps were behind me and I jerked back, turning, as he grabbed my arm. "I'm trying to fucking talk to you."

I let out one puff of a sarcastic laugh. "I thought it was Nick I'm supposed to be talking to?" I used my hand to peel his fingers off of my arm, meeting his angry eyes with my impassive stare.

"Don't go in there with this damn attitude. Just sit and listen to what he says, all right?" He stepped closer to me but didn't touch me again, his arms crossed over his chest.

And even now, the heat coming from him caused my stomach to dip and I crossed my own arms, just to keep from touching him. I had spent the ride wrapping my anger around all of my emotions and all my pain, but he still managed to untangle them with just a glance.

I nodded, tight lipped. I was fine with keeping quiet for now.

He opened the door for me, but stepped in front of me as we walked down the hall to Nick's office. Gage walked in without knocking, but nobody was in the room. He went straight to the drink cart and poured himself a shot. He slammed it, then opened the mini fridge and took out a beer and water. Walking back over to me, he handed me the water, then took a seat on the couch and pulled out his phone.

"Have a seat," he said, looking down at his phone as his thumbs bounced on the screen.

I sat in the chair opposite Gage, the one that gave me a better view of the door. Sliding my bag off my shoulder, I placed it between my feet, then opened the water and drank. The night's events were catching up with me and I needed something to ease the pain in my head.

Gage leaned back in his seat, eyeing me with a stern face as he sipped his beer. He leaned forward suddenly, about to speak, when Nick walked in.

He strode in, casual and confident. He flashed a smirk my way as he went to the drink cart and mixed a glass. "You managed to pull it off, little one. Maybe Silas was right about you."

He sat next to Gage on the couch, setting his glass on the coffee table between us. Side by side, both resting their forearms on their knees as they leaned forward, the resemblance between them was clear. I had thought Gage was nothing like his uncle and it pierced my heart to admit I'd been wrong.

Nick's eyes swiped over me and his smile grew. "Look at that bruise. Ya gonna feel that in the morning."

I nodded, putting a lid on the simmering anger that his delight caused.

"Let's get to business, all right?" Gage spoke up.

Nick looked to him and nodded, smirk evaporated. "Sure." Then he brought his focus back to me. "You ready to fight again? Silas worked out another fight in two weeks."

"I thought it was next month?" Gage cut in.

Nick's smirk was back as he took a slow sip of his drink. "That was earlier. Anatoli told Silas to find another fight, something sooner." He shrugged. "Everyone want's this done with."

Lines creased between Gages brows, "But she's going to need time to prepare and recover. She—"

"It's fine. I want this done with, too. Who is it?" I stopped his argument. I was skeptical of Rusnak's motive, but the one thing I knew it meant was that Gage was wrong. Rusnak would intervene on my behalf.

"Fuck if I know. Silas has all that information, he should be here soon." Nick leaned back in the chair sipping his drink.

The door opened, but instead of Silas, it was Rusnak. His black suit was tieless and the top buttons of his shirt were undone. Everything else about him was put together, though, not a hair out of place and perfect white teeth shown as he smiled.

"Congratulations Regan, I heard you had an impressive win." He sucked in air as he looked at me, "But you didn't go unscathed."

Maybe I should have kept my hair down.

Gage had stood up when Rusnak entered. "You got a minute to talk?"

Rusnak shrugged one shoulder. "Maybe later, right now I need to talk to Regan." He looked back at me and nodded his head to the door. "Come with me."

I looked towards Gage as I stood, stomach gripped tight. Didn't he say he wasn't leaving me alone? Now was the time to prove that, to prove he meant any of what he's told me. But Gage wouldn't meet my eyes. Instead, he was staring through Rusnak, face unreadable.

"Come on." Rusnak held the door open for me, waiting for me to listen.

I picked up my bag in one hand and walked out. As I passed by Rusnak, he slid his hand to the small of my back, guiding me where to go. The door closed as he let go of it, and then we were alone in the hall. I counted to ten in my head, waiting for Gage, but he never came.

Rusnak led me into another room, a bigger office than the one we were just in, with nicer decorations as well, dark cherry furniture with red accents. The smell of cigar smoke clung to the room and made the open space suffocating.

As the door closed and he clicked the lock, my heartbeat quickened and I gripped my bag closer to me.

He walked around his desk and sat in his leather chair as he opened a bottom drawer and rummaged through it. He popped up into standing and crossed the space between us with long easy strides.

"Here's your take from tonight." He held out a wad of cash for me, hundred dollar bills on the top.

"That should go to Nick." I stepped back from the money, not wanting to tempt myself.

Rusnak smiled and kept the money raised to me. "He's got his share already. This is for you. You're going to need money."

Not wanting to argue, I took it. Maybe it wasn't as much as it appeared. I would count it later. For now, I shoved it into my front pocket and nodded to him in acceptance.

His arm shot out and snatched the bag in my hand.

I tried to pull it back at first, keeping my grip tight, but thought better of it and let him take it. "What are you doing?"

"I'm checking something." He unzipped the top, then the inside pocket, and his smile grew. "I knew it. You don't wear the bracelet I gave you, but this," He slid my gun out and raised his eyebrow at me. "This you carry with you. It's illegal to carry out of its case." He clicked his tongue at me.

I rolled my eyes and took my bag back. He didn't need to see the rest. "It's illegal for me to have a gun. I'm not licensed."

His eyes were bright with amusement. "Well then, I'll have to get you one."

"Why did you tell Silas to schedule a fight sooner?" I asked directly, not in the mood for his banter.

He stared at me for a moment, and then he inclined his head to the couch along the wall. "Let's have a seat and talk."

I looked to the gun he still had in his hands, my gun, and walked to the seat. Damn, I don't think sometimes. What good did I think a gun in my backpack would do?

He sat next to me and followed my gaze to the gun. "Here, put it away. I was just curious." He handed it back to me.

This man confused the hell out of me. I took it from him and zipped it back into my bag.

He stretched his arm on the seat behind me as he leaned back, watching me. "I told him to speed it up because I know you want out, to be left alone when this is done."

That's the story he was going with. Fine. I still wasn't sure if I believed him, but I would go with it, for now.

He moved his hand on the couch, the tips of his fingers playing with the end of my ponytail. "Are you sore from the fight?"

I sat up further, moving out of his reach. "I'm fine."

His eyes narrowed and lip curled, his hand still floating where my hair once was.

"Was there something you wanted to talk to me about?" I kept control of my voice, not letting my nerves show.

"You wanted out of the deal with Nick last week. I wanted to see how you felt now."

"You said you couldn't do anything because my deal was with Nick, not you." I spoke slow, unsure of where to step or what to say. Certain I was being lured into a trap.

"Wouldn't do anything, not couldn't. I can do what I want. But I'm still not willing to completely interfere. I only wanted to know how you felt about it now that you won."

"I'm fine. I'm going to go through with it. So if that's all…" I stood up, wanting to end this conversation. I was tired of never knowing what to expect.

"No, that's not all" He stood up with me, grabbing my elbow and taking a step towards me at the same time. "Was there anything else you needed? Wanted?"

I jerked away by reflex. "Nothing. I don't want anything from you." I took a step back towards the door, still facing him but putting distance between us.

His eyes narrowed as he considered me, but a smile tugged at his lips. "I know you were looking for work this week, applying to different places. If you want more money, all you have to do is ask. I could give you a job."

"No. I'm all right." Agitation was building as I thought of working for him. I wouldn't.

"I insist. If you want to work, work at the gym. They'll work with your training schedule, they pay well, you can walk there, and they won't mind when you show up with bruises like this." He stepped close and ran the back of his fingers over my cheek.

"No." I pushed his hand off of me, but didn't step away. I didn't want to show any weakness. "I don't want anything from you. My deals with Nick, not you."

He had my ponytail in his hand before I even finished, jerking my head back, forcing me to look up into his angry face. "I have been nothing but nice to you. The least you could do is say thank you."

I met his eyes, unblinking. My fight adrenaline was back, coursing through me, tightening my body. "Thank you."

His lips curled up as his head dipped close to mine. He wound his hand up in my ponytail, pulling it tighter, my scalp burned as he forced my head back further.

"I think I like you better scared." His voice was low and his warm breath dripped in my ear.

His grip didn't allow my head to move, but I did my best to look directly at him. "Too damn bad." I tried to insert as much strength into my voice and glare as I could. I wouldn't give him the satisfaction of seeing me scared. Not tonight.

I knew I was only inciting him further, but at this point, I didn't care. I wanted to force his hand, make him show his cards. I was tired of this game. And he was finally showing himself.

He pulled his head back to look at me. His free hand moved to my neck, lightly wrapping around it. "I know you're lying, I can feel your pulse. But that's a good try." His hand in my hair didn't let up as the other one slid down my neck and over my shoulder to my back. He pulled me in close, against him, and whispered in my ear, "Or are you more turned on than scared. Is this how you like it?" His teeth grazed my ear lobe and then he sucked, sending shivers over my skin.

I moved my hands between us, gripping the firm fabric of his jacket, unsure if I meant to push him away or pull him closer.

A knock at his door made him release my ear and I dropped my hands.

"Another time then," he whispered as he unwound his hand from my hair and let me go.

He unlocked the door and opened it. "What is it?" he snapped.

Gage stood in the doorway. He glanced in at me before focusing on Rusnak. "The ones from last night are back, and Silas is here for Regan."

Rusnak took a deep breath and buttoned the coat to his suit. "Tell Boris to take her home when she's done talking to Silas," he ordered and walked out of the room, leaving me alone with a pissed off Gage.

I picked up my bag and walked to the door. Gage stepped back to let me pass but his eyes followed me the entire time.

"Back to Nick's office," he said as I walked down the hallway.

The knots in my stomach eased some as I stepped into the room with Silas and Nick, Gage right behind me. At least the night would soon be over.

Silas was the only one to speak and his information was brief. I would fight a girl named Brandi Glenn. This fight would have eight rounds, but they wanted me to end it in the fourth. With his trademark smile and confidence, he told me he trusted I could do it.

They were just as eager for me to leave as I was, and before I knew it Gage was walking me out the back.

"Where's Boris?" I asked as I stepped into the cool night air.

Gage walked past me, his SUV lights flashing as he unlocked it. "I'm going to take you back. Get in."

I almost thought about fighting about it, but I wanted to hear what he had to say, see what he would do. But mostly, I wanted to push all his buttons, make him react like I had made Rusnak, make him admit where he stood in all this.

16: Moving Forward

I SHUT THE CAR DOOR JUST AS the back door to the club opened.

"Where ya going?" Nick stood in the open door way.

"I'm taking her back." Gage didn't stop his path to the driver's side of the SUV as he responded.

"Ya sure ya should be doing that, kid?" Nick lit a cigarette, the flame glowing in front of his face.

Gage paused in front of the driver's door. Then he took a step towards his uncle. "Yeah, I'm sure. Now go worry about your own fuckin' business, old man."

His eyes narrowed, but a smile spread across his face. "Oh, you're in a right mood tonight." His voice dropped some as he added, "Just get your ass back here before time and ya won't have nothing to worry 'bout, not from me. After all, this ain't my business, right?" As he gestured to the car, his eyes met mine and I wanted to punch the smug, knowing look off his face.

He didn't know what was going to happen with Gage and me; he only thought he did.

I looked out my side window, breaking the stare down as Gage slid into the driver's seat.

Anger rolled off Gage in waves, hitting me with every movement he made, from snapping his seat belt to throwing the SUV in reverse.

I waited till we were on the main road and the muscles in his neck eased before I spoke.

"Look at you, talking back, ignoring orders." I smirked as I saw his muscles strain again. My flippant comment hit its mark. "Don't worry, I know you wouldn't go against any serious orders. You're a good soldier."

"Shut up." He stretched his fingers and re-gripped the steering wheel, focus maintained on the road. "You said you'd do whatever you have to, well so will I. Except I'm not fucking someone to get where I want."

His words stabbed me, right in the gut. But I rebounded with anger. "No? So where do you draw the line? Snorting coke off a stripper?" My voice came out just as loud as his. I was supposed to be the one pushing him, not the one reacting. I took a deep breath trying to pull back the emotions he pulled out of me.

His head jerked to look at me. "What?" He divided his gaze from the road to me, voice at a lower level when he spoke. "I am always thinking of you. Nobody else. Everything I've done, you're the reason." His voice thickened with emotion, coming out gravelly. "But you're throwing it all away, making everything I did pointless."

I had wanted him to be mad, but right now my heart was breaking. The chaotic rush of emotions he caused clouded everything. I couldn't think through them and I couldn't decide what I wanted. To ease his hurt, or to increase it?

"I can't do this with you." I decided on the truth and whatever that may result in. "This blaming thing. I can't. We both are doing things for ourselves, you just won't admit it, but you and I both know that's the truth."

He slowed at a yellow light even though he could have made it through. Once stopped, he leaned in towards me and gripped my chin, making me face him. "He doesn't care about you, he won't help you. Sleeping with him won't do anything for you, it's only making things worse."

I jerked back, slapping his hand away. "Do you think I'm stupid? I know he doesn't care. I know I'm only part of some sick fantasy he has about my—" I cut myself off, unable to speak of her. Although, I wanted to. I didn't want it to be a secret between Rusnak and me only. "But you're wrong, he can help me. He already has. He's moved up—"

"What fantasy?" His voice was icy as he interrupted.

I took a deep breath. Part of me wanted to tell him everything, he was the only person I had to talk to about all this. But a part of me wanted to completely shut him out, he was the person I was most scared of hurting and not knowing his motives frightened me.

"He knew the woman who gave birth to me." The words were acidic, burning my throat.

His eyes widened and mouth parted, but no words came out. I nodded to the light, it had turned green.

"What the hell does that mean?" he breathed, almost to himself, as he accelerated.

"I don't know. I really don't. He liked her, but I think he hated her too. And I don't know what that means for me. I don't know anything that's going on." Once the words started, I couldn't stop. "I don't even know what I'm doing. I had wanted out. All I think about is getting away, but then what? What the hell do I have left? How am I going to live with everything I've done, with everything I'm going to have to do?" My throat closed up with emotion, silencing my voice. I turned to look out the passenger side window, hiding the tears that started.

Get it together. Pull it back in. This wasn't supposed to happen. I wasn't the one that was supposed to be spilling.

Gages warm hand slipped over my arm, sliding to my hand. "What have you done?" he coaxed.

When I turned back to face him, my anger rose. Concern was clear on his face, but he was only worried about what I'd done with Rusnak. He wasn't thinking about the larger picture.

"I've killed someone." I pulled my hand from his as I shouted, wanting to shake him. "I'm responsible for other deaths too, indirectly. But I actually killed a man." I couldn't shake the image of me jerking the wheel into the man on the motorcycle from my mind, but Nan and Demetri's face was there too.

"And what's worse is I don't even care. I don't think about it except to wonder if I'll be caught, if I'll go to jail, 'cause I should. And I still want others to die." Damien's face burned in my brain. "What does that make me? It was never supposed to be like this. I wasn't supposed to be like this."

"You're only doing what you have to. People change, adapt to their environment." His sympathy took me off guard.

I watched him. His throat moved as he swallowed and he kept glancing over to me as he merged onto the highway from the ramp. I wasn't the only one adapting to my environment, changing.

"Obviously. Some are just better at it." I looked at him pointedly, wanting to get back on track. This car ride wasn't supposed to be about me. I felt bipolar the way my emotions jerked from one to the next.

His eyes flashed back to me, eyebrows narrowing. "So what? You're mad at me for not losing my shit? You want me to not do well in this? You want me to get myself fucking killed?"

My vision blurred as his words hit home. What did I want from him? I couldn't answer that. Like everything else with him my answer was divided. I wanted more, I wanted all of him. But I also wanted nothing, which was the safest path for both of us. It should be the easiest way, but that step felt near impossible.

We both sat in silence for a while, giving me time to put my thoughts in some sort of order. This was not a conversation to have while he drove. It was probably a conversation best not had at all.

As we hit the exit into DC, Gage broke the silence. "It's easier for me because I grew up in this. I was already part of this before I met you, so it was easy to slide back into it. You were never meant to be involved. I'm sorry. I should have never told you I was done with this life when we first met. I know now that was never true. You can never leave it behind."

There was an apology in his words, but not for the right thing.

"It's not your fault I'm involved. I did this on my own." My voice was as empty as I felt. This was just another dead end.

"Then why are you so mad at me? Why won't you let me in? Why are you turning to him?" His desperation was growing as his voice rose.

A current of shock shot through me. "Turn to him? I'm being jerked everywhere. I'm not really getting a choice in who I'm around."

"You can say no."

"Do you say no?" I cut myself off. This circular conversation was getting us nowhere. "Just stop. Stop expecting so much of me when you don't step up either. This is what I was talking about. We can't keep going like this. We each have to do things for ourselves, and it's better if we don't have to worry about the other. So just stop." I closed my eyes and leaned against the cool glass window.

The sounds of the city filled my head, blocking out his audible breathing. I couldn't allow myself to focus on him. This entire ride had crushed me, removed my fight. I'd lost. But I knew what I said was true as much as I wish it wasn't.

He pulled up to the curb of my apartment building but grabbed my arm as I went to open the door.

"Wait," his voice cracked. "I know you don't believe me, but don't give up on me yet. I have to go away this week, but when I come back things will change. Just wait a little longer."

He was ripping me apart. Concern pulled at me, concern about what he was doing, where he was going. And my weak heart held hope that things might change for us, but my brain reminded me that he had said that several times. He was always telling me to wait, but for what? And every change just seemed to be worse than before.

I swept my head towards him. "It's too late. I already gave up on you." I tried to pull my hand away, but he didn't let me.

"No," his response was desperate and suddenly his other hand was behind my head, holding me in place as his lips dominated mine, trying to silence my words, erase them.

But I felt dirty as I recalled Rusnak's hands in my hair, holding me in a similar position, except his lips were on my ear. As much as I wanted to let go with Gage, I couldn't. His words were always convincing, but empty, and I couldn't fall for it this time.

I shoved him off me and quickly looked away. The pain on his pinched face made me doubt everything I was doing. Sliding out of the car, I gripped my bag in my arms and found the strength to walk away. I had to keep moving forward.

* * *

"Nice shoes," a familiar voice called as long arms wrapped around my shoulders, pulling me into a hug from behind.

I spun around. "Dex what are you doing? I thought spring break was over?"

He shrugged. "I don't have class for a couple of hours, figured I could help you with the next fight."

I crossed my arms, leaning away from him.

He rolled his eyes and gave an exaggerated sigh. "Come on Rea, stop questioning everything. I like training with you."

I narrowed my eyes a little bit more and he huffed. "And Gage may have told me to check in on you while he's gone."

My jaw dropped. "Seriously? Where did he go?" I couldn't hold in the question.

Dexter's eyes shifted with nerves as he shrugged. "I think Florida. He left Saturday and should be back on Thursday, but he wouldn't tell me much. Just told me to check on you but I wanted to anyway. I like training with you, just wish it was still in Baltimore." He looked repulsed as he glanced around the bright gym, packed with toned bodies. He shuddered as he saw the kickboxing class in progress in the back and I laughed.

Rusnak must be with Gage. Kiera had said he went out of town on Saturday, and that news seemed to lighten the tension between us.

Dexter side glanced at me with a crooked grin. "I really like the black Nikes and this outfit. You get new training gloves too?" He knocked my gloved hands with his own.

I had to fill my time, sitting around the apartment wasn't an option. I used some of the money I made and bought new workout gear. I had to stay focused and any bit of confidence helped.

"Yup, let's get started. I looked into the girl I'm fighting and she's no joke. Much more experienced than me." I had to train through my nerves.

"Rea, she's the one that should be worried, not you. Let's do this," Dex said, building my confidence with his easy smile.

* * *

Walking into the apartment, I started to peel my sweaty clothes off of me, starting with my shoes and socks. I walked into my room and tossed my bag down as I slid my long sleeve shirt over my head, heading to the shower.

A throat clearing behind me froze me in my path. I spun around, thankful that I hadn't started taking off my tank top yet.

Rusnak leaned on the open door, a smirk pulling on his lips. "Don't let me stop you. Continue."

"I didn't know you were here. I thought you were out of town." I had already taken a step back when I first saw him, but I stopped myself from retreating further. My mind caught up with the moment. "Is Kiera here?" I usually didn't see her until the evenings.

"I didn't come to see her." He closed the door as he stepped into the room. His eyes brightened and smile stretched with each step he took towards me.

"What did you come to see me for?" My words stopped his path, and his smile dropped.

"Do I need to have a reason?" The edge in his voice made my skin tingle with warning.

"No, you don't." I tried to bring down his anger. "But I didn't expect you. I just got back from the gym. Can you give me a minute to shower and change?" I shifted on my feet. He was the type of person I needed to mentally prepare for, and I wasn't prepared for this right now.

His gaze slid over me, and it took all my strength not to run away or cover up, to stand still and let him devour me with his eyes.

"A minute? Sure." But he didn't move.

"You can wait in the living room." I put authority in my voice as I walked past him and opened the door for him to leave. It was bad enough I was about to get in the shower with him in the apartment, but I couldn't handle him waiting in my room.

His smile returned at my demand and he bowed slightly towards me with a soundless laugh. "Whatever you wish."

I closed and locked the door the second he crossed through. Then I grabbed my baggiest sweater, shirt, and jeans outfit I had and locked myself in the bathroom. Every sound I heard in the shower had me pulling the curtain aside to see if he was entering, but he never did. It wasn't till I was dressed that my jumpiness eased some. But anxiety still swirled in me, making me feel sick. I brushed my hair, but left it wet as I walked out into my empty room.

I know I was trying to make myself undesirable in my attire, but I was also psyching myself up for him to touch me. I wasn't sure if I could let him, but if it felt like a move that could get me anywhere, I might have to. Gage's face was tattooed in my thoughts, a constant that I tried to block. There was no room for him right now. I couldn't let him and my irrational feelings control my decisions.

I gave a second thought to concealing my gun on me, but dismissed it. That would only get me in trouble since I knew I wouldn't shoot him. I couldn't. I'd never get away with it.

Walking back out in the living room, I watched him, watching me. He was sitting back, relaxed in the corner of the couch, arms draped along the back. His long legs were stretched out in front of him and crossed at the ankles on the floor. His grey suit looked tailored for him, but he dressed it down with a black button up shirt, top buttons undone. If I had any doubt about why he came to see me, the look in his eyes and the way his teeth drug over his bottom lip as I walked closer eliminated it.

I stopped on the other side of the coffee table, my heart about to drill through my chest, and slid my hands in my pockets to cover their shaking. I was frozen, unsure what the next move should be.

He cocked his head at me as he sat up. "Are you feeling all right?" There was concern in his voice.

I swallowed and nodded, throat dry.

He shook his head, with a hesitant grin. "Then have a seat. Relax."

My stomach flopped, threatening to expel my light breakfast while my feet carried me to the other side of the couch and I sat. But it was impossible to relax.

He clicked his tongue as his fingers stretched, lightly moving over the ends of my wet hair.

I closed my eyes, waiting for his next move, forcing myself to sit still.

But his hand dropped away with a sigh. "Have I gotten it all wrong?"

I popped my eyes back open and looked to him.

He shifted in the seat and sat up as he turned towards me. "I thought after Friday things might have changed. I didn't intend to act that way but you were pushing me. And then, I thought you were into it. But now…" His hand floated between us, confusion wrinkling his forehead. "I don't force myself on anyone Regan. This won't happen till you want it to."

His words lifted a heavy weight from my chest and the room spun with the sudden lightness. But I didn't let the relief get too far and reminded myself of who was speaking.

"Okay." I nodded to him, acknowledging his words. As much as I wanted to tell him I'd never want him, I stopped myself. Letting him think he was getting somewhere, but not giving in, seemed the most powerful position I could take at the moment. I knew enough about men to know it would only get me so far, for so long. But I'd stretch it for as long as possible, until more was required.

I gave him a little smile and dropped my eyes to my lap, playing shy, and hating myself for the act.

The sound of water ran through the walls as the shower in Kiera's room turned on. So she was here, probably just waking up.

He scooted close to me. One arm stretched behind me and the other slid to my cheek, turning my head to face him. "Why don't you change into something nice, and I'll take you to lunch." His hazel eyes pleaded, with an urgent look.

He didn't want Kiera to see us together. I looked toward her door. "I don't know." I wanted to test his reactions, get a better read on this new situation.

He dropped his hand from my cheek. "I only want to talk" His smile was back, the one that masked so much, so effectively. "And you need to eat, don't you?"

I could say no. I saw that now, he gave me that option. But where would that get me?

"Okay." I stood up and went to my room to get ready.

17: Added Pressure

WHEN I CAME OUT, KIERA WAS SITTING on the couch and Rusnak was standing over her, his voice too low to hear as he scolded her. Or at least that's what I assumed he was doing; she certainly looked like a kid getting in trouble. Her eyes were rimmed red and face crumpled as she sunk into the couch.

He glanced towards me as I walked into the room and her hand shot up, grabbing his. He glared back down at her, flicking her hand off like dirt.

"We'll talk about this later." He stepped away from her, warning clear in his voice. Then he walked past me down the hall and paused at the front door, holding it open for me.

The look in Kiera's eyes as she swept them towards me tugged on my guilt, but I walked away. She wasn't my concern.

* * *

The tension between us was thick and the conversation was sparse on the way to the restaurant. It was at a business club in the city, on the top floor of a tall building. The room had a waterfall in the center and glass walls that gave a stunning view of the city skyline. Even though there were only a few other patrons, I knew immediately I wasn't dressed up enough. I'm surprised they even let me in with jeans on.

But Rusnak hadn't commented about my clothes, except to say he liked the color of my top, a dark blue chiffon blouse that hung loosely on me.

He ordered our meals, not even giving me a chance to look at the menu. But I finally spoke up when he ordered a glass of wine for me.

"I don't drink." I waited for the server to leave before correcting him, but his face still tightened in agitation.

His fingers tapped on the thick white tablecloth. "You need to relax, Regan. You take things too seriously."

I straightened up at the insult. "Are you relaxed?" I immediately regretted my tone.

His answering smile gave me some relief. "Touché. But that's what I want, for you to be able to relax around me." He drew a small circle on the table with the tip of one long finger and then leaned back, looking around the area. "What do you think of this place?"

"It's nice." The look in his eyes made me hesitate.

"It was your mothers favorite place to come." His voice was distant and soft, but his words were ice running in my veins.

"Talking about her doesn't help me relax."

His eyes narrowed at me, drilling into me, but I stood strong. This was an area I wouldn't give in. It might have been a card I should be using, but I couldn't. I wanted to burn any memory of her.

"I'm not her." I met his eyes, sure mine were equally as intense.

The room froze for a minute, holding us in place. And then his smile spread, sickly slow.

"Yes, you are. You're exactly like her, you just don't realize it."

"Go to hell."

"Sit back down," his voice was quiet but sharp with demand.

I hadn't even realized I stood up, but he's lucky I hadn't hit him.

His eyes drilled into me, his anger clear under his cool surface.

I wasn't anything like her—he had to see that. My blood raced hot through me and I wanted to choke him until he took back those words. I needed to leave before I acted on the impulse.

The elevator was already open when I reached the lobby of the restaurant; a group of men in suits were walking out. I slid in and pressed the button to close the door the second it was cleared. I didn't see Rusnak following, but rushed all the same.

Panic flooded in as the elevator descended to the first floor. I had just ruined everything, my only chance. I had just pissed off the only person who could help me. My body vibrated with nerves, but they burst when the phone in my pocket vibrated as well.

The number that lit up the screen was unknown. Rusnak had never called me personally before. I didn't want to answer, but I did. I couldn't risk making this situation worse.

I reluctantly slid the phone to my ear.

"You need to come back. Now." I could picture his calm, but dominate face as he spoke.

I'd already gone this far, if I went back now he would know he had full control.

"I think I should go. I'll take a cab back." I wasn't completely running, I hoped that was enough.

"Fine." The way he said it made it clear it was not fine, and then he hung up the phone.

My thoughts were on a downward spiral as I made my way back to the apartment. I couldn't be anything like her. I despised her, hated her more than anyone or anything, but he was the only person that would know if I was or not. And he said I was exactly like her.

* * *

Kiera stepped out of the kitchen at the end of the hall as I closed the door to the apartment. Her sad eyes met mine for a second, glistening as tears pooled in them. "What is it, huh? What is it that he likes better about you?"

I couldn't contain the groan and eye roll as I walked to my room. "Don't start this shit with me right now."

She moved with outstretched arms and braced her hand on my bedroom door to keep it from closing. "No, we need to have this talk. I've put it off too long."

I rounded on her, stepping towards her. "I'm warning you Kiera, back off now."

"I know there's got to be something. I mean, look at you, all bruised up. He can't find that attractive. So what is the real story?" The girl stood her ground, not budging from the door way as she gestured to me.

"Get out." I shoved her back, forcing her out of the room.

She slapped at me, but I grabbed her wrist before she could make contact.

My blood ignited and I shoved her back until she slammed against the hall wall with a thud.

She was shrieking with anger, trying to claw at me, but I held both of her arms. I jerked her forward and back, slamming her into the wall again. Her wild eyes met mine and I saw what she was about to do the second before her spit hit my face. A spray of liquid splattered my cheek, below my eye.

I dropped her arms and released my fist like a slingshot, right in the center of her face.

Her angry shriek morphed into a crying scream and she brought her hands up to her nose as she fell onto her knees.

My muscles pulsed, wanting to let lose. Especially when I wiped her spit from my cheek. But I stepped back away from her, restraining myself.

She was crying on the ground, folded over her knees. She was in enough agony and it wasn't me that caused it. But I had to get away from this psychotic bitch all the same.

I swung my door shut and left her crying in the hall. My destructive emotions needed a release, and I needed a distraction. There were bound to be consequences from my actions tonight with Rusnak and now Kiera. I couldn't wait around for them. Looked like this would be a double gym day and then a trip to the gun range.

Kiera had stopped crying by time I left my room. I heard her in the kitchen but didn't stop to check on her.

* * *

The gym released the tension in my muscles, but the gun range was a different type of stress reliever altogether. But it all came back tenfold as I exited the D.C Small Arms Range and was greeted by Boris. He took the toothpick out of his mouth and opened the back door of a town car with deeply tinted back windows.

I contemplated walking by. He hadn't spoken to me after all.

But Rusnak's smooth voice called out from inside the back seat of the car. "Regan, get in."

My breathing tensed and my senses sharpened, but I slid into the back seat. The smooth leather was heated and the cab was deceptively warm, comfortable. So was Rusnak's smile.

I didn't speak and I didn't look directly at him, just buckled my seat belt and focused on the dark partitioned glass blocking the front seats from view. The fact that he found me didn't surprise me, I had been waiting for it—but that didn't mean I was prepared.

"I'm sorry if what I said upset you earlier." Rusnak broke the silence as the car pulled away from the curb.

I flicked my eyes to him and nodded. His eyes never left me. My skin prickled under his constant gaze.

"I'm only going to tell you this once." He grabbed my hand in his hot ones. "Don't ever walk away from me again." He put pressure on my hand, squeezing the bones. "Look at me when I'm talking to you."

I turned towards him, my teeth clamped to keep from speaking.

"Today I let you leave without permission, but never again. Do you understand?"

"I have to ask permission to leave?" I had meant to say it as a statement, but it came out like a question.

His grip eased on my hand and his thumb moved a wide arc under my wrists, tickling the skin, making it crawl and my stomach turn sour.

"Hmm hm, everyone does." He was watching his thumb dip into the sleeve of my jacket as he caressed the skin underneath. "Only you could have gotten away with what you did today, nobody else."

His words were added pressure on my lungs. Even though I should have felt relief that he wasn't angrier, I was finding it hard to breath.

"Do you understand what I'm telling you?" He leaned in close, his upper body crossing the middle seat.

"I won't walk away again." My skin twitched under his touch, my nerves at rapid fire.

"That's not what I meant." His eyes glowed with amusement as he leaned back, resting his long torso against the corner of the seat and door. But he still kept hold of my hand.

At least the space he gave made a breath easier to take.

"I heard you hit Kiera when you went back to the apartment."

"I regret it," I said simply.

His fingers stilled on my hand and his smile stretched. "Why do you regret it? She needed someone to hit her."

I took the moment to pull my hand back and tucked them both between my knees. "I pushed her first. I shouldn't have put my hands on her."

He stretched his arm along the back of the seat, his fingers just above my shoulder. "Maybe it's time I move you to a new apartment. Or maybe it's time for her to get out."

My heart stopped for a moment. "I could get my own place."

"Could you?" his smile was arrogant as his fingers pulled on a lock of my hair.

I scooted away, shoulder lifted to block his touch. "I have some money saved and if I got a job…"

He shook his head no, smile growing. "Sweetheart, remember, I am trying to help you and keep you safe. That man is still after you. It's best you stay under my guardianship."

We pulled up front of the apartment building and I moved to get out.

"We're still talking." His stern words made me pause.

"I'm fine staying here with Kiera. I've just got to talk to her." I didn't want him moving me anywhere else. "Can I go now?" His face brightened with my request.

"Just a moment." He slid his hand into my hair, fingers running along my scalp until they curled around the back of my head, cupping it. "I want to see you tomorrow. Be ready at noon to be picked up."

His movements were slow. I saw it coming, but when his lips met mine, all air escaped me. His kiss was poison numbing my lips. I could barely get them to move with his and I prayed he'd stop at a kiss tonight.

He pulled away, gliding back into his seat. "You can go now. " He released me.

I needed a shower and then bed. I had thought I could go along with Rusnak, play along with whatever he wanted. But that kiss had shook me and now I doubted myself. I needed to get it together before tomorrow.

18: Win or Lose

"What's wrong?" I sat next to Dexter on the weight bench. He wasn't his typical high energy self and his silence was freaking me out a bit.

He lifted his head and gave me a closed lip smile. Something was definitely off.

"Just a lot on my mind." He nudged my knee with his own. "You want to hit up some stores after this? Get some lunch?"

"Don't you have class?" I had plans that I wouldn't share with him. It was nearly time for me to get ready to meet with Rusnak. But I wanted to stay and talk to Dexter, find out what was bugging him.

"Not going today." He leaned the side of his head on his hand, looking at me with that shadow of a smile.

"What's on your mind Dex? Is everything okay?" He didn't seem sad really, just distant.

He sat up, biting his bottom lip as his smile spread. "I'm going to be a dad."

My jaw dropped.

"Leona just found out." He slid his eyes to the ceiling with a small laugh. "Oh shit, I'm going to be a dad." His smile was larger than life when he spoke those words.

"That's something." I was at a loss for how to respond.

Dexter dropped his smile. "It's a good thing, Rea. I'm still shocked as hell, but it's going to be a good thing."

"If you say so." I stood up, wanting away from this conversation. I should just keep my mouth shut.

"I do say so." Dexter stood up too. "That's why I wanted to go out today, get a baby shirt or something for Leona. I thought you would be happy for us."

I didn't care for the disappointment on his face. "I'm worried for you two. This isn't a joke Dexter, that's a baby and you've got to be there for him or her."

"I know. I am." He was shaking his head, confused. "Rea, why would you think I wouldn't? I'm going to be a good dad and Leona's going to make the best mom."

The sincerity in his eyes calmed me some. "I hope so. But Dexter you need to stay away from trouble." I tried to give him a smile. "I think you'll be the best father, just put that kid first." I gave him a partial hug of reassurance but he pulled me in for a full one, wrapping his arms tight around me.

"I will, you'll see. And you'll be Aunty Rea," he joked as he rocked me back and forth.

"No." I pulled away. "You need to stay away from me and all this. I'll find a new corner man, be there for Leona."

"You can't replace me, I'm irreplaceable." He cocked his head, concern creasing his brows. "What are you involved in that I need to stay away from?"

Silas's arrival saved me from answering.

"What's up?" Dexter asked Silas with a lift of his chin.

He stopped in front of us, arms crossed but smile in place. "Wanted to check out the new gym, plus I did what you asked."

"Really, when's the fight?" Dexter's excitement was back and the disappointment was heavy in my stomach.

"Dexter," I cut off my warning when Silas glanced at me.

"Next month, I get you all the details." Silas nodded to me. "You need to go clean up, I'm supposed to take you to a meeting."

That pulled me from my thoughts about Dexter's baby. "What meeting?" Did Rusnak send him? Were we all meeting? Maybe I had made the wrong assumption, but I knew better than to believe that.

"A meeting about your fight. Now are you using the locker room here or going back to your apartment first?"

"If it's about her fight maybe I should come," Dexter said, and I could have slapped him.

"Dexter, go get your gift for Leona. Focus on that," I snapped, walking away to the locker room to get my things.

* * *

I should be happy at least that Dexter didn't come, but sitting in the car with Nick and Silas was more than uncomfortable. Nick always set me on edge. So when I saw he was with Silas after the gym, I made sure to conceal my gun on me, just in case. It was tucked in the waistband of my jeans and this time I wouldn't give it up to anyone.

"The fight next week, we need you to win in the second." Silas said from the front passenger seat.

"Second?" I sat forward as my heart bounced in my stomach. "That's too soon. Make it like my last fight; give me till the last round. I can do that."

"It's not your call to make." Nick's deep voice was thick with disapproval as he merged onto the highway, leaving DC.

"She's never been knocked out before. The odds are against me being the first to do that, especially so soon in the fight." We were meeting in Baltimore, which meant I had some time to try to convince them.

"The odds against ya are the reason we're betting on the second. More money to be made if ya win." Nick spoke as if I was an idiot.

"But if I can't do it, you lose money." My panic was rising, but I tried to keep it from my voice.

"Honestly, I don't give a fuck if ya win or lose. Your fights are barely worth betting on, the second's one of the only rounds we stand to make any money, that or the first. If ya win, we get the money, but if ya lose, I can be done with your shit. I'll figure out a different way for ya to pay, a different line of work."

His lips curled as he looked at me in the rearview mirror. "We could drop the boxing now if ya want, I know some guys who'd pay big bucks for a fighter. They're into the dominant bitches."

"Nick, stop. You know that's not an option." Silas's voice was almost too low for me to hear.

"For now, it's not. But if she loses, it will be, then maybe she won't be such a fuckin' headache."

The acid swirling in my stomach, burning the back of my throat, made it hard to speak. Not that I wanted to. This newest threat made my blood run cold. I may be willing to use sex to my advantage sometimes, but never in the way was he referring to. Never under someone else's orders. They'd have to kill me before they could make me do that, and I'm sure Nick would be more than willing.

"Regan," Silas twisted in the seat to face me, his face full of false sympathy. "Ignore him. You will win next week. You can do it, I know you can."

"Ignore me if ya want, but little one, you should know that no one will protect ya if you lose. It's my choice what happens." His eyes kept flipping to the rearview mirror, delight building in him as he spoke. "You might think you've got an advantage with Anatoli on your side, but he won't stop this and when it's done, he won't want you. So win or lose, I don't care."

* * *

We drove to a marina outside the city. Many of the slips were empty, but the few boats in the water were large.

I followed Nick down the dock to one of the larger yachts, and Silas walked behind me. The boat was easily two stories tall and nearly the length of a basketball court. As I boarded, Rusnak stepped out of the cabin and greeted us with a smile, dressed in his version of casual, tan pants and black top.

"Everything go okay?" He asked, looking between Silas and Nick.

They traded glances, but nodded.

Then Rusnak extended his hand to me. "Come with me for a moment. I'll give you a tour."

I stepped towards him, almost eager to show Nick that he could be wrong, except I knew he wasn't. Not yet anyways.

Rusnak paused to tell Nick and Silas, "Boris is in the marina office. Go check in with him." Then he pulled me through the door he had exited moments before.

He didn't really give me a tour, just paused to show me the controls to the boat. He said a bunch of technical terms that I paid no attention too, my thoughts sill consumed on what Nick had said. The room he led me to after had a low couch running along one wall with food laid out on the table in front of it, a large screen opposite, and a bar at the far end.

He gestured for me to sit as he poured a drink from the bar. "What would you like?" He raised an empty glass.

"Water's fine." I hesitated. Something stronger might be useful, but I threw out that idea. I needed to stay alert and aware.

"Do you like steak?" He gestured to the plates as he sat down next to me. He handed me my glass and slid closer, till his legs touched mine.

"I do." I took a sip of the water, trying to wash away the knot in my throat.

We sat in silence as we ate, or as Rusnak ate. I picked at my food, barely tasting it.

"How's training going? Are you ready for your fight next week?" He took a sip of his drink, watching me over the rim of it.

The weight of the fight was suffocating me, and I was drowning under Anatoli's scrutiny. Was he just making conversation or did he know what Nick had threatened?

He set his glass down and slid his arm behind me, so close now that I could smell the light alcohol on his breath. "Is everything all right? You seem extra quiet today."

"I—" I paused and turned my body to look at him, putting a slight space between us. "What is it that you want? I mean really want from me?"

"Don't you know already?" His eyes dragged all over me and his lip slid into a grin as his free hand gripped my jean-covered thigh.

"I'm not sure. There seems to be more to it." I desperately wanted to figure this out, him out.

He leaned in to me, lips brushing my ear. "I'll show you what I want." He dropped his head, sucking in the skin of my neck. His hand traveled up my thigh to my hip and the arm behind me curled around my shoulders, pulling me to him.

"Wait." I slid my hands to his chest, keeping a space between us, my heart pulsating. "I just want to be clear. That's it, really?"

He pulled his head back and gazed down on me with hooded eyes. "Do you want more?" one hand gripped my hip and the other slid up the back of my neck and tangled in my hair. "What is it you want?"

I took a breath, preparing myself. Once I took this step, there was no turning back, I only hoped it worked. "I don't want to work with Nick anymore."

The lustful look in his light eyes hardened and he sat up, but didn't release me from his hold. "I told you I won't let you out of that deal."

"I'm not asking to be out, I just don't want to deal with Nick anymore." I surprised myself with how calm and level I sounded.

His eyes narrowed and fingers curled around the back of my neck. "Who do you want to deal with, Gage?"

I shook my head, testing his grip. "No. Silas."

His hold relaxed some as the tension slipped from his fingers. "Silas is Nick's man. Nick would still be the one you had to deal with. What's wrong sweetheart, he not treating you well?" His hand circled around my waist and I moved my hand to grab the gun tucked into the back of my jeans before he could.

His eyes widened as I pulled it out, and his hand covered mine as we moved it to the table. "I'm only getting it out of the way," I explained carefully.

He nodded with a smile and grabbed my now empty hand in his. "I like that you carry it. But back to what you were saying. You don't want to deal with Nick, and you can't deal with just Silas, so who?" The glint in his eye told me he was willing to negotiate this and his hand was in my hair, tugging my head back to give his lips access to my neck.

I twisted in his arms and brought one leg over his lap to straddle him. Pushing down my screaming thoughts that wanted me to stop, I continued, "You. I only want to deal with you."

His hand gripped around my waist, holding me in place. He leaned his head back on the seat and shifted his hips beneath me, bringing my attention to how hard he was for me already. "Nobody else?"

I shook my head. "No one else."

His hands slid up my back, pulling me down to his lips. "I can work that out."

I kissed him with all I could. My body was in a battle with itself, responding to his touch but not wanting to. I had to block the memories of Gage's hands running over my skin, they were smothering me.

Rusnak's hands slid under the back of my shirt. Instinct took control and I pulled them down, off of me, as I moved my lips to his neck. He struggled against my grip, but I wasn't giving in. The one thing I wouldn't allow was his hands on my scars.

"Stop." He gripped my wrists, pulling them in front of me. "Are you willing to do this, or not?"

I shook my head, swallowing hard. "I am, but my shirt stays on."

His eyes narrowed and then realization transformed his face. "'Your scars?" At my nod his lips slid up, but his smile was dark and crushing. "I want to see what she did to you." He met my eyes, challenging me. "Take it off."

19: Promise

SOMETHING IN MY FACE MUST HAVE GIVEN away my next move. He was able to use the momentum of my escape against me. He moved with me as I tried to stand but then forced the movement, and in the blink of an eye I was under him, back flat on the couch but feet still on the ground. He was half straddling my legs, one of his knees bent on the inside of the couch, standing on his other leg off the couch. He pinned my wrists to my chest as he leaned over me, his position giving him all the power.

"Get off of me." My voice was loud and clear as I tested his grip and tried to move my legs up for leverage, but I couldn't budge.

"Shhh." He dropped his head close enough that his warm breath fanned over my neck. "I'm not going to hurt you." His voice was low and strained as he shifted more of his weight onto me, pinning me tighter into the leather couch.

The excitement brightening his face didn't give me any confidence in his words. I stayed completely still, but met his wild eyes as I repeated, "Get off of me."

All of my senses were turned up, ready to fight if need be, but I didn't want it to come to that.

"I won't make you show me, not today," he spoke slow and soft.

The strain in my chest eased slightly, but my blood still surged through me, pulse pounding.

"Is that the promise you need?"

My breaths were shallow and I was at a loss for words, unsure of how he had taken all control in this within seconds. I was a fool to think I ever had any to begin with. Closing my eyes, I nodded my head and barely resisted as he moved my hands, pinning them above my head.

I had walked into this willingly, and now he was going to let me have my way. But it still felt like I had lost everything, the already broken ground disappearing from beneath me.

He gripped my wrists with one hand, the other sliding down my arm in a light caress. He tilted my head back, and then his lips were on my neck.

"You are going to be fun… so… much… fun." He spoke between kisses and licks that shocked my skin and made my stomach twist. His hand ran over my shirt, squeezing one breast, almost painfully, before continuing its path down my body to my hip, fingers dug into my skin. "But I want you more than willing; I want you begging for it." He nipped at my collarbone and groaned as he shifted his hips into me. "I want you begging for me."

I opened my eyes, confused if I was hearing right. Should I beg now? I couldn't. Bile burned my throat just thinking about it.

He licked his lips and stared down at me with lust filled eyes. "You're not ready yet and I don't have the time right now to get you there. But believe me sweetheart, you will be begging me." He released my wrists and pushed himself off of me, just as quickly and smoothly as he had pushed himself on.

Unsure about the sudden change, I sat up and ran my hands through my hair, trying to calm my pounding pulse and even my breathing. I'd built myself up to go through with this and now it wasn't happening. The cool rush of relief tempered the hot sting of rejection.

He strolled across the room, seemingly unaffected, and slipped his shirt over his head, creamy skin stretching over lean muscles. I dropped my eyes to the floor, but not before I caught a glimpse of the silvery scar that only a bullet could cause, on the lower right side of his back.

"Sweetheart." He stood directly in front of me.

I raised my eyes, traveling over his long body. He was buttoning the top two buttons of a pale blue dress shirt.

"Are you ready to go?" His smile was satisfied, smug, like he had gotten exactly what he wanted today.

And I realized, I wasn't sure I was walking away with anything.

"What about Nick?" I stood to my feet, trying to cover my nerves about bringing this up again.

He cocked his head as he tucked his shirt into his pants. "What about him?"

"I don't have to go through him anymore?"

"We talked about this." He grazed the back of his fingers over my cheek, speaking as if I were a confused child. "From now on, you'll deal with me. What just happened doesn't change that."

His other hand came up and he cradled my head in his warm hands. "I can give you what you want. I can make you happy."

I dropped my eyes to avoid his green blue ones and bit my lip to keep in the insane laugh that threatened to spill out. What made him think I wanted, or needed, or deserved to be happy? I wasn't searching for that, and if I were, I wouldn't find it with him.

He dropped his hands and bent to pick up my gun on the table. I froze.

Stepping close to me, he hooked one finger over the front of my jeans and slid the gun inside the band. "If you're going to wear it, wear it at the front, not back." He pulled on the end of my shirt, covering the gun. Nodding to the door, he signaled for me to follow as he walked away. "Saturday we can go to the range again." He glanced at me out of the corner of his eye. "At my place."

"All right, Saturday." I tried to smile. I had cooled off some, but the last remnants of adrenaline still tingled my muscles. I had two days to figure something out because there was no way I would beg.

* * *

Silas finally emerged from the building at the front of the docks. Rusnak had told me to wait in the car while he went in, assuring me that only Silas would drive me home. And sure enough, only Silas was walking out.

After several minutes of driving, Silas turned down the radio, regret deep in his voice. "Since that day in my office, all of this has gone further than I ever planned for it to."

I wasn't sure which day he was referring too, my first day or the last.

"I feel the same way," I grumbled, already getting annoyed with where this was going. He had been giving me looks since he got in the car, disappointed and disapproving looks.

"Really?" His eyes narrowed and glanced towards me before focusing back on the road. "Because from where I stand, it looks like you've got one hell of a plan." He shook his head with a laugh. "It's actually pretty impressive, in just over a month you've managed to climb your way to the top. Got Rusnak doing things for you? But I ain't mad, just be sure to keep Gage out of it now."

Mentioning Gage took me by surprise and made my stomach hurt. "I don't want him in it either."

We were stuck in traffic and Silas used the moment to face me. "Good because he's finally getting back on track."

A bubble of hope rose in my stomach for him. "What do you mean? Is he getting back to just fighting?" I realized in that moment I would do anything to get Gage out.

Silas inched the car forward with the slow flow of traffic around us. "He's fighting again, but I didn't mean that. I meant in this business, he's finally stepping up and getting somewhere, like he was always meant to."

The bubble of hope burst painfully in my chest and I had to cover my mouth with my hand to silence the groan that wanted to escape.

"Jesus girl, you really don't get it." He shook his head. "I knew he didn't tell you the truth about his past, he warned me against speaking about it when you started. But I thought you would have figured it out by now."

I stared at him, holding my breath, waiting for him to continue.

"I got my start with his father and Nick when we were young. But Gage's father, Aaron, he climbed fast and soon we worked for him. He had a few people between him and the main guy, Nikolai, Anatoli's cousin. But then he went to prison, made a few connects there, and came out on top. After that, Aaron and Anatoli were Nikolai's right and left hand." His eyes flicked to me, checking that I was still listening.

I was hanging on every word.

"That's when Gage came in. He had his father's skill for getting jobs done, straight and quick, with very little mess. He rose up the ranks, especially when everyone saw his talent for fighting; he was notorious in the underground fight clubs. But about a year ago shit went down; Nikolai got locked up and Aaron was killed. Rusnak took over and Gage wanted out. But we all knew it wasn't for good, he just needed time."

He paused to look at me.

"That's when you two started the boxing club and he went pro?" I was struggling to make sense of what I knew about Gage, the little he had told me. He claimed he left the past behind, but I hadn't realized it had been such a recent past.

Silas nodded. "His father was my best friend. I promised to look out for Gage, that's what I've been doing, that's why I went in with him on the gym."

I scoffed. "You were looking out for him by getting Dexter involved in your drug deal, making Gage have to go back to Rusnak?"

His jaw flexed and his voice came out low. "He was always going to come back. That was always the plan."

"Why are you telling me all this?" I didn't want to believe Silas. Gage had told me something different. He had said he wanted a different life, and I had believed him. But now, I wasn't sure.

"I know you still care for him, that's why I'm telling you. Gage knows to put this family in front of all else, including you. He's shown that, and it would be best for you not to test it, you'll only get yourself hurt." His hard look softened as he sighed and added, "You're a smart girl Regan. Stick with Rusnak. For some reason he's taken an interest in you. He sent Dexter to be your corner man after I told him you two were friends. He moved up your fight, and now he's told Nick to stay away from you." Silas's smile was distant "You've got a good thing going, don't ruin it."

I nodded and stared out the window, heart heavier than ever.

* * *

My path to my room was blocked as I entered the apartment. Kiera was in the entry hall with a man, her face full of surprise at my arrival.

The man pushed his dark curls back as he cocked an eyebrow at me. "This the girl?"

He was only a little taller than me and I met his eyes, challenging him to say something else.

Kiera pushed him to the door and turned to me with wide eyes. "He's only a friend." She dropped her gaze and added softly, "I'm sorry about the other night. Can we talk tomorrow?" Her busted lip was swollen and quivered as she lifted her eyes to meet mine, concern clear in her features. "Please."

"Sure. Tomorrow." I closed the door on her as she stepped into the hall, following the mystery man I didn't want to know about.

* * *

I pulled the cord to my headphones, ripping the buds from my ears, silencing the beat as I walked towards Dexter.

He spotted me as he strolled into the gym, face brightening at first, then dropping as I stepped close to him.

"Go home. I told you yesterday you need to stay away." My muscles vibrated with anger and hurt. He needed to get it together and put that baby first, earn the title of parent.

"Whoa, Rea." He put his hands up in surrender. "I'm going to stick with you. I'm not getting involved in shit except boxing, it's fine."

"No, it's not." I wanted to physically shake him, my fingers clenched and my eyes burned. "Remember what happened to Leona? Now there's a baby too. You've got to stay away from me and from boxing for Silas."

He tentatively put his hand on my shoulder. "I need the money more than ever because of that baby."

I pushed his arm away and he shifted on his feet, agitation rising.

"I can't let Gage pay for everything. I'm trying to make my own way, and boxing helps." His voice was rising. "Don't you act like your actions are any better than mine. Last I checked, you fucked up more than I ever did, but I haven't called you on any of it."

I took a step back, wondering just how much Dexter knew and who he heard it from.

"Cool off before you lose the only friend you got." He yanked off the towel that was draped around his neck, tossing it in a laundry bin as he walked out the front door.

I watched him leave, my body icy and tense. Then I put my buds back in my ear and let the heavy beat drown out my thoughts, leaving me to focus on training. But training only increased my tension. My muscles were jelly and my punches lacked the impact needed to knock out an opponent. I kept pounding until I literally couldn't pick up my arm to swing again.

I held onto the body bag with both gloved hands, catching my breath, when a light touch to my shoulder pulled me from my desperate thoughts. Turning, I stepped back with surprise as my eyes rose over Gage, his muscles and dark ink on display in his sleeveless t-shirt. The room stood still as we locked eyes.

The corner of his mouth tugged up as he stepped towards me, arms open. "Come here. I missed you."

Then I was wrapped in his warmth, surrounded in the comfort of his arms, body, breathing in his fresh scent—heart breaking from the pressure on it. I pulled away and took a step back out of his arms.

But he didn't let me go far. He kept a hold on my hip as he tried to step back into my space again.

"What are you doing?" I put my hand up to keep him back as I looked around the crowded gym, muscles twitching from shock.

His eyes dropped over me, his soft, easy smile, infuriating me. "I told you when I got back things would be different, remember?" he pressed into my hand on his chest, closing the space between us. "I talked to Rusnak. This fight can be your last and then it's over."

My stomach was turning inside out, making it hard to speak. "You talked to Rusnak, when?" I didn't understand, Rusnak hadn't told me this fight would be my last. The idea made me dizzy, but seemed too good to be true.

Gage dropped his hands straight by his side and his face slowly began to harden, starting with his narrowed eyes. "I talked to him this weekend when he was with me."

The blood drained from me. They had talked before my talk with Rusnak.

"But he had to leave." He let out a huff and raised his chin, looking down at me. "He came back here to you didn't he?" His voice was too quiet and the slow clench of his jaw made it clear he knew the answer.

I would have nodded if I could have moved.

Gage was stepping away from me, slowly backing up before he turned and shoved his way out of the gym.

I wanted to yell for him to stop but I didn't. I couldn't. And I knew it was best to let him go.

* * *

"That's my laptop," Kiera accused with a slight edge as she stepped through her bedroom door into the living room.

"Is it, really?" I didn't even look up from the screen. I continued to scan the article about the sports camp Rusnak funded for underprivileged youth, probably the one Gage claimed to volunteer for. "Who paid for it then? You?" I looked up at her with a smirk, and her jaw dropped.

I knew I was being mean, but I didn't care. I was in a bad mood and her constant reminders that everything in this place was hers pissed me off.

And I was pissed that my Google search into Anatoli had given little information. He wasn't even present in case search, proving he had a clean record. The only black mark that could be found was an article linking him to his cousin Nikolai Rusnak, who was put in prison for drug trafficking. But Anatoli came out clean as a wealthy businessman trying to improve his community. Stupid Google.

I snapped the laptop closed and set it on the coffee table as Kiera sat next to me on the couch.

"It's mine. Doesn't matter how I paid." She huffed as she adjusted herself to look at me. She didn't look comfortable in her knee length snug skirt. "Maybe we should have some drinks before this talk."

"You always want a drink. Don't use me as your excuse." I pressed my lips together to quit speaking. I had to stop myself from taking all my frustrations out on her. She was an easy target, the only person I could get away with talking back too, but I needed to stop.

Maybe she could be helpful. Maybe she could give me some insight on Rusnak. But it was difficult to care about what she had to say. My thoughts were crowded and muddled, Gage's voice from earlier echoing in my head. I didn't dare call Rusnak and question him about whether my next fight would be the last in the deal I made. I wasn't willing to risk him knowing that Gage had come to see me. Gage had thought it was okay, but my instincts were buzzing, warning me that it wasn't.

A high-pitched growl came from Kiera as she stood up. "Whatever. I'm getting a drink." Her body was tense as she walked to the kitchen. She returned to the living room with a wine glass and a phony smile on her pinched face. "Let's start this over, try again. I really think I need to explain myself here."

I curled one leg under me and waited. I was dressed as her exact opposite; sweatpants, big t-shirt, and hair hung lose, un-styled. I planned on going to sleep right after I finished talking to her.

She sipped her wine, awkwardly trying to relax back against the cushion and then repositioning herself to sit up straight. She pulled her large wine glass, nearly half emptied, away from her mouth. "I am sorry for the things I said the other night, for blaming you for my relationship with Anatoli." That phony smile was back. It looked like it physically hurt her to hold the face, especially since her top lip was puffy and heavy makeup veiled her bruising.

"Okay. I accept." I sighed as she eyed me, obviously waiting for me to say more. I hope she wasn't waiting on an apology. "I'm stuck here for now. I don't want things to be awkward between us. You do your thing and I'll do mine. No hard feelings."

She flinched, but covered it with a gulp of her wine. Licking her lips compulsively, she set her empty glass on the coffee table before looking back to me. Her smile was much smaller now, but still there. "I don't want hard feelings. But I'd like to do more than tolerate each other, possibly help each other. Anatoli and I may have our ups and downs but he means a lot to me, and I mean a lot to him. Please, don't come between us." Her attempt to innocently blink at me made me want to laugh, but not from amusement.

"I'm sure his wife would have the same request." The words stabbed me even though they were meant to hurt her. I didn't want to be in the middle of any of their relationships, but I had to look out for myself above all else.

Her thin attempt at staying calm and friendly was slipping. She gritted her teeth as she moved to the edge of the couch, leaning forward but angled towards me. "Please. He is my only chance, I'm begging you to stay away from him, to let me have him." Her eyes shown with emotion, tears about to spill over.

I felt nothing when I looked at her. I had no compassion. I uncurled myself and slipped my leg down to the floor to mirror her position, but I kept at least a foot between us.

"Your only chance? At what? This lifestyle? Having your bills paid? Do you ever work?" I didn't give her a chance to answer, I already knew. "What you fail to realize is he's my only chance too. But my stakes are much higher."

She was leaning back by the time I finished, putting more space between us.

"Fine. I guess we have nothing to say to each other then." She grabbed her phone on the side table, stood up, and stomped out of the apartment, slamming the door behind her.

* * *

I threw myself into my workout, letting my anger strengthen my punches, but it didn't relieve any of my frustrations.

Kyle coached me as I batted his padded hands, moving in circles around the ring.

"Whoa, stop for a minute." He was wearing a goofier grin than usual as he pulled off his gloves and slid between the ropes.

I followed him with my eyes, then scanned past him to where he was headed. Gage was walking towards him, or towards the ring, but Kyle intercepted him. He pumped Gages arm in an excited handshake, face animated as he rambled.

Gage barely paused for him and stepped away, pulling the brim low on his black Orioles baseball cap as he walked towards me.

I climbed down from the ring, picked up my water from the edge, and took a sip to drown out the words that wanted to escape. Each and every time he showed up relief flooded me and I wanted nothing more than to touch him, to prove to myself that he's okay. But I had to play this a certain way, and jumping into his arms, telling him how much I missed him and feared for him wouldn't work. I let the cool water slide down my throat, till there was none left.

"You done already?" He was in front of me, glancing between me and the ring.

I looked to his left, where Kyle stood, grinning. "Sure man, she was just finishing up." He waved dismissively at me. "Did you want to use the ring? Damn, that would be something. I heard you use our sister gym in Baltimore, but this one's much nicer, all the best—"

Gages cool look silenced him. "No, I'll stick with my gym. I'm here to talk with Regan." He crossed his arms, tattoos and biceps on display in his thin white t-shirt.

Kyle looked at me with new interest. "All right, our session's over. Remember Regan, take the day off tomorrow. You need to give those muscles more of a break this week before your fight. I don't want to see you here in the morning, terminator." He laughed at his stupid nickname.

I didn't even acknowledge him, but kept my cautious gaze on Gage.

"Get back in there. I'll practice with you." He picked up the boxing pads on the edge of the canvas.

His request took me by surprise, but I climbed into the ring. I'd be sabotaging myself not to take advantage of his training.

He hit the top of each pad on the other one, securing them onto his hand. "This girl you're fighting, she's going to try to keep you at the end of her reach, she's got a longer one than you. So stay inside it, but don't let her hug you. She fights dirty and takes those kidney shots whenever she can."

He moved around the ring, keeping me on my toes, offering bits of advice on how to improve my form and softly praising me when I delivered strong punches. We barely talked, but the heat between us only increased. It wasn't long before several people, Kyle included, circled around the ring to watch and I ended our lesson.

He followed me, brushing off the spectators who wanted to talk to him.

Before I passed through the locker room doors, he grabbed my elbow, speaking low. "I'll be here when you get out. We have to talk." His eyes drilled into mine, still bright in the shadow of his hat.

I acknowledged his words with a nod but was unable to speak as I pulled away, unsure if he was here to talk to me for himself, or for Rusnak. Taking my time in the locker room, I built up my resolve to face him, to deny him if it came to it. When I walked out he was there with a small group of people, his head lifted, meeting my eyes as he excused himself and walked past them all.

He fell into pace beside me but didn't speak until we were outside the gym. The people traffic on the sidewalk was heavier than usual, the bright and unseasonably warm day brought everyone out.

"Can we go to your place to talk?" He nodded in the direction of the large apartment building, easily seen over the tree line and other buildings around us.

"I don't think that's a good idea." Anxiety pulsed in me.

His fingers curled by his side as he stretched his neck. "Walk in that direction." His voice was soft, but held authority.

"What do you need to say? Whose message are you delivering?" I started walking towards the apartment, but held my breath as I waited for him to answer. He could be delivering a message for Nick.

He pulled on my arm, making me face him. "God dammit Regan, I'm here for myself. I have things to say to you; we need to talk and get on the same fucking page." His words were strained with more pain than anger.

I stepped out of his grip and continued my path to the building. "We can talk in the courtyard, it's private enough." Public enough too. "But you can't be upset with me for asking that question. You haven't always come around for yourself." I kept my eyes forward, not wanting to see his reaction to my accusation. It was bad enough hearing his frustrated grumble.

Large trees surrounded the courtyard, making it a cool shaded spot during the summer, but a chilly place to be today. I found a stone bench that was in the sun and sat.

Gage didn't sit as he started, "Rusnak said you made a different deal with him that cancels out the deal I was making. So this won't be your last fight for him next week."

A heavy weight dropped painfully in my stomach, but I breathed through it. I hadn't really believed it was going to be that easy.

Gripping the edge of the chilled stone bench with my fingers, I looked up at him. The sun glowed behind him, shadowing his face. "Thank you for trying," I began carefully. "But from now on, just stay out of it. I'm handling this myself and don't want you involved."

He jerked back and removed his hat, hand running through his messy hair before he placed it back on. "What the fuck." He slid next to me on the bench, leaning forward to look at me. "I'm involved in this, whether you want me to be or not. If you would quit making your own deals, shit would be over. You're destroying everything I'm trying to do." He was heated, voice rough with anger.

"Stop doing things for me." I wouldn't back down, no matter how much fire he put off. "Worry about yourself and quit blaming me."

"I'm not—" he stood up again, frustration clear in his every movement. "This is—" he put his hands on either side of the bench, surrounding me as he leaned over me. "You don't know what you're saying." His voice was low and slow, his eyes searching my face.

It was like he lit my fuse, my body sizzled, pressure building. "I do"—I swallowed, my throat dry—"know what I'm saying." I forced myself to maintain eye contact and not back away.

He inched in closer, licking his lips, and my breathing hitched.

"You want me to go away? Leave you alone?"

I nodded, pulling both my lips between my teeth to keep from speaking.

He shook his head and moved one hand to the side of my face, stroking my cheek with his fingers. "Tell me you don't want me. Tell me you don't love me." His voice was soft, his breath a warm caress.

"I don't love you. And I don't want you. And if you keep coming around, I'm going to have to tell Rusnak." And I was thankful for all the scars on my heart, it made it stronger, gave me a thicker skin, so I could pull out the lie without flinching.

Gage snapped back like I'd delivered a physical blow. Several feet now separated us. He pulled his hat low and glared at me. "That's how it's going to be? After everything I've fucking done for you? You're going to threaten me with him?" he took steps back, still facing me. "You better hope you get out before he loses interest. He's only going to take what he can get, and then he'll throw you away when he's done. And I wont fucking wait around and watch." He turned and left.

I stayed on that bench until I couldn't see him anymore, and then I let the single tear fall. The only tear I would allow. Feelings had no place in all of this.

20: Preferences

"HEY, HOW'S IT GOING?"

"Thanks." I barely glanced at the man holding the door open for me.

He followed behind me as I walked to the elevator, not that strange since he lived in the same building. But then I decided to take the stairs. When the door opened and closed behind me, I picked up my pace, not pausing to turn around.

"You're Kiera's roommate, right?"

At that, I slowed my pace and turned slightly towards him. It was the guy she left with the other night. I recognized that mop of curly hair.

"Yeah," I answered as I stepped onto the platform for my floor. I pulled the door and he reached over me to hold it open.

"After you." He waved me through. "I live on the second floor, but I wanted to stop by and see if Kiera's home. She was really upset last night."

I kept walking during his talk and he kept following. He quickened his pace to fall in line next to me. "My name's Harrison, by the way."

I tried to give him a smile, but I'm sure it came across fake. There was something about Harrison I didn't like, something in those brown eyes that didn't sit right with me. Maybe it was that I knew the danger he was in by being involved with Kiera, or maybe my paranoia was at full tilt.

Pausing at my door, I turned to him. "Have you talked to Kiera, because she's usually not home this late." I had stayed at the gun range till closing.

"I was going to call her, but saw you first. Figured I'd stop by and check." He tilted his head and ran his hand through his curls, giving me what was probably meant to be a cute look. But my guards were up, and cute smiles did nothing for me.

He nodded to the door. "If she's not home, I'll call her and meet up with her that way."

I shook my head, gaging my ability to take him if it came down to it. "Call her. You're not coming in."

His eyes narrowed in an instant, but he took a step back with a surprised laugh. "She told me you were a—" He closed his mouth on his words and shook his head, curls sliding over his forehead.

"What?" I challenged with a grin. "What did she say I was?"

His hands were back in his hair as he looked at me through his thick eyelashes. "You know. But you'd just hit her when she said it, so…" He shrugged with a light laugh. "But maybe you're just smart. Girls can't be too careful, especially when it comes to being alone with guys." His expression darkened some. "Kiera should learn that too."

"Right." I shifted on my feet, adjusting my book bag on my shoulder "You can go. I'll let her know you stopped by."

"You didn't check if she was home yet." Persistent bastard.

"You can call her to find out." I lifted my chin, nodding down the hall. "Go."

"Okay, okay. Calm down, I'm going. Maybe I'll see ya around." He took a few steps back, still facing me, and then turned and walked towards the elevator.

I went into the apartment, and as I predicted, Kiera wasn't home.

* * *

I shouldn't have listened to Kyle. I should have gone to the gym. The run and room workout I did in its place didn't give me the same relief.

My muscles were pulled tight with stress as I rode in the back of Boris's town car. He had the partition up, keeping me from talking to him. Not that I would have anyways. The confined car ride left me alone with my thoughts, something I tried to avoid. Taking my phone out of my bag, I plugged in my headphones and let the music blast.

Boris walked me into the stables that served as a gun range. Rusnak stood at a table, three bottles of clear liquor and a stack of shot glasses in front of him.

"Taste these." He poured three shot's from one bottle. "I'm trying to decide if I want to invest." He waved his hand in front of all three bottles and then held out a glass for Boris and me. "This one is the smoother of the three."

The man to my left took the offered glass, swishing it in his mouth before swallowing easily. "Not bad." He set the glass upside down on the table.

I took the glass but set it to the table. "I'm not a drinker, I can't tell what's good or not."

Rusnak gave me curious smirk as he sipped his shot.

I shuddered just thinking about sipping the liquor that slow. The smell was enough to burn the back of my throat.

"I guess you can't tell the difference, but that doesn't mean you can't enjoy a drink. This one is infused with vanilla." He poured another bottle into three clean glasses.

Shoving my hands in the back pockets of my black denim jeans, I glanced around the stables. The cabinets on the wall were lined with guns and I shrugged. "Alcohol and guns? Doesn't seem like a good combination."

Rusnak laughed then brought a glass to his lips and sipped that painfully slow sip of his liquor. "You're in a fun mood tonight, I like this teasing side."

I wasn't teasing, but I shrugged one shoulder and attempted to smile. He seemed to like the idea of me joking around, so I wasn't about to correct him.

They took shots from the third bottle, and I looked out the windows as the sun skimmed the tree line, casting an orange glow. As Rusnak screwed the lids back on the bottles and discussed the pros of each with Boris, I walked to the first stull and began loading my gun.

After Boris left, Rusnak walked up behind me. I knew he was approaching, but each step he took wound my muscles tighter. I slid the magazine into the well of the gun, just as his hand brushed my hip.

"Eager to start?" He stepped behind me as his hand gripped my hip, pulling me back into him.

The back of my head rocked against his chest as I nodded. "The sun's setting, we don't have much time before the good light's gone."

His breathy laugh drifted through my hair to my scalp as he bent his head towards mine. "Scared to shoot when drinking, and now scared to shoot in the dark." He clicked his tongue and pulled on my hip, turning me around, his eyes bright with amusement. "What are we going to do about all these fears?" His voice was silk, wrapping around me, strangling me. Just like his arm, wrapping around my waist, drawing me tight.

I kept a grip on my gun as I rested it on the ledge behind me, bracing my hands there to keep my back from pressing painfully into the wood. He had me cornered. "I'm not scared." I shrugged, forcing a steady breath even though I was suffocating. "It's just preferences."

"Preferences?" His eyebrow quirked and his lip curled up. "I'd like to find out some more of your preferences." His seductive tone had my heart skipping beats.

He groaned with frustration, letting his knees dip slightly as his head dropped back. "There's one preference I have to clear up first." His body tightened, changing from alluring and warm to cold and intimidating in an instant. He snatched the gun from my grasp and turned me with a hand on my hip. Now he was leaning on the ledge, my gun in his hand, pointing to the ground.

He cocked his head, eyes narrowing slightly as he watched me. "Seems I have a bit of a dilemma."

I took a step back but didn't take my eyes from his as I waited for him to explain. My body vibrated with adrenaline, ready for fight or flight.

"Gage."

My heart dropped like a rock.

"He thought you two had something. Something worth confronting me over." He slid the magazine from the gun, turning it over in his hand. Then he slammed it back into the well with a loud snap.

"You are important to me." He took one wide step towards me, closing the space between us. "But he's more valuable, a bigger asset. And as much as I want you." His empty hand came up to my face, fingers trailing along my chin, leaving a chill. "I won't let it jeopardize my business." His fingers dropped away and he raised the gun, turning it as he inspected it from all angles. His eyes flicked back to mine. "Do you understand?"

"Yes." I didn't understand, but I wanted out of this conversation.

"Things are over between you two then? Is that what you told him yesterday?"

I nodded with what I hoped was a blank face. My mind was whirling, trying to think of what he might know, what might have happened with him and Gage. The thought of Gage in more trouble or hurt because of me was a knife in the gut. That's exactly what I had been trying to avoid.

His bottom lip dragged between his teeth. His voice came out low. "Nothing's happened yet. We can end our deal, you can go back to Nick and maybe Gage will help you with that, if that's your preference." He still had the gun dangling carelessly between us as he waited for me to respond.

Trying to discreetly suck in air, I stood up taller and shook my head. "No, I don't want that."

A smile reappeared, his face instantly changing yet again. But I could still sense the danger in him, just underneath.

"Good." He nodded, releasing air between his lips. "Good." He extended the gun to me, handle first. "Let's shoot some, before the sun sets, aye?"

It's impossible to relax when Rusnak has a gun in his hand, but a little easier when I have one too. As time passed, I was able to calm down enough that my smiles didn't feel forced, but they didn't come easy either. When he pulled out the rifles my nerves jumped back up, but after he shot a few rounds he left it to me, offering tips and positioning me to shoot. The sky was a deep purple when Rusnak pulled me back over to the table in the open area of the barn.

"There's something about you, and the way you handle guns, that is so damn sexy." His fingers slid through my hair, on either side of my head. He moistened his lips with his tongue and then they were on mine. He dipped towards me, knees bent to be on my level. His fingers flexed in my hair, holding my head pressed to his. His kiss was forceful and intense, but I didn't resist, even though my stomach flipped when his tongue slipped between my lips and the burn of vodka filled my mouth.

My tongue against his made him moan, and his fingers slid down my back. He moved his lips over my jaw to my neck, and his hands were suddenly tugging at the buttons of my shirt, trying to undo the top ones.

"Wait," It escaped in a breath and he froze, hands and lips still pressed to me, but unmoving. "I ah." I had to gather my words, think about them. I just knew I couldn't allow us to go further without getting something first. Gage's words replayed in my head, he would throw me away after he got what he wanted. I needed to make sure I had what I wanted out of our deal before that happened.

Rusnak inched back, questions clear in his cool hazel eyes. His fingers still held the chiffon fabric of my shirt.

"I"—I took a steading breath—"have some questions I need answered first."

Something dark passed through those eyes, but it was so fast I could convince myself I imagined it. Then he was shaking his head, his playful smile returning. "You want to bargain?"

He moved his hands to my hips, pulling me to him. "No." His head dipped to my ear. "I don't bargain with sex. That's something you have to give freely. And sweetheart, when you do you won't regret it." His breathy laugh tickled my ear, sending a hot chill through me.

He stepped back, suddenly releasing me, and I was surprised at the effort I needed not to stumble. I had been leaning on him more than I thought.

"I'm willing to bargain though, but in a different way. Have a seat." He gestured to one of the chairs tucked into the table.

I sat as he took one of the vodka bottles out of a cooler beside him and then laid two glasses on the table with a smirk.

"You can ask a question for every drink you take. Do we have a deal?"

My skin prickled with nerves, but it didn't sound like that bad of plan. My original bargaining chip seemed much higher than this one.

I circled my finger around the rim of the shot glass. "Do you have something to wash it down with?"

21: Keep Up

"I WANT TO KNOW WHAT'S GOING ON with Damien." I looked up from the shot in front of me, and a frown tugged at the corner of Rusnak's mouth.

He paused for a beat before sitting back in his chair. "That's not a question."

My jaw clenched with frustration, of course he wouldn't make this easy. "Fine. Is someone still going to kill him?" I held his stare and my voice didn't waver.

His lips glided into a sly smile. I could practically see his thoughts turning in those chameleon eyes, but couldn't read a single one.

He inclined his head, barely an inch. "Drink."

I held my breath and swallowed the shot, not daring to give myself a chance to taste it first. My throat and chest seared as it went down. Choking in a painful breath, my eyes watered as I chugged my chaser, trying to put out the flames that filled my mouth and nose.

"That's strong," I croaked, pulling the water bottle from my lips. It was still hard to breathe and the water was half gone. My hand rubbed my chest absently, with no relief.

Rusnak seemed to enjoy the show. He nodded at me with a satisfied smile.

"So Damien?" I gestured for him to go, it was his turn in this twisted game.

"I thought you didn't want that anymore." He spoke carefully, watching me like he could see all my thoughts.

His words forced me back in my chair. "What? That's not—" I had to look away from him to gather my words. Dim light streamed through the stalls and windows casting large shadows on the floor. "That's the entire reason I'm here." I turned back to him and took in a breath to make my voice stronger, not as distant. "I was willing to drop it. I wanted to drop it. I still would. But Nick wouldn't let me. And you won't let me." I leaned forward, bracing my forearms on the table in front of me. "If I have to keep to my end of the deal, so do you all. Otherwise this has all been for nothing. As it is, he's not worth all this."

"Is it that bad spending time with me?" There was a soft edge to his tone.

I couldn't tell the difference between the burn of the liquor and my anger. His question felt like a trap. "You're supposed to be answering my question, not asking one of your own."

His puff of a laugh was dry, without amusement. "Yes. Someone will still kill him."

I was stuck in limbo, somewhere between guilt and relief. The effects of the liquor were creeping over me, releasing some of the weight attached to the guilt.

"When?" It didn't sound like me talking.

He poured me another shot and then sipped the liquor from his glass, waiting for me.

Now that I knew the burn that would follow, it was harder to lift the glass, even harder to bring it to my lips. My stomach already clenched and throat closed, trying to block out anymore of the foul poison. But I pushed my body and tilted the shot back.

Even after I emptied the water bottle, all I could smell and taste was burning rubber, or maybe that was burning flesh, that's what it felt like. All the tissue in my mouth, nose, and throat had to be stripped, scorched away.

"You weren't lying about not being a drinker." He was laughing at me.

"That shit's horrible." I felt like breaking the glass in my hand, ending this game for good, but I still had questions. As the burn receded just enough for me to catch a breath, my confidence returned. I could do this, it wasn't so bad.

"When? That's a hard question sweetheart. Soon., After your fight." He poured more liquid into my glass, up to the very edge.

I turned his words over. All my thoughts felt like they were submerged in water, a bit slower, but lighter.

"That's not an answer." I called him out the moment the realization hit me.

He spread his hands, palms up and shrugged. "I have to talk to Nick."

"What's taking so long? What's the hold up?"

He chuckled. "Drink."

I hesitated as I picked up the shot, the vodka spilling over the side onto my fingers. "You didn't answer the question before."

"I'll answer both."

I was trapped in his icy gaze for a moment, time frozen as I made my decision. The burn was muted this time, my mouth numb, but the liquor bounced in my stomach and rushed back up my throat. I choked it down, but didn't have any water left to help.

Rusnak's smirk forced me to keep it down. I didn't want to give him the satisfaction of seeing me throw up.

"Patience." He took his time in producing another water bottle from the cooler, and then he kept a firm grip on it, not letting me take it. "These things take time." He released the bottle to me.

I sipped the water slowly, my stomach rebelling against everything. "I think I've shown a lot of patience here."

He laughed harder, slapping the table sarcastically. "Do you now? You think you've been patient? I think you've been pushing since you've arrived." His eyes dropped over me and his voice lowered. "You can't seem to stop yourself, always doing something." The look in his eyes chilled me as the alcohol heated my veins. "Just like her."

"Don't start this shit." I screwed the lid back on my bottle, but I couldn't cover my disgust. "What the hell is it with you? It's sick. And I'm not her." I stood up from the chair without thinking. "I'm done with this game, you aren't even answering the questions. It's a stupid fucking game." I didn't feel that drunk, I felt sick, but I watched the words tumble from me as if it was someone else speaking.

I slammed my palms on the table. "Quit fuckin' laughing."

He stopped with the stupid chuckle, but the smile stayed on his face. "Sit back down. The alcohol's getting to you."

"No shit. Maybe because I had three shots in three minutes."

"Twenty minutes," he corrected.

I glared at him. "It's not the alcohol, it's you."

His eyes narrowed and I sat down, clamping my lips between my teeth. The alcohol had thinned the cover on my anger, letting it show. I knew better than to let that slip any further.

"No more shots for you." He took away the small glass and replaced it with a larger one, mixing the vodka with seltzer water. "You can sip instead. But I owe you some answers. He will be killed, after your fight, but before the next one. It's taking a while because there's other business that takes priority first. Once that's squared away, this will be dealt with." He sipped from his glass. "Now, enough business. You have to have other questions. I know I have a few."

I sat still. The alcohol weighed down my limbs, but numbed all emotions, making me feel disconnected from myself. Not an unpleasant feeling.

"Why are you so against talking about your mother?"

I knew the sick bastard couldn't let it go. The question barely affected me, but I wasn't going to answer it.

"Why do you always want to talk about her?"

"I asked first and I've been drinking."

I actually laughed. "I couldn't give a shit about your drinking."

"Hm, you're being difficult." His smile made it seem like a good thing. He sighed and scooted the chair closer to me. "I loved her. And you're the only person that I can talk to about her. And as much as you hate hearing it, you remind me of her. You look just like her, and some of the things you do… you're impulsive." His eyes were intense and broke through the cloud of alcohol. "You should be thankful to be like her. That's why I want to help you."

I didn't like the return of feelings his words caused. I preferred the detachment, the not feeling. I took a sip of the drink in front of me, wanting to wrap myself in numbness again. "I don't believe you."

He sat up, pulling his hands off of my knees. I hadn't even realized they were there.

"I mean, you think you're helping me? Really? And why? Because of her? It doesn't make sense to me." I stopped myself from rambling further questions.

There was a shadow of a smile on his lips as his hands slipped back to my knees. "That's a lot of questions." He cocked his eyebrow to my drink.

"See! This is what I mean. If you wanted to help me then it wouldn't be so manipulative."

His teeth pressed into his bottom lip, excitement lighting his eyes. "You're right. You're always so guarded though, I thought this would help. It's clearly working."

My heart was pounding and I finished off my drink, trying to calm it. Nothing was clear, but if I had to choose a path, I'd take the one to emotionless drunk over being painfully sober and aware of my world spiraling beyond my control. I didn't really see a point in trying to stay in control when I obviously had none. For this one night, I was embracing oblivion.

"I drank. Answer the questions."

Something dark passed over his features, even with his smile in place. "I've helped you more than you know. I was there that night, the night she killed herself. I'm the reason you're not dead."

I picked up my glass, but it was empty. Fuck.

I watched as his hand surrounded my shaking glass, catching it before it dropped to the ground.

"I went there to make sure she was all right, I knew Nikolai had threatened her. I went there to help, but she took it wrong. She thought I was there to carry out his threats. She was already high and pulled the gun on me first. Then you walked out of whatever back room you had been in." He was talking fast, trying to get it out before—I'm not sure, maybe before I threw up on him.

I was trapped in my unmoving body, his hands holding mine.

"What happened next?" My quiet voice surprised me.

"You must have just woken up." His face pinched with the memory. "Your hair was tangled and ratty and you were wearing an adult shirt that covered you to your feet. I don't think you even knew we were there in the kitchen behind you. You came out and turned on the TV. Then she pointed the gun at you and shot, you didn't even turn around to see. She nearly unloaded the gun before you dropped, that white shirt turned red."

I pushed his hands off of me as they tried to move to my face. "Why?"

"Nikolai threatened to kill both of you, she did it before he could."

I sucked in much needed air. This didn't change shit, except now my buzz was ruined and I felt everything too heavily. I looked around the dim barn, the night sky closing in. There was nowhere to run. But I needed to escape. "I need a drink."

He poured me another drink and pressed it to my hands. "I tried to stop her, but by the time I realized what she was doing, you were down. I took the gun from her and called the ambulance that came. She'd locked herself in the bathroom. I left before the cops arrived and found out later she overdosed in there."

"Shut up." The way his voice broke talking about her overdosing made me sick. I gulped the rest of the drink and he refilled it. "I can't take anymore."

He met my eyes and nodded. "All right." He breathed out, hands up. "I'm done. I just wanted you to know. You're the only one who knows."

I nodded, hating the weight he just placed on me.

"I've got plans tonight. But you can come with me, I think you deserve a night out."

I shook my head. "I can't handle a night out, not now."

"It's a poker tournament, nothing big. It'll be fun. I'll buy you in."

What was wrong with him? "I'm not in the mood. I'll go back to the apartment."

"What if I make a deal with you?" He gripped my thighs, eyes intent on me. "You come with me and this can be your last fight, if you win."

What the hell, I couldn't keep up. Did I tell him that I knew about his deal with Gage? My thoughts were still reeling from his earlier revelation.

"Why?"

"So many questions. I told you I want to help you."

I grabbed my head, massaging my temples. "It always comes with strings," I mumbled to myself.

He smiled and stood, pulling me to my feet. "These strings aren't so bad. It's just a poker game. Who knows, you might even have fun."

22: Always A Choice

LAZILY SWIMMING THROUGH MY THOUGHTS, I REALIZED there was no one moment when I broke. But the pressure had cracked me and I'd been desperately fighting to keep the pieces together, a losing battle. Those pieces were now floating away in a river of alcohol and I didn't fucking care. And that's how I knew I was drunk. I didn't fucking care. And I was cussing in my thoughts. And now I was silently laughing to myself.

I swept my eyes around the back of the town car, the partition still up, blocking Boris from view. I rested my gaze on Rusnak and felt my smile slip from my face. He was watching me. Always fucking watching me, even when he wasn't around.

"How are you feeling?" He questioned.

"Some sort of way." I couldn't describe the disconnected feeling, it wasn't bad or good. It was nothing. I felt like nothing.

"Have another drink." He handed me the flask in his hand.

I sipped slow, taste buds long since burned away. I wanted to maintain the way I felt, not tilt it over the edge. I was comfortably numb, not concerned about what would happen next and there was a freedom in that carelessness.

"Thanks." I handed him back his flask with a nod of my head. As much as he controlled, I was at least sure that he wouldn't let things go bad tonight, or rather if that was his intention there was nothing I could do. So fuck it. I wasn't worrying. I was with the man with the most power in all this, it was all in his control. Right?

"This Nikolai, do you work for him still?" His name had been swirling in my head since Rusnak told his story.

He jerked the flask from his lips, wiping the back of his hand on his mouth. "What makes you ask that?"

I had surprised him. I pressed my lips together, keeping in the small laugh. "You use to. Does him going to prison change that?"

He eased the flask back to his lips, critically eyeing me as he sipped. "It changes everything. Under my control, this organization has gone farther than he could have taken it. It's better with me running things, and everyone knows it."

"So…" I turned to face him, leaning back on the door behind me. "This Friday will be my last fight?"

He pulled the leather flask from his lips and handed it back to me, with a slick smile. "If you win. I believe Nick already gave you those details about what round, that's all the same."

If I win. "In the second? That's a stupid bet."

His eyebrow rose, but smile stayed. "You don't think you can do it?"

I took another small sip, the liquor heating me, making me brave and untouchable. "I can. I can do whatever I want." I could. I stopped myself from kicking him, just to prove the point.

He chuckled leaning towards me, taking the flask from my fingers. "Can you now?"

Sighing I sunk lower in the seat, melting into the smooth leather. "Nope and you know it."

He shook his head, eyes dancing over me. "Sweetheart, I don't stop you from anything. There's always a choice." His hand slid into my hair. "And you chose to be here with me."

I closed my eyes, soaking up the feel of his hand gliding through the strands of my hair, sending chills over my skin.

"It doesn't feel like a choice." My eyes popped open after the words slipped from my lips. Crap, I shouldn't have voiced the thought.

"That's because you know it's the best choice. I'm the best choice." His fingers curled in my hair, gripping my head this time. "You should appreciate that."

I smirked, knowing where this was going. I leaned into him, hands on his chest, and slipped my lips to his ear and whispered, "I'm not in the begging mood." Laughing, I dropped back to my side of the car.

Biting my lip, I hid my smile. I felt more like my old self, my pre-Gage self, the me that knew how to separate sex and feelings. That's who I needed to be to survive Rusnak.

"That's all right. Now's not the time." He leaned across the seat to me and extended the flask to my lips.

I grabbed over his hand, keeping him from pouring too much into my mouth.

"I like this side of you." He tried to tip the flask back into my mouth again, but I pushed his hand away.

"No more." Gravity increased, pulling me into the seat. "I'm not going to be able to walk soon." I sat up as a brilliant idea struck. "I'll stay in the car." My voice was way too loud, way too excited.

He shook his head, laughing. "No. You're staying with me." He grabbed my hand.

"Why? What do you have planned?"

"What makes you ask that?"

"You always do." I just kept talking without thinking.

"Maybe this time, my plan is only to be near you." His fingers trailed lightly around my wrist. "Especially since you're laughing and smiling."

"I doubt that."

The car pulled around to the back of his club and my stomach dropped at the familiar location.

His grip tightened around my wrist, making my head snap to him. "Watch that mouth when we get in there," his voice was sharp.

"Then don't push me." I met his gaze with insane confidence, but a laugh slipped out. I was going crazy and knew it.

He gripped my chin with his hand. "I mean it. We'll be in mixed company, no shop talk." But his amused smile softened his harsh tone.

I nodded and he released me. That exchange sobered me slightly, but as I slid out of the car my claim of not being able to walk was tested. And it was difficult.

Rusnak kept an arm around me and I leaned into him for balance, not letting my mind jump ahead to where we were going and who might be there.

His arm was still around me when we walked into a large room, thick with smoke, and three poker tables set up in the center. Some people already sat around them, other stood in small clusters and talked with drinks in their hand.

He stiffened next to me and then his arm dropped away.

I lifted my gaze and was immediately drawn to where Gage was standing in the corner, his brown hair and blue eyes easily seen over the group he was talking too. He had a cocky smirk on his lips and the group erupted in laughter at whatever he said.

Then a woman stepped in front of Rusnak and me, blocking my view, and I realized this was the person that had affected him, not Gage. She was tall, thin, and very blonde. Her dress hung on her skinny frame with style.

"Elana, I thought you flew back yesterday."

She gave him a pointed look, with a no bullshit smile. "You never finalized your decision. No way I could go back to my grandfather with a maybe." Her bright blue eyes paused on me for a moment before traveling around the room. "Plus, I didn't want to miss one of your famous poker nights." She smiled sweetly at him. "I don't suppose you've decided yet?"

"I'm still considering." He put his hand on her bare shoulder and pointed to the bar in the corner. "Our bar is stocked with the Vysokiy Vodka tonight. I'll give you a definitive answer Monday."

I tuned out their conversation, shuffling on my feet. I could see beyond her now and was looking at him again. He was in a soft black t-shirt, with dark denim pants and a grey belt. He looked damn good, too good. It hurt to look at him, especially when he looked up and spotted me.

The small smile dropped from him, his eyes like daggers as they met mine. I snapped my eyes back to Rusnak and the blonde. The tips of her fingers drug over his shirt as she teased him about something. The scene made me want to laugh. If this girl stuck around tonight, and it looked like she was, then I would be off the hook.

Rusnak surprised me by grabbing my wrist as I stepped away, stopping me. "Where are you going?"

I glanced between him and her. "To get a drink."

"Excuse me a moment." He said to Elana and then guided me to a table with a hand on my back. "Sit here, I'll get your drink." He returned moments later with the same vodka tonic I had been sipping all night. I couldn't taste the alcohol anymore, but that didn't mean it wasn't there.

"We're going to begin soon." He patted my shoulder and then walked back to the tall blonde.

People filled the tables as girls in black, tight dresses began setting out poker chips and shuffling cards. A large biker with a full beard sat to my right. I spotted Nick on another table and was about to laugh at the sour face he gave me, but stopped when Gage sat next to him, not even acknowledging me.

Rusnak sat next to me, Elana to his left. The games began and I hung in for a while, but the alcohol blocked all strategy, I bet when I felt like it and folded when I felt like it, barely letting the numbers on my cards dictate anything. I loved the look on the men's faces when I would pull my winning chips into my pile, especially when I knew my hand had been shit. It didn't last long though, soon I was called on all my bullshit and after that my chips disappeared quickly. Since it wasn't real money to me, I didn't care. My drink kept being replenished, even when it seemed that all of Rusnak's attention was on that blonde.

After a while they combined the winners down to one table. Rusnak was one of the winners, so was Gage, and the bearded man sitting next to me.

Rusnak followed me as I walked away from the table, gripping my elbow to turn me back around. "Are you having fun?" He leaned into my ear to ask.

I smiled at him with a shrug. "Doesn't matter."

He gave me a curious look. "Elana, she's just business, you understand right?"

I laughed out loud, I couldn't contain it. "Doesn't matter." I meant it.

His smile was hesitant. "Good. Because she wasn't supposed to be here."

"It's fine." I looked past him to where she sat. She was talking to the bearded man but watching us. "She's waiting for you though."

His smile grew. "You're something else. So secure in your place."

I sucked down my laughter, not sure if he didn't get it or if I was the one missing the point. "Yup, my place. Right where you put me." I poked him in the chest, but it held too much truth to be the joke I had intended.

But he liked it. His grin spread and he winked as he walked away.

I sat on the couch along the wall and watched the game, trying, but failing, to avoid looking at Gage as he played. He didn't even seem to notice I was there, and I hated the way the female dealer's eyes kept raking over him and the way he acknowledged her.

He was picking up chips from the table when the bikers gruff voice began rising. "That's bullshit. You don't fucking call with a crap hand like that."

Gage met his red face with a cool look. "I did and I won."

"Well who the fuck are you anyways? A fucking idiot? That's bullshit, I should have won." The biker rose to his feet.

"Sit back down." Gage barely glanced at him as he straightened his chips.

The man reached over and slapped the chips across the table. "I said who the fuck are you? You've been pulling this bullshit all night. I think you're a fucking cheat."

Gage stood up and my chest tightened as the other man stepped around the table, some of his friends falling in line behind him.

I looked to Rusnak and Nick, both sat back in their chairs with matching smiles, watching the drama unfold.

"This is your last fucking chance to sit back down and shut up." Gage's voice was calm, his clenched jaw the only give away.

The man stepped closer. He was about the same height as Gage, but bigger, although not with muscle. Both of his hands shot out, reaching for Gages head, but Gage's fist slammed into his stomach and then face, making the large biker fall back.

His friends jumped in and one had Gage's arm as another attempted to hit him. Gage dodged the punch and threw his own.

I was standing now, looking around. Rusnak and Nick were still sitting as Gage was surrounded. The original man was on his feet with a broken bottle in his hand, rage in his bloody face. Before I knew it, without thought, I was there and my fist connected with his face, sliding across the already bloodied skin and spongy beard. My arm vibrated with the impact. I gripped the bottle with my other hand, yanking it from him as he stumbled back, shocked. Then his eyes locked on mine and I knew he was about to hit me back.

Hands grabbed my shoulders and pulled me away. A bouncer from the club stood between the man and me. My breaths strained as I looked around. Two other bouncers had arrived, breaking up the entire thing.

Gage stood on his own, only a couple feet away, one hand rubbing over his bloody fist. His gaze locked on me. His lip tugged up, eyes lit bright, and my heart nearly exploded at the way I inflated, laughter spilling from me. My mind was finally catching up with my actions.

"What the hell was that?" He asked, wavering between disapproval and amusement.

I flexed my hand, enjoying the pain after a bare-knuckled punch, and shrugged. "Fun?" It never failed, punching always gave me a high and mixed with the alcohol, I felt great.

Gage's smile disappeared fast as Rusnak pulled on my arm, leading me away.

"I think it's time for you to go." Rusnak's voice was level, but sharp. His hand gripped my upper arm, dragging me to the door.

The bouncers pulled the four bikers who fought Gage out of the room as well.

"Let go." I attempted to pull my arm free, but his firm grasp wouldn't break.

His grip tightened as he pulled me closer to him. "Shut up," he hissed in a threatening whisper.

Then Boris was in front of us and Rusnak released my arm. "Take her to the car," his voice was back to normal.

Rusnak's easily in control mask was in place as he walked back into the room, to where Gage stood with one hand covering his fist. Nick leaned towards him, talking in his ear, but Gage's eyes were on Rusnak, watching him approach with an unreadable, quiet look. I could see the storm in his eyes though, or maybe that was the alcohol in me.

"Come." Boris nodded his head to the door.

When I didn't budge, Boris pushed me with a hand on my back through the doorway, effectively killing my view of Gage nodding at whatever Rusnak said.

"Walk," Boris demanded with another nudge as we made our way out of the club.

As much as I wanted to be sober right now to process what the hell was happening, my blood wouldn't clear. I had to trail my hand along the hall wall to keep my balance while I walked, but it still wasn't straight.

I welcomed the night air, it was cool and refreshing after the smoke-filled room. It cleared my head some, but I stumbled when I stepped off the landing. Boris grabbed my arm to keep me up right.

"Am I in trouble?" I asked Boris, my silent stalker.

He snorted. "Sit in the car." He opened the door to the backseat. "Anatoli wants us to wait for him."

That deflated me and I flopped in the back, leaving the door open. I had thought he was going to take me back to the apartment.

"Are you sure?" I looked up at Boris after a moment of silence. I didn't remember Rusnak saying that.

He sucked in on his cigarette and blew the smoke towards me. "Yeah."

And like magic, the back door opened and out popped the man. He glanced at Boris, and then his eyes drilled into me.

Boris flicked his cigarette and walked away, disappearing around the side of the building. That started waves crashing in my stomach.

I stood up, adrenaline kicking in and giving me some strength, but I still had to lean on the car for support and I hated how wobbly I was on my feet.

He stepped close to me, his body flush with mine. "Why did you get involved in there?" his low voice was curious, but held a challenge.

I met his eyes, not backing down. "Why didn't you?" it came out too slow and sloppy.

He caged me in, his palms braced on either side of me. "I didn't have to. Neither did you. I have ways of dealing with those people, without tarnishing my reputation." One hand slid to my neck, fingers spreading to hold the side of my face as well. The touch was light, but the look that flashed in his eyes made it clear it was meant to intimidate. "Now answer me, why did you get involved?"

I shook my head, his hand followed. "I like to fight. It was fun." I shrugged. "I wasn't thinking."

His chest bounced with one laugh and his lips curled as he pressed his weight into me, leaning in close. "That was fun?" His other hand moved to cup the opposite side of my head and neck, all of his weight now pressing me into the car. "It had nothing to do with the man involved?"

"I wouldn't have jumped in for a stranger." I admitted with a smile, proud that my alcohol-laced mind was still working.

His eyes narrowed while he considered my words. Then his head dipped closer, lips almost brushing mine and I couldn't move back any further. "What if it had been me fighting? What would you have done?"

There was a whirlwind of answers I could have given, from the dangerously honest and bold to the safe lie. I didn't think I could pull off the lie, my poker face was drunk.

"You want to start another fight and find out?" I went with teasing and was rewarded with a laugh or was it only me laughing?

His hands slid over me, down my neck and arms, and then circled my waist. "Maybe another night." It was definitely him laughing, his hot breath bounced on me and made my skin crawl. "Go home and sleep this off. I'll call you tomorrow after your interview." He pecked the corner of my mouth.

Tomorrow was fuzzy to think about. Interview? I had a job interview with a nice restaurant; it shouldn't have surprised me that he knew about it. But that wasn't the most pressing question.

"Wait." I pushed on his chest, keeping him from kissing me further. "I'm still out after Friday, right?" I hoped my fighting hadn't ruined that.

He nodded. "That was the deal."

Then I wouldn't need the job interview, I'd be leaving DC after my fight. I kept my lips sealed on my thoughts, not wanting to get into that with him right now, especially since Boris was walking back around the building. I was ready to leave.

Rusnak pushed off of me with a sigh. "Taken care of?" he asked Boris as bright headlights lit up the back parking lot, passing through, towards the street.

"Yeah, going to drop them off now." Boris nodded to the taillights of the SUV as it pulled away.

Rusnak nodded towards me. "I told you I take care of things in my own way," he said cryptically, but I didn't want to ask what it meant. "Take her home." He tapped on the roof of the car and nudged me into the back seat, closing the door for me once I was in. His pace was quick as he walked back into the club.

I rode in silence, feeling like a caged squirrel. I couldn't relax. My stomach cycled and made me want to throw up if I sat back in my seat. I pounded on the partition to get Boris's attention.

The thick glass slid down and he gave me an annoyed look. "What?"

I paused. I didn't really have a plan but wanted to talk while I felt bold.

"How often do you follow me? Or watch me? Or track my phone? Or—or what is it you do anyways?" I asked conversationally, without accusation.

"Too often," was his short, bored response.

Ah, so he admits it, but that didn't really give me any new information. "Which do you do? And how often?"

He shook his head. "I don't have to tell you anything."

That sounded familiar. "Are you related to Demetri?" I was shocked at the way my heart ached thinking about him. I could almost say I was fond of him. At least he talked to me.

"No." His quick response burst my bubble.

I sat back in my seat. I shouldn't have thought about Demetri, now I struggled to stop the onslaught of bad thoughts and feelings that were surging just under my drunken calm.

"Have anything to drink Boris?" At the shake of his head I asked, "You want to go get something to drink?" I wasn't ready to let my heavy reality return.

"No." He wound back up the partition.

I sulked for a bit, brooding in my own stupor, but at some point, I passed out.

"Get up." Boris was pulling on my arm. "Can you walk on your own?"

I stood up and pushed away from his grip, almost falling on my ass with the effort.

"Yes." I stepped back, away from the car and him. "I'm fine. Thanks for the lift." I saluted as I spun on my feet, turning to face the front door. But the world around me kept turning. When would this end?

I walked past the doorman, to the elevator and Boris followed. He silently followed me all the way to my apartment but got right back on the elevator the moment I unlocked my door.

Dropping my bag and jacket on the floor of my bedroom, I stumbled out of my shoes and clothes. Pulling on my largest t-shirt, I crashed into bed, finding sleep as the room spun at dizzying speeds.

Pounding on the door woke me, the room rattled with it. My reactions were scattered and I jumped up, nearly falling over the sheets tangled around me. The pounding was coming from the front door. Knowing the lock would keep me safe, I scrambled to it without grabbing a weapon. It was probably Kiera, she frequently locked herself out, my mind was slow to remind me.

But through the peephole, I saw Gages brown hair as he braced himself with one arm on the frame. Then his head popped up and I was met with his bright blue eyes, burning into me like he could see me through the wood.

"You need to leave." My words would have held more impact if I hadn't opened the door.

My muscles vibrated with fear and excitement. My mind screamed that he needed to leave, but my body said just the opposite. The air was too thick between us, I couldn't breathe.

And in an instant, he had me in his arms, lips pressed to mine.

23: Collided

HE COLLIDED WITH ME, FORCING ME BACK, out of the doorway and into the apartment. He was all there was, filling all my senses. I breathed him in. I had been suffocating without him and didn't even know it until this moment.

The sound of the door shutting behind us made my heart skip, but it had only been him kicking it closed. My fingers ran through his hair, it was longer than I remembered and easier to grip. His kiss was intense, tongue swirling around mine, as he kept walking me back, further into the apartment.

The apartment I shared with Kiera, my mind whispered a warning.

I gripped his shirt. The soft black material bunched in my fists as I pulled him into my bedroom, out of the hallway where we could be seen.

He must have thought I was eager, and in a way a part of me was. He broke our kiss to slip his shirt over his head, and my mind had time to catch up. I had left it at the front door.

"Wait." I stepped back. My heart was pounding, tearing itself apart with the effort. "We can't." Another step back, my shallow breathing and his bare chest made words hard to speak. The back of my legs hit the edge of my bed, and I sucked in a steadying breath as he stepped towards me. "Stop. You shouldn't be here. Rusnak—"

"Don't," he snapped with a warning step towards me. "He's not coming, he left with that other girl." He raised his chin, looking down on me. "Is that who you want?"

I was captured and frozen in his gaze, and it was getting closer, more intense, as he stalked towards me. It gutted me that he even needed to ask, but all I could do was shake my head when I wanted to scream, no.

"Good." Relief flooded his voice and features, he melted with it and his hand shot out grabbing mine, pulling me towards him. "I should have come sooner. It should have never been him. You belong with me."

Everything ached in me, reaching for him. My arms circled his waist, pressing us closer together. I rested my head on his chest as his arms wrapped around me, his lips in my hair. I wasn't sure which was harder to resist, his hot consuming kisses, or this gentle soul-capturing embrace. But I knew I couldn't bring myself to push away, not physically. Besides it wasn't Gage who would get in trouble, Rusnak had said he was too valuable. I was the one taking a risk and this moment felt worth it. I was still drunk enough that I could turn off my concern for tomorrow.

He leaned back, using one hand to lift my chin to look at him. "I love you. And I know you love me."

"Shh. It doesn't matter." I tried to bring my lips to his to shut him up, stop his talking.

He stood up taller, too tall for me to kiss his mouth, so I kissed his neck and ran my hands over the hard muscles on his back, around his shoulders, tracing the tattoos on his chest and stomach. I licked and kissed his neck and shoulders as my hands dipped into the top of his jeans, hoping to spark that passion in him again. I was already burning.

The groan that rumbled his chest, vibrating my lips, as I took him in my hand was so damn sexy it sent shocks of lust straight to my core, causing a gasp of my own.

Then his hands gripped my shoulders and he tossed me back on to the bed. I was helpless to stop my free fall. He took me by surprise and my reactions were still dulled by the alcohol and his presence, I didn't know which was affecting me more.

As my butt bounced on the bed and I fell back against the soft comforter, I had my answer. It was this man that had me high, not the liquor. His eyes burned as he crawled over me and his fingers tugged my shirt up, hot kisses dotting my stomach, each one pushing me further over the edge.

His lips moved up me, lifting my shirt as he went. My brain warned me to push him away, reminding me that I was braless and the shirt was the only thing keeping my scars covered, but he quickly took it off me. And I didn't stop him, my arms even lifted to make it easier, quicker.

I closed my eyes, blocking the insecurities that tried to creep in. His warm hands were over me, sheltering me, keeping me safe. He wouldn't add salt to these wounds, under his touch it felt like I could be cherished instead of disposed of.

His lips wrapped around my nipple, sucking and tugging, burning away all other concerns, and his fingers moved down to my panties, sliding inside. He started a slow pump, in and out, and all thought combusted. I was left with only feeling and sensation.

His fresh scent surrounded me, his solid weight covered me, his sweet husky voice whispering words too low to hear, and his hands were all over me. He was all there was and all I wanted. And I needed more.

I moved my hands over his smooth, sensitive skin, and it grew under my touch. I ached for him to fill me.

"Say it again," he panted in my ear, sucking in a breath as I bit his shoulder.

My head swirled, his words forcing me to think, but his fingers continued their slow, rhythmic circles that made it impossible to recall anything else.

"Please," I begged, arching my hips to him and guiding him to me with my hand.

He lifted off of me, kicking down his boxers and dragging my underwear off with one hand, kissing my legs as he went.

The look and feel of his head between my legs as he paused, licking, tasting, on his way back up was too much. "Please, Gage."

His blue eyes lifted to mine, bright with desire as he rose over me, bracing his weight on one forearm. "That. Say my name again." He positioned himself between my legs, the tip pressing into me.

He thrust into me as I breathed his name, forcing it out in a gasp.

Rocking in and out, he commanded, "Again, again, again."

And each time I responded, my fingers digging into the skin on his back as the pressure mounted.

"It's only… my name… on your… lips… from now on… Only me," he demanded in between thrusts that got deeper and harder until it shattered my core.

I fell to pieces beneath him and he slowed his pace to a rock. He was slowly pulling me back together as he glided in and out of me, his lips over mine, drinking his name from them.

When my spasms slowed, he began that sweetly, torturous twist of his hips that started a fire, deep in my core, all over again.

"Only me," he lifted his upper body up, meeting my eyes. "From now on." His hips continued to move, stroking all the right spots.

The vulnerability he let show as he searched my face had me smoothing my hands over his head and cheeks, trying to soothe him, reassure him.

"It's only ever been you. No one else." I kissed his face and couldn't stop. My lips grazed over his forehead and cheeks. And once our lips met he dropped onto me, pressing me into the mattress as our kiss deepened.

We were tangled in each other, trying to melt into each other. He rocked into me, speed and strength increasing and intensifying, bringing me to the edge again and again before finally going with me.

Our fingertips ran softly over each other, leaving goose bumps in their wake. My head on his chest, I listened to his heart, a strong, steady beat. Sleep was taking over, a heavy blanket clouding everything. My fingers traced the letters on his ribs 'Rage' and then outlined the fire burning the top of the letters.

"I thought this was about boxing. It's not, is it?" My euphoric haze was slipping.

He sighed, lifting his head to look at the tattoo or me. I don't know which since I didn't take my eyes off the ink stretched over muscles. My head was too heavy to lift.

"Do not go gentle into that good night, Rage, rage against the dying of the light. It's by Dylan Thomas." My body shifted as he shrugged his shoulder. "It was for my Dad, but for me too. It's for everything, including boxing. It's a way of life."

His fingers were still on my shoulder, no longer trailing soft circles over my skin. I snuggled deeper into him, wanting to take back my question. I wanted to go back to ignoring everything else for a little longer. I don't know if it was the alcohol still keeping me from thinking or sheer hard headedness, but I wanted to stretch this night out as long as possible. But first, I needed him to relax again.

"I should get rage tattooed under my flame." I touched the tattoo behind my ear and closed my eyes as he laughed. "Then we could match."

His arms circled around me, wrapping me in his warmth, just where I wanted to be. Then I succumbed to sleep.

* * *

My head was throbbing. I was too hot, and everything was heavy. I could barely move. My lips peeled apart so I could lick them, my mouth dry and rough like sandpaper. I tried to rub away the sleep from my eyes, but my arm was stuck. Under Gage.

For a blind second, I was tempted to curl back into him. Then my present moment slammed into me and I shoved him away. "Get up."

Clear sunlight lit the room. The alarm clock read 9:23 am.

I was up, searching for clothes. My head split into two from the quick movements and I was forced to slow down. It was hard to slip into pants, my balance was still off.

"Get up," I said again in a panicked whisper, sitting on the edge of the bed.

He hooked his arm over his head with a groan. Then his other hand reached out for me, grasping at air. "Come back to bed, just for a bit."

I stepped back, away from him. "Get up and get out." Scooping up his clothes, I pushed them towards him, dropping them on his lap. "You shouldn't be here."

He sat up suddenly, his face pulled in confusion and annoyance.

"Last night was a mistake. Get out."

Threading his legs into his jeans, he remained silent. I had to turn away, unable to look at him and the frown darkening his face.

"You're scared. But you don't need to be." He was trying to calm me, his smooth voice sunk into me as he closed in behind me.

But it wouldn't work. I had to stay strong. Turning, I faced him, taking a step back. "So what if I am? It's not like that stops me from doing what needs to be done. Now leave." I pointed to the door. He was blocking me from opening it for him.

His eyes narrowed and he took one large step towards me, grabbing my arm. "That's the problem. It doesn't stop you, you let your fear control you. And that's a dangerous emotion to make decisions with." His other hand captured my shoulder and his hard look softened. "You don't have to be scared with me. I told you, things can be different. I can help you."

I pulled away, out of his grasp. "No. I don't want you to. I worked out my own deal with Rusnak. I'm out after my fight Friday. You'll only pull me in deeper."

He flinched back at my words. "Last night—I thought—You love me," it sounded like an accusation.

I shook my head and closed my eyes, trying to calm my pounding headache and block Gages fiery eyes. "It doesn't matter. I'm getting out and getting away. You're not. I can't do this. Now leave. If he finds out you're here…" I looked around the bare room, chaos and fear filling every cell of me. "He probably already knows."

"No, he doesn't. I took care of that last night. I told you, I can help you."

"I don't want your help." I was almost shouting, but knew I couldn't risk waking Kiera. "Now get out." He only stared at me and I knew I had to hit harder. With his scent still covering me, and the memory of his touch fresh, I didn't want to. But I had to. "Rusnak will be here soon."

"What?" He charged at me, quicker than I could retreat, but stopped short of grabbing me, fists flexed at his side. "If you fucking go back to his bed after what we had, I'm done. You can't go from my bed, to his, and back again."

My head was pulsing, white blinding pain, and I was going to throw up. I needed him gone and his anger was only feeding mine.

"Don't get it twisted, you came to my bed last night. Now get out." I swallowed the wave of nausea and tears that threatened.

His eyes seared into me for a heart stopping moment, his deep breaths rasping. Then he pushed over my dresser. It landed with a room-shaking thump, drawers spilling open as he stormed out of the room and apartment, slamming the door as he left.

24: Mistake

I WAS STILL FROZEN, STUCK IN PLACE, taking in the mess he made, mind reeling at the mess I just caused.

The tall dresser was knocked on its side. The few clothes I possessed hung out of the drawers that had opened at impact. I hoped he hadn't broken it because I couldn't think of a good excuse. I had been drunk and knocked it over, was the best I could think up, pathetic.

I sunk to the ground, limbs heavy and head throbbing. It didn't matter what excuse I came up with, Rusnak would know. Gage had said he wouldn't, but he didn't know everything. There was a lot I wish I could tell him—I wish I had told him.

Before the sadness could consume me, my stomach flipped and I was rushing to the bathroom. I hugged the toilet as my body turned inside out. I laid on the bathroom mat with a towel covering me, taking catnaps between bouts of hurling my guts out into the toilet. And so my morning passed, until my stomach felt calm enough, and body strong enough, to venture a shower.

* * *

I had several missed calls and texts from Kyle wondering where I was and if I was coming to train. I had missed our session this morning. I texted him back, letting him know I would be in tonight, but he didn't have to wait for me.

Dexter had texted too, asking where I was. I guess he'd finally come back to the gym for me. I didn't want that. I had decided this morning that the best plan was to stay away from everyone, only focus on the gym, until Friday. This Friday. I would fight and then be done with it all. I just had to make it through the week.

Kiera padded into the kitchen as I searched for Pepto Bismol or ibuprofen or any medicine to put me out of my misery. I was about to ask her, she had to have some remedies for as often as she binged, but her smirk stopped me.

She poured herself a cup of coffee, but kept glancing at me, laughter on her lips. "You sounded like you were having fun last night." She sipped from her oversized mug and leaned her hip on the counter as her eyebrow shot up. "Not so much this morning though."

An angry fuse sparked and burned, running through my veins. But my heart stilled, any chance of Rusnak not knowing about Gage and I, gone. Unless, I could get her to keep quiet. I stopped my instinct to get in her face and throw her to the floor. Perhaps she was only referring to me getting sick and coming in drunk? Her smug smile told me that wasn't likely.

"Your friend, I forget his name, the one with the curly hair, lives in this building." I had her attention now and her smile faltered. "He stopped by for you on Friday. We had an interesting conversation, I didn't realize you two were such…" I tapped my lips with my index finger considering my words, "good friends?"

The way her face paled and all expression dropped let me know I wasn't wrong in my assumption. I had been bluffing and it worked.

Now I was the one smirking as I stepped towards her. I placed my hand on the counter in front of her and leaned in, meeting her eyes. "Stay out of my business and I'll stay out of yours. Okay?"

She nodded, wide eyed. "I won't say anything, if you don't."

"Deal." Relief eased some of the tension in my muscles. I pushed off the counter, needing out of this place. We had come to a truce and I didn't want to ruin it.

I was already dressed in leggings and a long sleeve t-shirt, so I slipped on my running shoes, grabbed my phone, headphones, and some cash, and then I walked out the door.

Stopping at the convenience store across the street, I picked up my much needed medicine and equally needed fountain soda. I hadn't had soda in so long, not since Gage got me started on clean eating. Nan always said a coke was the best hangover cure, and she might be right. My hangover craved the carbonation and sweet, but refreshing, syrup. I had already wrecked my body last night, this couldn't do much worse; it felt like it was helping.

I was dragging by the time I walked to The National Mall. I sat on a grassy spot in the sun, watching the people go by. Many families and friends zigzagged happily across the lawn, going from museum to museum. A group of teens played Frisbee nearby and their laughter soothed and irritated me. All this life around me was proof that there was a whole insanely normal and happy world that I wasn't part of. How had I gotten stuck somewhere outside it all?

A charter bus pulled up, Tour America, written in big letters on the outside and paintings of different landmarks filled any bare space. As the group of tourist boarded I contemplated my chances of running on. I didn't even care where it was going. My body pulsed with the thought, adrenaline already flowing. But something kept me seated on the cool grass. I only had till Friday, then I would board a bus going anywhere and get the hell out.

Turning up the volume on my music, I leaned back in the grass and attempted to relax, attempted to block out all thoughts. I needed to rest now. Then I'd jog back to the gym and put in a good workout. I needed it.

My leg jerked as someone kicked my foot. Opening my eyes, I shielded my face from the sun. How long had I been out, a minute, an hour?

"Fuck," I groaned, sitting up, squinting at Boris.

"Get up." He kicked my foot again before I could move it away. He shoved his hands in his pocket, his face its typical bored scowl. "Anatoli's waiting in the car."

I thought I might get sick again. I pulled my feet under me, taking deep breaths to still the rising queasiness. My fingers pressed into the soft ground as I dug for enough courage to get up and face him.

"After you." He tilted his head to the dark town car parked in a fire zone on the side of the busy street.

Dread weighed me down, keeping my pace slow. Did he already know? The chill that ran through me was caused by more than the light breeze. But I kept my head up and walked towards the car and whatever was waiting for me. The fact that he found me here proved I would have never made it far on the bus earlier.

Rusnak put one finger up, silencing me as I got in the car. He was on the phone.

"Yes… Next week…Tuesday…"

His eyes were on me, watching me. I looked out the window as the car pulled away, feigning interest in the city passing by.

"He'll be there…So everything's still on schedule?" The tip of his finger touched the tattoo behind my ear and then trailed lightly down my neck.

I looked towards him. He was still on the phone but his finger trailed along the collar of my t-shirt. I pressed my lips together to keep myself from throwing up on him. My headache returned with a vengeance. Tangling my fingers in my lap, I forced myself to sit still. This was better than his anger, right?

"Good. Call me as soon as you know." He ended the call, but kept the phone in his hand, eyes never leaving mine.

"How are you feeling?" His finger retraced its slow path, dragging back up to my ear.

"Sick." There wasn't enough air in the car and my skin was getting clammy.

"I shouldn't have let you drink so much last night," He murmured, dropping his hand to my knee. He turned his attention to his phone, his thumb bouncing lightly over the screen.

I braced myself for him to say more, but he didn't. He kept a firm grip on my knee, but otherwise his attention was fully on the small screen in his hand. I let myself entertain the idea that Gage might have been telling the truth, that he somehow found a way to make sure Rusnak wouldn't know he came over. Or maybe he just didn't care? He had been with that other girl last night. I wasn't about to mention any of it.

"I still need to go to the gym. I was just about to go before…" I shifted in my seat, hoping my escape plan would work.

His eyebrow rose, but he didn't look up from his phone. "We can drop you off at the gym, but first I want an early dinner and you should eat something, it'll help with the hangover."

He lifted his head, looking out the window, searching the signs along the building. "And you missed your interview. You must have been feeling pretty sick this morning." He clicked his tongue at me, but glanced over with a smile and a wink. "Good thing I know the owner."

Recognizing the restaurant we pulled up in front of, I felt like I was in quicksand. It was the Italian restaurant I was supposed to have interviewed at today. I hesitated before following him out of the car.

"It wasn't that. I don't need a job there anymore."

He looked over the roof of the car at me with a curious smile. "Why is that?"

I closed the door and stepped to the sidewalk, out of the way of traffic. Boris pulled away as soon as I was clear.

"I won't be staying in DC much longer." I shrugged and tried to act as if my stomach wasn't tumbling painfully.

His eyes narrowed, but he didn't say anything as a dark haired waiter in a crisp white shirt opened the restaurant door for us.

"Welcome." His smile was bright. "Mr. Rusnak, your table is ready."

The main dining room was nearly empty as we walked through it. We were led to a back room divided by a large fireplace and sat in a secluded booth. After the server gave us our menus and walked away, we were the only ones in the room.

He set the menu down, eyes drilling into mine, but then he looked past me and his face broke into his perfect grin. "Francesco." He stood up. "Are you cooking tonight?"

Francesco extended his hand, shaking Rusnak's with warmth. "No, not for everyone. But for you Anatoli, of course." He turned his dark eyes on me and I stood up as he reached for my hand. "And this must be the girl who stood me up earlier." The laughter in his voice took the sting out of his words.

"Ah, yes. Well that was my fault, as I told you. This is Regan," Rusnak introduced.

I felt extremely uncomfortable as Francesco looked me over. This was the type of restaurant that would have a dress code, and I was in spandex and a large t-shirt.

The salt and pepper haired man smiled at me. "Well, when can you start?"

Rusnak's eyes were on me but he stayed mute as I decided how to answer.

"Next week." The lie came out easy, although I wasn't sure it was the right action.

"Wonderful. There is only a little bit of paperwork I need—"

"You two can handle that after we eat. I have somewhere to be soon," Rusnak interrupted, sitting back down in his seat. He picked up the menu. "We'll both have the Ossobuco di Agnello."

"Of course. And to drink?" Francesco immediately turned his full attention to Rusnak.

I sat back down, stomach twisting with the thought of alcohol.

"Two ice teas." Rusnak handed the menus back to Francesco.

Once we were alone again, Rusnak pierced me with a look. "So which is it? Do you need the job or not?"

Maybe I shouldn't have lied? "I don't—"

"Because you think you're leaving DC? When?" He cut through my explanation.

"After my fight." I spoke slowly, calmly.

"Then why did you tell him you would start next week?" He leaned back in his chair, voice icy.

I dropped my eyes to the napkin in front of me and shrugged.

"Look at me." He leaned in close, dropping his head to capture my eyes again. "Now tell me. Why did you lie to him?"

"I didn't want to make you angry." I was too flustered to do anything but admit the truth. I had thought contradicting him in front of Francesco would have angered him. And my nerves were already raw, waiting on him to explode about last night.

He pressed his lips together as a smile tugged them up. "Sweetheart, you should take the job. You can't go back to Baltimore, there's still a price on your pretty little head. Remember, that's why you're here with me. I'm keeping you safe."

I shook my head. The room was coming down around me. I was in the middle of a disaster. "You promised to let me out of all this when I was done fighting," I reminded him, the beginning stages of panic tightening my chest. It felt like forever ago that he made that promise, the first time I went to the gun range with him.

He nodded. "I did. And I keep my promises, but I can't let you get killed. When the threat is gone, you can go." He reached across the table, capturing my hand in his. "But I do want to stay in your life."

I looked down, avoiding his probing gaze. I didn't want him to see how much those words affected me. How hopeless he made me feel. He shook my hand slightly, and I knew he was waiting for me to say something.

"I…" I looked up at him. "I want to move to California." I chose the state randomly, somewhere far from him and this city. But it reminded me of the dreams Nan and I shared when we were younger. "I could move after the fight. There's no threat there." And once I arrived I would move somewhere different, somewhere that Rusnak couldn't find me either. I'd only told him this much because I knew it would make it easier to leave if I had his approval.

He dropped my hand as Francesco delivered our drinks. The man didn't speak or look at either of us, he must have felt the tension too.

"I have several connections there, in many of the cities. In fact, I own a winery in Napa Valley. I can set you up with an apartment."

He sipped his drink, always watching for a reaction. "What?" He smiled at me.

I swallowed the bile that was beginning to rise as I realized how far his reach went. "How many different businesses do you have?" I needed to turn the conversation. Stop talking about me.

"I'm a money man. I invest in whatever I think can make me money, with people I trust."

* * *

I lay in bed that night, embracing the exhaustion from a long day and hard work out. But I think it was the stress of dinner with Rusnak that wore me out the most. He never mentioned Gage and neither did I. Maybe he really didn't know.

Knocking on the apartment door pulled me out of my thoughts. Kiera's footsteps traveled down the hall as she went to open it. Then she was pounding on my door.

"Wake up," she slurred, annoyance clear in her voice.

The moment I opened the door, she was shoving a clothing box into my arms.

"It's from him. For you." The box crumpled slightly with the force, spilling the contents on the floor.

From a quick scan I saw the Lululemon symbol on some of the clothes and a running belt with a can of mace in it. The top of the box had a note that said,

For running in the city. –Anatoli

I met her glassy eyes and she backed away with a huff, running out the door.

* * *

The heavy anchor of dread followed me through the next day, gaining weight as the time passed. Nothing happened to add to the unease, but that was the problem, I kept expecting something that never materialized.

I tried to go to bed early. I tried to be thankful for the calm day. I had managed to avoid everyone with a slight change to my routine, Kiera, Dexter. The only person I interacted with was Kyle while I trained. Rusnak never tried to contact me, but I kept waiting, he had me on edge.

Pulling the sheets around me, I tried to remind myself I only had till Friday. Friday I would be out no matter what he said. But that promise did nothing to ease the weight around me, and it pressed into my dreams that night.

"Whore." Rusnak's face twisted in fury as he yelled at me, mere inches away.

I couldn't move. My body wasn't working. There was nothing but darkness and Rusnak.

"Stupid Bitch." His face morphed into Damien's, but it was Rusnak's voice laced with venom.

Then he disappeared and Gage stood in the darkness, too far away to reach. His mouth fell open as if to yell.

"Get out," the scream was Kiera's.

My eyes popped open, heart pounding.

"It wasn't me." Kiera's shrill voice echoed through the room and it took a moment to realize it wasn't part of my dream. "Please." Her sob was filled with pain.

I reached under the bed for my gun, not bothering to turn on a light, and walked cautiously into the living room.

It was empty, but her door was open. She was using the edge of her bed to lift herself off of the floor. Her face was red, streaked black as her tears ran through her makeup.

"It was bad enough you fucked someone else." He had his back to me, his voice deceptively soft as he stalked towards Kiera and lifted her into standing by her arms. "But then you had to bring my family into it?"

She was shaking her head, crying as he listed her offenses. "No, no, no. I didn't. I love you. No. Please."

"My kids found that letter, you stupid whore." His hands tightened around her throat and I hurried into the room, unable to stop myself.

He dropped her to the ground and spun on me with a backhand that I was able to dodge.

His eyes focused in on me, clearing, and he dropped his hand to his side. "This isn't your concern Regan. Get out. Now."

I should listen to him. My feet took a step back as I darted my eyes between Rusnak's cool anger to Kiera, sobbing on the ground with fear. She looked up at me, large green eyes now red and bruised, and I hesitated.

Rusnak's eyes dropped to the gun in my hand. "Don't be stupid. Put it away." His hand lifted his suit jacket, showing his own gun in a holster.

I slid my gun into the waistband of my spandex shorts, letting my large shirt drop over it all. Then lifted my hands, palms up. "I wouldn't. You know I wouldn't," I spoke carefully, slowly, trying to buy some time. I couldn't walk away and leave Kiera here with him like this.

"It was her, not me," Kiera suddenly interrupted. She was standing now, eyes as wild as her curly hair. "She probably wrote that letter. She—"

It was a slap in the face. I stepped towards her, fist clenched and anger rising, drowning out my concern for her.

"I know it wasn't her." Rusnak stepped towards her, snatching her arm in his grip. "She's smarter than that and—"

"She fucked some guy here, in your place, just the other night. She can't stand—" Kiera's tirade was silenced by Rusnak's fist. She dropped instantly, a heap of waste on the floor, unconscious and unmoving.

And for a second I was glad. I had been about to hit her, but he beat me to it. Then the new silence in the room wrapped around me, strangling me, and I reluctantly shifted my eyes to Rusnak.

His fists were still clenched, his back rising and falling as he stood over Kiera, looking down at her with fire in his eyes. Then his head twisted and I felt the burn of his glare, more intense than ever before.

My head was shaking back and forth, mouth opening to explain, but no words came out.

He lifted his hand, silencing me. "Enough." His hand dropped, pointing to the door. "I said, get out."

And this time I didn't hesitate. I stepped away, never turning my back on him until I reached the front door.

As I rode the elevator down, my troubles became obvious. I had no shoes, no money, no cell phone, and I was wearing only shorts and a too thin t-shirt. But at least I had my gun. There was no way I was going back into that apartment while he was there, but for the life of me, I couldn't think of what to do. So I walked out the front of the building, straight into Boris.

He paused when he saw me, inclining his head in acknowledgement with a slight smirk as his eyes dropped to my bare feet.

"Don't go far. We'll be gone soon." He patted my shoulder like he just told a joke and then walked into the apartment building.

My stomach twisted thinking about what it all meant. I should go to the police, but that would be signing my death certificate, if Kiera's words hadn't already done so. I wasn't going to do anything more to help her, and the only guilt I felt was over the fact that I didn't care.

I looked past the circular drive of the building to the city streets spotted with a few people. It must still be fairly early. The cold night air smelled of rain and the wind whipped around me, but I was numb to it, already cold from the inside out.

I couldn't walk around like this, so I sunk back to the building and sat on a bench in the shadows. I'd wait here till Rusnak and Boris left, and then I'd go back in and get some things. I couldn't think beyond that. I didn't even know if I'd make it that far. I tried to reassure myself, he had told me to go, if he wanted me dead or hurt he would have done it then. I needed to get a grip on my thoughts, think this through without panicking.

I don't know how long I sat on the bench, legs tucked into my shirt for warmth, thoughts spinning in circles that led nowhere new. But eventually, the sky began spitting icy drops of rain. The ledge above me protected me from most of the rain, but it was just another thing working against me, trapping me in my fate.

I watched the doors, ready to hide if I saw Rusnak, but they only opened a few times.

"What are you doing out here, like that?" a slightly familiar voice reached me, sounding distant as the wind carried it away.

Coming from the street, Kiera's friend walked along the sidewalk to where I was, an unlit cigarette dangling from his lips.

He huddled close the building, shielding his cigarette with one hand while he striked his lighter with the other. He brought the flame to his mouth and inhaled, the end of his smoke burning bright in the dark. He pulled it from his lips with two fingers and leaned against the wall. "So?" He gestured to me. "What's the story? You wanna bum a smoke?"

I hadn't spent any time thinking about an excuse for what was happening, didn't think I needed one.

"I'm locked out." I shrugged, sliding my legs out from inside my shirt and sitting up taller.

One eyebrow rose up and a dimple dotted his cheek as he looked at me skeptically over the end of his cigarette. "Kiera's not home yet? We can go in and get someone in concierge to unlock your door. I'll vouch for you." He blew out smoke as he talked.

"Umm, that's okay. Its, well…" I was trying to find an excuse but gave up. Why was I wasting my time with him? "I'm fine. You can go."

Now dimples were showing on both his cheeks and he sat next to me on the bench, bumping me with his shoulder. "I get it, she's busy with that boyfriend of hers." He took a drag of his cigarette, holding it away from me as he blew smoke into the air. "I'm surprised you're trying to cover for her. She wouldn't do the same for you."

My heart dropped at his words. She'd proved that tonight, but I had to remind myself that we weren't talking about the same things. This guy had to go.

I shifted away. "I'm not covering for anyone. I just don't need to explain myself to you."

He leaned against the brick wall behind us, his curls slick on his forehead from the rain. He watched me as he took a long, slow pull on his cigarette. Then he stubbed it out on the wall, even though it was only half way smoked, and flicked it into the bushes as he stood up. "All right, fine. You don't need to explain anything. But I can see you're freezing and… barefoot." Those dimples flashed as he pushed his hair back. "You can come to my place and wait."

I shouldn't, but I stood up ready to go. I was cold and his apartment seemed to be a good hideout until Rusnak and Boris left. Plus, he wasn't that big and I had a gun. He didn't scare me. He was the one that should be scared, but his smile grew as he realized I was accepting his offer. Guilt began creeping over me, but I was selfish enough to ignore it.

* * *

I stepped out of the bathroom in a pair of his sweatpants. He handed me a steaming cup of tea as I sat with one leg curled under me on his couch.

"Better?" His brown eyes met mine, a smile crinkling them.

I nodded as I took a sip. "Yes. Thank you."

"I would offer you something heavier to drink, but Kiera told me you don't drink. Is that right?"

"This is fine." It made me uncomfortable to know they talked about me.

Setting the cup on the table, I looked around the grey and red apartment. There was nothing to give away who he was, no pictures, no awards, nothing. Only a few frames of art hung up, black and white photographs of city skylines.

He sat back on the couch, legs spread wide, taking up as much space as he could. "Kiera thought they were breaking up. But I guess she was wrong. How long does this usually take them?"

I looked away with a shrug. "I don't know. But I can go if you wanted to go to bed." The clock above his TV shown it was nearly midnight.

"Where will you go? With no shoes?" He laughed and ran his hand through his hair, fluffing it. "It's all right, you can stay here. Sleep on the couch if you want. Kiera also told me you go to bed insanely early."

"Do you two ever talk about anything other than me?" I leaned back on the couch and turned to face him.

He nodded with a pacifying smile that I hated. "We talk about a lot of things, but lately it's been you." He tilted his head from side to side. "You don't seem as bad as she made you out to be." He nodded towards me with a smirk. "Although that gun at your waist is pretty bad ass."

I sat up and pressed my hand to my shirt, where the gun sat underneath.

"It's fine." Waving his hand at me, he continued with amusement, "A bit strange to leave with that and not your shoes though." His eyes appeared deeper, sharper, than I originally thought.

I stood up. "I'm going to go."

"No." He stood up too. "Really, you should stay. You don't want to talk about it, fine. Look, I'm going to bed. I'll leave you alone. Eventually, you'll realize I'm one of the good guys."

I paused at his words. I didn't really want to leave. I didn't want to face that apartment yet. But his claim to be one of the good guys sparked an all-new fear. What did he mean, how much did he know?

"Good guy? How so?" I dared to ask, sitting back down on the edge of the couch.

He plopped back down, relaxing into the cushions. "You know. Saving cats from trees, taking in shoeless girls from the cold streets of the mean city, paying taxes." He shrugged. "The usual good guy stuff."

"Okay." I wasn't buying it, but I didn't really want to know more. I didn't want to know him. I didn't need to know how he afforded this expensive apartment. I just needed a place to sleep for the night until I could get my stuff in the morning. "Good night, good guy." I still couldn't remember his name.

He took the hint and stood up, stretching. "Good night, trouble." He winked, then opened an ottoman and tossed me a blanket from inside before walking off.

* * *

I returned to my apartment before my host woke up and was greeted with silence. Checking all the rooms, I confirmed that no one was here. Then I forced myself to check my phone. There was only one text from Boris, at 12:47am telling me I could return to the apartment, Kiera moved out.

I needed to get away, but couldn't decide if that would make things better or worse. I didn't get a chance to find out because as I opened the door, wearing my stuffed backpack, Nick stood, blocking me.

His hand dropped away, surprised that the door had opened. He scanned over me and his eyebrow lifted with a satisfied grin. "Going somewhere, little one?"

25: Stay Put

NICK'S MASSIVE FRAME WAS BLOCKING THE DOOR, the only exit.

"I'm going to the gym." I pulled the strap of my backpack tighter on my shoulders and attempted to walk past him, but he didn't budge. It was like hitting into a wall.

"Not so fast." He pushed me back into the apartment with one hand.

As I stumbled back, I dropped my hand to my gun at my waist. But before I could even reach under my shirt he had his glock out, aimed at my face as he moved towards me. I shouldn't have waited, my instincts had told me to pull out the gun at first sight; I wish I had listened.

With my hands raised, I retreated into the apartment, slowly taking steps back as he took steps forward. Everything beyond the barrel of the gun was a blur, but I could see into it crystal clear. And I wondered if I would see the bullet fire before it killed me.

He took a massive step towards me and slammed me against the wall with a painful grip on my arm. The gun shoved into my neck as he released my arm and moved his hand under my shirt, disarming me of my weapon.

His large smile filled his face as he brought my own gun up to eye level. "This is nice. I wouldn't want ya hurting yourself though. I'll take it for now."

I ripped my eyes from the guns to look at Nick straight on. "Rusnak gave it to me." I used the only defense I had and it was a bluff. I knew I didn't really have his support anymore.

For a second, I thought it might have worked. He froze, eyes trained on me, but he started laughing, a bark of a sound that shattered any hope. He put my gun away, but I didn't drop my eyes to see where. His glock remained pressed to my neck, shaking as he laughed.

"He always did have good taste in weapons, but shitty taste in bitches." He sighed his last laugh and then his voice darkened. All amusement was gone as he inched closer, the gun sliding under my chin, forcing my head up. "He's getting smarter about that though. All that's left is cleaning up his mess; now don't make this harder than it has to be." His keen eyes watched me for any reaction.

The silence was too much, and my skin burned as the gun pressed firmly into it. I think his finger shifted on the trigger, but I couldn't pull my eyes from his dark ones to look. Nothing happened. I was going insane, the wait smothering me.

"If you're going to kill me, just get it over with. Do it already." I don't know where I got the air to speak, there was none in the room.

"Don't tempt me." He jabbed the gun deeper into the soft spot under my jaw, forcing my head back into the wall. "I'm not going to kill ya. Not yet." The gun dropped away slow, and he took a step back.

I was ready to shatter at the lightest touch, my nerves pulled tight. But now that the gun wasn't burning my skin, and Nick was giving me space, my mind raced to make sense of events and his words.

"Then what?" I asked, unmoving.

The gun disappeared at his waist, covered by his leather jacket. He pressed his lips together and nodded his head to the door. "We're goin' on a ride."

"Where?" I forced the question past my constricted throat. I didn't really need an answer. It didn't matter. It was nowhere good, I knew. I just needed to keep him talking so I could stay sane and think.

"Somewhere ya can't start more trouble." He pulled me away from the wall by my elbow and pushed me to the door.

"Why?" I tried to talk over the panic rising in me.

I was jerked back by my book bag. He was yanking it down, off of me.

"Enough talking. You're a shady little shit and I'm not fallin' for it."

But within a minute of riding in his car, he was back to talking.

"Anatoli and Demetri treated ya like a fuckin' toy, something they could play with, and look what that shit got them. You screwed them both over. I've got to put up with ya till Friday, but I'm not them, I'm not fuckin' trusting ya." He put a cigarette pack up to his mouth and slid the smoke out with his lips. "You're gonna stay put till your fight. Then this shit will be over one way or another." He mumbled as he lit the cigarette.

He seemed to calm down as he smoked. His movements slowed and he took deep breaths, smoke curling from his lips. He turned to me with a dark smile, pointing his light at me. "That's the one good thing about ya. There are people that are expecting ya to fight, but after that…" he took a deep drag of the cigarette, smirk growing. "After that, you've got no one that will file a missing persons report on ya."

I wish he would shut up. His words weighed on me, the truth in them pulling me down. But I had made it that way. I didn't spare any thought to giving him a response. My mind was already jumping to Friday. I had to win, but if I didn't, I had to have a plan. I had to escape.

* * *

I was back in the small room above Rusnak's garage, the one Demetri had first brought me to. It was one room with a couch, a small circle table, two dining chairs, and a bathroom. That was it. No windows anywhere and I easily lost track of time. There was only the one door, a solid thing that was locked from the outside. I'd been here long enough to determine that it was only a small fraction of the garage, I don't think the room even went to the main walls of the outside.

I lay on the small couch, too small to even fully stretch out on. My legs dangled over the ledge as I looked at the brown water stains on the ceiling, I could swear they were getting darker, but realized it wasn't likely. That's the sort of things I was thinking of, nonsense, since I had already decided the best plan for me was to wait and see what was going to happen.

I hated that plan. I hated not being able to do something. Anything. I had already worked out some, but quickly realized that as a mistake since I had no water or food. Nick had said he needed me till Friday, but I hope he realized I couldn't make it without water till then.

My stomach was grumbling, ready to eat. It's strange how quickly things had changed. A couple of months ago I could have easily gone a day without food and barely noticed, I had been use to it. But after meeting Gage and following his meal plans, my body had become use to eating regularly, it depended on it.

Still watching the water stains on the ceiling I did the only thing I could do to pass the time, I fell asleep.

I woke up at the turn of the door handle and sat up as Boris walked through, arms full with groceries. He kicked the door shut with his foot and dropped a case of water on the ground with a loud thump. Then he set the three bags down beside it.

He nodded towards the groceries. "This should last you till Anatoli gets back on Thursday." He turned back towards the door.

"Wait." I stood up, but he ignored me and left. I ran to the door, knowing he wouldn't be so careless as to leave it unlocked, but I had to check.

Kneeling by the groceries, I peeled open the case of water bottles and took one out. After a few needed sips, I inspected the rest. There was Total cereal, plain potato chips, crackers, Nutrigrain bars, and a bag of apples and oranges. At least I wouldn't starve.

But Boris's one remark confused me. Rusnak was gone, but coming back on Thursday. And he was going to come for me? After what Kiera told him and given my present situation, I was fairly certain his intentions wouldn't be to help.

* * *

I wasn't feeling well. The change in diet made my stomach hurt and the limited amount of food didn't provide energy. And stress ate away at what energy I did have, stress and depression.

It was hard to keep track of the time passing with no natural light to gage whether it was night or day. So when the door opened and Rusnak stepped through, I could only assume it meant it was Thursday.

He didn't come in with his typical smile. I always knew the smile was fake, but I still wished he was smiling. His blank face as he looked around the apartment, at everything except me on the couch, filled me with dread.

I stood up as he continued his slow perusal of the place, unsure of what to do in the silence and his odd entrance.

His eyes landed on me and he gave me the same leisurely once over. I only had the gym clothes I came here in, and by now they were well worn and sweaty from my mini workouts.

"Do you have anything to tell me?" He asked levelly, meeting my eyes.

I shook my head, choking on the words. "She was lying."

He nodded his head, lips pursing together.

"I didn't write any letters. I don't even—"

"I know." He put his hand up to silence me. "I know she was lying."

"Then why am I here?" My heart raced. Did he really believe she lied about it all? I hope so. I certainly wasn't going to admit to my night with Gage.

"Kiera tried to make the letter look like it came from you, but I have surveillance at my house and saw it was her. It was too late though, my wife saw it, and it said enough to get her angry and demanding things. I had to get rid of the apartment and take time to sort out that mess."

It didn't make sense. "So, you sent Nick?"

Now his smile was back, it slithered across his face as he stepped closer to me. "He didn't hurt you, did he?" It wasn't really a question. "I told you, I'd treat you well as long as you didn't give me a reason not to." He stopped just in front of me, eyes hooded as they dropped over me. "Have you given me a reason not to?"

"No. I haven't done anything." I didn't hesitate to respond.

The seconds were painfully slow as he stared at me, unmoving. "Good." His smile this time was more relaxed and less sinister. "You have your pre-fight physical and interviews soon. I have a change of clothes for you in the main house, in your room from before." His smile dropped some as he picked up a lock of my hair. "You can shower there, too. Let's go."

Boris was standing at the door to the garage, waiting for me to walk out. Rusnak nodded to him. "Take her to the room in the house." He stepped past me, but then turned before walking away altogether. "I'll speak to you more later, after." He spoke the words casually enough, but my skin still crawled as if it was a threat. And I had to admit, it probably was.

* * *

Rusnak had left me dark denim jeans and a thin Henley t-shirt. I was a little surprised that he had gotten me such casual clothes, very similar to my own style.

I was even more surprised to exit the bathroom suite and see Silas and Nick waiting with Boris. Nick stood by the window, watching the setting sun streak deep oranges and purples across the sky.

"Regan, are you ready?" Silas questioned with a smile.

I couldn't help the frown. "Yeah, let's go."

"What about for your fight tomorrow?" Nick pulled his eyes away from the window, meeting mine with a slight curl to his lips. "You ready for that?"

My chest burned with anger. He was trying to sabotage the fight. If the room and lack of food wasn't proof enough, his smug expression was.

"Yeah." I dismissed him by walking to the door. I wouldn't give him the satisfaction of getting to me.

"Good. Glad to hear it." His deep voice held a laugh as he walked just behind me, arm reaching over me to open the door first. "Remember, second round. You win and you're done." He waited for me to walk through the door he held open. "And little one, behave at the interviews tonight."

I kept walking without acknowledging him. My head began to pound, a crazy mix of relief and fear crashing in me. The agreement still stood then. Nick had just said, when I win tomorrow, I'm out. But everything around me seemed to say otherwise.

Once we walked outside, Nick broke away from the group and walked towards the garage.

Silas opened the passenger door to the silver car in the driveway and explained, "He's not coming with us."

That news let me breath slightly easier as I climbed into the back seat.

* * *

My fight tomorrow would take place at a large hotel in Baltimore. The physical and weigh-in today, was in one of the rooms there. The interviews were in one of the smaller conference rooms. My interview was second since I was one of the opening fights. But it was an opening fight for a title match, The East Coast Featherweight Title. In typical circumstances, this was a big deal. But I didn't feel it.

As I waited with Silas for our turn, one of the main boxers walked by and nodded in my direction. I tried to smile back, but fell short. Then Dexter was at my side and I nearly jumped out of my skin.

I grabbed his arm, heart stuttering. "Hey." I swallowed my words, I wanted to ask if Gage was okay, but Silas was watching and I didn't trust him. "What are you doing here?"

He pulled me into a hug. "I'm your corner man, I wouldn't bail on you. If you'd shown up to the gym this week you would know. Where have you been?"

I glanced at Silas, but he was his typical calm self.

"I was out of town," I lied easily, but I meant my next words. "I'm glad you're here." I knew I should be pushing him away, telling him to leave, but I couldn't. He gave me some comfort and some confidence and I selfishly was taking what I could get.

They called me up to the table and Silas and Dexter sat beside me. On the other end of the table sat my opponent, Misha Ballagio, and three people on her team. Her short-cropped hair was spiked with platinum highlights, but her makeup softened the look. I let her do most of the talking, she was cocky and funny in her boasts about winning, but I didn't pay any attention.

When asked directly what I thought about her saying it would be a quick fight, I responded, "I'm gonna try my best to keep it short. We'll see tomorrow." Tomorrow, I was going to end it in the second round. I had to.

As we walked out, Silas was stalled by some guy from another gym, and I jumped at the opportunity to talk to Dexter.

"Is your brother okay? Have you seen him?" I quickly asked in a low voice.

He frowned down at my hand clutching his arm. "Yeah. I just saw him this morning he's fine. Why? What's going on?"

Relief surged in me making me lightheaded. I took a deep breath. "Nothing. I just hadn't seen him. I wanted to make sure." He was okay. Concern for him had been eating away at me. I could let it go for now and focus on my fight.

"Rea, are you okay? Seriously, tell me. I can try and help you." Concern was etched in Dexter's face, lines forming between his brows.

"No." I shook my head. "I'm fine. Really. Once I win this fight tomorrow, everything will be okay." I was trying to convince myself as I reassured him.

Silas stepped up to us and clapped Dexter on the shoulder. "You go get home to that pretty girl of yours, take her some ice cream or something. I heard pregnant women love that. We'll see you tomorrow." He nodded to the exit and I followed him out, not wanting to look back at Dexter and see his worried face.

* * *

Nick met me at the car the moment Silas pulled up. He killed the hope of me sleeping in the comfortable bed in the main house when he pulled my arm, leading me to the garage. Silas and Boris didn't even get out of the car, and before I stepped into the garage, their headlights moved across the property as they pulled away.

I yanked my arm from his grasp. "I can walk," I demanded, tired of being pulled around.

He shoved me into the open door of the garage, making me stumble in. I straightened myself up and walked with much more caution towards the steps.

He closed the door behind him, shutting out the pale moonlight, as he followed me into the open space of the garage.

I paused, trying to let my eyes adjust to the new level of darkness. The soft thump of his boots on the concrete grew closer, and I immediately started walking again.

"Wait. You're not going up to that apartment yet."

I froze, senses heightened and muscles pulsing, ready to react.

"I'm trying to figure something out." He was close, I could sense him just to my left. "What are ya doing talking to the law? What do ya think you know?"

I jumped back, avoiding his grasp as he reached for me. But then he lunged, capturing me in his arms. One arm hooked around my neck and he pulled my back to him.

"Remember ya came to us little one. Ya started this shit. I should have told ya to fuck off then. But now, here we are. So tell me, what have ya told."

He loosened his hold on me, letting me breath in air. "I haven't said anything."

"Bullshit." His arm squeezed my neck. "Then why the hell do I have an officer locked up in the other room that knows ya?"

Anthony. My heart tore thinking of him. "He was only a friend, before I got involved with all of this. I promise. He doesn't know anything. I didn't tell him anything." I was pleading, but trying to keep it together, trying to remove emotion from my voice.

"Do you fuck all of your friends?" Nick's deep voice held a hint of laughter. "Doesn't matter. I know you're a fuckin' liar. He saw you the other night." He dragged me to the edge of the garage.

"No. I didn't." My feet struggled to touch the ground, and my lungs struggled for air as his grip tightened on my neck.

He shoved me into the next room and I cracked my knees and palms, sliding over the hard concrete.

A light flipped on and my eyes burned against it as I looked around. It was a tiny room with low cabinets and a counter along one wall and three chairs.

One chair had someone in it. Tied up and bloody. But it wasn't Anthony. The person's head was slumped forward, like he was asleep, or passed out, or possibly dead. But I recognized the curls, even though they were matted with blood. It was Kiera's friend.

26: The Worst Parts

THE SLAM OF THE DOOR UNSTUCK ME from my spot on the ground. I scrambled to my feet, barely feeling the pain in my knees from hitting the floor.

My eyes were glued to the guy in the chair. I wanted to go to him, check on him, see if I could help him, but Nick was stalking towards me. And my mind started working again, he thought I was involved with this guy.

Backing up, away from Nick and the cop in the chair, I tried to explain, "He was Kiera's friend, not mine."

Nick stopped coming towards me, his eyebrow lifted as he pointed to the bleeding man. "He says differently," his voice was conversational and it made me feel crazy. He walked over to him and gripped his head by his curls, lifting it up. "Agent Mathews, wake up."

The side of his face was covered in cuts and gashes, like it had been dragged over glass. It had been through something because dark bits stuck in the oozing blood. His mouth and neck were covered in the dark dried blood that had poured from his nose.

The slits of his eyes opened slightly and he groaned. His eyes rolled around in his head before landing on me and then cutting to

Nick, he was quickly becoming alert and rigid. "What is she doing here?" his voice rasped.

"I'm putting the story together, seeing what clean up needs to be done. What has Regan told you and who else have you told?" He pulled his head back, making him look up at him.

"It wasn't business. I didn't tell anyone."

Nick released his hair and walked to the counter, taking off his jacket. "What was it then?" He spoke so casual, like he had all the time in the world.

Agent Mathews looked towards me but no emotion could be seen through the bruises and blood. "We were friends."

The slow burn of anger crept into my frozen veins and I embraced it, encouraged it. It was better than fear. "That's bullshit. Why are you saying that?" I took a step towards him at the same time Nick waved a manila file from the counter.

"Why would ya have a file on a friend? We found this in your place after we caught ya snooping around the fuckin apartment like a dog in heat."

Nick tossed the file in the air and papers and pictures scattered over the ground. Air escaped me when I saw the black and white police photos of me when I was three, close ups on my gun shot wounds. Compelled by something beyond thought, I sunk to the ground and collected all the floating pieces of information on me.

My school transcript, police reports and suspension notices from fights at school, reports and pictures from the night I was jumped, but when I turned over the pictures of her, I dropped everything else.

There were two. One of her from afar, like a surveillance picture, she was walking out of a building with a man. And the other picture was of her dead, overdosed, on a grimy, laminate bathroom floor. My mother.

I looked up at the agent strapped to the chair. "Why do you have these? And why are you saying we're friends?" I stood up from the ground, aware of Nick's eyes on me and his growing smile. "I only talked to you one night, and I never said anything. I didn't know you were a cop. Tell him, it was Kiera you were with, not me."

"He's FBI." Nick had one hand lightly gripping the gun holstered at his waist. "What have you told him?"

I snapped my head to Nick. "Nothing. I haven't told anyone anything." My fists balled at my side. "I don't fucking know him. He's Kiera's friend, not mine." I tried to pull in my anger. I was shouting, but I couldn't think of how to prove what I was saying.

"You're lying little one." Nick's steps were slow as he approached me. "We know you slept at his place the other night."

I turned to face Nick head on, resisting the urge to step away as he got closer. "Only the one night, I had nowhere to go. And nothing happened. I just slept there. I only knew him because I had seen him with Kiera."

Nick turned his head to the agent. "Who's lying?"

Agent Mathews met my eyes again. "I'm sorry. I already told them we had a thing. You can't put this on your roommate."

I went up in flames and lunged towards him. I didn't care how bloody he was, I would kill him. Nick gripped the front of my shirt and flung me to the ground, keeping me from touching the liar in the chair.

My body was numb and I didn't feel the impact of the ground, but I landed with a smack on my hip.

"She's dead," I shouted at him, my brain finally making the connection of who he was protecting. "Kiera is already dead. Tell the truth."

His eyes shut, and then he looked towards Nick, who shrugged.

"What's it matter if she is? You don't know her." He had his arms crossed, smiling between the two of us. He was enjoying all of this drama.

The agent shook his head, murmuring low.

"What's that? I can't hear ya? You've got something to say?" Nick stepped towards him, lifting his head by gripping his hair again.

"Burn in hell," his sad voice caught fire with anger.

Nick tossed his head down and brought his gun up with his other hand, hitting him across the face with it, whipping his head back with force. He grabbed his hair again, righting his head on his shoulders.

Nick's voice was back to level. "Look, we know you're just a paper pusher in the agency. But what we don't know is why the fuck ya got involved in the first place. Whether ya fucked Kiera or Regan or both, doesn't matter to me. What matters is why the hell ya had files on her." He forced his head to look at me. "And who else ya might have told."

He was wavering in and out of consciousness, head only staying up because of Nick's grip in his hair. "Kiera wanted to know about her. I did it for her."

Nick dropped his head, forehead wrinkling. "Fuckin' serious?" He looked towards me with a laugh, pointing to the agent with his gun, like we were sharing a joke. "Who sent you to Kiera? I know you can't afford that place on your own."

His eyes were closed, more than they were open now. "Who killed her?" his voice was low, barely heard, and then he was out.

Nick shook his head. "Wake up. Harrison Mathews, wake up. We're not done talking yet."

His eyes pulled open, barely. "Please. Let me go. I'll work for you. I'll tell everything." Tears were coming down his face. "I can help you."

Nick sighed and took a few steps back, gun still wrapped in his fingers but pointing to the ground. "How can you help? You work in an office, Harrison. We've already got our people higher up than you. Who sent you?"

I was holding my breath, watching him. He was crying, shaking his head, eyes squeezed tight.

Then he exploded. And I dropped to the ground, vision wavering, covered in his blood and bits of tissue.

Nick stood behind him, arm still outstretched and gun aimed where his head had been. It was lulled forward now at an odd angle. His hair, the only part I could see, seemed to be fine. Still matted in blood, but fine. I couldn't figure out what I was covered in. A hot spray had splattered on me when Nick fired the gun. It had to be from his face. My eyes dropped to the concrete, a chunky pool of blood was forming under him.

I stayed slumped on the floor, not wanting to move, not wanting to acknowledge the horrific thing I just saw.

But Nick stepped into my vision, holstering his gun. "He was useless. And when they start crying and begging, ya can't trust a word they say." He crouched in front of me, dangerously close. "But you. What have you and Kiera been doing, little one?"

I pulled myself up and tried to block the sticky feel of blood coating me. "It wasn't me. I didn't know anything about this, about him."

He inflated larger and leaned in closer to me, eyes sharp. "I don't believe ya."

The door clicked open and Nick broke the heated stare down, turning his gaze to Rusnak as he walked in.

Rusnak glanced around the room, un-fazed, and stepped to where we were. He sunk down to our level, but stayed on his feet, never letting his suit touch the ground. His eyes scanned over me with a frown.

"Let's get you cleaned up. Come with me." He gently coaxed me with a light touch to my elbow.

I jumped at the chance to escape and rose to my feet.

Rusnak walked me to the door then turned back to Nick. "Clean this up. Call Boris if you must, but don't go far. I need to talk with you later." His soft demand reminded me that Nick may have been the one to shoot, but Rusnak had probably ordered it. I wasn't better off going with him.

I didn't want to look back, but I forced myself to as I stepped out of the room. Nick cut at the ropes binding Harrison hands with a knife, and his body slumped forward slowly as they loosened.

Harrison Mathews. I wouldn't forget his name any more. He was another name added to my growing list of people who died because of me.

My mind was blacking out, shutting down. The events of the evening were just too much. It seemed one second I was leaving the garage and the next I was in a large bathroom in the main house, and Rusnak was locking the door as he followed me in. My limbs were too heavy to move and my brain too clouded and slow to work. So I stood there as he stepped closer.

"Tcht," he clicked his tongue as his eyes slid down my shirt. "Let's get you out of these disgusting clothes and into the shower." His finger touched the edge of the thin material at the collar. "Nick must have ripped it." He raised his hooded eyes to mine, his smooth voice only added to the belief that I had to be stuck in a dream, or nightmare.

The sound of fabric ripping, as he used both hands to tear open the front of my shirt, sliced through my trance. Numb shock was quickly replaced with a surge of cold panic, and I wrapped my arms around my waist, keeping the sticky shirt pressed to me.

"Please," the word spilled out of me. I didn't even know what I was asking for, but I needed help.

He paused with a small moan, hands just above mine, gripping either side of my torn shirt. His eyes lit up as he raised them to mine. "Please?" One of his hands moved to my cheek, thumb moving over my skin, smearing whatever was there. "Let's get you cleaned up first. Okay?" He nodded and grabbed my hands, pulling them off of my shirt. "Then we can talk." He gripped my shirt again, tugging me to him as he ripped the bottom. Then his fingers ran over the skin of my chest and shoulders as he peeled the shirt away, off of me. His lips followed the path, softly sucking on the skin at my collarbone as his fingers moved to the back of my bra.

I pulled away, I would drown if I didn't, and he stiffened, eyes turned sharp.

He stepped away and opened the glass door to the shower, turning on the water before facing me again. His eyes dropped to the edge of my scars. "Take it off and get in the shower." He leaned back on the counter, watching me.

I dropped my eyes from his and undid the buttons on my jeans, quickly stepping out of them. I wasn't trying to put on a show or drag this out.

Keeping my bra and panties on, I stepped into the hot spray of the shower, heart racing. But I was glad to wash off Harrison's blood. I turned up the heat and stayed under the scalding stream until the water ran clear. Then I used shampoo and soap, scrubbing my skin and scalp raw. If he gave me scissors I would have cut off my hair.

Rusnak was the one to turn off the water, ending my shower. He wrapped a towel around my shoulders and pulled me to him. My wet bra and underwear soaked his clothes.

"Feeling better?" He asked, still using that hypnotic, low voice.

I couldn't answer. I didn't know what I was feeling. I didn't feel like me. I had no past, no present. There was only this moment and I didn't like it.

He moved his hands over the towel, drying me. Then he lifted it to the ends of my hair, soaking up the dripping water before tossing my cover to the ground, leaving me exposed.

He slid his jacket off and folded it methodically on the counter next to us. He licked his lips, eyes moving over me as he slipped the gun holster from each shoulder and laid it on top of his jacket.

His fingers slid under the bra straps on my shoulders, sliding them down. His tongue heated the top of my breast, leaving a chilled trail as he pressed me back against the counter. I forced my brain anywhere else, but only saw Harrison when I closed my eyes, and that was worse.

The pop of my bra clasp brought me back to the moment. His hands were cupping the weight of my breast, kneading them with his palms. I fought off the urge to push him away as he dropped his hands, lifting me by my thighs to sit me on the counter.

I moved my hands over his as he reached to pull my bra off, but his hazel eyes captured mine.

"Say please again." He was slowly sliding my bra away, sliding it down my arms.

I took a few steadying breaths, feeling unhinged at being so exposed to him. "Please," I whispered, not daring to look away or blink.

He smiled, eyes hooded as his fingers trailed over my stomach, making a slow path to the scars that spotted my right side.

"Please what?" His fingers froze at the bottom of my ribs.

And I choked on a cry, shaking my head as tears escaped. I couldn't think. My mind was shredded, barely comprehending after everything that had happened.

My head snapped to the side with a loud crack, white blinding my vision before I felt the sting of his hand on my face.

"Why do you have to be all the worst parts of her?" He had been quick in picking up his gun. "I should have let her kill you."

My world froze. Whatever I had thought was happening, wasn't. The look in his eyes now was one of disgust, not lust.

I shook my head, still not able to formulate words.

He caged me in with hands on either side of me.

"Nothing to say now?" He was smirking. "Come on. I can usually count on you for a good fight." He pushed himself against me and his lips dipped to my neck, sucking painfully. I stayed limp and he pushed away from me. "Always a disappointment. You're pathetic."

I covered myself up with my arms, wanting the discarded towel, but he was blocking my way. His other gun on the counter caught my eye, but he picked up the holster, slinging it on his shoulder.

He gestured the gun at me. "You don't think I know what you're doing? Using sex to get what you want? I'm not that desperate." He stepped towards me, pushing me back on the counter again, gun pressed to my chest. "I could kill you now. I was helping you out of respect for your mother, and I thought there was a chance for more, but you're just a self-serving bitch. You probably did sleep with that agent."

He pushed off of me and took a step back as he slid the gun away. "I won't kill you though, we still have a use for you. But my charity stops here. I'll keep my promise though because I'm not a lying whore like you. You either win and get the hell away, or you lose and Nick can deal with you."

He picked up his jacket with a malicious grin. "Get some sleep. You're gonna need all the energy you can get to win tomorrow's fight." He walked out the room without looking back.

I didn't breathe until I heard the bedroom door close. Then I slid off the counter and grabbed the towel on the ground. My bottom lip burned as I ran my tongue over the split on the side, tasting the coppery blood that had formed. And I threw up.

27: Inevitable

I didn't really sleep. I tried. I closed my eyes and wrapped myself in sheets, wearing only my bra and underwear beneath. But I couldn't shut off my mind. The events from the night flashed like lightning just behind my lids.

I repeated my chant. I will win. I will win. I will win. It was the only thing that would quiet the storm, the little bit of hope that I could hang on to and wrap myself in, letting me doze off. But when I would find sleep, it didn't last long. I'd wake up thinking I heard noises or someone coming, and then I'd have to fight the battle to find sleep all over again.

When the sun finally broke through the night sky I was filled with relief. Daylight meant my fight would be soon, and I wanted to get it over with, win or lose. I needed to win, but more than that, I wanted out of this purgatory I was in, this unknown place.

I stayed wrapped in my sheets and watched the sun rise in the sky through the window. It wasn't until it passed its peak and began sinking back down that the door opened and Boris stepped through.

He silently set a duffle bag on the floor and I didn't bother to get up or ask questions. I had already decided, I wasn't going to push anything or anyone today. I just wanted to make it to my fight.

"I'll be back in about an hour to take you to the hotel." He nodded to me and left.

Once the door was firmly shut I got up, still wrapped in my sheets, and looked through the bag. It had jeans and a t-shirt, my boxing outfit, a box of pop tarts, water, and several five-hour energy drinks.

I hadn't realized how hungry I was until I saw the pastries. Ripping into the blue box of strawberry pop tarts, I was on my second before I paused to drink water. And then I chugged a five-hour energy, wondering who had thought to give me these. The food and drink choices may not have been ideal, but I'd take what I could get.

After I showered and dressed, Nick came to the room sucking all the warmth from me. He sat on the edge of the bed with a small smirk tugging at the corner of his lips. I stood up, refusing to be near him.

"Let's get things clear about tonight," he began. "Rusnak told me if you win, you're free to go right after the fight." His laugh was loud, as if he told the funniest of jokes. With a few calming breaths, he braced his forearms on his jean covered knees, voice dropping to serious. "But when you lose, you'll be coming with me, and I don't want any trouble about it. So, I have something to show you." He reached into his pocket, pulling out his phone.

My heart dropped, mind spinning over what it could be. I kept thinking of Gage and prayed none of this affected him.

But it was my voice that broke through the silence.

"I want him killed." The recording was clear. And then Nick's voice asked who I wanted murdered, and I answered, "Damien Jallow."

Nick clicked the recording off. "Hiring a hit man can get you prison time. So if you try anything tonight, you'll not only have us after you, but the police as well."

I laughed. I couldn't help it. I had thought someone else I knew was going to be hurt because of me, but he was only threatening me with prison. At this point, I'd prefer to be in prison. I didn't care.

He stood up with a frown and I stepped back, cutting off my insane laughter.

"Remember, little one, we have people everywhere, so prison wouldn't be an escape for you."

He spoke directly to my thoughts, burning the thread of hope I had grasped.

Lifting his chin, he looked down at me, satisfied by my silence. "Good. Boris will be in for you soon. I'll see you after the fight," he promised with a wicked grin as he walked out of the room.

* * *

Kyle met Boris and I outside of the hotel and led us to my room on the second floor. His bright smile faltered when Boris followed us, but it returned when he entered the sitting area of my hotel room. Gage was standing in the middle of the room, stone still, with his hands in his pockets.

"Hey man, good seeing you again." Kyle walked up to him.

I froze in the door way and Boris pushed me, impatient to get into the room.

Gage's eyes flashed to him, but Boris only shrugged him off and walked to the mini refrigerator in the room.

Seeing him threatened the fragile hold I had on my emotions and I couldn't breathe.

"I need to talk to Regan, give her some advice." Gage looked between Boris and Kyle.

Kyle took the hint. "Sure man, that's cool. She's going to kill it tonight, I know. I know my girl, and I know Misha, this is Regan's fight." He didn't get a response to his encouraging words before he left.

Gage stared at Boris who sunk into the chair in the corner, sipping a soda. "Nope. I can't leave." He waved his hand in dismissal. "Talk."

Gage's jaw worked under the skin, but he sat on the sofa and nodded at the seat next to him for me to join him.

My legs carried me there, unable and unwilling to stop. I wanted to be near him, but it hurt to keep from touching him. My arms ached as they fought the pull to wrap them around him. My eyes ran over every inch of him, reassuring myself that he was all right. He was all right, and that's all that really mattered. His voice was smooth, but I wasn't listening to the words, just absorbing the sound of him, like a balm to my cuts and bruises. I wasn't able to focus on anything but him. I needed him gone, he was making me weak. But at the same time, I would shatter if he left.

"Regan, are you all right?" His voice cut through my thoughts. "Are you listening to me?"

Nodding, I tried to clear my head.

"Repeat what I told you," he demanded lightly.

I pulled my eyes from his, trying to search my brain to remember. "She'll try to attack the body first to weaken me, so I should keep my block low. She'll also try for kidney shots since she doesn't care about penalties. She's always won by knockouts. I should protect my body for most of the fight, but watch for her uppercut, that's her strongest punch." Stating the facts calmed me, focused me. I was impressed at what I recalled.

I peeked back at him. He was watching me intently but his expression was blank, controlled. His eyes were focused just below my face. The sound of his deep breaths passing through his full lips concerned me and when he picked his eyes up to meet mine, they were distant, chilly.

"Good. You were listening." He stood up.

I stood up with him, panic rising as he took a few steps away.

He turned around, but stopped himself from stepping back towards me. "You seem to know what you're doing. You'll do fine tonight." It sounded more like an accusation than encouragement.

When he walked out of the room he took a piece of me with him.

My heart was racing as I looked to Boris, he sat in the chair, eyes down on his phone. I opened the door closest to me and escaped through a dark green bedroom into the connecting bathroom.

Splashing water on my face, I tried to cool off. My blood was on fire, burning me. After taking a few drinks straight from the faucet, I looked at myself in the mirror, but couldn't meet my eyes. Instead, I saw what Gage had focused on, a dark purple bruise with red spots from where Rusnak had sucked, just where my neck and shoulder met. Guilt washed over me and I sunk to the floor under the weight. But I only allowed a second for indulging in pity before I picked myself up to get ready for my fight.

Boris's laugh nearly knocked me over again when I came out of the bedroom, it was a hiccup of a sound.

Dexter was on the couch, hands moving excitedly as he finished his story, Boris's laughter only increasing.

When he saw me, Dexter rose to his feet. I welcomed the hug he gave and even wrapped my arms around him, making it last just a bit longer.

Dexter noticed the difference and loosened his grip as he whispered in my ear, "It'll be okay. You'll see."

Stepping out of his hold, I nodded and tried to give him a reassuring smile. It would be okay. I was going to win.

"So are you going to be at the Poker tournament next week?" Boris asked, laughter still in his voice. "You missed the last one, lots of excitement." He nodded towards me. "Seems she can create more trouble than some of your friends even."

Dexter shook his head, his easy smile back in place. "Nah, I'm done with poker for a while. Gonna focus on my boxing and school. But if you're missing excitement, you should come out after my fight." He nudged me with his shoulder. "But for now, let's focus on the fight tonight." He picked up a grocery bag and handed it to me. "I brought you something."

I took the bag, glancing inside. "Gloves? Shouldn't I wear the ones I'm use to?" I asked, confused.

He nodded, taking a seat. "Yeah, but they could help you later. Just a gift."

I put the gloves in the duffel bag and sat next to him.

He frowned, studying me. At first, I thought he was focused on the bite on my neck, but then he spoke, "We'll have to put extra gel on that lip, keep the cut from reopening tonight."

I wonder if Gage had noticed the cut on my lip that went along with the bruise on my neck.

Dexter glanced at Boris, but he was back on his phone, pretending to mind his own business.

"You're going to win tonight. I can feel it. But whatever happens, I'm here for you."

"Dexter, don't," I warned him. He needed to focus on his family, not get involved in my mess.

"I mean it, Rea. I'm here for you." His voice dropped even lower. "I really am sorry for everything, for getting you into this."

Glancing between him and Boris, I put my hand up, cutting him off. Then I met his gaze full force. "It's not your fault," I absolved him, and I meant it. "All of this, I've been on this path my entire life. It was chosen for me before I was even born. It was inevitable."

He frowned, confused by my words, but I wasn't going to explain.

"Well that changes tonight. You'll see. You're going to win." He nodded with a reassuring smile. But his knuckles turned white as he gripped his knees, giving away his nervousness. He stood up. "I'm gonna go check on the first fight, but I'll be back to tape you up and stuff." He surprised me by pressing his warm lips to my forehead and holding it for a second. "Try on those gloves, you might like them better than yours," he added, just above a whisper.

Then he jogged backwards to the door. "Later B." He saluted Boris as he walked out of the room.

I picked up the duffel and went back to the bathroom to change. Pulling out the gloves Dexter gave me, my suspicion was confirmed by the weight of them. It scared me to see the gun though. Not fear for myself, but for my friend who was soon to be a dad. I moved the gun to the linen closet and tried to hide the evidence that could get him in trouble.

* * *

I kept my head down and arms low as I walked towards Misha at the start of the fight. She was skinny and tall with tattoos painting her body from the neck down. She was smiling, showing her black mouth guard as she approached me.

She jabbed the air, testing her reach and I revolved as she circled me. I struck as she jabbed again, hitting her cheek.

She shook it off with a step back. "Quick, but you're going to have to come harder than that to have a chance."

So I punched again, but she blocked with her forearm and struck me in the stomach with more force than I'd expected. She followed it with a couple more punches to my side before I recovered enough to block.

As a punch stung my shoulder, I hooked my left arm around, hitting her chin.

Her smile dropped as she stepped out of reach. Bouncing on her toes, she circled me and I moved so my side was always to her.

"You ready? Because I'm about done playing."

I tried to block out her voice. I wasn't use to talkers during a fight and didn't want her in my head.

She came at me, punching my arms. I absorbed them, but my body was pushed back with the force, until I was on the ropes.

She wasn't letting up so I returned punches, letting down my guard as I swung. Feeling my gloves connect with her flesh, encouraged more punches, and blocked out the feel of her hits. Until pain exploded on my back, making me remember Gage's warning about the kidneys.

The Ref pushed her away, but only gave a warning with no penalties. The needle pain radiated from the hit throughout my back and I was much more cautious as I approached, keeping my arms down, blocking my sides.

I stepped into her punches, giving her my shoulder to hit. Then crossed my left fist and hit her in the stomach, then the face.

She stepped back as the bell rung, wiping her nose with the back of her glove. "You made it through the first round, but if that's all you've got, you're not making it through the next one."

Her words repeated in my head as I sat in my corner. Dexter applied more Vaseline and Kyle gave me water. And her words repeated. She was right, not about me not lasting, I would last. She hit hard, but not that hard. She was right about me needing to do more, hit harder, faster. I had to knock her out next round.

Silas was outside the ring, yelling at the referee. "You've got to stop those kidney shots. Come on, you need me to do your job? Why weren't points taken away?"

The Ref was walking away, dismissing him. "Watch yourself. Go take care of your boxer, and I'll take care of the fight."

But Silas followed him.

I ignored the rest, refocusing on the fight. That's all I could think about. There was only Misha and me. No one else.

I charged her the next round, taking the punches so I could force myself inside her reach. I threw my own punches and her body gave with each one, moving back towards the ropes. I kept swinging, not letting up as each connecting punch charged me. I had her against the ropes, but she was still in control of her body, it was still resisting, not weakening. So I kept hitting.

She hit my back, pain lightning quick struck all the way to my toes. This time the Ref separated us and gave her a penalty of two points. It was no good though, it gave her time to recover and took her off the ropes.

Blood dripped from her eyebrow, but she smiled at me with a shrug. "My bad," she said, dismissing the Ref and walking a wide arc around me.

I didn't waste time, I jumped in again.

Her glove slid across my cheek, barely hitting as I dodged it. I came at her from below, putting all my force into a punch to her jaw. It shook her, but didn't knock her down. I felt her weakening as I stepped closer, delivering another punch.

She pushed me away with both her gloves on my shoulders. It gave her space to escape momentarily. I couldn't allow it.

I lunged at her as I threw punches, no longer worried about blocking. I needed all my force in my punches. She had to go down. With each punch, her energy and strength gave way beneath my glove. Her body jerked more and more with each blow. But she was still punching too and blocking several of my swings. I pushed harder, hit stronger, faster, blind to everything else.

Then the Referee was pushing me back. "That's a two point penalty for you. Stop with the back punches or you will be disqualified."

I couldn't focus on him. My lungs burned as I sucked in large amounts of air. She was bleeding from several spots on her face, but she was still standing. And now she was walking to the center of the ring, away from me.

I tried to wave the referee away, but he grabbed my hands. "Fight fair." I nodded and he stepped away.

She was ready for my attack and had her guards up. I barely got two more punches in before the bell rung.

But she was still standing and that wasn't supposed to happen. I needed her to be on the ground. To drop. I kept hitting her, thinking just one more punch should do it.

Arms pulled me away and the Referee was yelling at me. "That's it. Fight's over, you're disqualified."

"No. No. No." I stopped my begging as I saw that Misha was still standing. It didn't matter, even if the fight continued, I lost the round. I had lost everything.

Looking beyond the bright lights, I saw Nick standing there, just outside the ring in the first row.

Dexter was pulling me from the ring as the arena light's flicked on. The announcer named Misha Bilagio as the winner, by disqualification.

Kyle flanked the other side of me and Nick followed behind as we walked to the elevator. It wasn't till we were riding up to the second floor that the weight settled, and Dexter's arm felt like it was choking me. When the doors opened, I stepped away from him, out of the elevator.

"Go home Dexter."

He tried to step out. "No."

"Listen to her." Nick blocked him from getting off the elevator. "Go home." As the doors shut, Nick added, "Maybe I'll see ya at the next poker game."

I scanned the hotel room. Kyle, Nick, and Boris were the only people with me.

Nick sat on the sofa as Kyle took off my gloves.

"Hurry up with that. We have some people to meet tonight." Nick smirked at me.

Kyle cut away the tape in silence. No one spoke about my loss. He was too quiet and I wondered what he knew about all of this. He obviously knew enough.

As the tape fell away, I made my decision. It was my only chance.

"Where are you going?" Nick asked as I walked past him.

"To the bathroom." My words were absent of life.

He nodded as I stepped into the bedroom, closing and locking the door.

I hurried to the linen closet and grabbed the gun. Then I slid my jacket on, over my boxing clothes. The window was silent as it slid open, sounds of the city filling the space. I had to move fast.

The room faced another building, an alley down below, but the main street was only a few yards away. I was on the second floor so the drop wasn't too dangerous. I would have risked higher.

Sliding my feet over the ledge, I dropped into the darkness, bending my knees as I hit the cement below. I landed on my feet, ready to sprint to the street, but stopped short. Gage was at the opening of the alley, back to me, talking to someone.

I turned and ran in the other direction, cutting right behind the other building. I didn't bother to turn and see if he saw me, I knew he did. The sound of his boots closing in behind me only made me run faster.

28: Weak

MY LUNGS BURNED AS I PUSHED MYSELF beyond the limit. I kept running, legs gone beneath me. I turned right, down a skinnier path, trying to get to the main street. If I could get to the main street, I would have the safety of a crowd.

But I was running towards a dead end, and I couldn't turn around. I knew someone was behind me, even if I could no longer hear the sound of boots. My mind screamed with the prayer that another cut or door would appear before I reached the gate in front of me. But nothing ever did.

I launched myself onto the wrought iron bars and tried to find a grip to climb. My muscles fired, shaking with the need to keep moving forward. But the gate was too tall. Just beyond it, a building, doors open, lights on, perhaps the back of a restaurant? But I couldn't reach it, and windowless slabs of brick were on either side of me, offering no escape.

Now that I wasn't running, I could hear sounds outside my body, and the boots were back.

"Regan stop," Gage's voice was further away than I expected, but still too close for me to make it over this impossible fence.

If it was only him, I might still have a chance. Forcing myself to give up on the gate, I dropped back to the concrete, twisting to face him as I did.

He was the only one walking down the alley, but that didn't mean the others weren't waiting.

I sucked in air, searing my lungs, and faced him fully, the gate at my back. "You have to let me go, please. I can't go back there. Nick's—" my voice broke with panic.

"There's nowhere for you to go, Regan." His voice was too calm as he strolled towards me, coming out of the shadows of the buildings.

"Please," I begged again, I had to. This was my last chance. "Just give me a chance to run, that's all I'm asking for." If he just let me get to the street.

His phone ring echoed through the cool night air. And he twisted the knife in my back when he answered it.

"It's all right, I've got her." He took slow steps forward, voice low.

His words killed me and I pulled the gun from my pocket, muscles steady as I aimed it at him.

"I'll call you back." He stopped walking and put the phone away. "What are you going to do? Shoot me?" He wasn't taking my threat very serious.

But as gravity settled on me, my muscles shook. I wouldn't shoot him, I couldn't. Why the hell did the one person I couldn't hurt have to be the one to catch me?

And he must have seen the answer in my face because he started walking towards me again.

"Stop." I pushed the gun further forward, but my strangled voice didn't hold much confidence.

The closer he got, the more I shook. And my vision blurred as tears burned in them, but I could still see that he was getting closer.

And I couldn't shoot him. I'd kill myself before I hurt him. I'd kill myself before I let Nick kill me.

With that thought, I bent my elbow and put the gun to my temple, unlocking the safety at the same time.

"No." He folded like he was hit in the gut with a crow bar.

The tears were dripping down my face now and my arm vibrated with barely enough strength to hold up the gun.

"Don't. Put the gun down."

"He'll kill me." He needed to understand. "And now you've told them you found me. If you let me go they'll hurt you." I closed my eyes against the thought. I could see it now very clearly. Instead of Harrison, it would be Gage in that chair.

"You think killing yourself is the answer? Trust me, Regan. Don't do this." His voice was thick and his arm was out, reaching, but too far away to touch me.

My thoughts spread in all directions, but it was Rusnak's voice that sliced through the storm. I was just like her, all the worst parts. And it was crushing me that he was right. I sunk to my knees, broken and no longer able to stand under the pressure. My vision only a blur of silent tears.

My finger burned over the trigger, testing the spring. I just had to press a bit harder. Just a bit harder and it would all be over. But I couldn't find the strength and that crushed me all over again. I wasn't just like her. I was weak. Weaker than her. And Rusnak was right, he should have let her kill me when I was little.

"I can't." And I wasn't sure if I meant trust him, kill myself, or go back. Everything probably.

Then his hands were on mine, pulling the gun from my fingers. His warmth surrounded me. Choking me.

I pushed away as my silent tears intensified to sobs, but he pulled me tighter to him, muffling the sound with his body. He sat on the concrete and pulled me onto his lap, cradling me, arms securely wrapped around me.

"It's going to be okay… Shhh… no one will hurt you… I'm here." Bits and pieces of his soft murmurs reached me through the screaming filling my body.

I needed to pull it together. Stop crying. Get away. But it was useless. Hopeless. I couldn't escape, I couldn't even kill myself. I could only hope that Nick did it fast. That he was going to just kill me and nothing else.

A slam made him perk up and his hold tightened. The door behind the gate had closed, but nobody was seen. They probably didn't notice us in the shadows.

"We've got to go." Gage's hands ran over me as he shifted me off his lap, pulling me to my feet.

I followed him, lifeless. Tears all dried up. It was as if I had pulled that trigger, killing any fight left in me. I was already dead, but now I'd make sure Gage wasn't hurt for it. He could take me back without a struggle.

He kept his arm around me, pointless because I wasn't running. But I soaked up the warmth and support, too close to the end to deny the fact that I loved being near him. I would take this last moment.

We walked in silence to the parking garage. It would have been quicker to go to the main road, but Gage kept to the darkness of the back alley. And then he was placing me in the SUV, in the backseat. I tested the door, just to be sure, and it had the child safety lock on, it could only be opened from the outside.

My head rested on the tinted glass and I closed my eyes, willing my thoughts to stop. I wish I could take one of Nan's pills, the ones that made reality disappear. Or the drugs that had killed the women who started this. My stomach twisted and I stomped on the thoughts.

I wasn't like her. I couldn't be. Didn't want to be. And I wouldn't end my life being her.

I pulled myself out of my dark pit just enough to make the decision that, whatever happened, I wouldn't be her. I would fight when I faced Nick. But I wouldn't take Gage down with me.

Opening my eyes, I sat up. We weren't on the road to DC or the club or anywhere I recognized. There were barely any cars on the highway as we drove past signs for the Bay Bridge toll. He took the last exit before the toll, making a few turns before he pulled into a hotel parking lot. I stayed silent until he opened the door for me, reaching into the SUV to pull me out.

"What are we doing?" I scooted across the seat, out of reach.

He dropped his hand onto the seat next to me with a sigh. "We're going to stay here tonight and figure shit out in the morning. I'm not trying to go too far."

Icy fear was back, cracking my bones and shaking my muscles. "No." My breathing was shallow. "You can't do this." I had wanted to run on my own. He wasn't supposed to come with me.

"Regan, trust me." He frowned and slid into the back of the SUV with me, but didn't close the door.

I scooted away further, pressed to the opposite door. If he touched me, I knew my resolve would dissolve like sand.

"What are you so scared of?" He reached his hand out and I flinched. "Don't be scared of me, please?" He slid just a bit closer, eyes penetrating me.

The pleading in his voice cracked my heart open, and I strangled the cry that wanted to escape.

"No, I'm not scared of you. I'm scared for you." I was gravitating towards him, moving closer little by little. "Helping me will get you killed. You should take me back, I'll go and face them."

His smile confused me, his light laughter even more so. I felt desperate, near tears again, and he was laughing?

"What?" I attempted to move away from him again, but his hands shot out around my waist and pulled me closer.

His shallow breaths fanned over me in waves as he dipped his head to mine. "That's probably the closest thing to an I love you that I'll ever get from you." He moved his hands to the sides of my head, turning it up to meet his eyes. "But you don't have to be scared for me. I can handle this. What I can't handle is losing you. You don't want me hurt? Then don't leave me or push me away. Let me do this. Let me help." His eyes darted around my face, his lips opening and closing as he breathed.

I had no response. Had I really never told him I loved him? But I couldn't now, not when I needed him to save himself and get away. I would have to hurt him, to keep him from getting killed. But being so close made him hard to resist.

Shaking my head, I moved my hands to his chest, intending to push him away but unable to do so. Instead, I let the feel of his heartbeat steady my own, calming me and terrifying me.

"You don't need to say anything now. Just come with me into the hotel." His blue eyes were clear and open, and I wanted to trust that he knew what he was doing.

I met his eyes for a moment, the air still around us. His presence was calm and reassuring, where I was chaos and fear. Right or wrong, I was clinging to him like a buoy in the storm.

At the slight nod of my head he pulled me out of the SUV and walked with an arm around my waist into the hotel.

He checked us in and the lady behind the counter smiled sweetly at us. I'm sure we looked like young lovers the way he kept one arm around me, my arms wrapped around his waist, and him placing kisses on top of my head as he waited for his receipt and room key. She didn't react as if she thought anything odd about my messy appearance, although my jacket was long enough to cover most of the outfit.

I showered straightaway, needing, but not wanting, the space to think. But I couldn't think, thoughts weren't coming, my mind was locked up or blown to pieces beyond repair. I couldn't decide which.

The hotel was nice enough to have plush robes hanging on the door and I wrapped myself in one, not wanting to put back on my boxing uniform. Gage was waiting for me as I stepped out and his eyes dropped over the robe.

"You can wear my shirt to sleep in. I'll get you clothes in the morning when stores open." he hesitantly approached.

I stepped into his arms, wanting his security again. He was already talking about tomorrow, but I couldn't.

His hands crossed my back, rubbing up and down over the robe. "Everything's going to be all right. I promise."

I blocked out his voice, he couldn't promise that. And I didn't want to be lied to. I just wanted to be near him now, while I could. Squeezing him tighter, I pressed my cheek into his shirt, feeling his warm muscles underneath. "Don't make promises."

He pulled back and I met his gaze. After a moment, he nodded once. "You've got to be tired. Let's get some rest, all right? We'll deal with tomorrow in the morning, together."

I nodded, more relieved than I should be. The idea of facing it together was sounding better and better. He would probably already be in trouble anyways for bringing me here; I knew he turned his phone off when it rung in the car.

He pulled me to his chest, lying back on the bed and I rested my head on him. The sound of his heartbeat quieted everything else in me, holding the panic back. But it was a fragile hold, and the frenzy of emotions were beginning to seep through with each passing second.

My breathing quickened as it shallowed, unable to pull in enough oxygen to remain calm. I tried to still myself and focus on breathing deep, calming breaths to push back the panic attack.

Gage sat up beneath me, keeping his arms around me. "It's all right, baby. Everything's all right. You're safe here with me." His voice was meant to calm me, but it only stirred the panic.

I pushed away from him, trying to curl into myself, protect myself from how weak I became near him. I hadn't cried the last several weeks. I'd only shed a few tears last night when Harrison was shot, but Gage pushed it all to the surface.

He didn't let me go though. Instead, he picked me up onto his lap.

"I'm sorry," I tried to speak through the tears. "I didn't—"

"Shhh" He was stroking my hair. "Shhh. It's all right. Let it go. You've been strong long enough, you don't need to keep it in with me."

But I couldn't let it go. I kissed his neck, hands sliding under his shirt as I tried to fight down the sadness. I don't know why, but I was sure this could overpower my breakdown. I pulled myself up onto him, wrapping my legs around his waist.

But he pulled his head back as I tried to kiss his lips. He gripped my wrists, holding my hands away from his skin.

"Don't," he warned me.

I could tell by his force that he wasn't budging. "You don't want me?" I was desperate, my muscles shaking, quivering as it sunk in that he was rejecting this, me. And my tears were returning, burning my eyes but not falling. He melted in my blurred vision.

His grip loosened and he pulled me to him again, gently holding me. "I always want you. I love you, but you can't do this. Not tonight. Not like this. Not yet."

I fell apart. I didn't want to, but he didn't give me a chance to pull away and block the flood of tears. He kept me wrapped in his arms. He held me as I cried through the night. He held me, comforting me in a way that no one ever had before. And I cried in a way that I never had before. Soul bearing sobs drained me. But it made me lighter, releasing weight that I had held onto, on my own, for too long. And at some point, I fell asleep, satisfyingly empty and surrounded in warmth.

I woke up to bright sunshine and an empty bed. My stomach dropped momentarily, but then I saw Gage on the balcony. Only the side of his arm could be seen from where he stood in the corner, looking over the bay in the distance. I hadn't realized last night that we were so close to the water.

Climbing out of bed, I walked to the slider and paused. I could hear his conversation as I got closer, muffled through the glass.

"She's with me… She's not going anywhere… At that hotel by the bay… Later." His voice was getting sharper, frustration seeping into his tone with each reply. He turned around, leaning against the bar, and his eyes widened as he spotted me.

I was stuck in place, all the weight from last night crashing back over me.

29: Learned Your Lesson

THAT BRIEF LOOK OF SURPRISE DROPPED FROM his face in an instant, and he gave me a slight smile, phone pressed to his ear. Then he lowered his head, speaking into the phone.

"I told you…" His voice dropped, too low to make it through the glass, and then he hung up.

As he slid the door open, I stepped back, headed to the bathroom. I needed to get my clothes on, get out of the robe, so I could leave.

"You hungry? I ordered room service, it should be up soon." He walked towards me with an open arm.

I couldn't respond. Any hope I had was now crushed with his lie.

"Hey." He braced his arm on the bathroom door to stop me from shutting it on him. "What's wrong?" He pushed into the bathroom with me and I stepped back, wanting to keep the space between us.

"Who were you talking to?" it came out in an angry hiss.

He stopped walking towards me and stood up tall, realization sinking in. "How much did you hear?"

He just kept making it worse. "Everything." I could lie too.

For a second, the small room was sucked of air as we stared at each other in silent challenge. I broke first, pushing past him to escape the confined space.

He grabbed my arm as I passed by, twisting me to face him. "I'm doing this for you."

I jerked back, out of his grip and into the main room. "Lying to me? How is that for me?"

He ran his hand over his hair in frustration as he followed me into the room. "I haven't lied to you." He put his hands out to still me. "I don't know what you think you heard, but let me explain."

Standing in my robe, with him blocking me from the door, I didn't really see that I had any other choice. And I wanted him to explain. I wanted him to have a good excuse, something other than taking me back to Nick. I had been willing last night to go back, to face everything. But that was last night. I wasn't willing to do that now. Not now that I had a little time and space.

"Explain." I crossed my arms around my waist.

He scratched his head, watching me with cautious eyes. "I…" He sighed and sat on the edge of the bed. "I had to call him back. These aren't people you can run from. Direct is the only way to deal with this." It sounded like an apology.

"Be direct with me too." Anger was constricting my chest and I pulled my arms tighter around me.

His eyes narrowed for a moment. "All right." He was conceding. Nodding his head to the spot next to him, he said, "Sit and I'll tell you."

"Just tell me." I was too rigid to sit.

He leaned forward, forearm on his knees, reminding me of Nick.

"I made a deal to get you out." He reached for me as his words hit me, making me unsteady on my feet. He grabbed my arm and pulled me closer. "You're safe, all mine. I told you I was helping you. You have to trust me."

I was outside myself, lightheaded and unsure. It couldn't be that easy. The rest of his words sunk in, and I sat down. "What deal?"

He shook his head, a sad smile pulling on his lips as his hand ran through my hair. "Don't worry about it. It doesn't involve you."

He kept pulling me in just to hit me again. Standing back up, I slapped his hand away. "Stop. You can't keep hiding things from me." I felt dizzy and pressed my hand to my head, trying to think through this new information. "This does involve me. Whatever the deal is, it's because of me." I took in a few breaths and met his eyes. "You said last night we would face this together."

He was on his feet now. "I meant it. I want you with me."

I stepped back and put my hand out, keeping him away. "That's different. Wanting me with you is different than doing things together. And you should know by now that I'm not going to sit around in the dark."

He took a step towards me, his own anger rising, seeping from his pores. "And I would have thought you learned your lesson by now, especially after last night."

"What Lesson?" I returned his sharp tone, ready to say more but he cut me off.

"To trust me."

"You haven't done shit to earn it. You say—"

"If I haven't done anything, then why are we here?" He swung his hand around the room as he stepped closer, yelling over me.

"I don't know, you won't explain. I woke up this morning to you telling someone where I was and I'm supposed to trust you?"

He stopped me from passing him by pulling on the upper sleeve of my terrycloth robe. "Where are you going?" He spoke between clenched teeth.

Trying and failing to jerk myself free of his grip, I replied, "To the bathroom." I needed to get dressed and get away before who ever he spoke to showed up.

He pulled me closer to him, using his other hand to grip the other side of my robe. "And then what? Where are you going to go?" His voice was low and cold, creeping under my skin. His eyes, still bright with anger, dropped to my neck and I knew what he was looking at, the mark Rusnak left. His eyes narrowed and my skin burned under his glare.

"Do you think Anatoli told you everything? You think you can go back to him for help? He won't help you." He tugged me closer, his heat pressing into me "Or are you going back to your cop? Or is there someone else? I can't keep up with you."

He might as well have spit in my face. I shoved him off of me, but he dropped me at the same time.

"How dare you." I was shaking in my shock and anger. "You wouldn't say that if you knew."

He spun around with a growl, taking a few steps away, and then he turned back towards me. "I don't know because you haven't said shit either. I'm not the only one not talking." He stopped in front of me, and I could see him wrestling with his anger. His voice strained as he tried to control it. "You're mad at me for the same shit you do. You haven't explained anything to me. The difference is, I trust you." He grabbed my hand, his voice and body softening. "I trust my feelings for you and I've been patient with you. But fuck, can you do the same with me?"

His words extinguished my anger. I met his eyes as he squeezed my hand, my voice heavy with truth. "I didn't ask you to trust me, but you're asking me to trust you with my life."

He grabbed my other hand, lacing our fingers together. "I would protect you with my life, trust that."

I was lost in his open gaze, it looked honest and felt real, but I was scared. "I don't want that. I only want you to be honest, to talk to me."

His eyes slid down me to our hands. He blew out air and looked back up. "All right. But you're going to talk too."

A knock at the door had me jumping back and the corner of his mouth lifted.

"It's probably room service." He jogged to the door as the knocking continued.

I ran to the bathroom, stepping inside just as Gage pulled a cart into the room. He had been telling the truth about ordering room service at least. And that small victory went a long way in trust, more than it should have, probably.

"Regan, come back out. I'll get you new clothes." Gage yelled through the door.

I finished changing into my shorts and sports bra. Then I zippered up my jacket and pulled it securely around me, covering the mark on my neck.

"Who were you on the phone with earlier? What if they come here? I don't want to stay," I started as I stepped out of the bathroom.

"They won't. It was Nick, but we made a deal, one that him and Anatoli have been wanting. They won't break it." He walked closer to me, putting a hand on my hip. "We can go though."

I didn't like that he called him Anatoli and not Rusnak. But I didn't want to fight anymore. I wanted him to talk.

I nodded. "Let's go."

* * *

Knocking on the SUV window from the inside, I called out to Gage. "All right, done." I had changed into the blue sweat suit he bought me.

He opened the front door and slid into the driver seat as I climbed over the center console to the passenger seat.

He moved his hand over my cheek and through my hair. "God, you're fucking beautiful." His eyes dropped to my sweater and he laughed. "Even in a crab shirt."

I pulled away. I wasn't ready to pretend things were okay. "Tell me what the deal was."

He pushed himself back in his seat, hands gripping the steering wheel. "Do we have to do this now? Let's go back to my house."

"Back to—" I shook my head, tension building in my muscles. "No. What if they come there? I need—"

"They won't. I told you." He raised his eyes to the ceiling and blew out air. Then he rolled his head to face me. "Or I guess I didn't, not really."

I nodded, relieved that he was finally getting it.

"They've been wanting me to set up more fights. Get the title and throw it to another boxer. I'm going to do that."

"That's it?" I asked when he paused.

He shook his head, staring straight ahead, out the front windshield. "There are other things. Some deals I have to take over, some runs I have to set up." He squinted at me out of the corner of his eyes. "That's the stuff I really can't talk about. It's better for you not to know."

I rubbed my palms over my sweat pants. "And Nick's just letting me walk away?"

"I had to promise you wouldn't talk. But yeah, he didn't really want to deal with you."

A dry laugh bubbled up. I could believe that. "So they traded me like property? Does that mean I have to stay with you?"

"No." He moved his hand over mine, on my knee. "I bought the assurance that they wouldn't come after you, nothing else. You can do what you want."

I wasn't convinced but decided to move on. "What about you? After you finish these jobs, you'll be out too?"

When he swept his eyes to meet mine, I could already see the answer in them. "No. I told you before. This is who I am now. This is my life now."

I tried to take my hand away from his, but he held onto it. He used his other hand to pull me to face him, his eyes begging me. "I have no right to ask you to be with me after everything that's happened. But I want you to."

My heart ached as realization hit. Gage was the black hole. I had been circling it since I met him, running around the edge, slipping in, and clawing the sides to get out. But now, he was asking me to fall into the darkness willingly, knowing what monsters lived there. And a part of me was willing to, if it was the only way to be near him. But a hissing whisper at the back of my mind reminded me that it wouldn't stay like this. Gage would leave, and I would be stuck.

30: What's Best

DEXTER WALKED INTO THE KITCHEN WITH A Pampers box under one arm. He smiled and set the box down on the table in front of me.

"This is stuff you left at the house, there's some clothes in here."

"A diaper box already?" I asked him. I knew he was going to be a dad, but seeing the reality of it in front of me felt surreal.

He smiled shy, so very unlike him. "Yeah, we're already setting up a baby room in our new place. Got tons of these boxes in all different sizes. Great for packing." He nudged the sturdy box. "They've got a new roommate in your old room, but Leona's moving out at the end of the month if you wanted to move back."

Gage straightened next to me, glaring at his brother while he chewed a bite of food.

I hadn't answered Gage in the car the other day. I couldn't make any promises, still unable to think beyond the moment, and I couldn't make decisions when I didn't have any options. I needed to build myself back up and get things together before deciding if I would stay with him.

But what I did know was I would not go back to living with those girls. I couldn't bring them into anything, and I didn't trust I was really out.

"No, that's okay." I dropped my eyes to my plate and stabbed a scallop with my fork. "Thanks for the offer though."

Gage's hand gripped my thigh under the table and then fell away as he stood, picking up his empty plate. Leaning down, he kissed the top of my head as he walked by to the sink.

Warmth radiated from the spot he kissed, but guilt chilled the rest of me. I hope he didn't think that meant I was agreeing to stay here with him for good.

Since we arrived yesterday, we both stayed in the house, not going anywhere, but not talking much either. We spent most of the day watching a marathon of movies in bed with breaks for food. Good food that Gage cooked. He would disappear sometimes and panic and paranoia would kick up, making me wonder what he was doing or who he was talking to, but he never stayed away long.

I knew this pattern in myself, something bad happens, I melt down, take a day to recover, and then I'm back out. Except, it had never been to this level. I wasn't sure I would ever recover and that scared me the most. I would never be the girl he fell in love with again, and I think he knew it. He had been giving me the little kisses and touches, like he just did, but nothing more.

"There weren't many clothes left at the house, we could go shopping. You know I'm always down for a mall trip."

Except, I had no money. I had nothing except whatever was in that small box Dexter brought. The stuff I hadn't packed when I left, the leftovers. Rusnak had everything else; it was as good as gone.

"Maybe you two could go tomorrow," Gage added as he loaded the dishwasher.

The idea gave me chills. I wasn't ready to leave the house, not yet, and I didn't think I would be ready tomorrow.

"You're going to be here all day tomorrow, right?" Gage shot a look at his brother. "I have to go out, remember?" he was speaking carefully.

I could tell they had discussed this before and I could also tell it was me he was concerned about. Dexter was supposed to be my babysitter and that made me feel even more broken. Not even capable of being on my own. But it was the truth. Thinking of Gage leaving tomorrow was sending me into a panic, it whirled around the edges of my mind, closing in.

"Sure." Dexter plopped into the chair across from me, picking a scallop off of my plate with his fingers. "Where do you want to go shopping?"

I tried to focus on Dexter, but I was barely hearing him. I shook my head to shake off the feeling. "I can't go. I don't have money." The whirlwind of panic was picking up speed.

"Don't worry. I've got it." Gage sat back down next to me, hand gripping and stilling my bouncing knee.

"Plus, you should still be getting money from your fight, right? Or do you not get paid if you're disqualified?" Dexter's brows scrunched as he questioned.

Gage shot daggers at his brother with his eyes. "It doesn't matter. I said, I'll cover it. Get whatever you want." His grip on my knee tightened.

I popped up to standing and walked out of the room. I needed to get away from their concern and offers. I needed to stop the tornado of thoughts that were wrecking my brain even further. And I was thankful neither of them followed me to the bedroom. I needed the time alone. Curling up in the bed with one of Gage's too large shirts on, I tried to quiet the storm in me, minimize the path of destruction. Even though I was certain there was nothing left to protect.

Sometime later, Gage quietly entered the room, removing his clothes. I stayed curled on my side of the bed as the mattress dipped, giving way to his weight.

I kept my eyes closed as he scooted behind me, then his arm slipped around my waist and pulled me into his chest. A feeling of complete safety seeped into me, warming me from the outside in. And I hated that I needed him for that, but that was the fact I couldn't deny.

I turned in his arms, wanting more, wanting him. Needing him to make me feel more, to bring me back.

My head rested on the crook of his shoulder, both of his arms around me now. I trailed my hands along his torso, following the lines of his muscles, feeling them clench and his skin goose bump as the tips of my fingers glided over him.

One of his hands played with the ends of my hair, tickling my scalp, and the other was rubbing up and down the length of my spine, over my shirt still, but with enough pressure to keep me pressed to him.

I let my fingers trail down his stomach and ran them along the elastic of his boxers. I knew he wanted me, I could feel him growing against me, his body flush with mine.

"Regan?" He leaned back slightly, hand over mine, but not pulling it away.

My heart broke all the same and I tried to roll away, but he locked his hold on me, not letting me.

"Hey, don't." He dropped my hand so he could get a tighter grip on me.

I struggled in his grasp for a moment and then gave up, frustrated and embarrassed. "What is it you want then?"

"I don't want you like this."

I turned my head, unable to look at him. I wish he wasn't looking at me either.

"No, look at me." He pulled me in tighter, but I moved my hands to his chest to keep space between us. "I meant, I want you, but I want it to be different. I want to know it's real."

His fingers tangled into my hair and he guided my head back so our eyes met. "I want more than just your body. I want your heart, your soul." His eyes were reaching into me and I'd let them take the things he wanted. "You already have mine."

His face blurred and my eyes burned with tears. I had no defenses left and I nodded my head, unable to find a voice.

He sucked air between his teeth. "Are you sure? Babe, I don't know if you can make this decision yet." His hands were back to stroking the length of my back, from my neck to the curve of my hip.

"I know I need you," I admitted in a breathy whisper.

His hands felt great; I focused on the feel of them running over my body and tried to ignore the prickle of anxiety under the skin.

He was still hesitant, I could feel it in his movements, see it in the way his eyes darted over me. He sunk down, moving his head to be parallel with mine, our noses almost touching as his hands moved to cup my face. "I don't want you to choose this because you think you need me, that will change. I want you to love me." His fingers slid down my neck and then shoulders, over a spot that caused me to cringe with memory. "I know you chose others because you needed them. And I don't want this to be the same. I want more."

I had to close my eyes against his gaze and the truthful accusation in his soft words. "I'm sorry. I'm sorry." There was no point in telling him that I didn't have sex with Rusnak, because I would have, and that was just as bad. I opened my eyes, trying to make him understand, believe. "This is different. I feel different about you. I know I shouldn't be in any relationships right now. My therapists all told me that when I was younger, I can only imagine what they would say now." I tried to smile through the tears, but it wasn't funny, not really. "I don't think I have anything left in me to give. I have nothing to offer but broken pieces. It's yours though." I moved my hand to his cheek, feeling the rough growth of hair there. "And I think you're the only one that I trust to help put them back together. You're the only one who can understand." This was me being as open as I could, spilling what was left of my soul for him and I hope he realized it really was all I could offer.

He trailed light kisses over my face, speaking in-between, "Babe… I will cherish…and protect… whatever you give me… You're everything to me… you're stronger than you know… I love you." Then his lips covered mine, and I was able to breathe.

His slow movements were torment and pleasure. Hands rubbed over all of me, absorbing every curve and his lips followed. His body was just as open to me and I re-familiarized myself with it, taking more time than we'd been afforded since the start of our relationship. I found new scars on his skin, reminding me that I wasn't the only one who had changed. But I blocked the bad thoughts from seeping into our moment. I needed this, more than I needed my next breath. He was the only reason I could breathe.

As he filled me, deliciously moving slow circles with his hips, I let myself give up all thought. There was only him, only me, only us. Our bodies perfectly fit, perfectly moved, pleasure and pain mixing in an intoxicating way that felt like perfection. He brought me to the point of climax and pushed me over and over. Then his movements lost control, becoming faster, harder, reckless. He handed control over to me as he pulled me on top of him and I rode him with the same intense pace he had started, feeling the power in bringing him to his own edge, making him lose control until he busted. He pulled me to him with hands on my bare back and our lips met as we panted into each other, sharing in ecstasy.

I slept better that night than I had in months, wrapped in the security of Gage.

* * *

It felt good to work out again. I wasn't training, I wasn't ready for that, but lifting weights helped me to feel stronger, putting a little bit of me back in place.

Setting down the hand weights on the rack, I saw Gage approaching in the mirror. His arms circled around me from behind, his lips pressed to the back of my ear, over my tattoo.

"Have a good workout?" His sultry voice sparked a flame low in my stomach.

I nodded and leaned back into him, my hands gliding along his arms.

"Try to get free." His grip tightened on my waist and I froze.

"What?" My heart skipped a little faster, unsure.

He moved one arm higher, re-wrapping it over my upper arms, pinning them to me. "I said," he breathed into my ear. "Try to get free." There was no trace of humor in his voice.

"I don't—" I wasn't sure what I meant to say. I still felt safe in his arms, even pinned to him, but I wasn't sure I liked this.

"I want you to be safe. I want you to know how to protect yourself. If you're not ready for this, that's all right. But I want to teach you."

I nodded, blowing out air, trying to calm myself. I could do this. It was just us, just practice, just a workout.

I tried to twist in his arms, but his grip only tightened.

"You're giving me an advantage by moving, letting me get a better hold."

I paused, thinking. I knew this. I just had to remember. I moved my foot, pressing lightly on his.

He laughed in my ear. "What's that going to do?"

"I would do it harder, I just don't want to hurt you."

His chest vibrated behind me. "You wont hurt me. I want to see what you've got."

I brought both my feet up, throwing my weight back on him and slammed them down, still too cautious about hurting him. But I had taken him off guard and put him slightly off balance by my quick motion, earning myself a little room to move in his arms. I twisted and he released me, backing up.

"All right, all right." He put his hands up in surrender. "That was a good start." His eyes were lit bright with excitement and his genuine smile encouraged me.

"All right, lets try again. You know to go for vulnerable spots, like feet and groin, but the bottom of the ribs is another one. If you can manage to grab them and pull, you can get free." He hesitated before putting his arms around me again. "Just don't really do it, all right?"

We practiced a few holds, ending up on the ground as I tried to wrestle free. We both lay back on the mat, exhausted from fighting. But it felt good. And I knew from our last position, when he'd been pressed against me, that it felt good for him too.

"You're a quick learner. I might have to stop taking it easy on you tomorrow." He turned his head to me, with a teasing grin.

"Oh?" I felt bold and confident in this moment. Swinging my leg over to straddle him, I gripped his forearms beside his head. "Maybe I've been taking it easy on you." I rolled my hips on him, his hardness stroking between my legs. I moved my lips to his ear as he groaned, sending an electric current through my veins. "Try to get free," I whispered, sucking his ear into my mouth.

"No fucking way. You've got me trapped babe, what are you going to do?"

I silenced him by capturing his lips in mine and hungrily moved against him. His hardness grew beneath me, warming and teasing, desire increasing. Another part of me fell back in place as I slinked down his body, drinking in the power he gave me. The power to make him react, to make him shake, to make him weak beneath me.

* * *

I paused at the bottom of the steps as Dexter and Gage's voice reached me. At first, a crazed relief flooded me to hear Gage. When he left today, all of that confidence he built in me disappeared like the illusion it was. And I was glad he was back. But his tone wasn't happy and they were arguing about me. I stayed out of sight, listening.

"—barely lasted twenty minutes in the store," Dexter's voice was strained.

He was talking about our shopping trip. I had tried, but wasn't ready to be in public, paranoia creeping into every movement and thought.

"What exactly happened?" Gage's voice was grave.

"Nothing really, but she wasn't her. She just looked so…I don't know. She barely looked at the clothes, just kept watching everyone in the store. She was freaked out, but trying not to show it. So I didn't make her stay when she said she was tired. She's been upstairs sleeping since we got back—Wait," Dexter called.

Gage's heavy stride stopped.

"She needs more help than you can give her, man."

Gage walked back into the kitchen. "It's only been a few days, she just needs time. It'll get better. Look at Leona—"

"Leona was a wreck and that was only one night of bad memories. She still has issues and she does see a therapist." There was a pause and then some movement. "Has she talked to you about what happened at least? Do you even know what you're dealing with?" He sighed. "Jesus man, she hasn't has she?"

"We've been working out our shit first, I'm gonna get her—"

"Your shit? You two can't have anything if she doesn't talk. Gage, I don't think she should stay in the city. She needs—"

"She needs me." His voice roared, interrupting Dexter. "It's only been a few days. Do you think I don't care? I'm doing what's best for her."

"And what about next week when you leave?" Dexter softly warned. "You think she's going to be better by then? That she's going to be all right with you leaving for days? I won't be able to stay around twenty four-seven, I have class. The fact that you want someone around her all the time should show you how bad this is."

My world tilted. He was leaving next week? But he hadn't told me that. And Dexter's words rung true. The fact that I was so shook up by him leaving proved how messed up this all was, how messed up I was. I was fooling myself to think being with Gage would be enough. Not when I couldn't even step out of the house.

But I couldn't think too far, not with the weight of Gage leaving pressing on my lungs, taking away my air. I walked to the kitchen, getting no relief from being near him now. "Where are you going?"

Gage's eyes lit on me as I spoke, then crossed to Dexter, drilling into him for a moment. But he let his anger go as he stepped towards me. "I have to go next week, but only for a few days then I'll be back."

I stepped back as he got closer. "Can I come?" Somewhere I recognized how desperate that sounded, but I didn't care.

His face melted slightly as he reached for me. "Regan, you can't come. It's not—" He stopped as I pulled away again. "Let's talk about this, all right?" He grabbed for my arm again. "Let's go upstairs and talk."

I hated the rollercoaster of emotions in me. I hated that I was already near tears. This was not me. This was not who I was supposed to be. I wasn't the girl that needed a guy for all her strength. And being near him only made it harder to find her.

"That's okay. There's nothing to talk about. I'm going to be moving anyways."

He turned sharply, eyes piercing into me. "What?"

"I'm going to move out of the city. Out of the state. I don't think I should tell you where."

31: Destroyed

DEXTER GOT UP FROM THE STOOL AND walked out of the kitchen. He squeezed my shoulder as he passed but didn't look at me.

I had Gage's full attention, and the look on his face made me want to pull back the words I just spoke. Except I knew I couldn't and I knew I shouldn't.

"When? Have you set this up already?" He was on the edge, voice carefully blank of emotion.

I shook my head. It had been a thought, a possibility in the back of my mind, but I hadn't really considered it till now—now that my emotions crowded out every other option.

He let out a stream of air between his lips and took a step closer, hands grabbing my elbows. "Then you're not doing it. I'll think of something else, another plan." He was trying to convince himself.

I pulled back from him. "You'll think of… No, this is my life. I make the plans and I made this one."

"What happened to doing shit together? You agreed last night and now you're leaving? And why wouldn't you be able to tell me where?"

"You were planning to leave this entire time and you never told me." My voice was rising, anger covering the ache in my heart.

He stepped back, hand running over his hair, voice rising with mine. "So you're fucking moving away? You find out I'm leaving for two days and decide to move away?" His hands spread out in front of him. "Do you not hear how crazy that sounds?"

I took all of a second to think about it. "Yes. I do. And that's exactly why I need to do it. I am going crazy here. You are making me crazy. This city is making me crazy. And I can't take it. I can't." I couldn't hold on to the anger, it was slipping through the cracks in me, consumed by my fear. I truly was losing my mind.

His arms wrapped around me and I struggled against them for a moment, but he only held tighter.

"Don't decide this right now. You said last night that you trusted me to help you. Trust me. Let me help. Don't run away." His voice sounded as desperate as I felt. "Talk to me. Tell me what's going on. Tell me how you feel." He pulled back, meeting my eyes. "But don't shut me out."

"I don't know how I feel. This morning I felt… all right, like things could get better. Then I went out and…" I shook my head, dropping my eyes down between us. "I was scared." I closed my eyes, voice barely a whisper. "And now, I'm terrified of you leaving. I've never felt so weak, so out of control."

He pulled me back in again, hands rubbing up and down my back. "But you feel better when I'm around? I make you feel better?"

He did, I was already beginning to relax in his arms. But my emotions were too wrapped up in him, so I pushed away, separating us. "I need to feel safe on my own. I can't rely on you."

His frustration was rising. He ran his hand through his hair, pulling on the ends. "Why not? That's what relationships are. We're supposed to rely on each other, be there for each other, make each other stronger. You felt better with me, that's a good thing. Don't punish me for that."

"I'm not punishing you." This wasn't about him. But his words were slowly sinking in, confusing my thoughts and making me doubt myself even more.

"Then why would you not tell me where you'd move to? It's one thing to move from the city, I could help. But why exclude me?" He bent his head down, leaning forward to be on my level. "Do you not fucking trust me?" He sounded so self-righteous, like he had never done anything to make me doubt him.

"I don't trust the people you're with. And I don't trust myself. I need a clean break."

His face hardened and lines creased around his jaw as he straightened himself up, looking down on me. "From me. Say it. You need a break from me." Before I could respond, he continued, voice cold and low, "Have you even thought about this? Where are you going to get the money to move?" He shook his head, lips pressed together. "I'm not giving you any. Not if this is what you're doing."

My own anger was returning, surging in me. "I didn't ask for you to. I'll figure it out on my own."

"Like you always do?" The fire in his eyes went to a new level as he stepped towards me. "You don't think. You keep making all these stupid, dangerous choices, and I have to get you out of it. How many times? For what?"

"I never asked you to," I yelled back at him, heart banging erratically in my chest.

He flinched back, chest rising and falling heavily as he tried to control his temper. He pointed his finger at me, voice rough, "You—" He curled his finger back into his fist and lifted it up as he pressed his lips together. "I've got to get out of here."

Every movement screamed pissed off as he walked out of the kitchen. He turned with his hands raised as he passed by me, making a show of not touching me, before stomping down the hall. The front door opened and slammed close.

I let out the breath I was holding, sitting on a stool at the kitchen counter to recover, to process what was said and what just happened. Gage's anger still hung in the air around me, making it thick. Slumping, with my head in my hands, I let his words and accusations replay in my mind. Everything he said stung with truth, making me doubt my decisions.

But panic was pressing on me now. He had left, and I was stuck, paralyzed in my fear about where he was, who he was with, and if he would come back. It reminded me why I needed to leave to begin with.

I couldn't stand the way I was being torn apart. I got up and went to find Dexter's computer. The first step in deciding would be to research options.

As I walked towards the living room, the front door swung back open, freezing me.

Gage looked up as he walked in, sliding his arms out of his jacket. His eyes met mine, something flashing in them before they hardened again and he walked past me, down the steps to the basement.

He had only been gone for a few minutes, not long enough to go anywhere. My heart pulled from my chest, wanting to follow him down those steps, but that distant look he gave kept me in place. He needed space and so did I. I had enough to think about. But the relief I felt knowing he was in the basement was undeniable.

* * *

"How'd you figure out the password?" Dexter came up from the basement with a smile and dirty dinner plate.

I forced a slight smile. "The password hint says, 'cat' and your password is Rocky. I thought it was an invitation."

He put the dish in the sink and sat next to me at the table. "What you looking up?" His eyes scanned the screen and then swiped to me. "So you're really planning on leaving?"

I pointed to the screen and the grey hound fairs listed on it. "I'm looking at options, But…" I shrugged. "I'm not sure. I can't afford it anytime soon." Wrapping one arm around myself, I added, "I was just about to start applying to jobs here again." It came out calmer than I felt.

"If it's money, I can lend you some for a ticket." He twisted the laptop towards him, fingers moving over the keys.

He said it so casually it took a moment to register. I shook my head. "Thanks, but that's okay."

A sly smile pulled up his lips, reaching his eyes. "It would only be a loan, you'd have to pay me back. But I mean it Rea, if you think you need to leave, I'll help." Swiveling the computer back to me he pointed to the screen. "You should go to Vegas. Airfare and hotel packages are cheap. Lot's of work options, I even know a few people that work there. And we'll be out there for Gage's fight in June."

I ignored the screen, turning towards him. "So you think I should leave?" He had to have been downstairs with Gage and I wondered what had been said.

"Nuh-uh, you're not trapping me into that answer." He scooted back from me with his hands raised. "I didn't say that. I think you need to do what you think you need to do." He squeezed my shoulder. "But I'm here, whatever you decide."

I nodded, a bubble of sentiment choking me. I stared at the screen, Vegas was a horrible idea.

"A piece of advice though, don't move and cut everyone off. I can understand getting away, but being alone won't help. If you stick around, I could give you Leona's therapist information, she really likes her."

I was listening until he mentioned therapist. "Do you see a therapist?"

My tone made him hesitant. "No."

"Does Gage? Does Boris? Does Silas? Does anyone else you know?"

"I know a few people that do and maybe those others should too. But we're not talking about them, we're talking about you. We didn't go through the same things you did."

I crossed my arms, leaning back in the chair, keeping myself from walking away. "You're right, you all didn't. But you went through other things and dealt. I can too."

He nodded, genuinely acknowledging what I said, and the bit of anger building in me receded.

"Everyone's different, Rea. Everyone deals differently. But it's okay to need help. It's okay to feel however you feel. Don't force it, this shit takes time." He flashed a grin and then looked down at his phone and back up. "I've got to go back to Leona's, are you all right here? Gage is downstairs, but I'd leave him be for the night."

My stomach squeezed at his warning, but I nodded, letting him know he could go.

Standing, he tapped the table in front of me. "Another thing, with Gage, I'm not saying you have to stay with him, but if you want to, you have to let him help."

I focused on the laptop, not seeing anything on the screen and let his words settle.

"You'd want to help him right?"

I nodded. I did want to help him. I didn't want to be a burden.

"Good." His bright smile spread over his face and he pivoted, coming down for a hug. "I'll see ya in the morning."

"Wait." I stopped him before he walked out the kitchen, my stomach flipping. "Thank you for the other night, but why would you do that?" I sounded more than disappointed so I tried to explain. "You could have been caught, and it could have made things worse. Please focus on your family. You need to be there to protect your child, its entire life. Stay away from those people. It—"

He came back to the seat next to me, worry pulling his face down. "It wasn't like that. You're here now and no one was hurt. You're right, things could have gone bad, but I couldn't let you face it with nothing. I had talked to Silas that morning. I'd known you were setting up the fight, I knew you were in some trouble, but I didn't realize it was that bad until I talked to him. Something he said, about it all being over after the fight… the way he said it though. I don't know what was going to happen, but I knew I couldn't let you face it with nothing. I couldn't." He was speaking low and fast. "I would have wanted something to fight back with if I was in that situation, even if it didn't work, even if it was a risk. Sometimes, you just need a little chance." He nodded at me and let out a breath.

"I shouldn't have left on the elevator though, I'm sorry." He picked at the seam of his pants for a moment and then looked up at me. "I did call Gage though. And I went back to your room and listened from the hall, waiting for you to come out. When I heard Kyle say you were gone, I got out of there."

"Thanks." I wanted to say more, but couldn't. Just talking about that night brought back all the fear, as if I was there again. I wasn't far enough away from it yet.

Dexter hesitated for a moment and then wrapped his arm around me again. "It all worked out. Take your time, things will get better."

I wish I could believe that.

* * *

I was done tossing and turning in an empty bed, even though I hadn't done it for very long. Kicking off the sheets, I made up my mind, I was going into that basement to find Gage. I'd prefer to argue with him than lay here and continue my pretend arguments in my head.

My blood warmed my veins as it rushed through them, anticipating seeing him, both nervous and excited. By time I reached the top of the basement steps, nervousness had taken a large lead, especially as the creek of the stairs boomed in the silence and gave away my presence.

His glassy eyes met mine the moment I turned the corner of the stairs, but he didn't move. He was sitting back on the couch, handle of rum in his hand. But the destruction around him stopped me in my path. The framed posters from the wall were broken and torn on the ground, trophies and other things lay in pieces all around.

"Did you want something?" He spoke slow and deliberate, no hint of an alcohol slur, but the bottle in his hand was nearly empty.

"To check on you, make sure you were okay."

He puffed a sarcastic laugh. "Me? Since when do you care about me? You're only worried about yourself." He finished his bottle off, rising to his feet. "And now you're down here ruining my night of drinking alone." Gesturing the empty bottle towards me, he continued, "But you ruin everything, right? Should have expected you to ruin this too." He tossed the bottle to the ground and stepped on the frame to one of the posters, shattering the glass under his boot. Plopping back on the couch he smirked at me. "Might as well come on in now."

"I do care about you. I worry about you all the time." I took a few steps into the room, but didn't pass the pool table, hoping it would be a buffer. He was using his words like weapons and they were already slicing me. "I don't mean to ruin anything, but it happens."

He sat up on the edge of his seat. "Don't mean to? More like you don't care if you do. Look around. I have given up everything for you, to protect you, and you only care about yourself." He rose to his feet and stepped closer, the table still between us. "You are so fucking selfish, it makes me sick."

I took a few steps back, retreating to the stairs. I had made another mistake by coming down here.

"No." He came around the table in an instant, grabbing my arm. "You don't get to leave now. You don't get to come down here, stir up shit, and run away. Not tonight."

I reached for that girl inside me, the one who wouldn't shrink from his stinging words. The one who would stand up for herself. But I could barely find her.

"I'm not running. But you're being mean and going to say things we both will regret in the morning." I could smell the liquor surrounding him, seeping from his pores and rolling off his breath. I tried to remind myself it was just the liquor talking, but I knew he was saying the things he wanted to say.

He jerked me closer to him, turning me to face him completely. "Too late for that, I regret a whole bunch of shit." His breathing was intense, and his eyes fell over me, unreadable. His voice dropped, low and raspy. "Mostly I regret giving my soul to a woman who doesn't give a fuck." He pushed away from me, turning to the pool table. The eight ball went flying across the room, smashing into the mirror behind the bar, knocking it from the wall.

Bracing his hands on the felt of the table, he took a deep breath then turned his head towards me. "And I can't even take it back. I don't even want to. I'm so fucking pathetic." He flung another ball and then another, smashing glasses and bottles that were organized on top of the bar.

"Stop." The shattering sound vibrated in my bones as I placed my hand on his back, keeping him from grabbing for more. His anger was breaking my heart. But I wasn't scared for myself, I was hurting because he was.

"Stop?" He spun around on me. "Stop what? Am I doing something to you? Am I ripping out your heart and tearing it to fucking bits?" His hands gripped my shoulders and he pushed forward as I tried to step back, till he had me pinned to the wall. "You won't even try to make this work."

"I try." I shook my head, unbelieving. He actually believed what he was saying, I could see the clarity in his eyes. It wasn't just out of spite and that was a punch in the gut. "I tried."

"Bullshit." He cut me off. "You always pushed me away. And I'm the stupid one for coming back, thinking it would be different. Even when you'd run to the cop, then to Rusnak." He spit the names out with disgust, letting go of me and stepping back. "You'd go to them for help, but never me." His eyes ran up and down me as if seeing me for the first time and not liking it. "And I was fucking blind and gave up my life for you."

He took another step back, looking around the room. "I don't even have boxing anymore. I agreed to give up my title for you. The one good thing I had going for me, the only thing I ever dreamed about. I gave it up for you. And I'd fucking do it again." The hot, loud, anger was draining from him, a cool, quiet rage seeping into his words as he stalked closer to me. "But you'll never commit, even before you wouldn't. You can't and I'm a fool for trying when all you do is destroy me."

He was blaming me for everything. It was too much of a weight to bare. I stepped towards him, my own anger strengthening me, setting fire to my blood.

"I destroy you? Fuck you. You left me. You left me in New York when I had committed to you." I stepped closer, pushing his chest to back him away, but he didn't budge. "I committed to you. I would have stayed by your side through it all, but you left me." I met his eyes, returning every bit of intensity he was giving. "You started this, not me. You. Destroyed. Me." I jabbed my finger into his chest with each word.

He captured my wrist in his hands, electricity running through him, brightening his eyes as he pushed me against the wall again. "You never fucking listen. I was protecting you from this."

"I didn't want protection. I wanted you." I snapped my wrists out of his grip like he taught me that morning.

His lips crashed into mine, hands moving to my legs as I wrapped them around his waist.

Just like that he'd taken me from scared, to sad, to angry, to passion in the space of a minute. But I threw thought away as his hands glided up my shirt, over my back, sparking fire. He turned us, sitting me on the pool table. His tongue traced inside my mouth, filling it with a cool spice as he used one hand to sweep away the balls still on the table.

Then he broke the kiss, pulling my shirt off over my head. I tugged on his, lifting it over his smooth muscles and tossed it to the ground.

His chest rumbled as he looked over me, hot lips pressing to the top of my chest. He undid the clasp on my bra, as I ran my hands through his hair.

"You have me. You've always had me."

His breathy promises and scrape of his teeth on my skin made me ache, and I wrapped my legs tighter around his waist, raking his back with my nails.

His hands found the button to my pants, pausing over them, the tips of his fingers already sending currents through my skin there. He pulled back, blue eyes piercing into me.

"But do I have you?" He pulled on my pants, pressing me against his hardness, and I nodded. Dipping his head down to me, he groaned in my ear, "Say it. And mean it."

"I'm yours. You can have me."

He sunk to his knees, pulling my pants down my legs. Looking up at me with a triumphant grin, he darkly promised, "I will have you. And you'll be screaming it so all the neighbors know you're mine before I'm done."

32: All I Needed

HE WASN'T GENTLE, OR PATIENT. BUT HE wasn't fast or cruel. He just stopped treating me like I'd break.

And I didn't. I came alive under his rough touch, bites, thrusts.

Meeting him blow for blow, we both marked each other's skin with nails, smacks, and teeth. Making the outside a bit more like the scars we'd given each other on the inside. We were covering every painful memory with exquisite pleasure.

He had me leaned over the pool table, my hands gripping the edge to brace myself for each thrust of his hips as he slammed deeper into me. His hands gripped my hips, pulling me back into him, forcing me to take in every sweetly painful bit of him.

Leaning over me, pressing his sweaty chest to my back, he slid his firm hands up my sides. One hand slid to the front of me, cupping my breast, rolling the nipple between his fingers. The other hand twisted in my hair, pulling my head back as he sucked on my neck, making me moan as his hips circled into me.

"No more Regan," he growled in my ear. "No more leaving." He yanked my head back, keeping me pressed to him as he straightened up. "No more pushing me away." His hand unwound from my hair, and his hips slowed as he slid his fingers down my body, between my legs, barely touching. "Say it."

Sliding my hands behind me, I glided them along his abs, around his waist, to his backside, squeezing the firm muscle. Drunk from him, his touch, his words, he had me so wired I could barely speak. I moaned my agreement.

He applied pressure with his fingers and his hips dipped and rolled back into me. His deep growl in my ear vibrated over my skin, sending all my nerves into a frenzy. His hand disappeared all too soon and he pulled out, spinning me to face him.

His cool blue eyes held so much heat, I thought I'd melt. I might have because before I knew it, I was on my back, the smooth felt of the pool table under me. And he was over me, hands running up and down my body. But when I tried to touch him, he pinned my arms back.

"No. I need you to say it Regan. No more." His lips wrapped around my nipple, sucking and then biting, eyes never leaving mine. He released me and I whimpered for more of his touch. He was hovering over me, but we were only connected where his hands pinned my wrists.

His eyes penetrated deep in me as he promised, "You have me. I won't leave you again. I only want you." His face dipped closer to mine, nose trailing over my cheek, followed by a surprisingly sweet and gentle kiss that didn't match the fire in his eyes. "Now you."

I raised my hips, trying to make contact between our bodies, any contact. I craved his skin on mine. "I'm only yours and I'm not going anywhere, not without you." And I meant it.

I'd realized the moment I said, 'I didn't want protection, I wanted him,' I was a hypocrite. I had been denying him me, to protect him. I was done and I hoped he was too.

His lips devoured mine and his body pressed me into the table as he filled me in one hard thrust, to the edge of pain. I gripped his shoulders, nails biting into his skin.

Being together might get us hurt—by others and probably each other. But I'd step into the fire with him, just to feel my soul burn, the way only he could make it.

"Only mine." He raised himself up, driving into me. "Mine," he grunted as he pushed deeper. "No one else's."

The table shook beneath us as he slammed harder, but we ignored it, too consumed with each other, being in each other, laying each other bare.

I didn't fall apart beneath him when I reached climax, I came together. He filled me, shaking over me, muscles hot, sweaty, and covered in goose bumps as we released into each other.

I was completely drained, exhausted. Physically and emotionally. I could have been content passing out on the pool table, but Gage picked me up, leaving our clothes behind, and walked me up the stairs to our bedroom. He curled around me on the bed, arms wrapped around my waist, keeping me pressed to him.

"I love you, more than anything else," he whispered into my hair, his hold tightening on me.

I slid my hands over his forearms, closing my eyes, feeling overwhelmed by his warmth and raw intimacy of the moment.

"I love you too. More than I ever knew possible." It wasn't the earth shattering confession I'd imagined it would be. But it took every last bit of my strength to say it. The admission passed from my lips quietly, joining the warm, still air around us.

And I didn't break.

His chest sunk in as air escaped him in a gasp. "That's all I need." He kissed the back of my head and repeated, lips still in my hair, "That's all I need."

If I just gave him a part of me, the last piece, he returned so much more. I felt stronger, somehow more, because it was no longer just me.

And that's all I needed.

33: Easy

THE SOUND OF RAIN FALLING ON THE ROOF and blowing against the windows enveloped the room. Letting in only a dim grey light, but also making the cocoon of sheets and man I was wrapped in feel even warmer. I didn't want to move, but my arm was asleep and I had to pee.

As I pulled the sheet down and began to unwrap myself, Gage jerked awake and I froze.

He sat up, blinking away the confusion, as he looked at me and took in our naked bodies.

"Fuck," he groaned and fell back on the pillow, one arm draped over his eyes, the other still under me, around my waist.

It was only then that I remembered the empty handle of liquor. He may not even remember last night, or worse, he may regret it. My heart was in my stomach as I went to slide out of bed again.

Strong arms wrapped around my waist, pulling me back down. When I looked up at him, from my new spot on his chest, he had his eyes closed but a smile on his lips.

"Shhh, don't move, don't talk. Just lay with me," he whispered.

So I did, for as long as my bladder would allow. When I returned from the bathroom, freshly showered and dressed, he was still in bed.

"How are you feeling?" I was a bit hesitant to ask as I ran a brush through my hair.

He sat up, sheets pooling around his hips as he stretched his arms out. His hair stuck up in all directions. "My head is fucking killing me, but I feel better than ever. Now get your ass back over here."

I couldn't resist the sleepy look in his eyes mixed with a lazy grin, but I went back into the bathroom to grab him two pain relievers and a glass of water first.

He strolled in after me. "What are you doing? You're not listening very well this morning," he teasingly admonished.

I turned towards him, giving him the water glass and medicine.

"Thanks." He swallowed the pills and gulped the water, setting it on the bathroom sink when he was done. Then he pressed his naked body against me and wrapped his arms around my waist, lips slowly moving against mine.

Breaking the kiss, he rested his forehead on mine. "Tell me last night really happened," he pleaded quietly. "That you're really not going anywhere." He pecked my cheek, hands moving up my back. "That you love me."

I nodded, tightening my hold around his waist. "I still don't want to stay in the city though, I can't."

He kissed my forehead, hands sliding into my hair. "I understand. We can start looking for other places together."

My heart stretched with relief and I brought my lips to his again, feeling every bit of him against me.

"Now let's get you out of these clothes." He smirked as he pulled away, lifting my shirt at the same time.

* * *

"What's wrong, babe?" Gage slid under the sheets and scooted closer to me over the king mattress.

I sat up to face him, pulling my bottom lip out from between my teeth. It was time to talk. There was still so much unknown between us, too many questions casting a shadow over the security I found with him.

"Where did you go today?" I was testing the waters before diving in. Dexter had come over and "hung out" while Gage ran "errands."

Acceptance crossed his features, he knew where this conversation was going.

"I had to see Anatoli, work out some plans, and then I went and met with a real estate agent."

The first part twisted my stomach, but the second part was a surprise.

"What?" I turned myself on the bed to face him completely, sitting on my knees in front of him.

"If we're going to move, we need an agent. She's coming by tomorrow to look at this place to see about putting it on the market or possibly renting it out." His hand spread over my knee. "Isn't that what you wanted?"

"Yes, but I didn't know. I wish you would talk to me, include me on decisions."

He raised his hand off of me. "So now you're mad that I talked to a real estate agent without you?"

"No. I'm not mad." I grabbed his hand. "I'm just saying, talk to me, include me in decisions instead of making them for me."

"You said you wanted to leave the city. Do you not want me to sell my house?" He spoke slow, frustration running under the question.

I sighed, my own frustration rising, but this wasn't supposed to be the conversation we were having. "I do and I'm happy you are willing to, for me." I rose up on my knees in front of him, wrapping my arms around his shoulders. "Thank you."

He relaxed some, sliding his arms around me tentatively, and then he rested his chin on my shoulder. "I'll talk to you first, keep you included."

I hummed with relief as he turned his head and dragged his nose down my neck, his breath tickling the skin. I pulled away and stopped the moment before he could distract me away from the real conversation we needed to have.

"What about Rusnak? How did that meeting go?" I spoke quickly, to stop Gage from grabbing me again and to force the words out before they got stuck in my throat.

He stilled, different thoughts crossing his features, and then he nodded and leaned back against the headboard, getting himself comfortable.

"We were only going over details for a shipment I'm in charge of next week. The reason I was going to have to leave."

Goose bumps covered my skin and I wrapped my arms around my legs. "Are you still leaving?"

"I might have to for one night. I'm going to try to get back as soon as I can."

"Where are you going?"

"Florida." He met my eyes and I could tell he wasn't willing to say more.

"Can I come too?"

"It's not like I'm staying in a hotel. I'll be at the docks the entire time, if I'm not on a boat in the middle of the gulf. And Nick will be there." He leaned towards me, hands on my legs. "We'll be in a new place by then. It might only be temporary, but somewhere else. You won't be in the city."

I tried to smile, to reassure him. Whatever he was doing sounded dangerous, he didn't need to be worried about me on top of it. "Okay. It'll be okay. I'll be fine. But, what about you? You said Nick was going to be there? How can you trust him or Rusnak?"

His eyes searched my face. "Don't worry about me. They won't do anything. Maybe I haven't said enough, but they need me. This deal that's going down is a big one. And the," he paused, searching for a word, "distributor is picky, OCD actually. He only wants to deal with me." He smiled, like it was something to be proud of. "He doesn't like Anatoli, doesn't trust his methods, but he is willing to work with me. He only did small shipments when it was Nick and Anatoli. But since I took those over, he's willing to increase his supply. It'll make Anatoli a lot of money. It'll make him the largest distributor on the east coast. This is what he's wanted and I am delivering it." He paused, watching me as the words sunk in.

"But when it's done, what's stopping them from coming after you then?"

He narrowed his eyes. "Why do you think they would?"

I shook my head, unsure if I could put it into words. "Nick is mean, vicious. He hated me and wanted to hurt me, I know. And you helped me get away."

His features dropped and hardened as his arms wrapped around my waist. I pushed on his chest to keep him back so I could finish.

"And Rusnak." His arms fell back as I spoke his name. "I don't know what to expect from him. Until the end, he was never mean, but he was…" I couldn't find a word to express what he was. "Sneaky? I don't know, I never knew what to expect, but he always seemed to have a plan and be in control. And he didn't want me with you. I just—"

"What did he do at the end?" He interrupted me.

"I'll tell you everything, but first, I need to know what might happen now. I keep thinking something has to happen, that it couldn't be so easy to get away."

"Easy?" He flinched. "Shit's not easy." His features softened, and he ran his hand through his hair. "But I'd do anything to keep you safe." He sighed. "I told you from the start, the whole reason they kept you was to get to me. Except that shit you told me about your mom and him? That was something else. But Anatoli puts business first so I don't think that will change anything." He dismissed that confusion with a shake of his head.

"It started with them only wanting me to agree to throw my fight and some small jobs, but I knew those weren't enough, not really. When I saw the opportunity coming with Xavier"—he paused, eyes flashing to me—"the distributer, I knew that would be the only real way to keep you safe. Because it's not a one time deal. Anatoli is going to want to keep the partnership going and he'll need me. He won't want to mess that up by retaliating against you."

It was starting to make sense. Sort of. Rusnak wouldn't risk his money, and he made it clear at the end he was done with me. But it still sounded dangerous for Gage.

"And Nick, he's paranoid. There's something going on, we knew that when things went wrong with Demetri. Someone is leaking information to Rock, so we've had to close ranks, keep everything close. And Rock's crew is doing the same. They've gone underground completely and we haven't seen or heard from them since that night." Concern was clear in his eyes and that worried me. He slid his hand to my hair. "Nick doesn't hate you, but he doesn't trust you. He doesn't trust anyone. He won't come after you, but I'm not letting you anywhere near him either. I'm not taking you anywhere near any of this. We should go look at places tomorrow."

I nodded, dipping my head to rest on his chest, circling my arms around his waist. "Okay. I want that. I think I'm starting to understand, but what about Damien? If Rock has disappeared, does that mean Damien has too?"

He let out a breath, hands running up and down my back. "Yeah, we haven't seen him. That's how I know it was never about you with Nick and Anatoli. After Demetri, they never even tried to go after Damien and they never actually bet anything on your fights, it was just a game."

A cold chill skittered over my skin, raising the hairs on my arm. That scared me the most, that they could be so cruel and terrorize me to that extent, over things beyond my control, over Gage. But I didn't blame him, I couldn't, not when I was laying in his arms, knowing what he would do to keep me from it all.

His hands trailed lightly over my skin. "Now you need to tell me what happened."

I took a deep breath and pulled away. Sitting up, I stared at the covers twisted in my fingers as I spoke. I couldn't stand to look at him or have him touch me while I told my story, I wouldn't be able to continue if he did.

I told him everything. I told him about the guys on the motorcycle, I told him about Nick's threats, I told him about Kiera, and I told him about Harrison. I only skimmed over some of the more intimate stuff with Rusnak. And he didn't interrupt me till I finished.

"Jesus," he breathed, tentatively reaching for me and I fell into his arms, burying my head in his chest. "I didn't know. I really didn't know that's the way it was. I'm sorry I didn't step in sooner." I pulled away and he tried to press me back to him.

"No, don't apologize. I didn't let you do anything. I wouldn't have. I was so scared it would be worse for you, that I would get you killed." I choked on the word, eyes burning as I curled back into him. I needed the reassurance of his body and heart beating in my ear, assuring me that he was still here. "That still scares me."

I could feel my story sinking into him, his body slowly tensing under me.

"Fucking Nick." He scooted up to sitting. "He better not have been serious about…" his jaw clenched, teeth grinding. "I could kill him for even threatening it, for even thinking he could hurt you."

I sat up on my knees, hands going to his face, forcing him to look at me. "I'm fine. I'm here. Please, don't make it worse. Please, I don't want anything more to go wrong and you have to work with him."

He grabbed my wrists, pulling my hands away from his face. "You don't get it. He can't hurt me. He fucking has to answer to me now. And I'm going to make him pay for this, for what he would have done. He's only lucky he didn't go through with it."

The determination and anger hardening his gaze made me breathless. I wasn't sure if he had a right to be so cocky, if he was exaggerating his power, but it scared me how much it actually excited me.

He must have saw it in my face. Or maybe in the rise and fall of my chest, because he licked his lips as his eyes dropped over me and I inched towards him, core tightening with anticipation.

"Wait." His voice was low and rough with desire already, but a different sort of need creased his brows. "Anatoli and you—you never—he never had you?"

I dropped back at the question, guilt punching me in the stomach. "Only because he didn't." I don't know why I couldn't have just told him we didn't have sex, except, I don't think I deserved to be forgiven for it.

Gage either didn't notice the distinction I made or didn't care because he released his breath with a groan and wrapped me back in his arms.

"Thank God." He buried his head in my hair and neck, pulling me to straddle his lap. "Thank fucking God above." His hands moved to my butt, cupping each cheek as he pulled me tighter on him. "You're my fucking girl. Only mine, and that sick fuck will never touch you again."

And I don't know how he did it, but he made me believe the words. Then he made me scream his name, over and over.

* * * *

We moved to an extended stay hotel an hour from the city while we looked for places to live. Dexter and his friends helped us pack and put stuff in storage. And we enjoyed several days in a fragile bliss, pretending to play house.

I knew Gage had to leave and it was a dark shadow over our time. I tried to reassure myself that he would only be gone for a day or two, and then he would be back. But the anxiety over his departure only increased as the time grew closer.

He would have to leave in the morning, so I tried to make the night before special. Focusing on cooking dinner for him helped to distract me from my fears.

"You can't ruin it from here. Just be sure to take it out of the oven in twenty," Dexter instructed, pulling out his phone again. "You sure you're going to be okay?" He looked up from his screen with concern.

"Go, you don't want to be late for the ultrasound. I'll be fine." I waved him away, walking towards the door.

"You can come with, if you don't want to stay alone."

"Your brother should be back soon. You go, enjoy the moment with Leona." I smiled at him, slipping an arm around him for a hug. "I want to see pictures tomorrow and call if you find out the gender."

"They say it's too early for that, but I'm sure Leona will have lots to tell you tomorrow. You're still staying with us for the next couple of days right?"

"Yes, now go."

"I'm going, I'm going." He raised his hands up with a grin and jogged back out of the door.

Locking the door behind him, I went back to the kitchen to set out plates for dinner. My anxiety didn't even have time build before there was a knock on the door.

The pounding grew in intensity, never stopping, as I walked to the door. Checking the peephole, I saw Silas's baldhead, and I reached for the gun in the entry hall closet.

"Rea, you there?" Silas yelled out, voice at an odd pitch.

"What do you want?" I asked through the door. None of them were supposed to know where we lived.

"Open up, we've got to talk, it's important."

My heart was pounding as I gripped the glock in my hand and dialed Gage with the phone in my other hand.

"It's Gage. Things went wrong."

Silas's words stopped my heart at the same time Gage's voicemail picked up. Fuck was I to do?

34: Eyes Open

"WHAT HAPPENED?" I ENDED THE CALL AND tried texting Gage.

Silas is here. You okay?

"Gage sent me to take you somewhere safe. He's going to meet us there." His voice was growing tense and louder as I finished typing.

My heart was squeezing painfully in my chest, making me lightheaded. I wanted to open the door and go with him, see where Gage was, make sure he was okay. How else would he have known where I was if Gage hadn't told him?

I reluctantly dialed Dexter's number. I didn't want to bring Dexter into this, especially since I didn't know what this was. But I needed to make sure someone knew who I was with, in case he was here for Nick or Rusnak.

"Rea, what's up?" Dexter's cheery voice spoke over the phone.

"Silas just showed up here. He said your brother sent him, but I can't get a hold of Gage. Do you know anything about this? About Silas?" I spoke low and quick into the phone.

Silas continued to yell through the door as he banged on it again. "Rea, we don't have much time. The others are on their way, and we need to leave before they get here."

Bile burned the back of my throat as Silas's words drowned out Dexter's.

"I haven't heard anything. Stay there. I'm coming back now," Dexter ordered.

"No, don't come here. I think I'll be leaving." I'd take my chances with Silas over waiting for the others. "But stay on the phone. I'll keep it on." I slid the phone into my pocket, unable to make out what Dexter said as I pulled it away from my ear.

Gripping the glock with one hand, I opened the door with the other.

Silas's fist fell away from the door. His face dropped with relief and then instantly hardened as he spotted the gun in my hands, aimed at his chest. The memory of Nick getting the upper hand when I didn't pull the gun soon enough was fresh in my mind.

"Put it away Regan, we've got to go."

"Where?" I asked him, unmoving.

A gun was put in my face as another, taller, man rounded the edge of the door and pushed me back into the apartment. Silas twisted the gun from my hand and turned it on me.

I stumbled back when pushed, but found my feet quickly. Standing away from the two men with guns aimed at me, my brain tried to catch up.

"Get her, we've got to go." The tall man looked vaguely familiar as he gestured to Silas and started searching the room, gun pointed at me wherever he went. "You sure she's alone?"

Silas looked at me with guilty eyes as he pulled a plastic tie from his pocket. "He's in Florida with Rusnak."

The tall one peeked inside the bedroom, arm still extended towards me. "That's what you said about Nick," He threw back at Silas. "Now come on man, do it quick. I want to still search the place."

I wasn't going to correct them, and I wasn't going to let Silas handcuff me with that tie. I watched him, waiting for him to move, wondering why he wasn't.

He looked down at the tie in his hand. "I'm sorry, Regan. I always did like you, but…" He shrugged as he took the first step towards me.

"Fuck's sake man." The other man approached from behind.

Then it hit me, he was the tall one from that night at the gym, when Rock's crew robbed Dexter and Silas.

I darted to the open door, quick and low, before the men could close in on me. The bright sunshine blinded me as I sprinted towards the stairs. I was going to leap down them, it was only one flight, broken into two by a landing. But something jerked me back by my shirt and yanked me to them. A rough rag blocked my vision and a sickly sweet smell filled me before I disappeared.

* * *

Everything hurt and I couldn't move. I was laying in the backseat of a car, arms and feet bound. My throat burned, head throbbed, and the metallic tang of blood filled my mouth.

Opening my eyes, the world slowly came into focus. It was only Silas driving the car. The taller guy wasn't around.

"What?" I forced the word out of my dry throat and mouth, my lips peeling apart.

"Don't move yet, you might feel sick," Silas advised, like he was a friend.

I couldn't move if I wanted to, my arms and legs were tied together behind me. All I could do was wiggle and that caused the ties to bite into my skin. But I couldn't help but jerk against them a couple of times, as pointless as it was.

"Stop doing that," Silas cautioned.

My muscles began to shake as shock wore off, or picked up, I don't even know. But I was shaking and the air was thin.

"Why?" I was almost yelling. "Why are you doing this?"

I rolled to my back, but that was worse than my side so I fell back. Taking deep breaths, I tried to loosen panics grip on me.

"I have to." Silas was breathing heavily. "Nick and Rusnak pushed me to. They were getting suspicious, questioning everything I was doing after the night we were robbed. Rock offered protection and pays much better."

"What's that got to do with me?" Talking was keeping me calm, but only barely as I realized the phone was gone from my pocket.

Moving my arms, I discovered one tie was strapped to the seat belt. He was going to have to cut it loose to let me out. If he was going to take me out. Shifting my wrists back and forth, I tried to use the friction of belt and tie to cut through one, as unlikely as that was.

"When Gage came back, he was picked for the jobs I was supposed to get. I've been with them for twenty fucking years and they chose the kid over me?" His anger was rising, straining his voice. "But I don't blame him. No, I'd take the jobs too, if I could. But if they aren't paying me, I'd make my own money."

He turned back to check on me, and I froze. Then he put his eyes back on the city traffic.

"You know they didn't even bet on your fight? No one told me. I thought we were all working together, but those fuck's crossed me. They sabotaged it with that crooked ref and didn't fucking tell me. Well, two can play that game." He made a few turns and tall buildings dropped away to row home rooftops.

Now that the traffic was gone, I could hear the motorcycle engine in front of us. Silas was following it.

"What's the plan? They don't care about me. This doesn't hurt them."

He turned down another street. The sun glowed bright red behind run down and boarded up buildings.

"No, but you're a form of payment. Sorry Regan, I had no problems with you. But you're not making me money anymore. And after what happened today I need Rock's protection more than ever," his ominous tone got to me more than his words.

"What happened today?" I was still working my hands and the belt was beginning to tear as I prayed that Gage wasn't there for whatever happened.

The motorcycle engine cut off and Silas pulled the car over.

He twisted to face me. "Don't be stupid, Regan. These people won't kill you. They don't want you dead. Just do what they say."

The car door opening made my skin jump and heart burst. The tall one yanked me up by the cord at my hands, nearly twisting my shoulder from my socket. The quick saw of a knife cut the seat belt, but the ties stayed in place. Then the point of the knife pricked into my neck, burning as it punctured skin. The guy crouched low to look me in the eyes. "Don't yell, don't move."

A thick wool dropped over me, covering my body, and I was scooped up awkwardly between two people. I didn't try anything. If they dropped me, I couldn't run, not with the ties. And I saw enough of the neighborhood to know it was abandoned, there was no help to scream for, only a knife waiting for me if I tried.

I heard other voices as they carried me up stairs and then I was dropped on a hard floor, knocking the air from me as my knee twisted with a shot of pain.

The wool was ripped off of me and Damien was in front of me, hands already on my legs, sawing at the tie. It snapped away and he yanked me to my feet, wrapping his arms around me and keeping me balanced. Fire shot from my knee, up my leg to my hip and spine.

"I thought this wasn't happening for two more days. What happened?" The thick man to my left asked, his face tight with anger.

"Nick and Boris caught us talking. We had to take them out, move up the schedule," Silas explained, eyes shifting around the group.

Damien's raspy voice spoke behind me, "So you got her, but what about him? What about the shipment? If they don't have that yet, everything's fucked."

The tall one spoke, "We killed Nick and Boris, hid their bodies, it should be a while before they're found. The shipment should be coming through now."

"But why is she here already?" The angry one interrupted.

"In case Nick or Boris told anyone before we got them. She's insurance." Silas's eyes flashed to me and then behind me as he swallowed. "And he wanted her." He spoke only to Damien now. "You said you'd pay if I brought her."

Damien's chest rose and fell against my back and his arms tightened around me. "Hmm I did. I will." Then he pressed his lips to my ear and whispered, "Keep your eyes open."

And I saw something I never wanted to see again.

The angry one whipped out his gun and fired at Silas. Three clicks of his finger; the silencer on the tip making the shots whisper soft.

Silas dropped to the ground, bright red blood spreading on his chest then pooling on the floor under him. His eyes, wide open, turned to face me, realization filling them. He coughed and spluttered up blood, red foam spilling out of his mouth. His chest fell one last time before he stilled, all life gone from his eyes.

35: Crashing

DAMIEN'S HOT BREATH BLEW IN MY EAR as he laughed. But I was stuck watching the pool of blood around Silas spread, causing my own blood to drain.

"That's what snitches get. He turned on his boys for green, he would have turned on us." Damien twisted his head to look at my face. "You're not going to fucking cry, are you?"

The one that shot Silas was crouched by his body, checking his pockets and boots.

I ripped my eyes from Silas to look at Damien, letting him see how far away from tears I was. I wouldn't cry over Silas, not after he brought me here. The only thing I was in danger of doing was throwing up. But I'd keep it down.

Damien's eyes flicked over my face with a slight grin. "You think you're a bad ass bitch? But you'll find out, you and your boy ain't got shit on us." He kept one arm around my waist and used the other to pull on the cord around my wrists, yanking my arms up behind my back, making them burn under the abuse.

"Clean this up, Jay," Damien ordered the tall one.

The angry one rose from the ground with Silas's wallet, cell phone, keys, and two guns. He tossed the keys to the tall one, Jay. "Drop it in the cut."

Damien pulled me down the hall, the other guy followed.

We passed a room on the left and a female voice yelled out. "Dee, whose here?"

Damien didn't stop, just kept pushing me forward. But extra footsteps join our group as he pushed me up a flight of narrow stairs with peeling paint and graffitied walls. The air was thicker, mustier, as we climbed the stairs and my knees ached with each step. But if I flinched, Damien forced my arms up higher behind me and pain bit into my shoulders.

"Go get the rope, Des," Damien ordered. "The thick one in the work room."

A thousand little needles stabbed into my stomach at his words. I jumped back off the stairs, pushing into Damien behind me, not caring about the fall.

We were both stumbling back, then Damien's body fell away from behind mine as his friend grabbed him, twisting him to the side and flinging me down the steps on my own. I hit the edges of the stairs and sharp pain stabbed into my arms, sides, and hips as I bounced down them, landing at the bottom with a breath-stealing slam to the back. But I rolled to my feet, ignoring my body's protests against the movement.

The thundering of boots on the stairs filled the air around me, making me push beyond my limit. But Jay was blocking the exit, Silas's body still at his feet. If I had my hands free I would have risked running by him, but they were still stuck behind me. I ducked into a side room, but there were no windows, no escape.

Two girls stood from the table they were sitting at, one already raising her gun at me. Bricks of marijuana were stacked to the side of a scale on the table. I gasped, air burning my lungs as any hope went up in flames.

Damien stepped into the room behind me, jerking on my arms. "Stupid bitch. Did that fall feel good? Was it worth it?" He hissed into my ear as he lifted me off my feet by my arms, making me cry out as my shoulders exploded and burned.

The other guy stepped in and grabbed my legs, immobilizing me completely between the two of them.

"You're not going anywhere. Not till we say so." The thick, short man warned.

They took me back up the stairs and turned into the second room on the left. There was nothing there but a few wooden chairs and pallet of crumpled blankets in the corner.

Setting me in a chair, Damien pulled my arms over the back of it until Des came back in with the rope. And that's when I recognized her, Destiny, Damien's sister. She smirked wickedly, eyeing me as she handed the rope over to her brother.

She crossed her arms over her large chest, watching as I was tied up to the chair. Rope was wrapped around my legs, torso, and arms.

Damien tied the last knot and the other guy jerked on the rope at my chest, testing it.

"We need to call Rock, update him," his yellow eyes slid to Damien.

"He's already on his way. I just talked to my man." Destiny took a step towards me and leaned forward with a fake grin. "My man, Regan, you hear that? You ain't fucking with this one."

I met her eyes. I guess she hadn't got over high school. I'd told her I had sex with her boyfriend, in the same sentence I told her I slept with her brother and her dad. I wasn't serious, only trying to piss her off when she kept calling me a whore. I could have slept with him though, he came up to me the next day offering to make the statement true, but I sent him away.

"Want another hair cut?" She asked, overly sweet.

My hair use to reach my lower back, but she had cut a chunk of my it in science class the following week.

"Want another nose job?" I responded with the same sweetness.

I'd broke her nose immediately after she cut my hair. She got suspended, but I got expelled, my third strike with the school. That's when I dropped out. I wasn't going to a delinquent school.

Destiny's eyes flashed with anger and I knew what was coming. She slapped me across the face.

My head jerked to the side, but I brought it back to look at her with a smile. "Try that when I'm not strapped down." I knew I should have kept quiet, but there was no getting on these peoples good side, and all tied up, my words were all I had.

"Fuck you." She slapped me again.

I laughed.

The two men in the room seemed content to just watch the show.

"Glad you find this so funny you stupid whore." Her eyes blazed into mine. "You're gonna get to use that talent of yours real soon. Get to spread your legs for all kinds of men, see how much you laugh then." She straightened herself up as another girl walked into the room, the one who had pulled her gun on me earlier.

The new girl, with red streaked hair, stood beside Damien. She looked between Destiny and me with a raised eyebrow.

"Have you met Harley?" Destiny turned to her and then looked back at me. "She's a big improvement over Nan. Can't get over that my brother would stoop so low, with filth like her." Her lip twisted up. "So damn glad that girls gone. If only you would fucking die already."

Explosions went off in my head and I jerked against the ropes, but they didn't budge. "Fuck you." I pulled back my words as she smiled. I couldn't let her get to me, that's what she wanted.

The third girl walked into the room, she was tall and cut. Her arm was extended, my phone in her hand. "Jay just left, but he gave me this. It keeps going off."

Damien snatched the phone from her, eyes dropping to the screen, and then he looked up at me. "Looks like someone's worried about you." He moved his fingers over the screen. "What's your code?"

I told him as he aimed his gun at me, not thinking it worth dying over. I hoped Dexter had heard enough to know the phone wasn't with me anymore.

Damien continued to press on the screen. "He's not in Florida yet?" He frowned, looking towards the other guy. "I thought our guy at the docks said it was going down today?"

He stepped towards me, pressing the gun to my head. "What do you know about this? When is the shipment coming through?"

I met his eyes, looking past the gun. "I don't know."

"Bullshit."

The gun cracked my face, blinding pain exploding my jaw and blood filling my mouth.

My phone vibrated in his hand and Damien focused on the screen, reading the message. "Fuck," He groaned and signaled to the guy to walk out with him. The girls followed him, Destiny flashing one last smile before closing the door on me, leaving me in the musty darkness.

I immediately tested the binds, ignoring all the pain that radiated from multiple joints. I couldn't think about what damage I may have done. I knew nothing was broken to the point of not being able to move, and that's all that mattered. Destiny's threats scared me, but their interest in Gage's shipment worried me more, what were they planning for him?

The more I moved, the tighter the ropes became and the pain in my wrists increased, I was rubbing the skin raw.

Pounding boots from the hall stilled me. The door creaked open and a new guy walked in, the whites of his eyes glowing in the dim light. He held out my phone with a tattooed covered hand. As he stepped close to me, it became clear his dark skin was covered in tattoos, only his face was clean.

"She's here." His deep voice had a rasp to it.

"Regan?" Gage's voice spoke from my phone. That one word held an ocean of concern, washing over me.

"Yes." My voice cracked, unsure what I should say.

"I swear to fucking God if you hurt her—"

"No one's hurting her." The man standing in front of me in jeans and leather jacket cut him off. "Not as long as you do your part. Get that shipment, I'll call tomorrow." He pressed the end call button.

He slid a chair over the floor, placing it in front of me and sat down. "Looks like you're staying here longer than expected" He rocked his chair onto the back two legs, fingers pressed to his lips. "That chair won't do, but I heard you already tried to escape." He slammed his chair back down onto all four and leaned forward towards me. "Don't try that shit again."

Damien silently walked into the room, standing along the back wall. "We could always keep her under, to the point that she can't fucking think."

The man in front of me nodded, eyes hooded as he looked over me. Then he stood up and walked towards the door. "Do it," he ordered before exiting.

Damien smiled at me, nodding his head. "Stay there. I'll be right back." He was breathless with excitement.

He came back into the room with the short guy that shot Silas, a little black bag in his hand. Damien sat on the ground and took a baggie of white powder, spoon, and needle out of the black bag. "Shit, Quin, we need a lighter."

Quin laughed, stepping back to the door. "Des must have been in the bag."

Damien laid out the items and attached the needle onto the syringe. "You're gonna love this shit. It's gonna take you on a good fucking ride." Scooping out some of the powder, he added, "This is that stuff that'll have you begging for more, willing to do almost anything for it. You're lucky we're willing to do it this way."

Excitement ran through his words, like he believed what he said. But I was feeling anything but lucky. My stomach swirled painfully and my heart pumped out of my chest, my veins already collapsing on themselves in preparation for what was coming.

Quinn came back in with the red haired girl, Harley.

She kneeled down behind Damien and ran her hands over his shoulders. "Here, Daddy." She slid a lighter into his hands.

He smirked up at her and she went in for a kiss. He leaned into it and used one hand to hold the back of her head, his eyes cut to mine as he swept his tongue into her mouth. Then he pulled away, flicking the lighter with one hand.

Picking up the spoon, he held it over the flame. "Tie her off." He nodded to his girl.

Harley picked up the rubber band and scooted to where I was, tying it around my upper arm.

"No." I tried to jerk away, but couldn't move. "No," I yelled louder, panic gripping me. I rocked in the chair.

"Hold her," Damien said, syringe drinking up the liquid now in the spoon.

The other man hovered over me and pressed down on either side of my chair, holding me in place.

The sting of the needle broke into my skin and in the next second a wave of sensation crashed into me, turning me to liquid.

It was like I was trapped in an endless land inside myself. My mind spread out before me alight with pure feeling. My head rolled back with the overwhelming high.

"Feels good, right?" Voices echoed around me and the hands on my stomach were electric as they moved up me. "Give her more."

But the feeling lost its good effects almost immediately, the waves crashed over me too fast, too strong. My heart beat too fast, too strong, bursting with the effort.

An explosion. Suffocating darkness and pain.

36: Only Chance

"IS SHE BREATHING?" A GIRLS VOICE.

My brain had no control over my body. My brain had no control of anything. My eyes wouldn't open. But I wasn't in the chair anymore. I was laying on something, hands and feet untied.

"She stopped fucking shaking." A guy.

I was untied. In my wreck of thoughts, I grabbed that one. I couldn't even see straight but I jumped to my feet.

"Whoa."

"Stop her."

Voices swirled around me, streaking past me. Flying by as I ran through them.

Monsters grabbed me. I pushed them away. Throwing punches. Clawing. I could hear them shriek as they fell.

A burst of light. I slammed into darkness.

* * *

"You can't give her anymore right now. What the fuck, you'll kill her. We need her alive." A girls voice was talking.

I was back in the chair, tied up. My skin was crawling, itching, tingling, without relief. I kept bobbing in and out of consciousness, trying to grip onto the moment, but losing the battle.

"This isn't for her. That shit was intense, I need a fix."

"Me too." More voices agreed with Damien, swirling into a hum of nothingness.

* * *

I don't know how much time passed, minutes, hours, days? But when I fully woke up, the room was empty besides the tall one, Jay.

He sat in a chair to the side of me, foot rested on the edge of my seat, smoking a blunt. Thick smoke rolled out of his mouth as he watched the end of it burning in the dark room. The door was open and let in light from the rest of the house.

I blinked, trying to align my vision.

"Finally." Jay took a hit, the smell of weed filling the space around me. "How you feeling?"

I pulled my eyes from the floor and looked at the guy next to me, holding in a groan. It hurt to move my neck. It hurt to sit. It hurt to breathe. All of me hurt.

"What time is it?" I asked instead of answering, voice scraping out of my raw throat.

"Almost six." He held up the cigar. "You want a hit?"

"No."

My limbs felt heavy, beyond heavy, but the heaviest weight was on my chest. It was hard to take a full breath.

"In the morning?" I don't know why, but it felt important to know when I was. Nothing else made sense.

He laughed, a soft squeak of a sound. "Yeah, in the morning. You missed the party. Slept right through that shit." His words meant something, but I couldn't figure it out.

"I have to use the bathroom." I don't know what they expected me to do.

"I'll get the others." He knocked the burning tip off of the blunt and stood up with a sigh before walking from the room.

My stomach soured as I looked over myself. They had changed me. Instead of my clothes, I had on a large t-shirt over my bra and underwear—that was all.

I turned over his words, what could have happened while I was out? It was even worse to think about what would happen today, now that I was awake. But the worst was to think about what was happening with Gage and his shipment, when would that drop off be and what would happen then?

The guy that had been on the phone with Gage yesterday stepped into the room first, followed by Damien, Harley, and the taller girl.

"I thought the plan was to keep her high so she didn't have to be in the chair." I think this guy was Rock. He seemed to be in charge as he stood in front of me.

All I could do was stare back, waiting for something to happen.

"She tweaked hard. I dosed her and she started fucking shaking and throwing up. We took her out of the chair and she went crazy, straight fucking crazy. So we tied her back up." Damien stepped next to him and stared down at me too.

"That's because you gave her too much. You almost killed her." The taller girl said, face severe as she accused Damien.

"You should have let her die, Jade." Harley sneered at the tall girl.

"What the fuck are you even doing up here? Learn your fucking place." Jade took a threatening step to Harley.

Rock turned his head to Damien.

Damien stepped between the girls and walked Harley out of the room with whispered words. Then he came back to stand with the other two.

"She can't die. Not until we meet up with her people tomorrow. They're expecting to see her." Rock's raspy voice was calm as he instructed the other two. "And even then, the plan is to sell her to Shadow after and make some more money from her."

"Whose Shadow?" My voice was calm, but my legs and arms were still shaking from the drugs or nerves. They weren't planning to trade me for the shipment, I already knew, but this confirmed it.

The three looked at me, like they had no clue why I would talk and didn't understand a word I said.

"I think it's time for another dose," Damien said, not taking his eyes from me.

"Are you trying to kill her? " Jade whipped her head to Damien and then turned back to me with a critical eye. "What drugs do you take?"

My chest was tightened, pulse already picking up from fear of another shot. "I don't."

"No fucking wonder. You can't give her anymore of that shit," Jade ordered.

"That's bullshit. She runs with Rusnak, of course she uses," Damien defended.

Rock turned to leave, "Jade you take over dosing her. It's gonna take Shadow a while to get her feening, but we can start the process. Take her to the bathroom too." He looked between the two of them with a warning look. "I don't want any more shit, she's out of here this time tomorrow."

Jay came in as Rock walked out.

"Harley's pissed." He nodded to Damien. "You should go."

"She can fucking wait," he responded.

"Keep the gun on her, I've got to untie her to take her to the bathroom," Jade said to Jay as she bent down and untied my legs from the chair.

My muscles tingled as the ropes loosened. But Damien and Jay kept their guns on me. Damien kneeled down to grip my legs as the ropes came undone, his gun pressed to my stomach.

Jay grabbed my arms as Jade undid the ropes on my hands, gun pressed to my back.

Damien pulled me to my feet and moved his arm around mine, holding them to my side as he walked me out of the room. My body felt drained of energy and ached with every movement. The other two followed behind. I didn't see a way of escaping as they closed me into the bathroom, and I knew I didn't have the energy to fight. They only gave me a couple of minutes of privacy before they were in, escorting me back to the chair.

I felt like a zombie as they tied me back up. My only hope was that something would happen tomorrow. Gage would fight for me, Rusnak for his drugs, and I hoped they would win, because I didn't see a way out otherwise. This hope was the only thing keeping me going.

Especially when Jade left to go get that black bag of poison, my mind nearly broke with hysteria but I kept it together, somehow.

"How pissed was Harley?" Damien asked, pulling the blunt from Jay's hand.

He shrugged. "She don't want you up here, not after last night. You should go down there."

My blood froze at the way Jay's eyes slid down my bare legs, reminding me that I was only in a long shirt. What happened last night? My head pounded as I racked it for memories that weren't there.

"She's overreacting. Nothing happened, not yet." Damien twisted the blunt, sticking the lit end into his mouth, and then he leaned towards me and blew the heavy sweet smoke into my face.

I held my breath, but he made it impossible to avoid inhaling some, it filled the air around me.

Jade walked back in, only a filled needle and rubber tie in her hand. "What the fuck are you two doing?" She waved away the smoke around me.

"What?" Damien smiled innocently. "That will help keep her calm."

Jade rolled her eyes as she secured the tie on my arm.

I was shaking so bad the chair vibrated under me, my heart pounded in my chest. I squeezed my eyes, bracing for crash that was sure to come.

The prick of the needle stung as it broke my skin inside my elbow, and my heart was already flying out of my chest, but nothing else happened.

The girl leaned into my ear, speaking soothingly, "Just close your eyes and relax. You'll be fine."

"You swing that way Jade? Always wondered about you."

She pulled back from me, cool air filling the space she had been. "I'm easing her into it, Ass, making sure she don't seize again."

I was breathless from anticipation, my eyes still closed. But after a couple of moments with no effects, I began to relax, unsure what had just happened. I knew I wasn't high, but I wouldn't let them know, in case they decided I needed more.

"I think she'll be fine. Let's go, Rock wants to talk before he leaves," Jade said and then they trailed out of the room and I opened my eyes.

I still wasn't feeling anything, except the same pull of exhaustion and pain from before. I didn't waste my time alone, I tried to twist the ropes, but they were knotted securely. I don't know how long I tried to loosen them, but my skin began bleeding on my ankles. Even though I couldn't see them, I knew my wrists were bleeding too, they burned worse than my ankles.

Music started from somewhere in the place and I paused, listening. I could hear people yelling, but not in anger.

The more time that passed, the more desperate I became. I took the risk and threw myself to the side, the chair crashing with me. It was wooden and I hoped to crack it, but nothing happened. I rolled it to the back, hands burning as they crushed under the weight, but not enough to keep me from trying. The chair didn't have armrests, my hands were tied behind it. No matter which way I rolled, it was my body taking the beating, not the chair. Tears pricked my eyes as I twisted and flopped, I couldn't put enough force into my movement to even crack the chair. I was stuck, and in more pain than ever.

After a while, footsteps came down the hall and Jade came back in with Jay. She had the syringe in her hand again and didn't seem concerned that I was on the ground.

Jay smiled as he righted me in the chair. "You might need to double it, she's tearing up her skin. Look at this."

"She's had enough already. I don't want to push it." She brushed off his suggestion, coming behind me and tying off my other arm.

He pulled at the bottom of my shirt, fingers lingering on my thighs. "Relax, stop hurting yourself. 'Cause even if you get out of these ropes, there's nowhere to go."

I put as much fire into the glare I shot him as I could. But I couldn't speak, dread choked me as the needle pierced my skin.

Jade slid the needle out and stepped back. I felt nothing, but I closed my eyes and pretended I did. Jade squeezed my shoulder briefly and walked away, Jay following her.

Maybe it was my adrenaline coursing through me that kept me from feeling the drugs, but whatever it was gave me hope. I needed to be able to face what may come with a clear mind.

I should try cracking the chair again, but the floor wasn't enough. Eyeing the room for anything that could help, I also listened to the noise downstairs. I couldn't make out what was being said over the music, but I could hear knocks and bumps as they moved around, and laughter and shrieks that followed.

I tried to scoot the chair to the wall, but only moved an inch when footsteps outside the room stopped me. Damien slipped in, barely opening the door and then closing it softly behind him. He paused, chest rising and falling, and a grin on his face that drained my blood.

I was supposed to be high, but the fear gripping me made it hard to act on. I closed my eyes and counted in my head, trying to keep calm, silent. My senses were in overdrive and my skin tingled as the air shifted around me and the floors creaked. But when his hands touched me, I flinched.

"Shh" He slid one hand over my shoulders, down my body to my waist. His breath on my neck and then ear. "Can you feel this?"

I nodded, eyes squeezed tight. There was only so much he could do with me in the chair and ropes around me, I kept reminding myself.

"Good, I want you feeling this." The tip of something sharp poked into my stomach, just nicking the skin.

I hissed, opening my eyes, the silver of a large blade shone in the dark.

He moved it under the ropes at my stomach and cut them away. As they slid off me, my courage built. It was only him. If he cut me free, I might have my chance. But he had to cut me free.

My breaths were heavy and ragged, the sound filling the empty space. I couldn't bring them down. They only increased as his hand slid up my thigh and under the shirt, fingers grazing my underwear. I gritted my teeth to keep from yelling out, but couldn't contain the cry when the knife replaced his hand, dragging down the skin of my inner thigh, the heat of blood spilling over the shallow cut.

He growled low in his throat, or maybe it was a laugh. "I may not be able to kill you, but I can hurt you. And I'll show that boy of yours what I did before I kill him tomorrow." He cut the rope at my ankles, yanking it off.

I held my breath, keeping in any reaction.

My chair was suddenly tilted back, Damien's hands on either side of the backrest. "He said he'd kill me for touching you." He licked along my jaw, tongue like sandpaper. "Well, he'll die with my blade in him, knowing that I fucked you and cut you, and that soon you'll have a different guy fucking you every night, and worse."

Setting the chair down, he undid the top of his pants and slid them off. He pulled himself out of the front flap of his boxers and gripped his erection in one hand as he dragged the blade of his knife around me, from my stomach to arms. He bent down and cut the rope there, releasing me of all restraints. But his arm quickly wrapped around both of mine and he pulled me to my feet, blade pressed to my neck, the tip twisting into the skin just below my ear.

He yanked my arms behind me. "Maybe I won't hurt you too bad if you keep quiet. You've been a good girl so far." He slid his fist with the knife in it down my body then up under my shirt. "Let's take this off."

My breath was faster than ever, senses pricked for a fight. The spots he cut burned, but only fed my adrenaline.

He released my arms, bringing that arm to the bottom of my shirt and I waited for him to begin tugging it up. When I should move my arms up so he could lift it off of me, I twisted and kicked him between the legs, forcing him back. But he lunged towards me before I could jump away, knocking us both to the ground.

My hands gripped his, struggling to keep his blade from my body.

"Stupid Bitch, you just made it so much worse for yourself." He forced my arms back, pinning them to the floor with a triumphant grin, moving his hips to wedge between my legs.

I twisted my hips and bent my legs, getting one foot to his stomach. I kicked him off enough to roll away from him. But the space was only for a moment, then he was on me, and I was face down. I grabbed behind me, gripping the bottom of his ribs, fingers digging into his skin. I pulled with all my force, feeling the bone bend under my grip.

He roared, body twisting with pain, and I grabbed for the knife in his hand, yanking it from him in his weakness. I slammed the blade back, low in his stomach, up to the hilt. It wasn't till the sticky heat of his blood poured around my hand that I realized what I had done.

I yanked it out of him, pushing myself away and to my feet. He stayed on the ground, gripping the spot where I stabbed him.

I ran to the door, but it didn't open. I unlocked it just as I heard heavy boots in the hall. But Damien was struggling to rise up, getting a leg under him.

Gripping the knife in my hand, I pressed myself to the wall, just to the side of the doorframe, ready to fight whichever attack came first.

The door flew open, and I swiped the knife as I tried to pass the person. But my wrist was gripped before the blade could make contact. And I choked on relief as my eyes met bright blue ones.

Gage was breathing heavy, holding my arm away from either of us. His face collapsed just before he pulled me to him.

"Oh shit," He breathed and wrapped his arms around me for a second, filling me with an indescribable sense of safety before he pulled back, but still gripped me. "We've got to get you out of here." His eyes darted over me and then flashed to Damien, who was just rising to his feet.

Lightening fast, Gage pulled his gun from a side holster and shot Damien in the chest.

Damien's arm floated to the bullet wound for a second, and then he staggered forward and collapsed.

Gage pulled me behind him through the door and handed me the gun in his hand.

"Take this. They'll know someone's here now that I fired." Even as he spoke, footsteps were coming up the stairs.

Gage pushed me behind him, taking his other gun from its holster.

Quinn, the short one who shot Silas, was up the stairs first and Gage shot him in the side of the head before he even rounded the corner. He fell back and I heard the shriek of the girl behind him as his body fell down the steps.

"Fuck, how many people Regan?"

"There were three girls, four guys if Rock is here."

"Last room on the left, there's a window, go out it. I'll meet you at the car," he spoke without turning around, gun aimed at the steps.

There was commotion below, but nobody had attempted the steps again.

"Go. Now," Gage ordered.

"Are you here alone?" I asked, still not moving.

"Come down, show yourself," Jay yelled from the bottom of the steps.

Gage nodded to me, taking a step closer to the stairs.

"Come with me. We can both go out the window."

He shook his head. "It's too late, someone just went out the front. I heard the door." He grabbed my hand. "Stay up here. Keep the gun out and shoot first. These bastards aren't getting away. I'll be back for you." He turned briefly and kissed me on the forehead, then was moving down the steps.

My breath left me as a shot blasted through the house. I crept to the top of the steps to look down at where he had disappeared.

Nothing was seen, then Destiny popped into view, gun in hand, and I shot her. The gun had a greater kickback than I was use to and the bullet went high, hitting her in the neck. Blood splattered the wall behind her as she dropped on top of Quinn's body at the bottom of the steps.

"FBI, cease fire." Jade's voice bellowed through the house. "Police are on their way."

Another shot.

I couldn't take it. I ran down the steps, keeping to the wall to stay out of view. Rounding the corner with my gun raised, two more shots went off. I slid down the hall to the first room.

"You fucked up," Rock's raspy voice traveled over the rap music that was still playing.

I edged to the open door and peeked around the corner.

Jade lay on the opposite side of the room, breaths gurgling in her chest, blood pooling around her from an unseen shot. Rock stood, back to me, with his gun raised and aimed at Gage. Gages gun was aimed at Jay, who was shot on the ground.

Adjusting my aim for the kickback, I fired at Rock. Pressing my finger on the trigger till he dropped, I filled his side and chest with bullets.

Gage dropped his arm, eyes meeting mine, and then he lunged for me. I thought for an embrace, until I was knocked to the ground and shots rung through the air. Gage twisted his body, firing his own gun at the girl in the doorway, Harley.

She bounced back as the bullets hit her stomach, slipping out of view as she slid to the ground just outside the front door.

Gage was half covering me with his body, but a liquid heat surrounded my bare legs. The bright red blood surrounding me scared me, but the pain in Gage's face was shattering.

He had his hands pressed to his upper leg, blood erupting out like a fountain. It was too much blood.

"No, no, no, no." I twisted from under him, laying him back. "We've got to stop the bleeding." I slid my shirt over my head, thankful for its size. I wrapped it around his thigh, just above the bullet hole, tying it off, trying to stop the continuous flow of blood. But it didn't stop. "No, no, no." Tears were clouding my vision.

He moved a bloody hand to my face, words slipping from his lips, too low to hear.

"Put your hand back on your leg, help stop the blood," I demanded, pulling away from his touch.

He gave me a smile that only panicked me more. "Shh, it's okay. You'll be okay. That's what matters." His eyelids were closing, breaths shallow.

I pulled the shirt tighter on his leg and then pressed my knee on top of it, putting all my weight there to stop the blood. "You'll be okay too. We'll both be okay." My heart was about to explode as his eyes closed.

His lips moved, but I couldn't hear him as he mouthed, "I love you."

I was yanked away by my hair, and a searing heat sliced my side. Damien tossed me to the ground and jumped on top of me, hands around my throat.

"Stupid whore, I'ma fucking kill you." He was spitting blood.

All I could see was Gage, unmoving. I was still stuck there and not caring for my life, except knowing his only chance was if I kept pressure on that leg. My vision was wavering from lack of oxygen and the coldness overtaking me. Heat poured out of my side. I moved my hands up, pressing on his face, trying to get his eyes, but his reach was too far. My sight flickered

His bloody smile and his venomous voice filled my head as he hissed in my ear. "Nan put up a harder fight than you. Took me almost an hour to kill her."

My vision flashed red and I dropped my hands, bringing them to his chest and stomach. I dug my fingers into his stab wound and where he was shot, tearing open the gashes.

He screamed, but his hold on my throat tightened. Then loosened as a gun blasted.

I kicked him off of me and ran to Gage, taking the gun from him as his arm dropped.

Turning back to Damien, I emptied the gun into him, until there were only blank clicks.

I fell on to Gage, putting pressure on his leg, but I felt weightless as my own blood mixed with his.

My head collapsed to his chest, energy drained, and my heart shattered when I didn't hear his strong heartbeat. His blood was warm as it spilled out, surrounding us. Sirens filled the night air and I slipped into unconsciousness.

37: Always

MY STOMACH ITCHED. BAD.

I jerked against the ties and my arms flung with the effort since they weren't bound. I sat up. Pain seared through me, tearing my side and slicing my stomach. But I ignored it and pushed away the hands that reached for me, forcing myself to get to standing.

"Regan, it's okay, it's just us," Dexter's voice cut through my panic.

My heart beat wildly, banging in my chest, and I gulped air as I tried to still my body. Feet on the ground, but sitting on the bed, pain radiated everywhere.

Dexter was to one side of me, Leona on the other, both with the same shocked expression.

It took one breath for the memories to come back and my heart to crush under them. "Gage," I croaked, looking toward Dexter.

He closed his mouth and reached his hand out to grab mine.

I snapped my hand back as he blurred because of the tears in my eyes.

"He's getting a transfusion now. He lost a lot of blood," Leona spoke, hand on her still flat stomach.

"Oh God." I closed my eyes, shuttering as the news washed over me. "He didn't die." I opened my eyes, looking between them. "He didn't die."

"Lay back down, Rea." Dexter stepped towards me, placing a gentle hand on my shoulder. "You look like you're going to fall over. You've just had surgery yourself and shouldn't be up."

I didn't let him guide me down. I gripped his hand on my shoulder and pleaded with him. "Tell me about Gage. Everything. What are they saying?"

He swallowed, throat moving with the effort and I noticed how tired he looked. His blue eyes were absent of their usual spark and warmth.

"I'll tell you, just lay down please, before the nurses come in and make us leave." He flashed a barely there smile.

My stomach throbbed as Dexter helped ease me back. I gritted my teeth against the pain and hoped I hadn't torn anything when I woke up. It burned like I had.

"Here, this button will give you another dose of pain medicine in your IV." Leona handed me a little switch that was hanging on the IV stand.

I kept it in my hand, thumb running over the button, but not pressing. I might later, but first I needed to hear about Gage.

Dexter sat on the edge of the chair that was already pulled close to my bedside. "The main artery in his thigh was nicked by a bullet. They operated to repair it but he lost a lot of blood. They've been giving him a transfusion for the past hour." He leaned forward, arms resting on his bouncing legs. "The doctor knows to find me here. We're just waiting on news." He looked at his spread hands. "How much blood can they give him? How long can it take?"

A lady in light pink scrubs walked in, wheeling a cart with a laptop and equipment on it.

"You're awake?" She was surprised, but gave me a forced smile, sadness clear in her eyes.

I didn't like that look. "Is Gage out of surgery?" I asked.

She straightened up and looked to Dexter and Leona instead of me, as if they could explain my question.

"Gage Lawson. He's my brother. He came in with her." Dexter's words were tight with frustration.

"Oh." She walked to my bed and put a blood pressure cuff on my arm. "The others that came in with you, right? One moment, just relax," she instructed as the cuff tightened with air and then released.

She undid the cuff and gave me a shaky smile. "The police want to speak with you first, as well as Dr. Smit, our psychiatrist. I'll leave it to them to explain more."

I was cold. The blankets on the bed couldn't touch my bone deep chill.

She turned to Dexter and Leona. "Please, step out for a couple of minutes, I need to change her bandages and check her over."

They stood up and it was hard to breath.

"Dexter." I didn't want them to leave.

He stepped to me and grabbed my hand. "I'll be right back. I'll go see what I can find out about him," he promised before walking out with Leona.

She didn't talk except to ask about my pain level as she changed my bandages. There were bandages covering the superficial cut on my leg, and my wrists and ankles. But there was a large, red tinged bandage on the lower right side of my stomach, covering a jagged stab wound that had been stitched up. It stung as she pulled off the dressing and it still oozed blood through the scab that was forming. I turned my head away, unable to look at it for too long.

"You've got to stay still, try not to move too much as this heals. Your medicine should kick in again shortly and you'll feel sleepy. Rest, it's the best thing for you at the moment." That forced smile was back, hiding none of the pity that was clear everywhere else.

I closed my eyes to block out her look, but soon fell asleep again.

I woke up to a different nurse. She was tapping the bed beside me. "Sweetie, everything's okay now. You're at the hospital. I'm Elaine, your nurse. It's safe here. You're okay." She repeated this speech, soothingly low, pulling me gently from sleep as she eased me into wakefulness.

When I opened my eyes, she smiled, a genuine smile. "There, sweetie, see everything's okay. You must have been having a bad dream."

My mind was thick and dark, nothing coming to surface, but when I rubbed my eyes, trying to wake up further I felt the slickness of the tears that covered me.

She moved around the dim room, using only the light from the hallway and monitors as she changed out the pouches attached to my IV.

"Your friends were here earlier. Dexter, he left you that note." She nodded to the table beside me.

I grabbed the folded white paper, regretting the twist when it pulled on my stitches.

"Careful now. You've got to listen to that body, go easy with it." She nodded and lifted the gown from me as she changed the bandage. Her fingers were swift and gentle and within moments, I was covered again.

"I'll be your nurse for the next"—She checked her wristwatch—"ten hours. I wrote my extension on the board there, call if you need anything." She smoothed the sheet over me. "I mean it, anything at all, you just give me a call, that's what I'm here for." She stepped away.

"I'll let you sleep now, give you at least five hours of uninterrupted sleep before tomorrow begins."

The clock on the wall read 2:20 am. I had slept too much already. My lungs strained to breath. I had slept while Gage was in surgery, he had to be out now, and I shouldn't have been sleeping. The weight of that was worse than any other wound I had.

Unfolding Dexter's letter, I read his large slanted print.

He's out of surgery. Hasn't woke up yet. In room 223b. Only one hall over from yours.

I sucked in air as I swung my feet off the bed, holding in the pain my movements caused. It didn't matter. Using the IV cart to help brace myself, I walked to my room door, pulling my gown around me to cover my back end. But it didn't really matter. I only had one goal, and that was to see Gage.

Scanning the hall, I saw the direction the room numbers moved in and followed them down, spotting his number mounted outside a door down the hall to my left.

The nurse's station was to my right and Elaine lifted her head from the computer, spotting me.

She popped up. "Ms. Sommers? What are you doing, you could hurt yourself walking around." She was quickly closing the space between us.

My legs shook, but I forced them steady. I forced all of me to stay steady even though my insides were a whirlwind of panic.

"Please," my voice was thick and shaky. "I've just got to see him. Gage. I just need to see that he's okay. Just for a moment."

She pulled her lips between her teeth and searched my face with her eyes. Then she cracked a slight smile. "I should have guessed, you're Rea, aren't you?"

I paused, unsure, but nodded.

"He was asking for you, too." She slid her arm around my waist, helping to support me to walk, but she didn't make me turn back to my room.

"When was that?" I tingled with excitement. If he was asking for me then he was all right, surgery had gone okay.

"When he was first brought in. One of the medics on duty told me, in the ambulance they had to sedate him because he kept yelling for Rea." She smiled at me and stopped in front of his door. "You." She opened the door, leaving me standing while she checked his chart. "He hasn't woken up since surgery. It's his left thigh, so be careful. I'll come back for you in a little bit, okay?"

"Thank you." Emotions were spilling out of me. I could have hugged her for her kindness, but didn't waste time getting to Gages side.

He was laid on his back and even in the moonlight from the window, I could tell he was pale. But I could see the steady rise and fall of his chest, and hear the constant beep of the machines attached to him, and that was enough. Except it wasn't, not really.

I stood next to the bed and rested my hand on his chest, my desperate heart healing as I felt his beating. Before I knew it, my head was on his chest, arms holding him, stomach burning as I bent over him. But I couldn't let go.

"I love you. I love you," I repeated, crying into his chest. I couldn't stop. I should have said it to him more. There was so much I should have said to him and never did. I needed the chance to say it to him, and if given that chance, I would never waste it again. It was a prayer. A promise. I would never waste the time I was given with him again. Never.

I eased onto his bed, sitting beside him, lessening the pressure on my wound. I traced my fingers over his face, but he didn't move. I kissed over his eyelids, cheeks. Nothing changed. I ran my hand along his arms and grabbed his hand to lace his fingers with mine. But they were limp. A knot formed in my throat when I kissed his lips, only to be met with no response.

Lifting his blanket, I slid beside him, careful not to shake him in any way. But I rested my head on the crook of his shoulder and laid my hand on his chest, feeling it rise and fall steadily and the beat of the heart underneath.

I didn't try to stop any of my tears, but I spoke through them. Telling him how important he was, how much I loved him, and how I needed him. Until eventually, my own breathing steadied, matching his, and I fell asleep on him.

* * *

Arms circled me, sliding around my back, and my heart burst. Relief flooding me, surging with so much love it hurt. It hurt to be in his arms, but I only gripped tighter because it hurt worse to be anywhere else.

"You're safe." His voice was rough and breathless. "And you're here, with me." His hand stroked over my hair. "Thank God you're all right."

His lips pressed to the top of my hair and I lifted my head, moving my lips to meet his. My hand slid over his wet cheek, our tears mixing together where they fell.

I pulled back, finally finding my voice. He gave me the air I needed.

"I love you. Oh, I love you so much. I thought I lost you." I couldn't keep talking, my throat closed off with emotion. But I pressed my face into his neck, breathing him in, absorbing comfort in his breaths.

"I know, I heard you."

I could hear the smile in his voice and looked up at him, confused.

He adjusted himself on the bed and his face pinched with the movement. Then he looked down at me. "Or at least, I think I heard you. I've had your voice in my head, saying things, but I couldn't move. I wanted to, but I couldn't get to you." His chest rose and fell heavily under me, picking up speed as he talked. His hands were pressing me tightly to him. "But you're here, and we're okay. I was so fucking worried, scared, I couldn't get to you."

I knew he was talking about more than last night in the hospital. But I couldn't offer words to make it better, I only held him tighter.

"I was scared too," I began tentatively. "That you were going to die. I thought you gave up, you took your hand off your leg. You stopped trying." I tried to breath down the anger building in me, but it was a fire consuming the pain.

His chest bounced with light breathy laughter. "You're mad at me for that?"

His laughter picked up, extinguishing my anger, forcing me to smile through the tears with him.

"Yes, I am. I would never have forgiven you if you died." But I couldn't keep the smile up as much as I tried. The words were too close to being real and a new wave of tears welled up.

"Shh." His hand was back in my hair, stroking my face. "I didn't give up. Don't you know by now, baby, I will always fight to be with you. But I had to touch you one last time, say I love you one last time, just in case." He kissed away a tear on my cheek. "It was important."

I dropped my head back to his chest, taking a moment to let his words settle, to let my heart calm. "It's not as important at staying alive, staying with me. Don't do it again." I slid my arms back around him, snuggling close. "I already knew you loved me, you were there. You saved me. Thank you."

"You saved me too." It was barely a whisper as we both closed our eyes, sharing the comfort of being together, laying in each other's arms.

When Nurse Elaine came back into the room, neither of us were ready to separate.

"She's staying here. Her doctors can see her here." Gage kept his arm on me, but I wasn't going anywhere.

Some small part of me knew it sounded unreasonable, but I didn't care. It was unreasonable to separate us after everything we went through to be together.

"I'm really sorry Ms. Sommers, but you have to get back to your room now, the police are waiting to speak with you. I'll bring you back to see him after." Elaine's words struck a new fear.

If the police were here to talk to me, they were probably going to talk to Gage too. And I had to face the truth, we both killed people the other night.

I pulled back, meeting Gage's alert blue eyes.

"It's going to be okay. You didn't do anything wrong." He squeezed my hand. "Just tell them about Damien."

And I read between the lines, keep Rusnak's name out of my story.

38: Living

I BARELY GAVE A STORY. I TOLD them the names of the people in that house and that Gage saved me, but little else. I couldn't, not to a room full of strangers, probably not to anyone, except maybe to Gage. The cops didn't press for more. They already had it decided, I was the victim, Jade told them so.

The police officer told me, Jade had survived. Her real name was Serena Woods and the FBI filled in the police on Rock's crew. She had been undercover, trying to infiltrate the human trafficking ring. Trying to find out who "Shadow" was. They had been hoping to discover his identity at the exchange.

And that's what got me. That's what stopped me from seeing her as good. She may have had good intentions and kept me from overdosing, but she had still used me as bait.

Once everything happened, she had to pull her gun, blowing her cover. Jay shot her in the chest, but the surgeons were able to repair her lungs. She still hadn't woken up from her most recent surgery though.

The officer promised to come back later, when I was ready to talk. It sounded like a threat.

I didn't get to go back to Gage though, not like Elaine promised. Instead, they moved me to another wing of the hospital, to get emotional treatment. I tried to explain that if they wanted to help me, they needed to let me be with him, but they didn't listen. They only gave me things to calm me down, drugs I didn't want.

I saw it spinning out of control and heard the storm in the things the nurses and doctors said to me.

"You can't see him."

"He is being questioned by the police."

But the worse, was seeing the way they talked in hush tones outside of my room, the looks they gave each other when I said I just wanted to talk to him on the phone. The response of, "You need some space, time to process everything away from the people involved."

And there was nothing I could do. Not when they had me sedated, in and out of sleep.

It wasn't till the next day that visitors started. But I had nothing to say to them or their fake smiles. Leona, Aliya, and Zoe came by without Dexter. He was with Gage.

"How is he?" I asked first thing.

I could tell by their traded looks something wasn't right and my blood dropped.

Leona grabbed my hand, but I pulled away.

"The doctors told us not to talk to you about him for now," Aliya explained, head lowered.

"That's—" I was at a loss of words. "That's crazy. Why? What's going on?" I pulled myself up on the bed, careless of the stitches in my side.

The girls traded glances. "The cops are investigating his involvement," Leona explained.

"He saved me. He didn't do anything wrong." I grabbed for Leona's hand on the bed. "Please, go get my doctor. Tell them to come in here. I'm ready to talk. I'll talk to the police. Anything. He didn't do anything wrong," I was panicking. I should have said more sooner.

I had already told them he saved me. That was one of the only things I had said. But maybe they needed more details. I had to try. I had to do whatever I could to help him.

But even after I told the story, from Nan to Silas to Damien at the end, they still arrested him. He was sent to prison, charged with murder, with no bail.

And I was released from the hospital.

* * *

I stayed with Dexter and Leona, trapping myself in their apartment. I was stuck, unable to take a step forward without knowing what was going to happen to Gage. As bad as it sounded, I didn't want to move past anything without him with me.

I lived for the brief phone calls from him. That and the news were the only reasons I got up.

"The Star says they were part of one of the largest human trafficking operations on the east coast," I summarized the article I read earlier. "They are giving all the credit to the FBI's human trafficking task force. Their operation removed large quantities of drugs and the shoot out resulted in seven deaths of notorious gang members that plagued the streets."

"How many times do I have to tell you, stop reading those things? You know the story. Don't drive yourself crazy."

I could picture him running his hand through his hair simply by his frustrated tone. I ached to see him.

I obsessed over articles and news reports about Gage, and there were many. My name was absent from all of them, just referenced as a young woman rescued. Gage's involvement was unclear, under investigation. Some claimed he helped, but others suspected he was part of it, or a member of a rival gang. Either way, his name had been dragged through the mud with all of this.

"Anything new from your lawyer?" They had scheduled a grand jury indictment for the following week.

"He thinks they don't have enough evidence to charge me with murder, at least not first degree. And the FBI agent is awake now. Her report should help." His sigh blew into the phone.

"I'll go back up there. I—"

"No." He cut me off. "Stop, you've done what you can. If it goes to trial, you'll have to talk, but not now. Are you okay? Dexter told me you haven't gone back to the therapist."

I lay back on the bed, only a slight stinging from the movement now. "They're the ones that wouldn't let me see you in the hospital. I'm done with them. Stop changing the subject. I'm fine. I just can't wait to see you on Sunday." I closed my eyes, picturing his strong features and light eyes.

"About that."

I sat up with the warning.

"Don't come here. You need to do what we talked about. Move out of state, get away. I'll come to you when I get out."

"No, I already told you, I'm not leaving you here."

"Good to see you still have your attitude," I could hear the smile in his sarcastic tone.

"My attitude and I are staying." I wasn't going to back down and I wasn't going to let him push me away.

"Regan, listen to me," his voice was softer.

"Your indictment is so soon, why are you pushing this now?"

The weighted pause was driving me crazy.

"Anatoli was arrested. He was brought in yesterday, I don't want you coming here."

I was struck with the news, speechless. But my emotions pulled, a tug of war between relief and fear. "What does that mean? Why?" I was already going to Dexter's laptop to look up this news.

"I can't talk about it here, but…" There were voices behind his, requesting the phone. "Back the fuck up. I'll be off in a minute." He dropped his voice when he spoke to me. "I'll fill you in when I can. Just don't come here, not yet."

He ripped away the only thing I was looking forward too. I was being crushed, but I forced myself to think past my emotions. "Is there more? Does this affect you? Me?"

There was no news that I could find on an Internet search.

"Maybe not, but I don't want you taking any chances. Tell Dexter. I've got to go. I love you."

I took a deep breath, not wanting to say goodbye. "You be careful. I love you."

Typing Anatoli Rusnak into case search, 56 charges popped up. All surrounding drug possession, distribution, trafficking across state lines, and smuggling over the border.

* * *

"I shouldn't have let him go. I shouldn't have told him where." Dexter tossed his phone on the couch next to me, frustrated by the article he just read.

We were all on edge since we arrived in New Jersey. Leona was sleeping off her frustrations.

He pinched the bridge of his nose, sweeping his eyes to me. "I'm sorry, I didn't mean he shouldn't have helped you. I meant I should have made the police go instead. If I would have went to someone other than the detective he sent me to, there would be no question of his motives."

I nodded, arms wrapping around myself. There were a lot of what ifs to this, but I couldn't help but feel that since we were both alive, this scenario wasn't so bad. Sure, I was lost without him, but at least there was still a chance for us.

"Why didn't you?" I asked, more to keep him talking. I'd heard some of this story, but not enough.

"I may not always listen to him." He smiled slightly. "But his plans are usually good. He's always taken care of things. Of me." He shook his head and shrugged, despondent.

We were both missing him.

"After you called me, and I heard Silas and that guy take you, I was freaking out. I went back to the apartment, but you were gone already. And they had turned off your phone so I couldn't track you. Gage called back just as I was about to call the police. I'm sorry I hesitated." He shifted his eyes away from me. "It's only, I didn't know if that would make it worse." He deflated with a sigh. "He had been out of signal, setting up for his delivery at a warehouse. I told him everything they said, about them thinking he was in Florida, but I didn't know who the other guy was. I didn't have a fucking clue what to do. Gage gave me a police detectives name and number, told me to go to him and tell him everything. Said we could trust him."

He shook his head, leaning forward. "He helped, he found out where Rocks' hideout was, but he never reported any of it. I got the feeling he was doing it more to keep Rusnak's shipment safe. Whenever he talked to Gage, that's all he cared about. Wasn't till the drugs were secured in Florida that he even told us the address. Probably knew it all along."

Dexter stood up, pacing. "Then I thought Gage was going to that place with Nick or Boris or even Rusnak. I wouldn't have let him go alone."

"It's better you weren't there." I could only say that since Gage lived.

He paused his pacing and looked at me. "Maybe. We'll see if they have enough evidence to take him to trial."

* * *

They didn't.

They dismissed his charges after Jade—I mean Serena—filled her report. They gave a one-sentence press statement, clearing his name. It was deemed self-defense. But that was it.

I didn't question it too deeply, not when all I cared about was seeing Gage.

As soon as we got the call, we drove back to Maryland to pick him up.

The day was hot for May, and the sun was high in the sky when we pulled up to the prison and waited for him to be released. The moment I saw him, walking down the sidewalk in his faded jeans and soft t-shirt, I thought I would burst. It had only been a couple of weeks, and he looked the same, but at the same time, he looked better than ever. I wanted to run into his arms but his slight limp stopped me. He was still recovering.

He had the oddest smile as we walked up to him, it almost put me on edge, but I was too relieved that he was getting out, for good, to let it bother me.

"You weren't supposed to come here. You never could listen, could you?" He softly questioned, pulling me into his arms at the same time.

His fresh scent overwhelmed me, both allowing me to finally breath and stealing my last breath at the same time. He made me light headed.

I wrapped my arms around him. "I make my own decisions, and I want to be wherever you are."

"Good because that's where I want you." He pulled back and kissed my lips gently, his hands rubbing over my black maxi dress.

Dexter cleared his throat and Gage broke the kiss, but didn't take his arm off me as he greeted his brother with some sort of handshake.

"Do you want to drive?" Dexter held up the keys to Gage.

"No, you can." He opened the back door for me and slid in after, placing his arm back around me.

"So," Dexter started the SUV, grabbing Leona's hand in the passenger seat. "Where to? Can we go home now?"

Leona shot him a look, but stayed quiet.

"Yea, you two can go home. Things should be fine."

"Rusnak's not an issue then?" Dexter questioned.

Gage looked around the SUV, I could see him carefully considering his words. "He'll be away for a while. Won't cause any trouble for us."

My nerves started to prick and I captured his eyes with mine, silently questioning him.

"It'll be okay. I promise." He mumbled to me and pushed back a piece of my hair.

Leona let out a sigh. "I hope you're right because we just need to finish this semester then get the hell out of this town."

This was the first I heard of their plan. "You just moved into your apartment."

She rested her hands over her tiny baby bump. "I don't want to raise a baby here. We need somewhere new."

"Where?" I asked, eyes glancing at Gage.

He didn't seemed surprised, just kept looking down at me.

"Vegas." Dexter squeezed Leona's knee. "I told you Rea, great opportunities there."

Gage shook his head, but sat back and pulled me back with him, keeping me under the warmth of his arm.

* * *

Gage put my suitcase in the back of his SUV while I buckled up.

"Where are we going?"

"Not far." He pulled a hat low on his head, shading his eyes from the afternoon sun.

"Then why not stay at Dexter's?" I questioned. His silence was unnerving me. He hadn't talked much on the rest of the ride back and then immediately said we were leaving.

He shook his head, but stayed silent.

"Is something going on? Is it about Rusnak?" I spit out my fears.

That pulled his attention from the road and he looked at me. "No," his voice was thick and he moved his hands to my knees, rubbing over my dress. "Don't worry. I'll explain. We're not going far."

I tried not to worry, but his lack of words didn't give me confidence.

By time we walked into the hotel room I was vibrating with anxiety. "Can you please talk to me?" I turned on him the moment the door closed.

He stepped towards me, sinking to his knees as his arms wrapped around my waist. "I have missed you. I have wanted you. I have needed you. Not just the time in jail, the hospital wasn't enough."

He pulled his head back from my stomach, his hands still gripping my hips, and his eyes glistened with unshed tears as he looked up at me. "We've talked and I knew you were okay, but…"

I sunk down to meet him on the floor and moved my hands to his cheek. "I am all right. I'm fine."

He shook his head. "Seeing you, I don't know what I was expecting. But damn, you showed up in this dress and you smiled and I didn't know if we were going to get time like this again." His hands were running over my hair. "In my brain, I knew you were okay, but my soul needed to feel it. I need to feel it."

His lips captured mine, putting all his emotions into it. I had needed this just as much as he did and I rose up onto my knees to press into him, returning every bit he gave me.

"This is okay? You're okay with this?" His eyes searched mine, showing me his fear and need.

I nodded, keeping my hands on him. "I need you. I need this. I need to feel it too." I needed him to make me believe everything could be all right again, for both of us.

Our lips collided again, making my soul ache with how much I missed him, how close I had been to never feeling this again. But I pushed away those fears as he took off his shirt. He was here and this was real. He was here.

I ran my hands over his bare chest and trailed my lips over his skin.

He pulled the straps of my dress down as his lips slid over my neck to my shoulders. Then he stood me up, letting the dress fall. He guided me back to the bed as my fingers unbuckled his pants, undressing him. His hands caressed my skin, but I flinched when they crossed my newest scar. The knife wound was still an angry red, even with the stitches removed.

His gaze dropped over me with a rasping breath, and then he slid down my body.

I closed my eyes, shuddering, as he placed a gentle kiss over the mark.

"This is nothing to be ashamed of." He grabbed my hand when I tried to pull him back up to me. "That's our mark. Just like this is our mark." He gestured to the wound on his leg. "We fought for each other. These scars show that. More than any fucking tattoo or anything else, these show how much we love, how much we're willing to do for each other." He kissed the mark again and I didn't stop him. "Be proud of it. Because it's proof that we'd go to fucking war for each other." He gripped my shoulders, raising himself back up me to eye level, his lips grazing mine. "We fight. And we win."

"Together," I added, breathless.

"Together," He agreed before collapsing onto me, pressing me into the mattress as his teeth trapped my lips with soft nibbles.

We gave up to each other, challenging each other with every move. A dance of control where neither of us held it for long. Our bodies responded to the other's demands, reassuring us both that we were still us, whatever issues may still be there. At our core, in our souls, we were still us. And we would fight together to keep it.

* * *

I hadn't slept so well in a long time. And both of us were enjoying our morning in bed, wrapped in a naked embrace. His fingers traced over my curves and scars. And I traced over his.

"Are you all right?" His fingers paused over my bellybutton.

I squeezed him to me, regretting having to break the moment. "I just need to know what happens next, with Rusnak, with you." He stiffened beneath me and I continued, "I'm staying with you, whatever it is. I just need to know."

He nodded. "It's over."

I sat up, unbelieving.

He sat up with me, wrapping his arms back around me from behind. "He didn't trust me. I had to set up the shipment to find out where you were, but then I left and Rusnak wasn't happy. I gave Rusnak the plan, told him about the checkpoints and routes the drivers should take, and I warned him that Rock was after the shipment. He thought I was setting him up and changed it." He gave me a lopsided grin and pulled me to straddle his lap. "He got new drivers and a new plan. And one of the trucks got caught. From there they were able to track the truck and warehouse back to him. When they searched his house, they found even more evidence. He's not getting out anytime soon."

I felt lighter than ever before and wrapped my legs around him. "So you're out? For good?"

But his face darkened, pulling me back into my body. "I am. But Rusnak's family, they see an opportunity here and are sending others over to fill his spot. They want to rebuild with all new people. I don't want to stick around for that."

I cupped his face with my hands. "Done. Let's leave. I want to leave too."

His smile faltered. "I have something else to tell you."

I waited, holding my breath.

"Rusnak wants to talk to you. He wants you to visit him in prison."

I sat back, pulling the sheets around me. "Do I have to? Will this help you or—"

"No." He gripped my hips before I could pull away completely. "No you don't have to. I—well, I'm leaving it up to you, If you want to. But there's no reason you have to."

His hand dropped away and he watched me cautiously.

It took only a second to think about. "I don't want to." I still wasn't sure it was okay to say no.

"Then you're not going." He put his hands back around me. "I didn't want you to, but didn't want to tell you what to do. I'm glad you decided not to."

Nodding, I thought out loud. "I have nothing to say to him and I don't want to hear anything he has to say. I don't care what he knows about my mom or my past. I want to leave it all behind."

"We will. We can. Where do you want to go? Anywhere. We can start over anywhere."

"I already told you. I just want to go wherever you go." I paused thinking, "Where's a good place for your boxing? You've got a belt to win."

He kissed my lips with a burst of passion. "New York? We could leave today. You could start training tomorrow."

"I want to see James first, let him know about Damien and Nan."

He nodded, eyes searching mine. "I'll go with you."

Sliding my arms around him, I hid my head from my words. "I'm not ready to train again. I don't know if I want to anymore." It hurt to say it since I still remembered the joy and power I felt boxing, but now it was all tainted, all the good sucked out.

"That's okay. You don't have to, not until you want to." He smoothed my hair with his hands. "Babe, are you really okay? If there's anything you need—"

I pushed my finger to his soft lips. "I think I'm okay, now that you're here."

He cracked a smile and pulled me to lie back on his chest. "I can't believe my independent girl just admitted that." He kissed my head with a light rumbly laugh and then added with a whisper. "Does that scare you?"

I laid my head on his chest, thinking it over. "Maybe, but I don't care. Not anymore. I thought doing things alone was the only way to go, that it made me strong, better. But…" My stomach clenched thinking about where that got me. "That didn't work. Now I want this. The way I feel right now. It's the only time I feel like I'm living."

"Loving," He corrected with another kiss to my forehead. "You're loving, that's why it feels good. Why it works."

My fingers coasted over his chest and I returned the question he had asked me so many times. "Does it scare you?"

He sucked in air, nodding his head back on the pillow. "You scare me all the fucking time. But I'm learning to live with that."

"I thought we were loving not living." I poked him and he captured my hand with his.

"It's because I love you that you scare me. You've got my heart in your hand." He placed a kiss on my palm. "But I don't want it back. It's yours."

I climbed over him and pressed my body to his, our eyes burning into each other's. "You're mine. And I'm yours."

He sealed the words with a soul-igniting kiss. And I knew it didn't matter where we ended up or what we ended up doing. As long as we were together, I had a chance at living. We had a chance at living. We could fight any obstacle and win, because of the way we love.

39: All That Matters

THE ARENA WAS ALREADY FILLED AS LEONA and I took our seats next to Jace and Aliya. My stomach twisted and bubbled with excitement and nerves.

"Hey, finally you two get here." Aliya had to yell over the buzz of the crowd. "You missed a fine looking man. That last fighter, gah." Aliya fanned herself, giggling as Leona slapped at her. "You're a mom, not dead. You can look." She looked between Leona and me, wide eyed. "Everyone should be able to appreciate a fine body."

Jace rolled his shoulders back and swept his hand across his chest, showing off, and Aliya rolled her eyes.

I didn't even bother responding as the lights dimmed and people began filtering into their seats. I still appreciated fine bodies, but not many compared to my mans.

"How's the ankle biter doing?" Jace asked.

Leona pushed him with a smile. "He only bit you that one time, quit calling him that. But he's good. Trouble, but good. You should have seen him tonight, took forever to get him to sleep. All he wanted to do was play. Had to get him down before I left though or he would have never went to bed." She smiled like she didn't mind.

I brushed away the concern over who he was with, that was Dexter and Leona's choice to make. Picturing his chubby cheeks and head of curls never failed to make me smile. And recalling the way Gage played with Felix that morning in the pool made me weak in the knees at how sweet he looked, but it also terrified me to my core, nearly sending me into a panic attack.

"Girl, can you imagine? When he wins tonight you get bragging rights to dating the cruiserweight champion of the world. That. Is. Crazy." Aliya squealed, leaning over Leona.

This was the fight he had been training his entire life for. And it had been a hard road. His reputation had been struck at first, but after his name cleared and the news stories stopped, he returned to boxing. The allegations of murder only made him that much more intimidating to opponents. The past year and a half had been spent in physical therapy and the gym. I had no doubt in his ability; he had trained his ass off for this.

The minute Gage walked out he had my full attention. Seeing him now, with his tattoo's shining, gloves on, and his confidently cold expression made me weak in a completely different way. A fire burned low in my stomach for him, and I couldn't pull my eyes off the grace of his hard body.

He was with a small entourage, only Dexter and his trainers, Brady and Ian. As they approached the ring he captured me with his eyes, making everything else in the room lose focus and my nerves disappeared. He still had that effect on me. Every time. I got a little stronger every day and could finally be on my own, but he was the only one that made the anxiety go away completely. Even now.

He climbed into the ring and the crowd cheered, feet stomping a thunderous beat. The energy in the room fed my excitement, I vibrated with it. He turned and winked at me, my body pulled towards his so I could barely focus on the other man entering the ring.

His opponent, the current titleholder, was shorter than Gage, but with thick muscles that made him look like a bull.

The first round was a test. They sparred, neither giving their all, sizing up each other and their reflexes.

My muscles twitched, reacting with each move as if I were in the ring, willing Gage to take a punch or dodge a certain way.

The second round started the same way, easy. Then the bull stepped it up, attacking with the speed and strength he was known for. But Gage blocked and threw his own punch. Gage was having fun, I could tell by the light in his eyes and his slight smile. But the other guy was living up to his nickname, fuming red with anger, I almost expected him to blow smoke.

Gage's lips were moving, he was saying something to him that caused him to charge again. But Gage dodged with a roll of his shoulder and returned a punch to his stomach, then his chin.

The man folded slightly but recovered, putting his arms up to block as he tried to retreat.

Gage was still so casual about it all, it excited me, the control he had in the ring. It was clear he owned this fight. He didn't let his opponent back too far away. He stepped to him with a hook that sent him back to the ropes, followed by a combination that had him bouncing against them, knocked off balance. Gage used one gloved hand to keep him up and the other to slam into his cheek, dropping him to the canvas. The bull knocked out cold.

There was no need to even count, the guy was out. And I was on my feet, stomach tightening. I knew what was coming and so did the others. Cameras had already found my seat.

The last two fights, Gage had repeated that kiss from Atlantic City, and now it was expected. Even knowing it was coming, I still pulsed, body still lit, as he climbed out of the ring.

This time though, he paused by Dexter who cut his gloves off of him, only making the adrenaline in me build. I couldn't wait at my seat and started the path towards him as he pushed through others to get to me.

My shaky arms immediately found his face as he approached, lifting me into his arms.

"You did it," I breathed, lips tingling with expectation, heart exploding with pride.

"No, I didn't. Not yet." He put me down, shaking his head, stepping back from my kiss with his arms still around my waist. "This was my dream, but…" He sunk to his knees.

I would have collapsed then and there if his hands weren't still on my hips, making me stand. I was trapped in his blue eyes, his words the only thing I heard.

"None of this matters without you. You're my life. My future. I fucking need you by my side through it all, the good and bad. You saved me and gave me a life worth living. I fucking love you." Somehow there was a ring in his hand. I don't even know when he pulled it out or when he grabbed my hand. "Stay with me forever. Be mine forever. Marry me."

I was shaking and I couldn't breathe, but I had no hesitation. I just couldn't form the words.

Sliding down to his level, I fell into him, lips crashing into his as my arms wrapped around him. We burst like a firework, the kiss exploding all my emotions, our love sizzling around us. His hands slid to my face, pulling back slightly, stilling the kiss.

"You need this." He held up the ring, a shiny thing that I could barely look at, not when his eyes shone brighter, unshed emotions sparking in them.

But the feel of it sliding onto my finger was more than I expected. I hadn't thought it would matter, I knew we had already made this commitment, but that ring felt like safety.

* * *

"Dude," Dexter began, pointing at Gage. "You said fuck"—he paused a moment, thinking—"lots of times. You're not supposed to say fuck when you propose." He turned to me with that grin I loved. "Rea, make him do it again."

I grabbed Gage's hand next to me, leaning into him as I shook my head.

"Was it okay?" He asked softly, too low for the others around the table to hear.

"Better than okay," I assured him, raising my head to meet his lips briefly.

"You're crazy." Aliya pushed Dexter. "That was great. I swear you two are too hot, I can't even handle it." She slid into an open seat next to me.

"All right, well let's celebrate." Dexter grabbed the tray of shots from Jace.

When I waved away the shot he handed to me, he coaxed, "Come on, you just got engaged, one drink, you've got to celebrate."

"Nope." I shook my head sliding my hand a little further up Gage's thigh under the table.

His breath hitched and his fingers grazed the skin under my skirt, but he looked towards Dexter. "She's got her fight next week, she can't drink tonight."

My heart was already speeding up as his fingers glided up my thigh, but his mention of my fight made it trip. It would be my first time back in the ring.

"All right," he let it go and everyone else took a shot to our engagement.

"Did you ever agree on a name yet?" Aliya asked with a strained voice from the liquor.

Dexter took his seat, wrapping his arm around Leona. "I'm trying to convince her to be Regan Raging Sommers"

"What about Regan Lawson?" Gage squeezed my thigh, sitting up to face me.

"What?" The intense look on his face left me breathless, I couldn't even focus on what Dexter was saying about it.

"Let everyone know that you're mine, and I'm yours. That we're a team. Fight with my name next week. Marry me tonight, here in Vegas."

I'm sure I had the same spark in my eyes. The idea excited me.

"Hell yeah!" Dexter shot up. "That would be a fucking epic night. And everyone's here. We could even go get Felix and Mom to come."

Gage tensed at that and Dexter realized his mistake. "Or not, I just thought you two were doing better." He waved away his words. "Never mind. Felix can stay with her, they don't need to come."

I pulled on Gage's shirt, bringing his attention back to me and his tight expression eased into a smile. Dexter moving to the city where their mom lived was a sore subject that I never pushed. Even if she had been in recovery for years, Gage couldn't forgive her yet.

He searched my face. "What are you thinking?"

"Let's do it." I couldn't contain my smile, didn't even try to. "It doesn't matter if we get married tonight, or tomorrow, or a year from now." His hand tightened on my waist with that. "All that matters is we're together and I fucking love you too."

Continued in book three: OtherSide Of Fear

(First chapter excerpt is included at the end of this book)

OtherSide Of Fear *Excerpt*

Book Three of Outside The Ropes

This preview for OtherSide Of Fear is still in editing and may be changed or modified before publication.

1: Almost

MY STOMACH ROLLED AND SKIN WAS CLAMMY. Hot and cold warred inside me, erupting in beads of sweat on my skin. Bright orbs danced in my vision, blocking the small audience from view.

Closing my eyes, I swallowed hard, forcing saliva down my dry throat and replayed my conversation with Gage in my head.

"You don't have to do this if you're not ready, but I know you can."

"I feel like I'm going to throw up. What if I throw up?" Panic had already taken up residence in me, a strong vine twisting and choking out everything else.

"Then you throw up." He lifted his shoulders easily, a beautiful smile on those full lips. His hands circled around me, pulling me into his body and I was able to relax slightly.

I opened my eyes, the spots gone, the ring clear. Coach was behind me, removing my silk robe. Sylvie next to him, encouraging me.

"You've got this Regan. You're ready, more than ready. That girl doesn't stand a chance." She squeezed my shoulders with her strong hands. "Loosen up some."

"Babe, look at me." Even with the dim lighting of the changing room his blue eyes were bright. But all amusement was gone, his tone serious. "You've been training. You're prepared. You know physically you're the better boxer. The only thing that can get in the way is your fear." His hands slid over my shoulders, down my arms. "If you're not ready for this, we can leave right now." His grip tightened, keeping me from pulling away. "You can do whatever you want and I'll be right there. Go out there and try, but if it's too much, walk out."

I shook my head, dropping my eyes from his. I couldn't allow myself to think of an escape. "I can't do that. The team is counting on me. If I don't do this, they'll probably kick me off the team."

He lifted my chin with his fingers, making me meet his eyes, a cocky glint sparking in them. "Do you know who your husband is? You don't need that damn college team, you could throw up all over that ring and I'd still have you boxing next week if that's what you wanted to do."

Rolling my shoulders and shaking my arms, I turned around, facing the audience. I found Gage in the front row and my nerves slowed their rapid-fire assault. He inclined his head towards me and I could see the question in his eyes. Was I all right, could I go through with this?

I nodded and gave a tight smile in reassurance. Just knowing he was there was enough. Turning back towards the ring, I stretched my neck as I faced my opponent and waited for the announcer to finish.

The bell cut through my anxiety, my body propelling me forward without thought. I stepped towards the girl. She was tall and thin, and held her body awkwardly, like she didn't fit her long legs.

I leaned, dodging her glove as she jabbed towards me with her right, and blocked a left jab with my arm. She quickly pulled her arms back to cover her face. Her reach was long, but punches sloppy. I almost felt bad for what I was about to do. Almost.

Her attack, no matter how weak was enough to spark my adrenaline. No longer fear and anxiety, but excitement, pumping through me, energizing me.

I jabbed her stomach and followed with a wide hook to the side of her head. She crumpled forward, but stayed on her feet, her eyes wide. I swung again connecting with the opposite side of her head and she dropped to the canvas with a thud.

Stepping back, I didn't take my eyes off her. She wasn't knocked out, but she was curled up on the mat. Her mouth opened and closed like a fish, no air reaching her lungs. I kept anticipating her pushing herself up, returning to the fight, but she didn't. The ref reached ten and declared me the winner and I was almost disappointed that it all ended so quickly, just as I was getting into it.

For a second, I wished Dexter had been there, to shake me out of my thoughts and pump me up about my win. But the rush soon came on its own, flooding me with excitement. I did it. And it had been easy. I could keep doing this.

Sylvie was in my corner, rubbing her hands together. "Ragin' Regan, this might be our year. With you, we might have a chance of making it regionally."

Coach slid between the ropes, smile bright as he smoothed his grey hair back on the sides. "Hell, even maybe nationally." His face lit up with his dream, but I'd be lying if the idea wasn't enticing. I wanted it too.

But I looked past them as Gage pulled himself up onto the canvas. Everything else faded away and only then did I feel breathless. The match hadn't touched me, not like his presence did. His lips curled and he extended one arm to me.

My body was already there, gravitating towards him.

"I told you—" He started but I gripped his collar, pulling him towards me, silencing him with my lips.

For once, I was able to kiss him after my fight, and I wasn't going to waste the moment. I could feel his laughter bubbling out of him, his breath bouncing over my lips. So I slid my hands around his neck, pulling him in closer, sliding my tongue in his mouth.

That stopped his laughter, and he wrapped his arms around my waist, lifting me to him, off of my feet. The ropes pressed into my stomach, wedged uncomfortably between us, but I didn't care about that, only that it was a barrier from his body. He lowered me down until my feet were firmly back on the mat, reluctantly returning me to the ground and letting the outside world back into our bubble.

* * *

"Lawson, hold up." A voice cut through the buzz of the gym, just as I exited the locker room.

Gage pushed off the wall he had been waiting on, saying a quick goodbye to the group of people he had been talking too. He grabbed my hand as he turned to the caller. "Yeah?"

At the same time, I turned towards the voice with a raised eyebrow.

Coach pushed through the concession line, stopping in front of Gage and I.

"Lawson," He paused looking between us with a small laugh and shrugged. "Both of you. You leaving already? Not going to stick around for the next fight?"

"Not tonight."

"Hey, Lightning. Good fight last week." Someone yelled as they passed by.

Gage nodded to the person and then continued, "We've got plans."

I didn't know about that, I hope it was a lie. I wanted nothing more than to get him alone and work out this adrenaline and energy coursing through me. Gripping Gage's hand tighter and stepping closer to his body, I smiled politely at Coach Finnegan.

"Well, I'll see you at practice Sunday then?" At my nod he continued. "Hell of a job tonight girly. Hell of a job."

Gage dropped my hand and slid his arm around me, turning me away from the old man and towards the door.

"Thanks, see you Sunday," I called over my shoulder with a giggle as Gage whispered in my ear.

"I need you alone, now." His voice was low and heated, breath sending chills down my skin.

Escaping out of the side door we made our way to the deserted parking garage. Even with the crazy city traffic, Gage insisted on us driving. The garage was filled with cars, but empty of people. Our whispered teasing echoing in the concrete space, our steps even louder, bouncing off the walls around us.

He laughed into my neck, swinging me in front of him so I was forced to walk backwards as he dragged his nose over my skin.

"Babe, I knew you could do it." He growled as his lips reached my ear. "You were hot as hell in that ring. That girl didn't stand a chance." His lips claimed mine, hands sliding to my ass, easily lifting me onto him in an instant.

I gripped tighter to him, wrapping my legs around his waist with a small moan. The slow burn that had been simmering low in my stomach, erupted.

About The Author

Ashley Claudy is a mother, wife, teacher, proud UMD Terp, and perpetual Learner with a wild imagination fueled by coffee. She's also an occasional runner, a late night book junkie, and a daytime dreamer.

She loves to interact with her readers and can be found on most social media. Go to her website for more information about her and her books, including some fun extras for this story and sneak peeks at future novels.

Please visit: AshleyClaudy.blogspot.com

Made in the USA
Monee, IL
18 August 2022

11866526R00236